1918: We Will Remember Them

Book 5 in

Griff Hosker

1918 We Will Remember Them

Published by Sword Books Ltd 2015
Copyright © Griff Hosker First Edition

The author has asserted their moral right under the Copyright, Designs and Patents Act, 1988, to be identified as the author of this work.

All Rights reserved. No part of this publication may be reproduced, copied, stored in a retrieval system, or transmitted, in any form or by any means, without the prior written consent of the copyright holder, nor be otherwise circulated in any form of binding or cover other than that in which it is published and without a similar condition being imposed on the subsequent purchaser.
A CIP catalogue record for this title is available from the British Library.

Cover by Design for Writers

Contents

1918: We Will Remember Them i
Dedication iv
Prologue 1
Chapter 1 3
Chapter 2 9
Chapter 3 17
Chapter 4 25
Chapter 5 33
Chapter 6 40
Chapter 7 46
Chapter 8 55
Chapter 9 61
Chapter 10 69
Chapter 11 79
Chapter 11 85
Chapter 12 94
Chapter 13 99
Chapter 14 104
Chapter 15 110
Chapter 16 117
Chapter 17 124
Chapter 18 130
Chapter 19 135
Chapter 20 144
Chapter 22 153
Chapter 23 159
Chapter 24 166
Chapter 25 173
Chapter 26 177
Chapter 27 185
Chapter 28 192
Chapter 29 198
Chapter 30 204
Epilogue 212
Glossary 214
Historical note 216
Other books by Griff Hosker 222

Dedication

To the British and Commonwealth soldiers and their allies who, then and now, put themselves in harm's way to protect their country. May we never forget them.

Prologue

I had been awarded the V.C. to accompany the Military Cross I had won earlier in the war. The rest of the squadron and my family at home thought it was a great honour. I suppose it was but the loss of so many of my friends and comrades added to those who had become maimed had left a sour taste in my mouth. I would have traded all of my medals to have Charlie Sharp, my first gunner and the love of my little sister's life, back alive. I would have swapped them both for Lumpy Hutton's arm or Johnny Holt's eye. I would have exchanged any of the honours I had received for Lord Burscough; the man I had first served and my mentor. It was a ridiculous notion to think that a lump of metal could be exchanged for something human but after the battle of Passchendaele in 1917 my spirits were at their lowest low ebb. I was not certain if I could go on. The only bright spots were the letters from the love of my life Beatrice, and the birth of Gordy's son, Billy. Gordy was one of my oldest friends and the birth of a boy seemed to give hope.

As we toasted the baby in the mess with the rest of the squadron I wondered at that. The two things which made me feel good were nothing to do with the war. The medals, the fact that I was a major and one of the leading British aces of the time, none of those things made me happy but the birth of a baby hundreds of miles away and the thought that I was in the mind and heart of a beautiful woman did. I had found that my values had changed as the war had gone on.

In England, we call the drunken binge when a baby is born, '*wetting the baby's head*'. It was a traditional rite for the father and his friends. Had the poor little mite been in the mess that night he would have been drowned. I, however, drank little. I was now the second in command and I did not wish to appear foolish before the men I commanded. More importantly, Gordy and Ted were my oldest friends and someone had to watch over them. There were mainly new pilots in the mess that night and many of our old comrades were either dead or in the hospital. That sobered me up more than anything. It would be me who would have to put them to bed.

I was not alone with that task; Airman John Bates was my batman and he helped me to put my two friends to bed. He organised the batmen of Gordy and Ted too. He told me they would have been happy to do it for me but I had shaken my head. "They are my friends, John. I owe it to them."

When they were safely tucked up in their beds with heads draped and pointed towards the floor I retired. Bates came to my room to lay out my uniform. He noticed my face and ventured, "Sir, if you do not mind me saying so, you do not look happy and yet you should be."

"How so, Bates?"

"Major Harsker, you have won the V.C. You single-handedly stopped hundreds of Canadians being slaughtered and you are the most respected pilot in this most distinguished of squadrons. In addition, you have a beautiful fiancée. Many men would trade places with you in an instant."

"I know, John, and I should be but when I see pilots like Mr Holt being blinded and decent chaps like Lumpy Hutton being maimed I wonder if this is all worth it."

"You mean the war, sir?"

I nodded, "Yes the war."

"Well in that case, of course, it isn't worth it. There is no sane reason for all the slaughter, the deaths, the injury and the hurt. This war has affected people who have never set foot in France. People like your poor sister who lost the love of her life." I must have looked surprised at his words. "But none of you gentlemen does this for the armchair generals and the politicians, nor the pernicious newspapers and the profiteers at home. You do it for each other and that, sir, is worth it. I am not a warrior sir, but you and the other pilots are and I am proud to be associated with you. Take pride in your medals for they are recognition that we… you are doing a wonderful job."

I patted his arm as he turned to leave. "You were right with the '*we*', Bates. You are as much a part of the success of this squadron as me, the pilots and even the bloody Camels. Thank you. I can always rely on you to show me the way ahead."

"I just try to do what I can sir. Goodnight."

Before he left he made sure that my uniform was laid out; my clothes were put away and that there was a glass of whisky and another of water by the lighted nightlight next to my bed. He was the most ordered and organised man that I knew.

Chapter 1

It was good to be back in our old base. The old field with the wooden buildings built by my brother Bert and the other engineers was home. I hated sleeping in tents and here we actually had defences to protect our aeroplanes. We were, however, pitifully short of both pilots and aeroplanes. Newly promoted Colonel Leach had allowed Gordy leave to visit his wife and new son. He had no bus to fly anyway. We were down to two Camels and three Bristols. It was not so much a squadron and more of an extended flight! I was lucky in that Bates had sorted all the domestic arrangements for me allowing me and Freddie to make sure that the two Camels were in tip-top shape. They had been the difference between the squadron's survival and destruction. They had proved to be the most effective fighters to keep the menace of the German Jasta at bay. The camel was as near to perfection in the air as it was possible to get. At least I thought so.

The colonel was keen for us to get up in the air but he had me in his office before he issued the orders.

"Bill, we need a patrol up and I need someone to lead it." He watched my face keenly, "If you aren't up to it then I can take your bus until my new one is delivered. I know you have been through a great deal."

His soft Scottish tones showed the concern he had for me. I have to admit his offer was tempting. I felt as though I had ridden my luck too much lately anyway. Perhaps I should let someone else take my bus up for me. I smiled, "No sir. It is my bus. Besides, I remember when I was in the cavalry. If you fell off you had to get straight back on the horse."

He nodded and I could see the relief on his face. He had never flown a Camel. When the new ones arrived, he would need a day or two to get used to them. They flew a little differently from the Bristol two-seater he was used to. Many pilots new to camels had managed to crash them the first time out.

"When do the new buses get here?"

"By the end of the week. The priority went to the chaps up at Ypres but they are sending us a mixture of Camels and Bristols."

"That is a relief. We are getting short of gunners as it is."

He laughed, "And besides all the new pilots want to fly the Camel just like the leading ace."

I shook my head. "Don't you start, sir. It is just luck you know."

"No, it isn't. You are damned good. Stop being so modest. Anyway, let's find out where you are off to. Randolph!" Captain Marshall came in with the maps closely followed by Ted, the other Flight Commander. "Where are we sending Bill and Ted this morning?"

"Headquarters want a few photographs of Cambrai."

"Cambrai? We haven't had any action there yet."

"I know. Headquarters want to know what the likelihood is of a German attack. Our front lines are some three miles south-west of Cambrai so they want you to take photographs between the front lines and Cambrai."

"Are there any German Jastas in the area?"

Randolph looked up. "That is what we want you to find out. No one has any idea since we went to Ypres. This has been a quiet sector. Perhaps they moved north with us."

"Perhaps." I felt a little more hopeful. The battle of Passchendaele was over but there was still fighting going on. I hoped that Baron von Richthofen and his Flying Circus were giving someone else a hard time. He had killed too many of my friends for me to be happy about bumping into him. I would know soon enough. He always flew a red aeroplane. Having met him I knew the reason for that choice: it drew attention to him and he liked the colour.

I looked at Ted who had just finished his cigarette and was stubbing it out. "Ted, you and the Bristols are taking photographs today. Freddie and I will be your guardian angels."

Ted was a dour man and always looked on the dark side but I had flown alongside him for most of the war and I knew what a redoubtable and doughty fighter he was. His face might look hangdog but, in his heart, he was a bulldog.

"Righto, Bill. What's the plan then?"

"We need to fly east of our front lines as far as Cambrai. Freddie and I will climb to five thousand feet and keep watch for any Hun who might be about. That should give you the chance to take as many photographs as your gunners can manage."

We left the office and went to our aeroplanes. We fussed over them the way a gardener would with a prize rose. The difference was that these could save our lives.

Freddie Carrick had grown from the callow youth to a confident and successful pilot. He had already shot down more aeroplanes than anyone in the squadron except for me. He and I flew the only Camels we had, at the moment. When Johnny Holt returned from the hospital and his Camel was ready then our hunting flight would be back to full strength.

"How is the leg, Freddie?"

Freddie had been wounded at the same time as Johnny had lost his eye. "Oh, it is just a little stiff now and then. Still, the more I use it the easier it gets."

"Three hours in a cockpit may make it give you more trouble than enough."

"Don't worry, sir. I will be fine. At least I still have two eyes and my leg will get better eventually. Others are a lot worse off than I am." War made a man mature early; Freddie was old beyond his years.

After I had checked the bus and spoken with the mechanic I was about to climb aboard when Bates appeared with a flask. "Here you are, sir. I got some soup from the canteen. The other officers told me how high you fly and this will keep you warm!"

"I have my flying coat, you know, Bates."

"It can't hurt and as I recall a similar flask saved Flight Sergeant Hutton's life so let us call it a good luck charm eh sir?"

He strode purposefully back to my quarters as Freddie came over. "It must be like having your mother with you, sir."

"It is Freddie and it is just as comforting." I pointed to the skies. "There are just two of us today so stick to me like glue. I do not intend to fly straight and level for too long. We have no idea who is in this sector so until we do we assume it is the Flying Circus."

"Righto, sir."

That would be all that I would need to say to Freddie. He was experienced and he was good. I did my last-minute check of my pockets. I had my two guns, my hip flask with whisky, my compass and three bandages; one never knew. Once we took off I began to climb. Ted and the Bristols were marginally slower but they would be flying at a lower altitude. We had learned long ago that it was better to fly low and get the photographs right the first time rather than having to go back a second time when the Germans would be waiting. I did not envy Ted. The Camel was much smaller than the Bristol. We were harder to hit with ground fire. The Bristol drew bullets like moths to a flame.

The front looked to be remarkably quiet as we flew over. Some of the crater holes made in the last push showed signs of grass growing on them. The summer had dried the land and the small lakes had evaporated. If it had not been for the scars that were the trenches crisscrossing the land then it could have been a summer's day before the war began. We spiralled up to our patrol height. I glanced down and saw Ted and his companions as they flew across the front in straight lines. They looked like three ploughs as they kept to a rigid formation and traversed the ground to photograph every inch of it.

Higher in the sky, I flew figures of eight; then ovals and even reverse boxes. I could not see an enemy but if one came then I did not want to hand him the initiative. Both Freddie and I scanned the sky above and below. In the early days of the war we would have been well above any enemy at five thousand feet; now we could fly as high as nineteen thousand and the Bristols even higher. The Germans were equally good at climbing. The problems with the higher altitude were the cold and the lack of oxygen. I was grateful that Bates had been so thoughtful. An hour into the flight and I poured myself a cup of the soup. It was very warm rather than hot but welcome for all that. He had put some curry powder in with the bully beef soup and it soon warmed me up. I had just replaced the top when I caught a movement in the distance. I dropped the flask to the floor and peered east. There were three aeroplanes rising towards us. We were further east than Ted. It was Freddie and I that they had seen.

I waggled my wings to attract Freddie's attention and waved east. He nodded. He had seen them. We had learned that offence was the best defence and I cocked both Vickers as I began to descend to close with them. As we closed I noticed something strange. One of the aeroplanes rising to meet us was an unusual shape. It had three wings. I had heard of a Sopwith Triplane but I did not know that the Germans had them now. It would be some new information for Randolph. As we descended many questions ran through my mind. Did it have twin machine guns like the two Albatros it was accompanying? Would it be more manoeuvrable and what sort of speed did it have? I knew that we were superior to the Albatros but this new element was disturbing.

I had little time to worry about that for I had to deal with the threat of three German aeroplanes screaming through the skies towards me. They were flying three abreast whilst I had Freddie on my tail. It meant that they could split up and attack us from the side but we would be able to bring the fire of two Camels to bear. With the added speed from our dive, I hoped it would work to our advantage. If we could take one of the three out then we would have a chance. We would have a parity of numbers. I breathed a sigh of relief when I saw that they were not the Flying Circus. They all had a yellow tail and were painted camouflage green.

Suddenly the triplane we had been flying towards lifted its nose. It was certainly fast and manoeuvrable. I adjusted my nose so that I was aiming at the port Albatros. The second one fired a hopeful burst of his 7.92-millimetre guns. I did not feel any impact and I assumed that he had missed. As the second Albatros came into my sights I fired. I saw my bullets strike his fuselage. I checked my mirror and saw that Freddie had fired but the triplane had performed an Immelmann Turn and was lining up on Freddie. Two could play at that game and I pulled my nose up, giving Freddie a free shot at the Albatros in front of me. Instead of copying the turn I side-slipped as I came around and fired at the tiny target that was the triplane. In my mirror, I saw the smoking Albatros heading east and Freddie was coming around to attack the second Albatros.

I do not know if I managed to actually hit the triplane but it began to climb. I swung the Camel around to follow. The triplane was even smaller than my Camel and could turn on a sixpence! As it climbed I realised that it had a faster rate of climb. What was its ceiling? I was grateful to Bates for, as we climbed up into the icy heights, I was still sustained by the warming soup. I watched as he climbed away from me. He was just too far away for me to fire at him but I did not want to be the one to begin to descend. If I did so then I would have this unknown triplane upon my tail. I was relieved when it stopped climbing and headed east.

I had just enough fuel to get home and I turned gently and began to descend west. I saw Freddie's downed Albatros and his Camel as he circled and waited for me to join him. I saw nothing of Ted and the Bristols. They must have finished and gone home.

After I had landed I found Ted waiting for me. He was puffing on a cigarette. "What the hell was that? It was a nippy little bugger!"

"And a fast one too, Ted. I couldn't catch it. It had three wings like the Sopwith, it was a triplane. I wonder why he headed east. I don't think I damaged him. He looked to have the ability to outfly me and he had all the sky he needed."

"He might have had a problem with his guns."

"Perhaps that is it."

We were both grateful to the eminently reliable Vickers which, as Flight Sergeant Richardson had told us, would never jam. Sometimes the Lewis gun did and perhaps the German guns suffered the same problem although the twin Spandau appeared to be as reliable as the Vickers.

Freddie walked over to us with a grin like a Cheshire cat. "Another kill sir! Unless you want to claim a part of it?"

"No, Freddie. I did not damage him enough to bring him down. Have it with my blessing."

He looked relieved that he could claim the kill. "That triplane looked a little handy sir."

"It did that. We had best go and see Captain Marshall. Did you get the photographs, Ted?"

"Aye, mind you there was bugger all to see. If they are planning owt they are keeping it well hidden. There was nothing on the road and they didn't have any guns to stop us snooping."

As we wandered up to the office I thought about the tunnels we had dug before the Arras offensive. I hoped they were not copying us in that area too.

Randolph frowned when he heard of the new aeroplane. "This is the first we have heard of it. The Sopwith Triplane was phased out. Not reliable but very fast and very agile. Let's hope that the new German one is unreliable too."

Colonel Leach had been listening. He tapped his pipe out, "Well at least the Hun doesn't appear to be preparing anything just yet. I think we need a quiet time to train the new pilots and get used to the new buses." He waved his pipe at me, "The new lads will be here tomorrow. Their buses will be here by the end of the week. You are the training officer what do you suggest we do with them?"

I turned and grinned at Ted. "Well sir, what always used to work was sending them up in an FE 2 but we don't use those any more. We could send them up as a gunner in the Bristol; have some mock fights using the Camels."

Ted actually smiled, "Oh yes! Let's have some of that." He sometimes had a wicked sense of humour. Many new pilots ended up being violently sick after having to sit in the open cockpit and being thrown around by another pilot.

Chapter 2

We used the new pilots as gunners before they went into combat just to show them what it was like. It also gave them a healthier appreciation of someone who might be sitting behind them unable to make any of the important decisions. When we had flown the Gunbus it had been even more important for there the gunner had to stand and fire without any safety belt. The Bristol was not as bad but the gunner still had to stand and fire sometimes.

We spent the morning putting every new pilot through the ordeal of being a gunner. Freddie and I dived, swooped and generally gave them a hard time. Two of them vomited the moment their feet touched the ground. The gunners, all of whom were sergeants, found the sight of the young pilots shaking as they climbed down from the aeroplanes hilarious. It would be the only time they would experience it but Ted and I knew that it would make much better pilots of all of them.

The colonel waved me into his office. "How did it go, Bill?"

I smiled and nodded, "As it always does, sir. They will have far more respect for their gunners." I took my pipe out and began to fill it. Archie poured me a large malt.

"It might be a little wasted on some of them. Half of the squadron will be flying Camels."

"Well, that is good news at least."

"You may be right but it makes it harder for the ground crews. The two aeroplanes are as different as chalk and cheese." He held up his glass, "Cheers."

"Cheers."

"Anyway, it will mean some reorganisation. Ted is getting his majority. Don't say anything just yet but I will have him leading the Bristols. You can command A-Flight. I am afraid that will be made up of new pilots. Your old flight, well I was going to ask you about that. Who would make the better flight commander? Freddie or Johnny?"

That was an easy question. "Freddie."

"Good. You can tell him then. We will see if we can get him promoted. We have a lot of goodwill at headquarters. We might as well use it, eh?"

"Do we fly any differently now then sir?"

"We are on our own here Bill. It is Archie, remember. It wasn't that long ago we were the same rank." I nodded. "You are still the hunters. From what you say these new triplanes will run rings around the

Bristols. We are fast but we are much bigger than they appear to be from your description. They would have a field day with us. I have a feeling that we will have to do the observations. The RE 8 and the new FK 8 look like they are too easy to knock out of the skies; even by the Albatros and old Fokkers. At least the Bristol is a fighter."

"Any chance of getting more Camels?"

"I think the powers that be favour the new SE 5 or the SPAD. We will just get what is given."

"Righto Archie. Well, I had better pop along and see Freddie and then get my new pilots together."

"Send Ted to me when you see him, will you?"

Freddie was by his Camel talking to his mechanic. We both appreciated our mechanics. They had the ability to get an extra mile or two an hour out of the buses and that could make all the difference in combat. Once the riggers had done their work they could leave a bus alone until it was damaged. The engines were different; they seemed to be almost organic and they changed as they became older. They needed attention every day they flew.

"Could I have a word, Lieutenant?"

"Yes sir. I'll see you later Bert." His mechanic went back to his work and Freddie joined me.

"Trouble, Freddie?"

"No, sir. It was just that the old bus misfired once the other day. Bert thinks he knows what it might be but it will mean stripping the engine. I won't be up again today."

"That is not a problem. The front appears quiet."

"Good. We could do with the rest. Any idea when Johnny will be back?"

"That depends on the base hospital. Doc Brennan reckons it will be sooner rather than later. We will just have to use him sparingly when he gets back." Freddie was quick on the uptake and he had read a message beneath my words. "Yes, Freddie I need to speak with you about the flight. The Colonel is giving me A Flight. That means C Flight is yours. Can you handle it?"

His face gave me the answer. "If you think so sir then I'll give it a go. What about Johnny? I mean is this because he has lost an eye?"

"No, not at all. Even a fully fit Johnny would not make a difference. You were my first choice all along."

"Thank you, sir. I won't let you down."

"I know. That goes without saying. Now you will have Alldardyce and Duffy from A flight. They are good chaps. That means you will only have two new fellows: Carpenter and McDonald. You will all be flying Camels like A Flight. Their gunners can go to the other flights. The new pilots will need the experience of good gunners."

"Do Duffy and Alldardyce know yet?"

"No. Would you like me to tell them?"

"No, sir. If it is my flight then I need to take command."

"I have no need to tell you that we can't afford to lose new pilots so it is up to you to keep them alive. Train them the way I trained you and they should be all right."

He nodded. "That means you will have five new pilots to train sir."

I laughed, "Yes it looks like I will be running the kindergarten again. Oh, see if the gunners who are now redundant want to transfer to other squadrons or be part of the defences of the field."

"Sir." The new pilots were in the mess busily looking at the identification charts for the enemy aeroplanes. It would have to be updated to accommodate the new triplane. Freddie nodded. "I'll go and see Alldardyce and Duffy sir."

"Righto. I'll have a word with Ted and then I'll see all the pilots."

Ted was in his room smoking and staring at the ceiling. He missed Gordy. They had been friends even before I had joined the squadron and they were inseparable. "Ted, the Colonel wants a word with you. He has reorganised the flights. I now have A-Flight. I am going to have a word with the new pilots. Freddie is being given C Flight. If you join us after the colonel has seen you then we can get the new pilots organised."

Ted frowned, "Why does the Colonel need to see me?"

I laughed, "You are getting the sack of course! Just go and see him eh, you miserable old bugger!"

He stood shaking his head. "Nothing good ever happens to me. It will be some shitty little job I'll be bound!"

He was incorrigible. I could not wait to see his face when he returned. The young pilots in the mess were still engrossed in their homework. I tapped my pipe on the table. "If I could have your attention for a few moments…" Silence descended. "I know that you are all still full of the excitement of being gunners." I looked pointedly at the two who had vomited. The others laughed at their discomfort. "We need to get you organised into flights. Your buses will be here in a few days. When they get here we will have to hit the ground running." That grabbed their attention. "I will be commanding A Flight and we will be flying the Sopwith Camel. The officers in A Flight are: Lieutenant Fall, Lieutenant Clayson, Lieutenant Hickey, Lieutenant Jenkin and Lieutenant Hazell." The slapping of backs and the smiles did my ego a world of good. It was allied to the disappointment on the faces of the ones, not in my flight.

Freddie came in, "Lieutenant McDonald and Lieutenant Carpenter, you will be in C Flight also flying Camels with Flight Commander Carrick." Until Freddie's promotion was confirmed it would not do to give him his new rank. The two pilots looked pleased.

Ted came in with a big smile on his face. I walked over to him and shook him by the hand. I said, quietly, "Congratulations, Major."

"Don't jinx it, Bill. It might not happen."

"Of course it will. I have taken the Camel pilots. You have B and D Flights left. I will leave them to you."

"Thanks!"

"A and C Flights come with me."

Freddie and I led the new pilots out. "We'll show them the bus and tell them how it flies. It is a couple of hours before dinner. We should be able to give them enough information to keep them awake all night eh?"

"Yes sir!"

The eager young faces stood staring intently at me. All that is, except one, Lieutenant George Jenkin looked a little bored. I put it down to the fact that they had had a busy day up to that point.

"The Camel is a wonderful little aeroplane but it can be, sometimes, a little difficult to control. I hope you all have enough hours in the type. If not then please tell me or Mr Carrick and we will bring you up to speed. You and the aeroplanes are both too valuable to lose before you get into combat." I clambered up to the top wing. "We will have your Camel fitted with a rear-view mirror. Why Sopwith do not fit them I have no idea but we find them invaluable. Use it at all times. It will tell you where your friends are and, more importantly, where the Huns are."

"Before we go to the aeroplanes a few words on how we fly. The Germans like to fly three abreast. Sometimes they fly five abreast. We fly in line astern and echeloned so that we can all fire quicker." I demonstrated by putting my hands one above the other. "The twin Vickers will not jam and they have a good range. It will mean that the second can fire without hitting the Camel in front. I lead one column and Mr Carrick the other…"

"That's a little unfair isn't it sir?"

I saw that it was Lieutenant Jenkin who had spoken. "I beg your pardon?"

"Well I mean, sir, how are we going to become aces if it is you who are shooting down all the Germans?"

I was dumbfounded and I struggled for words. It was Freddie who turned on him. "It means that Major Harsker will have to bear the brunt of the enemy fire and you will all have more chance of survival!"

I put my hand up. "And this is not about how many aeroplanes we can all claim. We are a squadron and we fly together. We, as a squadron, shoot down as many German aeroplanes as we can. Who shoots them is irrelevant."

"Yes sir but the fact remains that you are an ace. I want to be one too."

Some of the other new pilots gasped at the effrontery of that statement. "I will be happy, Lieutenant Jenkin, if you manage to survive your first aerial combat."

He smiled, "Oh don't worry about that sir. I will. It's in my blood, don't you know. My uncle was Major Lanoe Hawker."

"And if your uncle was here now he would tell you what I am going to tell you. You obey orders and fly as we tell you to or you will be grounded. Is that clear Mr Jenkin?" I had raised my voice and I left him in no doubt that I meant what I said. I saw Freddie fuming in the corner. He nodded sullenly.

One good thing about the interruption was that no one else dared to interrupt for the rest of the afternoon. We let them go to get changed for dinner and Freddie walked with me. "If you like sir I'll have young Jenkin in my flight. I'll teach him how to follow orders."

"No, Freddie. I have met pilots like him before. I will make sure he is in the middle of the flight with a more reliable pilot fore and aft. That way he can't get himself or anyone else in trouble. I must confess his arrogance and his confidence are something unexpected."

We used the time well before the new buses arrived and the men were drilled into the systems Freddie and I wanted them to follow. We watched them as they did take-offs and landings. We saw who the good pilots were and who needed work. Jenkins was satisfactory. We would get a better idea of how they might fare in aerial combat once the buses arrived and we could get them all in the air at the same time.

Annoyingly it was the Bristols which arrived first but it gave me the opportunity of watching Ted and his two flights. The new pilots all had an experienced gunner who was worth his weight in gold.

Gordy also arrived with the new Bristols, having cadged a ride in the rear cockpit of one of them. He was like a dog with two tails and bored us rigid with his tales of nappies, his gurgling son and the boy's smile which Ted assured him was wind. He was so full of his son that he seemed oblivious to Ted's promotion and the fact that we both outranked him. Perhaps fatherhood would do the same to me; if that day ever arrived.

Archie decided that the Bristols could have a short safe patrol to the east while we waited for the Camels to arrive for our younger pilots. Freddie and I took off with the Bristols. I was anxious to see how the new pilots fitted in with the more experienced fliers.

I noticed Lieutenant Jenkin watching with the rest of A and C Flight as we took off. He had been withdrawn since I had snapped at him and the others had distanced themselves from him. It had not been a good start for the young man. However, others had had poor starts and turned out to be good pilots. We would have to wait and see.

We climbed to get above the twelve Bristols. Compared with the tiny Camels they were huge. They were a very tempting target for the Hun. I hoped that it would be an easy day for the new pilots. Ted and Gordy would not venture much beyond the front lines but it was important for them to know where it was. Freddie and I would do the same with the Camels when they arrived. It was a glorious August morning. The sun blazed down and there was not a single cloud in the sky. Back in England, the farmers would be taking advantage of the sun and the long days to get the harvest in. In this sector, there were no farmers. It was a wasteland of mud and wire.

As we climbed we saw the Tommies waving to us. I knew from my brother, Bert in the Engineers, that the men on the ground appreciated our presence. I had thought that they might resent it but they found it comforting. Now that we had ground attack ability we could actually help them.

B and D Flight were two hundred feet apart and flying up and down the front. Ted would have his gunner telling him which of the new pilots was out of formation and the issue could be addressed once they landed. We climbed a little higher and flew in a figure of eight. We were on the western leg when I saw the flash in my mirror. What had caused it? I waved to Freddie to tell him that I was heading east. He acknowledged and climbed above me to cover my rear.

We crossed over No Man's land and I saw them. There were five Triplanes and they were diving out of the sun. The mirror was not good enough to pick out aeroplanes that were hidden by the sun and the five of them screamed down at us. I pulled my nose up and cocked my guns. I prayed that one of the Bristol gunners would have seen the enemy but I knew it was a long shot. It had been pure luck that I had seen the flash. The new aeroplane was as small a target as we were. They came on in line abreast. Swooping like that they would make mincemeat of the Bristols unless we disrupted them.

I opened fire at five hundred yards. At the speed, they were descending it only allowed me a short burst. I saw my bullets hit the fuselage of the leading aeroplane and then I heard the chatter of Freddie's guns as he joined in. I felt my bus judder as 7.92-millimetre steel-jacketed bullets hit my wings and then we were in an empty sky as they continued their dive below us.

I banked to port. We would now have extra speed but I had a feeling that these new aeroplanes were faster than our Camels. They were certainly faster in the climb. Our turn had given them a lead over us and I saw them descending towards the Bristols. As the Bristols were turning I guessed that someone had seen them but these new Triplanes were much faster than the Bristols. I saw the tracer from the twin guns as the bullets arced towards the twelve aeroplanes of B and D flight. The machine-gunners in the rear sent up their own cone of fire but there were ten German machine-guns raining death and destruction.

I opened fire at long range. My tracer showed me that I was close enough to hit them. The Hun I had fired at began to take evasive action. It meant he could not fire accurately. Freddie joined in. One of the Bristol gunners must have got lucky for I saw the triplane on the extreme right pull up and bank away with some smoke coming from the engine. It gave me hope. We needed hope for the Bristols had lost all formation. Perhaps the new pilots had panicked. Whatever the reason it suited the remaining four aeroplanes which fell amongst the two-seaters.

I focussed on the one I had nearly hit and I fired again. This time the bullets hit the tail. When it began to bank I knew I had his attention. I guessed that he would turn right to head home and I followed him. I kept my finger on the trigger and watched as the bullets stitched a neat line along the fuselage. I briefly stopped firing while I pulled even harder in the turn. The triplane was manoeuvrable but so was the Camel and I managed to turn inside him. As soon as the Hun became a cross in my sights I pulled on the triggers and hit him. I must have hit the pilot for it did not try to pull away. I fired again and this time I hit the engine. It began to dive towards the German lines. I glanced behind me and saw that the remaining three aeroplanes were climbing and heading east. We had driven them off. Once again they had left early and I wondered why.

I climbed to join Freddie and we watched the rest of our squadron head west while we kept our eyes on the departing Germans. I could not see any of our own aeroplanes on the ground but that did not mean that we had escaped Scot free.

The doctors and medical staff around the Bristols told me that we had casualties. No one had died in the air but the loss of gunners and pilots meant a depleted squadron. We had been surprised and we had paid the price. Two Camels were not enough. We needed two flights and as soon as possible.

Chapter 3

Three of the new pilots were hospitalised, although none of them seriously and one new gunner had died of his wounds. Doc Brennan had spent hours trying to save him but even he could not work a miracle. It was a sombre mess that evening. The new pilots and gunners had had a baptism of fire. Lieutenant Jenkin apart, the new Camel pilots were all shaken. The aerial battle had taken place close enough to the field for them to see it unfold. They had seen the power of the new triplane. Jenkin seemed to take it all in his stride. He obviously believed that aerial combat could be in your blood. It was not. You learned it through experience or you died.

Randolph sat at dinner and we talked shop. Normally that was considered bad form but the new triplane was on all of our minds. Any new German fighter was. "Well, we have a name for it now. It is called the Fokker Dr.I. The cheeky buggers copied it from a Sopwith Triplane they shot down. The RNAS chaps used them."

"Well they can out-climb us and they are faster. Not by much but if they run away then we can't catch them."

Freddie was on the opposite side of the table. "Sir, why do you think they leave so quickly? They must know they have a better bus than we do. Today they could have shot us down and then gone after the Bristols."

I had been thinking about that. "The only explanation I can come up with is that they do not have the endurance to stay aloft for much longer."

Ted nodded, as he lit a cigarette. "That makes sense. I mean the smaller the aeroplane then the smaller the fuel tank. We will have to try to take advantage of that."

"Yes we can make them waste fuel climbing but we still need a way to shoot them down. They are hard to hit."

Archie laughed, "Says the pilot who shot down the first Fokker Dr.I on the Western Front."

"Luck."

"You keep saying that but I say you have a killer instinct."

I hated it when they spoke like this and I changed the subject. "What happened to the formations today? If they had kept their lines then we might have had fewer casualties."

Ted shook his head and I saw annoyance in his eyes. "I think the young lads panicked and tried to fly them as a two-seater and not a fighter. It might have been me and Gordy too. I was nervous about attacking with the new pilots."

"We need to practise that. When do our Camels arrive?"

"Tomorrow."

"We need to check them out first so we will practise the day after tomorrow unless we get orders to patrol."

"I'll find out tomorrow but we appear to be a quiet sector at the moment."

"Let's hope it stays that way then."

Of course, it didn't. As Ted morosely pointed out, if they were giving us new buses in such a hurry then they wanted something doing with them. The Camels arrived and we were immediately given orders to support the French to our south. We would be at the extreme range of our fighters but the French had suffered at the hands of the new Fokkers and we had to show our presence. Archie also flew with us giving us twenty-one aeroplanes. I was less than happy about throwing my new pilots in at the deep end and, in the hours before dawn, I impressed upon them the need to keep in a tight formation and to follow my standing orders.

"Every one of you needs to watch the tail of the man in front. C Flight will not be watching our tails this time; they will be looking after D Flight. Lieutenant Fall, you are the last man in the line. I am, relying on you."

The earnest young man nodded, "Yes, sir."

I had picked him out as the most reliable of my new pilots. Part of it came from his background. He came from Lancaster and his people were farmers. He was both quietly spoken and careful. In fact, he was the opposite of Lieutenant Jenkin. I had Jenkin in the middle where I hoped he would learn from the others.

We took off half an hour before dawn and headed into the rising sun. I wanted every advantage that we could get. We would be flying from the dark and any German fighters would be silhouetted against the sun's rays. We flew a thousand feet above the Bristols. They would ground attack the German positions while the French aeroplanes bombed the rear areas. We hoped to draw the German fighters. I prayed that we were right about the German fuel consumption. We would be flying on fumes, too, when we got home.

The day was not as clear as the previous one and there were annoying puffs of cloud on the horizon. They would be perfect for the Fokkers to hide amongst. I felt nervous with so many new and inexperienced pilots. Archie and Ted had a much easier task; most of their pilots were seasoned veterans. It was their gunners who were new.

I spotted the French bombers; they were the Sopwith Strutter. It was not a good aeroplane but it could carry a decent bomb load. The SPAD fighters escorting them were reassuring. On the face of it, the Bristols would have an easy task that day. They just had to ground attack the trenches and the roads. The reality was that they were a large aeroplane and the German gunners had a good chance of hitting them.

We climbed towards the clouds. I was gambling. If I was waiting for bombers or fighters then I would wait there. I heard the chatter of machine guns and saw Archie and Ted leading B Flight to attack the German trenches. The popping of anti-aircraft guns soon filled the air around them with puffballs of smoke. I looked in my mirror and saw some of my pilots watching them and drifting off line. I would need to have a word with them once we landed. I scanned the sky ahead of me and I was rewarded by the distinctive shape of the Fokker Dr.1 as the ten aeroplanes dived on the Bristols. Behind them were another eight Albatros DV aeroplanes. They were a good and reliable aeroplane but we were faster. It gave us an edge. The danger would be the new nimble Dr. 1.

My calculated guess had given us an advantage. We were now above them. I turned to dive towards the middle of the flight. I would leave Freddie to choose his target. I cocked my twin Vickers and hoped that the triplanes had not seen us. They began to open fire on the Bristols. The rear gunners sent up a spray of bullets as the pilots took evasive action. Our extra height had given us greater speed and we began to overhaul the Fokkers. These were not the Flying Circus but they were a large Jasta. I hoped that they were alone or we could be in trouble.

I gave the aeroplane with the bright green tail a short burst. Although I missed, the pilot reacted by pulling up the nose. They were a nippy little bus and he flew out of my line of sight. I followed him around and Nat Hazell behind me took the opportunity to send a hail of bullets towards him. He was luckier and his bullets struck the tail. Again the German twisted and turned to evade Nat. He flew directly into my sights and I fired another burst at him. I was luckier this time and he began to tumble to the ground.

The German formation had broken up and I was seeking my next target when I felt the judder of bullets as they struck my fuselage. Looking in my mirror I saw that Lieutenant Hazell had been hit and was peeling off west. I began to pull a loop. I heard the bullets as they struck the body of my aeroplane and my wings. I saw that it was an Albatros. I breathed a sigh of relief. I could outrun and outclimb the Albatros. I threw the Camel onto one wing and then began a loop to bring me around inside the Albatros. I do not think I could have managed it against a triplane but the D V was not as agile. I felt a slight shudder as the engine missed. I frowned. That had been the problem Freddie had had the other day. The revs picked up again and I found myself on the tail of my pursuer. I gave him a long burst and saw his tail shredding as my bullets tore holes in the skin. I kept after him, firing as I did so. The Albatros was a tough little fighter but I watched his hand come up as he surrendered. I followed him down as he landed behind the French lines and I turned north and west. I had just enough fuel to get home.

I kept at a lower altitude to save fuel and I felt the engine as it began to judder and shudder more and more. My engine was definitely poorly. That worried me. My mechanic was extremely conscientious. Was it a fault with the engines? I looked into the skies and saw the rest of the squadron as they headed home. I saw the field approaching and wondered if I would actually get down in one piece. The engine sounded as though it was being struck by a hammer. It was too late to fire the Very Pistol and I bumped over the hedge at the end of the field and, as the wheels touched the ground, the engine stopped. I had to use the ailerons and rudder to keep me from slewing around. The grass was not the smoothest runway in the world.

I saw Senior Flight Sergeant Lowery racing towards me with his mechanics. As the Camel lurched to a halt I closed my eyes and sat back in the cockpit. That had been close.

"Are you hit, sir?"

"No, Flight. I had some damage but the engine started playing up. It might be the same trouble that Mr Carrick had the other day."

"The irregular running?"

"Two of the Bristols reported that too. I hope there isn't a fault with these new engines."

"I thought they had totally different engines." Flight Sergeant Lowery nodded. "Well, it needs sorting." I climbed out. "Any damage to the buses?"

"Three of the aeroplanes in your flight are pretty badly shot up sir. Mr Carrick's flight looks to be safe and sound but we lost one of the new pilots I think. At least he didn't come back with the others."

"Who is that?"

"Lieutenant Harvey sir. Still, he may just be having engine trouble." I saw him take his tunic off and roll up his sleeves. I had no doubt that he would get to the bottom of this problem.

I saw Freddie hurrying over to me. He waved to one of his chaps. "Sir, I need to speak with you."

"Of course Freddie, what is it?"

"Your new chap, Jenkin, he pulled out of formation to chase a Fokker. That is why the Albatros was able to hit you and Hazell and the others."

"The others?"

"Yes sir. When he pulled out Lieutenant Fall followed him. You can't blame him. The orders are to follow the bus in front."

"Thanks, Freddie. I shall have a word with the two of them later on." I had a sudden flash of memory. It was like déjà vu. I had had pilots do this before. They jeopardised the whole squadron with their self-centred and selfish behaviour. First, I reported to Randolph. Archie, Ted and Gordy were there and the whisky was open.

"You are right Bill, those new Fokkers are handy little buses. They cleared away a bit quickly though."

I began to fill my pipe and I nodded, "I reckon they do have shorter endurance. The others hung around a lot longer."

"Sorry about your chaps, Gordy."

He nodded glumly. "It wasn't anybody's fault either. The Bristol was hit by groundfire just as he began to pull up to escape the Fokkers. I thought he had made it but he didn't seem to have enough power to escape and he nosedived into the German lines. They wouldn't have known anything about it, either of them."

I frowned. Our engines had been reliable for some time. Why this sudden loss of efficiency?

"I will have to have a word with Jenkin and Fall. Freddie said they pulled out of formation."

Ted nodded, "I saw that. I figured something must have happened."

"Something did. Lieutenant Jenkin decided to go after a triplane and Jack Fall followed him."

Archie nodded, "Use my office. I am going to take a leaf out of your book and have a bath."

"Thanks, sir." I went to the ante-office and said to Senior Flight Sergeant Jameson, "Could you send Lieutenant Jenkin and Lieutenant Fall to the Colonel's office? I need to have a word with them."

"Yes sir."

I filled my pipe as I sat down in Archie's chair. I needed to calm myself down. They were both young pilots. I knew that many pilots, these days, came directly from school and to them, war was a game; an extension of cricket or rugby. We did not, however, have the luxury of being able to give them a long period to settle in. They had to hit the ground running. I struck a match to light the pipe.

Jameson tapped on the door and said, "The pilots you wish to see Major."

"Come in!"

There was a huge contrast in the attitude of the young men. Lieutenant Fall looked distraught while Jenkin had a confident almost happy look.

"Sit down." My pipe had gone out and I took a moment to relight it.

Lieutenant Fall burst out, "I am so sorry sir. I couldn't see beyond the other buses and I didn't know that the Germans were there."

Jenkin gave him a superior look and shook his head. The pipe was drawing well and helped to keep me calm. "The fact remains, Jack, that you have a mirror and can see what is behind you. You knew that the air was clear there. Your job is to follow the flight. I accept that the orders are to follow the bus in front and that somewhat mitigates your actions."

"Mitigates? I am sorry sir, but we are here to shoot down the Hun not to fly in nice straight lines. I saw a German and I went after him."

I nodded and gave Lieutenant Jenkin a smile, "You shot down the German, did you?"

"Well, no sir. I mean it was my first time up I had to get my eye in."

"And while you were getting your eye in, four of our aeroplanes were hit and two of our pilots were wounded. If we have to go up tomorrow we will be down to half our numbers. Yes, you need to, as you say, *get your eye in*, but the first thing you need to do is learn how to fly in combat. I am disappointed in you both, especially you Jack. I had high hopes for you. I will not make this a written reprimand but any more deviations from the standing orders will result in punishment."

"Yes sir."

"Sir that is unfair. I was only doing my best. I should not be punished for that!"

"And you are not being punished, however, if that is your best then I am not impressed, lieutenant! Get out of my sight before I do ground you!"

My bath, that evening, was more than welcome. Bates gave me a disapproving look as he poured a kettle of boiling water in to warm it up. He prided himself on the perfect temperature of the water. "Will you be flying in the morning, sir? I was talking to Senior Flight Sergeant Lowery and he thought there might be a problem with your aeroplane."

"I am not sure. It may be we are not needed tomorrow. Certainly, I could do with another couple of days to find the mettle of these new pilots."

He stuck his finger in the water and nodded his approval. "They are schoolboys, sir. They are like the boys in the first fifteen at my school.

They were all told by everyone that they were the brightest and the best and they believed it. They bullied those not in the team and they were insufferable when they were successful."

"You hated them then?" I stepped into the bath which was just the right temperature.

"At the time I did but then I felt sorry for them. There is no way that they can live up to the dream they all hold. I saw the same men at Loos and Ypres. They came back shivering wrecks or didn't come back at all. I found myself admiring those who fought back against the nerves and became damned good officers. Beg pardon, sir."

"No, Bates I understand. So you are saying that I should go easy on them?"

"Oh no, sir. I am saying that they can handle it. Their egos will be bruised but better a bruised ego than a shattered body. The ones who fail to live up to your standards, well that is life isn't it sir? But mark my words, sir, more of them will end up like Mr Holt and Mr Carrick and that, in the long run, is a good thing."

My philosopher servant left. I had only ever been to a village school and I had learned what I knew in the cavalry but Bates was right. I could not spare the rod. It might cost men their lives.

I was on my way to dinner when Senior Flight Sergeant Lowery buttonholed me. "Have you got a moment, sir?"

The Senior Mechanic never bothered me at dinner time and I knew that it was important. "Of course, Raymond."

He led me towards the aeroplanes. They were all neatly parked although there was plenty of space between them in case of air attack. He waved the sentry away and took me to a workbench.

"When I spoke to the lads they told me about problems with the engines. They all said the same thing. Engines were misfiring. So far, it has been irritating rather than dangerous. I looked at your bus sir because I know the lads take the best care of that one. The engine seemed fine. I thought it might be the fuel, you know, dirt in it or something like that and then I recalled that we filter it all before we put it in." He pointed to a metal tank. "That is your fuel tank, sir. I had it taken out."

"A little extreme eh Flight?"

"I wanted to be sure. Now you didn't have much fuel left. You could have only lasted five more minutes in the air so we drained your fuel and then washed it out." He held up a metal dish. "This is what we found in your tank."

There were tiny pieces of metal in the bottom. "Isn't this normal?"

"For an old engine and tank? Probably but yours is brand new. Mr Carrick has a brand-new aeroplane, only been up twice and we found the same in his."

"I may be being thick here Flight but explain it to me so that I know exactly what you are saying."

"I am saying sir, that we have a saboteur on the base. Someone is putting pieces of metal in with the fuel. The further you fly the more chance you have of the metal getting into the engine and making you crash. Today was just such a day."

"So Lieutenant Harvey could have crashed because his engine was sabotaged, rather than being shot down."

"I think so, sir."

"Who else knows about this?"

"No-one sir. I sent the lads to dinner while I checked it myself."

"Keep it that way. I will make sure we have no operations tomorrow. I want every fuel tank taken out and cleaned before we fly again."

"With respect sir, if you do that you will tip our hand and the saboteur will know we are on to him. We need to find him or them first."

"You are quite right. Then I will see the Colonel and we will devise some way to solve this problem. Thank you, Flight."

"Sir, this is my squadron too and I will have that bastard's nuts in a vice when I find him."

I smiled, "I am not certain that the powers that be will allow that but leave it with me. Come to the colonel's office after breakfast in the morning." As he walked away I frowned. The men in the squadron were the best I had ever served alongside. I could not countenance that one of them was an enemy agent.

Chapter 4

I was almost late for dinner and I saw a frown crease Archie's face as I entered the mess. He knew that it was not like me to be late. I gave the slightest shake of my head and smiled at everyone. "Sorry, I am late. Bates wanted the temperature of the bath to be just right!"

Everyone smiled at that. They all knew Bates and his ways. I stood behind my chair as Archie said Grace and the mess orderlies hurried in as soon as we were seated. I spoke quietly so that only Randolph and Archie, who were on either side of me, could hear what I said. I saw that Ted and Gordy were curious but they knew I would tell them later if it concerned them.

"We have a saboteur. Sergeant Lowery found metal in the fuel tanks. It explains why our engines have been running badly lately." I paused while the steward ladled the soup into the bowl. When they had gone I continued. "It has only begun since we returned to this field. It explains why young Lowery crashed today. I told Lowery we would not fly operations tomorrow."

"Good idea. Bit of a bugger though. I thought all of our chaps were good fellows."

"They may be. It could be someone coming from outside the base. Equally, it could be someone new."

Randolph shook his head. "There are only the new pilots and gunners who have joined us since we returned. All of the other ranks have been with us all the time. Certainly, they have been with us when we had no sabotage. I can't see pilots and gunners sabotaging the engines. Their lives are on the line."

"Are you sure about this Bill?"

"I saw the evidence with my own eyes. There are pieces of metal in the tanks of the new aeroplanes."

"Perhaps the sabotage is in England where they make the aeroplanes."

"There are metal pieces in the older aeroplanes too. I used mine at Ypres and there was no problem. I think that Harvey died today not because his bus was damaged by German fire but because he used so much fuel that the metal got into the engine and it stopped."

"Could it be one of the new pilots?"

"It could be but they would have to have a death wish. They fly the buses too."

We paused again as the soup was taken away and the main courses came. "We better have a drink and chat about something else sir, everyone is watching us."

Randolph was right. We looked serious and conspiratorial; it was not our way. "You are right. Join me in my office after the port then."

As we left the mess I nodded for Gordy, Freddie and Ted to join us. Once in the office hut, which the office staff had vacated and was empty, Ted asked. "What's up?"

I told them. The looks on their faces showed what they thought. Ted summed it up succinctly. "It's bad enough going against those triplanes without having to worry that someone has damaged the bus you are in. What do we do?"

"I have been thinking about this over dinner. It seems to me that there are two possibilities: one is a saboteur coming in at night and doing their deadly deed. The second is that it is one of our chaps. We can eliminate the first one."

"How?"

"Increase the number of guards we have around the aeroplanes at night."

"But if it is one of our chaps then won't that tip them off?"

"Not if you receive a telephone call from Headquarters warning them of possible German infiltrators close to our airfields. You will have to warn Headquarters anyway."

"Good idea, Bill, but we can't ground the squadron for long. This is the time when the Hun is out and about. They have been quiet in this sector for a few weeks and that normally means that they are planning something."

Archie was right. I filled my pipe and the others stared at the walls for inspiration. Suddenly Randolph smacked his hand on the desk. "This saboteur is a clever fellow; are we agreed?" We nodded. "He has not been spotted by the mechanics which means he is doing this when the mechanics are not around. I know that Lowery keeps the same mechanics on the same buses. They all protect their own aeroplanes very jealously. The times when they can get to the buses are after the mechanics finish and before they begin again."

"That would be any time between six in the evening and four in the morning when they do the pre-flight checks."

Randolph shook his head. "No, we can narrow it down even further. I think even the doziest sentry would see someone when there was daylight. That means it is between eight at night and three in the morning. Between dusk and dawn."

"Then I have an idea. Tomorrow we work on my bus and say we have a special mission over the German lines. As it is a long flight it will explain why Flight Sergeant Lowery has to flush out the tank to make sure that we have the maximum range."

"And what happens then?"

"I spend the night in the cockpit."

"Suppose the saboteur is from outside the camp?"

"Then the extra guards will spot them."

"Suppose it is one of the guards? How will you get into the bus?"

"That is easy. Sergeant Wilson parades the guards before they begin their duty and explains that there have been rumours of German soldiers attacking bases at night. It will put them on their toes."

I saw agreement forming on the faces of the others. Freddie nodded and said, "It would make more sense if it was two buses. I normally fly as your wingman anyway. I will spend the night in my bus too. It will not seem unusual."

Before I could disagree, Archie said, "Capital idea and I am happier with two pairs of eyes and ears."

"I will start to go through the records of all the men in the squadron. There may be clues in their background."

Ted shook his head, "I can't believe it is one of our blokes. I reckon it is more likely to be someone coming through the hedgerow."

I was not so sure. Whoever it was, knew aeroplanes and knew how to damage aeroplanes and make it hard to detect. "Well, I will get an early night. I asked Flight Sergeant Lowery to meet us here after breakfast. We can explain my plan to him then."

I lay in bed, unable to sleep. It was earlier than I normally retired but, more than that, my mind was filled with the horrific thought that we had a traitor in our midst. I could hardly contemplate it. We were a tight team and fought as one, ground and aircrew together. I began to doubt everyone. Who could I trust?

I was bad-tempered from the moment I woke up. I snapped at Bates. Amazingly he smiled at me as though he had expected it. When the war was over we could tour the music halls with his mind-reading act. I sat sullenly through breakfast. I was tired and I did not like the thought of a traitor in our midst.

We explained our ideas to Flight Sergeant Lowery who nodded approvingly. "We need this weasel winkling out sir. If the lads knew we had a saboteur..." Shaking his head he said, "I think they would string the bugger up from the nearest tree." He rose, "Well I shall get the buses sorted." He paused, "Do you think it might be a saboteur from outside the base?"

I shook my head, "Personally I don't think so. We don't always park the buses in the same place and only someone who knew aeroplanes would know where the fuel tank was. I reckon the odds are that it is someone on the field but Sergeant Wilson and his chaps will be on their toes tonight."

Freddie and I took ourselves out to the buses to watch the mechanics working on the Camels. I studied every face for deception or for signs of guilt but I saw none. The young pilots came out, full of curiosity. "Something special then sir?"

I tapped my nose, "I could tell you but then I would have to kill you, Lieutenant McDonald." I said it with humour and they all laughed. The mechanics were both diligent and careful when they took out the tank and cleaned it thoroughly. Sergeant Lowery was right it couldn't be one of the mechanics. They regarded each aeroplane as their personal possession.

We heard the sound of an engine approaching and looked to see a Sopwith Camel approaching from the west. We did not recognise it but Freddie knew who it would be. "That is Johnny! He's back."

The last time we had seen Johnny was just before they took him to the base hospital after he had lost his eye. I frowned. He was flying the Camel solo and yet I thought he had to be passed fit before he could return to active duty. I suspect my bad mood was still with me. I had flown a Gunbus with a broken arm! My nerves were getting the better of me. The spy in the camp was unsettling. It might be good to have Johnny back. Freddie was always happier when his old friend was around and I knew that Johnny would be good for the younger pilots. He spoke their language.

The Camel rolled to a halt and Johnny leapt out. When he took his goggles off, I saw the black patch covering the wound. Freddie burst out laughing. "You look like a damned pirate!"

I held my breath. I would never have dared to make such a comment. Johnny laughed too. "Well, I thought I had better come back and keep my eye on you lot! My good eye, at least!"

I breathed again. Johnny was neither self-conscious nor worried about the wound. I held out my hand. "Good to see you, Johnny. How is the eye?"

He gave me a deadpan look. "I have no idea. I haven't seen it since the doc took it out!" He burst out laughing as did Freddie. Suddenly my bad mood disappeared like early morning mist.

"I take it you have more of these jokes stored up for us?"

"Oh, hundreds sir. Enough to see me through the week at any rate."

I shook my head. This was death by the pun. "Has the doc cleared you to fly then?"

"Yes sir. I was ready to return a week ago but the new bus hadn't arrived and the medicos wanted to make sure I could manage it. I went up in a two-seater with a major from 56 Squadron. He was well satisfied. He gave me a clean bill of health."

"No problems then?"

"Not flying the Camel. I just aim the bus at the Hun and pull the trigger. Bob's your uncle. I have to turn to the right a little more to see behind me, that is all. The doctor said something about a loss of periphery vision; whatever the hell that is but I didn't have a problem getting here."

"Good. Well, Freddie will fill you in on the changes that have been made. You are his number two now and he should be a captain in the next week or so."

Freddie didn't know about his promotion; the news had only come in that morning and both he and Johnny were equally delighted.

"Well Captain Carrick, as you are now a higher rank and have more pay then you can buy me a drink in the mess to celebrate." I gave the slightest of shakes of my head to Freddie and he nodded. "Let me fill you in first, old chap. We have lots of time to have that drink!"

Johnny could be trusted to keep his mouth shut but I did not want Freddie sleepily drunk if we were to keep our vigil that night.

Had we actually been going on a mission deep into enemy territory then I would have been delighted with the diligence of the mechanics and riggers. When the Camel was started it purred like a kitten. Senior Flight Sergeant Lowery wandered over to me. "Now that is what the Camel should sound like. My lads do good work."

"I know Flight and there has not been a whiff of criticism. This is a saboteur."

"I know, Major Harsker, but it could be one of my lads and that doesn't sit well. It was me as spotted the problem but I wish I hadn't. I was up half the night going through my men in my mind and working out who it could be. None of them fitted. I'm stumped."

"If no one comes tonight then we know it is a German from beyond our airfield and we can do something about it."

Lowery went away happier but I knew, in my heart that the man who had tried to kill so many of us was within sight and sound of me. The news of a German infiltrator coming from outside set everyone looking towards the roads, hedges and nearby buildings. It was as though each of them housed a Hun.

Before dinner, I loaded my Luger and my Webley. I had Bates fill the flask with hot black coffee. He did not question my request. He was the perfect servant. After dinner, I returned to my quarters to wrap up in my greatcoat. I waited until I heard Sergeant Wilson marching the nighttime sentries to parade them and give them their instructions. Then I slipped away to the aeroplanes. It was remarkably quiet. The sun was setting in the west and the field was filling with shadows. Sergeant Lowery was giving the mechanics and riggers a talk about maintenance and the sentries were being paraded. I saw Freddie as he came from his quarters. I nodded to him and then, after checking that no one was watching, we both climbed aboard. There was no one around and the sky was quickly darkening. I hoped that we had managed to do it without being observed.

It was a tight fit in the cockpit but by pulling my knees up and hunching my back I was able to hide beneath the sides of the cockpit. I could not remain like that all night but I only had to do so until night fell and then I would be hidden by the struts and the shadow of the upper wing. I decided to wait until it was completely dark. I heard Sergeant Wilson as he marched the guards and allotted them their positions. There were twice as many as normal. They had been told to watch the perimeter for Germans and anyone who approached the Camels would be suspect. I heard the Sergeant tell them to call him if they saw anything suspicious and not to leave their patrol area. He terrified me and, I dare say, did the same for the men who guarded our airbase.

When it was dark I slowly raised my head. It took some time for my eyes to become accustomed to the dark but soon I was able to pick out the other aeroplanes and, eventually, the sentries. They were detectable when they moved. I moved my head slowly so that I could see all of them. I was happy when I had identified their positions. Sergeant Wilson was the one walking around them all. I heard him as he snapped at any inattention or glowing cigarette. He was good at his job. I could not see how a saboteur could hope to get close to an aeroplane. He would be spotted by the sergeant or one of the sentries. Perhaps there were two of them. That would make sense.

I could not see the face of my watch but I detected the noises from the messes which gave me an idea of the time. I heard the sergeants return to their quarters and knew it would be about 10.30. When the young officers noisily headed home then I knew it was about 11. The senior officers would not be drinking and they would be sleeping either dressed or half-dressed. All of us were anxious to get to the bottom of this.

Randolph had given us disappointing news. Apart from the new officers and gunners, he could not find any record of any airman joining us in the last month either before we left for Ypres or since we had returned. That made the likelihood that the saboteur had been with us for some time even higher. Neither was there any evidence that there was anything suspicious in the backgrounds of the men. None had either Continental or Irish connections. Since the 1916 uprising, many Irishmen had been investigated for their possible sympathies to the IRA. Apart from a couple of Welshmen and half a dozen Scotsmen, everyone was English. It was perplexing.

I had a drink of coffee as I heard the officers retiring. It gave me something to do and the movement brought the circulation back to my legs. The coffee was still hot and I felt more awake. I decided to wait an hour for my next drink. It was a sort of treat for myself. I had put the flask in the bottom of the cockpit and looked up when I noticed a shadow was missing. I looked to the left and to the right. The shadows of the sentries were still marching up and down. There was one missing. I wondered if he had gone to relieve himself and I carefully and slowly scanned the field for someone doing just that. As my head turned towards Freddie's aeroplane I saw the shadow and he was approaching the rear of the Camel. I withdrew my Luger. I wanted to have a bead on him before I shouted. I raised my head and arm so that, if I had to I had a clear shot.

I watched as he moved towards the fuel filler cap. Freddie had not seen him. It would be up to me. I raised the Luger and aimed it at his back. I could not bring myself to shoot a man in the back. There might have been a harmless explanation. I could not think what it might be but who knew?

I shouted, "That man! Stand still or I will shoot." I had a powerful voice when I was a sergeant. The figure spun around and I saw a gun in his hand. It was a pistol. He fired and the bullet cracked into the spar above my head. I fired three quick shots. The gun fell from his hand and he tumbled to the ground clutching his chest.

Freddie was out in an instant, his Webley aimed at the man. Sergeant Wilson was racing over with a handful of sentries and I heard the commotion as officers and sergeants ran from their quarters.

By the time I had clambered down Sergeant Wilson had his rifle pointed at the soldier's head. "It's Tommy Devlin, sir! I never would have believed it!"

The dying man opened his eyes and laughed. A tendril of blood dripped from the corner of his mouth. "And that's because you are an ignorant, stupid Englishman. I am just sorry more of you murdering bastards didn't die. Another week and…."

We heard no more, for he expired there and then. Archie and Randolph arrived. Sergeant Wilson said, "He was only new sir but he was really popular."

Randolph said, "New? That is impossible. When did he arrive?"

"He was here sir when we came back from Ypres. He said he had been sent from Headquarters." We stared at him. "He had the uniform and…." He shook his head, "He was right, sir, I am stupid. I was so busy organising rosters and tents I didn't check his transfer papers I assumed he had shown them to an officer. He just walked in as bold as brass and I didn't check him. I am so sorry, sir."

"Well, we have all learned a lesson. Tomorrow morning, we hold a parade and Captain Marshall here will check every man on the base. We lost two good men because of this spy. It could have been worse. We nipped his antics in the bud. He might have used more metal in the fuel and killed many more good men than he did. Well done Bill. You have saved a trial and a firing squad."

It had been some time since I had seen the face of someone I had killed. As I returned to my quarters I decided to have a whisky to help me get to sleep.

Chapter 5

Poor Sergeant Wilson was a broken man. A career soldier he normally followed the King's Regulations to the letter. Tommy Devlin had been very clever. He had obviously been sent by the Germans as soon as the squadron left for Ypres. It was a skeleton garrison we had left and there was no officer there. It was mainly the stores' staff and a few guards. They were more than happy to have an extra pair of hands. It helped that he was a popular soldier who pitched in with anything and everything. He seemed very curious and happy to listen to the stories of the squadrons and the pilots. It helped him to blend in. Once the squadron returned he volunteered for the night duty saying that he disliked the sun. We found his pockets filled with metal filings and pieces of metal. He had helped the armourers out by sweeping their workshops. Until we discovered his true vocation there was not a more popular soldier on the base.

We examined his quarters and found nothing at first then Randolph noticed one of the floorboards was not as tight as the ones around it and when it was prised up we found his German identification. It was obviously there in case he was captured by the Germans. The codebook was useful but Headquarters had other copies of it. All of his belongings were gathered together as evidence which might help other squadrons.

Archie was summoned to Amiens where he briefed the other squadron commanders. The trick could have been repeated almost anywhere. As soon as investigations began four other spies were discovered, three of whom fled before they could be apprehended. They were all members of the IRA and had been enlisted by the Imperial High Command. They had exploited the unrest after the Easter Rising of 1916. In late August and early September, military police were drafted in to every airfield to oversee security. It was difficult at first but we lived with it. Anyone of us could have died at the hands of the saboteur.

When Archie returned it was also with new orders. We were to clear the Germans from the skies. It was a tall order but something of a relief. Dealing with spies and saboteurs was not usual. Fighting high above the skies was. Archie also brought us news of new developments for our buses. Some squadrons had been issued with oxygen to enable them to fly higher. At the moment it was limited to bomber crews but eventually, we would have the ability to fly to our ceiling. We could reach almost twenty thousand feet!

Johnny was keen to fly again. I had been tempted to ask for him to be my tail-end Charlie but that would not be fair on Freddie. I decided to persevere with Jack Fall. The night before our first flight I took him for a walk around the aeroplane park. I noticed the increased security. It felt reassuring.

"I am leaving you as the last aeroplane in the flight because I have faith in you. But you have to concentrate. You must watch in your mirror and make sure we are not jumped. You must watch what I do. I realise I am four aeroplanes up from you but you have to do it. If Mr Jenkin decides to be an Australian and go walkabout again you have to ignore him. You are there to protect the flight and not Mr Jenkin."

"He won't do that again. He has promised me."

"Well, I will take that statement with a pinch of salt. I hope he means it because we need every pilot we can get at the front. All of you are more valuable now for you have survived your first flight over the German lines. Every time you land your value goes up."

"Really sir? We are valuable?"

I put my arm around his shoulder, "Of course you are and you will be a good pilot. I am confident in that."

The one order I did not like was the one which separated the two halves of the squadron. Archie was less than happy too but he had to follow the orders. The Bristols would fly one sector and the Camels another. The Bristol had been a good fighter in its day but the new German buses could fly rings around the old two-seater. I forced the thought of my friends dying from my mind and we ascended to our sector and flew east looking for Germans.

I glanced in my mirror and saw that my flight was keeping formation. I would soon have a stiff neck watching out for the troublesome George Jenkin. I knew that I could have him transferred but that seemed like admitting defeat to me. He had the makings of a good pilot but I needed to change his attitude. Aerial combat needs complete concentration and I forced myself to look to the east. Our mission was to eliminate the threat of the Jasta. To do so meant flying over their lines. I knew the inherent dangers of this. We would have less time to fight them and the Triplane, which we assumed had a shorter endurance, would not flee as fast. I hoped my young pilots were up to it.

I glanced to port. Freddie and his flight were on station. They were my ace in the hole for they represented the best combat pilots we had. I could rely on them. I saw Freddie wave forward and I saw the black dots climbing to meet us. I frowned as I waggled my wings to let my flight know we were about to go into action. We were barely over the German lines and yet the German aeroplanes were closing with us.

They must have had airfields which were closer to the front than they had been.

I cocked my Vickers and kept flying at the same altitude. Height was precious and you did not lose it until you had to. We would maintain our position. I had learned that timing was all. Sometimes fortune smiles on you for no reason. On that morning a sudden shaft of sunlight picked out the ascending flight. They were a rainbow of colours. It was the Flying Circus. I had the greenest of pilots to face the best that the Germans possessed. I had to get my flight back to safety as soon as possible. I knew that Freddie would have recognised the livery and would react accordingly but I had no way of telling my flight of the danger. They would be excited to be finally facing the Germans.

We had closed to within a mile or so. They were climbing in their normal formation and I would have to endure the fire of five aeroplanes. I decided to climb a little. It might confuse the Hun but, more importantly, it would allow us to sweep from the north and then turn west. It would also burn up valuable German fuel. Almost all of the Germans were the new Fokker Triplane. I saw, in my mirror, that some of my aeroplanes were a little slow to react to my formation change. It made me level out a little sooner than I wanted. I banked to starboard and started to descend.

I was closing with Fritz at a combined speed of over two hundred miles an hour. At that speed, you have less than a couple of seconds to fire and hit your target. My dive was shallow. I saw the German guns as they spat flames. I had learned to ignore them. You could not worry about them hitting you. You prayed that they would not. I waited until the Fokker was in my sights and I pulled my triggers. It was a small target and only in my sights for a second but I hit him and then he was gone. I pulled up my nose and was rewarded with the sight of the underbelly of a bright green and yellow Albatros. I fired a short burst. This time I knew that I had hit it for it began to peel away. Then I felt the judder of bullets hitting my fuselage. I kept climbing. If we could regain height then we might still have an advantage. Looking in my mirror I saw that the Jasta had disrupted our formation. There were just Fall and Clayson behind me now and they were no longer tight to me.

The air was filled with aeroplanes. It was a confused and chaotic melee. I looked ahead and saw clear sky. My compass told me that I was heading south. I banked to starboard. The red Triplane appeared from nowhere. I had to pull hard on the stick to avoid a collision and we passed within the width of a wing. I was so close that I saw the pilot's face. It was the Red Baron. He cheekily waved at me as he recognised me too and then he was gone.

I saw Jenkin and Hazell below me. They had lost the precious altitude and three Fokkers were chasing them. They were jinking across the front as they tried to evade the deadly twin machine guns. I dived down to go to their aid. Lieutenants Clayson and Fall followed me. The Camel was so responsive that we began to close rapidly with the three Huns who were now two thousand feet below me. I saw Lieutenant Hazell's bus judder and begin to smoke as he was hit by the Huns' guns. I was too far away to fire. I saw Jenkin as he started to climb. I prayed that Nat would not try to emulate him. His rudder was a mess. One of the triplanes climbed after Jenkin.

The smoke was now pouring from the Camel. At a thousand yards, as I saw the tiny target of the blue and yellow triplane cross my sights, I fired a hopeful burst. As luck would have it, my bullets arced above him. Although I did not hit him it warned him of my presence and he pulled his nose up a little. It gave Lieutenant Hazell some respite. I heard Roger Clayson's guns as he fired at the rear of the two Fokkers we followed. I fired a second burst and the Fokker's new flight path took him across the twin lines of tracer. I saw the bullets thump into his rudder. It clearly affected his control and he began to edge east. I fired another burst which, although it missed, encouraged him to depart. His wingman left with him.

Lieutenant Hazell was in trouble. I waved to Clayson and Fall to follow him while I scanned the skies for Jenkin. I knew that I would not have long to search for him. I was running out of fuel but I could not abandon him. I banked to port and saw the two of them. Jenkin was heading east! He was flying towards the German airfield. All that I could think was that he had forgotten to look at his compass. I was still above them and I dived to intercept. The Fokker was closing inexorably with my young pilot. Jenkin was doing all that he could to shake both the German and his aim. Bullets were still striking his Camel. I saw pieces of his undercarriage fall to the ground as they were hit. I came at the Fokker obliquely and it gave me a longer shot. I fired three bursts as I closed with him. One of them hit his bus close to his middle wing. I saw the Fokker wobble in the air. I fired a longer burst. My guns clicked empty but I saw a small plume of smoke come from his engine.

Lieutenant Jenkin must have realised he was flying the wrong way for he pulled hard to the right and the German kept going east. As I banked I saw the German pilot wave his arm at me. He must have realised that I was out of bullets for he had been at my mercy.

As I headed west I watched the erratic course the lieutenant was flying. His controls had been damaged. My bus was also feeling the effects of combat. The holes in my wings were making it more sluggish.

As soon as I saw the field, in the distance, I fired the Very pistol. The ground crews would be ready for the Camel. I knew that the undercarriage on Jenkin's bus was gone already. This would not be a pretty landing. I watched as the lieutenant fought to keep the Camel on as straight a line as he could. He was showing me now what a good pilot he was. The Camel was not a forgiving mistress. As I circled the field I saw Doc Brennan and his staff as they dealt with the other casualties. Then I watched as the stricken Camel bumped down. The damaged wheels collapsed as soon as they hit the grass. Jenkin was lucky. His tail hit the ground first. The damage he had received meant that it swung the aeroplane around and then the tail detached. It stopped him cartwheeling but it made him spin until the propeller dug into the ground and he stopped.

I banked and began my approach. I had to avoid his Camel which was in the middle of the runway. I hoped I did not catch a hole on the little-used left side of the field or I too would have a written-off Camel. God favoured me that day and, although it was not a smooth landing I came to a rest with the bus intact and I was able to climb down to the grass safely.

I took out my pipe as soon as I landed. It had been a lucky encounter but, as I counted the aeroplanes which had landed already I saw that we had been hurt. I saw Nat Hazell being carried off on a stretcher and the mechanics shaking their heads at the state of his Camel. Others were trying to cut Jenkin free from his almost destroyed Camel. I got my pipe going before I walked over. It helped to calm me. Archie was striding down from the office. I saw Freddie and his flight as they began to land. I saw that Lieutenant Carpenter was missing. Freddie and his men would need all their skills to land successfully until the field had been cleared.

Archie reached me, "Problems laddie?"

I nodded, "We ran into the flying circus. It was the Red Baron himself. We managed to wing a couple of them but they made a mess of the young lads."

"That's all we needed. Still, it could have been worse. If they had jumped the Bristols then it might have been a disaster."

I allowed myself a wry smile, Archie was definitely seeing the glass half full if he thought that there was anything good to be gleaned from this encounter.

With Lieutenant Jenkin on a stretcher, the mechanics and riggers began to move the two damaged aeroplanes. In the distance, we heard the throb of the Bristols as they returned. As they did so Freddie and his flight landed. We watched Freddie and his men taxi and then park up their buses. I counted the Bristols. They looked to be intact. Although, as they began to land we saw that they too had run into trouble. September had started badly.

Freddie came over to join us. "What happened to Carpenter?" I knew that Freddie would not be happy to have lost a pilot.

"He was forced down behind our lines. He walked away from the bus but I think it is a write-off. Mr Lowery and his scavengers might be able to rescue some of the bits but…"

"Did we get any? I was too busy to see if we actually managed to shoot any down."

"I am not certain. It was confused up there. I think we damaged four or five of theirs but I didn't see any crash."

Archie nodded, "Honours even then."

"More like advantage Hun, I think sir."

"No, Bill. You went up against the most formidable Jasta the Germans possess and we got all of our pilots back. You had young pilots out there. They will be better next time."

"He is right sir, your young lads, Lieutenant Fall and Roger Clayson did exactly what you asked and they followed you remarkably well. I think the colonel is right. We have positives to take from this."

I was not so certain but I began to see that they might be right. Senior Flight Sergeant Lowery reported. "Sir, two of your flight will need a week of repairs to be airworthy. One is a write-off."

"Make that two, Flight Sergeant. You will need to take a lorry and collect the remains of Lieutenant Carpenter's bus. It is three miles east of here."

"Sir." He looked at the Bristols which coughed and wheezed their way along the grass. "And God knows how many of these will need work, sir."

Archie smiled, "Do your best, Flight. That is all that we can ask."

As we walked to Randolph's office to report Ted and Gordy told us how they had been jumped by a Jasta. "We were outnumbered three to one. "We had to use the old Lufbery Circle." Gordy chuckled, "I am not certain that the German pilots had ever seen it before. It worked."

"Did you knock any down?"

"Damaged a few but we were just glad to get out alive." Ted pointed to the damaged Camels which were being taken to the hangar. "It looks like you ran into a meat grinder."

"The Red Baron and his Flying Circus!"

"That is all we need. I kept hoping he would be up around Ypres."

We had reached the office and we sat around the table while Archie poured us a whisky each. "I think he will stay in this sector as he can have a go at the French as well as us. There is more glory for him."

"You met him, didn't you Bill?"

I downed my whisky and poured a second, "Aye and the others: his brother Lothar and Werner Voss. They are both almost as good as the Red Baron." I shrugged, "The thing is only the best get into the Flying Circus."

Randolph nodded, "Sort of like the German first fifteen."

"A good analogy, Randolph and we are going up against him with the best fourth formers we have. It is boys against men."

Archie must have sensed the air of depression which had descended. He banged his hand on the table. "Right go and get cleaned up and put this from your mind. Tomorrow is another day. I will go up with you tomorrow and we will fly as one squadron. Damn the General. We will not spread ourselves too thinly in the future. I want us to have a fighting chance."

Surprisingly that little pep talk seemed to work and I went for the bath I knew Bates would have drawn feeling better. My spirits rose even higher when he greeted me with a bundle of letters. "We have mail, sir!"

That was always a reason for optimism. A letter from home was better than anything for raising spirits.

Chapter 6

When I returned to my room after my bath Bates had put a glass of whisky next to my bed. "I will see you are not disturbed, sir." Bates knew the value of the letters. As the door closed I sipped the whisky and picked up the envelopes. There were four letters. I rearranged the orders. I would read Lumpy's first then my mother's, Alice's next and I would save the most precious one for the end. Beattie was my fiancée and I saved hers for last to savour. I had been the same with the Sunday roasts my mother cooked when I was a child. The roast potatoes and the meat were left until last as a special treat.

Stockton August 1917
Dear Major Harsker,
Just a quick letter to tell you how proud I was to read of your promotion and your VC. No one deserves them more than you. I feel privileged to have served with you. The lads in the pub wouldn't let me buy a drink when they heard of the medal. They have never met you but they have heard all about you from me and Jack's widow. To them, you are a hero because you come from the same background as they do. You are an ordinary bloke to them.

The wife and I pray that this war will be over soon so that you can all come home. We see too many women in widow's weeds and there are too many bairns without dads.

I am doing well and the missing hand never worries me!
God Speed, sir, and look after yourself,
Your old gunner
Lumpy

I could almost hear Lumpy's voice as I read the letter. I was pleased that he had found happiness with Jack Laithwaite's widow. He would be a good father to her children. I always got a warm feeling when I thought of Lumpy surviving the war. It gave me hope for the future. The finest young men in England had been sacrificed and when the war was over the ones who remained would have a mountain to climb to make Britain great once more. We had suffered much and the whole country would bear the scars for generations to come.

Burscough
August 1917

Dear Bill,

Your father and I are so proud of you. What an honour to be awarded the VC. Lady Burscough came over to the cottage especially to tell us.

Things are not going so well on the estate. We are doing well so don't worry. Her ladyship has promised us that we can have the cottage for as long as we need it but most of the other estate workers have had to be let go. There is just our Sarah and Cedric at the big house now. They both have to work far harder than they used to. We look after little Billy every day but he is a canny bairn and no bother.

I haven't heard from Bert lately. I know you are both busy and writing letters isn't a priority but you manage it and you are an officer. I hope he is safe.

Your dad and I have had enough of this war. It has taken too many already. Poor John and Tom died so long ago but our Alice is still grieving for her young man. I know that he was a friend of yours and would have been a fine husband but we never got to meet him and I don't think our Alice will ever get over him.

John writes regularly and tells us how well you are doing. You are lucky to have such a good servant. You look after him!

You take care of yourself,

I pray to God each night to keep you safe. He has taken enough from us.

Your loving mother

xxx

I found myself dreading reading Alice's letter. I drank the whisky and poured another in preparation. I slit open the envelope and then lit my pipe. I knew I was delaying reading what I thought might be a sad and depressing letter. I felt a little guilty about Alice. If I had not introduced her to Charlie then who knows how her life might have turned out. She might have been able to find some happiness.

Burscough
August 1917
Dearest Bill,

I hope you are keeping well. Congratulations on the VC. Charlie always said that you were the bravest and the best and I know that he was right. He worshipped you, big brother and he was right to do so.

I noticed that the next lines were a little fuzzy as though they had been wetted.

I still find myself bursting into tears when I think of the life that Charlie and I might have had. It isn't fair. I know it upsets Mum and Lady Burscough but I can't help it. I want to hit someone or scream or I don't know what.

Your young lady, Beattie, is a godsend. She writes to me every week and she is always so positive. The main reason I am writing this is to tell you, big brother, that you must marry the girl and do it sooner rather than later! I know Charlie and I were like a pair of runaway horses but you never know what is around the corner. I don't want Beattie cuddling a pillow in her bed at night because you aren't there.

Don't worry about me, Bill. I know everyone is concerned but I will get through this. I know that I can never be truly happy again but, at night, I can still close my eyes and hear Charlie's voice and I can't wait to see you for that will bring him alive again too.

You have to survive this war! I can't lose you too!

I saw another patch of fuzzy writing.

This ink isn't very good, is it? It must be the war!

I pray for you, Ted and Gordy each night. I pray you will all come home safely,

Your loving sister
Alice
xxx

I found my eyes filling up. I missed Charlie too but for Alice, he had been her whole life. I sniffed the envelope before I opened it. Beattie was in the room. Settling back in the bed I began to read; savouring each word.

Hyde Park
August 1917
Dearest Bill,

I hope this finds you safe. The casualties who have been pouring through our doors after the battles of Ypres talk about the airmen who braved the skies to protect them. I knew that it would be you they were talking about- you are too reckless! They don't give the VC to careful soldiers. You cannot win this war alone! I want you home when this war is over. I have plans for us!

Speaking as often as I do with your sister, Alice, I know what I have and how lucky I am. Please God that our luck does not run out!

The Germans have begun sending bombers over each night to bomb London. One of the nurses on our ward was killed when her house was blown up. It is so indiscriminate and so cowardly. The Huns must be a cruel and heartless nation if they use poison gas while shelling and bombing civilians. I know that you and your pilots would never inflict such carnage on civilians. That is why I know that we shall win this war. We are in the right!

I am sorry that this letter is not the usual happy, chatty letter but I do not feel that way at the moment. I feel lost and alone and I miss you.

I know that is selfish; there are many people in our position but I feel like being selfish.

I cannot wait for your next leave.

Take care of yourself and be careful!

You are in my prayers each night but I see so much horror coming through the doors that I sometimes question if there is a God. I know that is an awful thing to say but why does God allow so many who are good die and allow evil men to live?

I love you now and forever,

Beattie xxx

Beattie's letter upset me more than I could believe. I just wanted to fly my Camel home and rush into her arms. I knew I would not but I felt angry. I dressed for dinner. We had to bring this war to an end and do so quickly. Our people at home were suffering and none of us had gone to war to allow that!

I called in at the sick bay on my way to the mess. My two pilots had survived but, even had their aeroplanes not been damaged, they would not be able to fly for a few days. Lieutenant Hazell tried to rise when I entered.

"No, Nat, rest easy. You did well today. Those new Fokkers are very nifty."

"Thank you, sir. I appreciate you coming to my aid."

"Nonsense we are one squadron here and we all fight for each other." I turned to Jenkin, "And how are you, George?"

"Feeling like a fool."

"How so?"

"When my compass was shot out I flew in the wrong bloody direction, sir!"

I smiled, "An easy enough mistake to make. I have seen pilots flying upside down because they became disorientated. A little tip; have a spare compass in your flying jacket and always look for the sun. We normally fly in the morning so the sun should be ahead of us; that tells you where east is. Don't berate yourself, you acquitted yourself well today."

"But still no kills!"

I sighed and shook my head, "We had no kills in the squadron today but as all our pilots made it back, then it is not a bad trade-off. You two take it easy. Your new buses will be here in a week. You are under Doc Brennan's orders now, not mine."

I knew that we had made important strides with Jenkin but he was not the finished article yet.

Everyone was in a better mood thanks to the delivery of letters. Gordy insisted upon reading them out so that we could hear every breath his new son made. We smiled. It was harmless and the baby promised hope. We had perilously little of that.

The talk was of the trenches. The Canadians were still bleeding for every inch of land at Passchendaele and we saw little progress. Flying high over the lines meant you could see how little land had been gained in over three years of war. There were also rumours of trouble in Russia. Randolph, who had many contacts in the intelligence community, was particularly sombre. "We are making little progress here on the Western front but if the Tsar makes peace then the Germans will have more men and materiel to send here. If that happens this war could go on for another ten years."

Johnny scoffed, "A thirteen-year war? I think you are exaggerating sir."

"We had a war with France that lasted over a hundred years. The Napoleonic wars lasted over twenty-five years. There was a war in Europe which lasted for thirty years. No, do not assume that this war will be as quick as the Zulu War or the South African War. We were fighting tribesmen then. We are fighting people like ourselves now. Our king, the Kaiser and the Tsar are all cousins!"

"People won't stand for it, sir."

"I'm afraid, Freddie, that the powers that be are like gamblers gathered around a table. The table stakes are so high that no one dares to be the one to leave first. They just keep raising the stakes and we are the chips!"

We were having a glass of port when Ted sidled over. "What is the problem, Bill?"

"How do you know there is a problem?"

"Because I have known you too long. If Gordy wasn't so full of Mary and his son then he would have noticed too. I have bugger all but for the squadron. You are like my family and I can tell that something has upset you." He gestured to the port. "You are drinking more than you used to for a start."

"We all drink."

"Aye, but you used to drink the least out of any of us. Now you drink as much and sometimes a little more. So come on, out with it. You know what they say a problem shared is a problem halved."

I nodded. He was a good friend and he was right. "It's Beattie. She is getting upset. The Germans are bombing London and she is worried about me. She was the only one not happy about the VC. She sees it as a sign that I am being reckless."

He nodded and stubbed his cigarette out. "Well, you are."

"What?"

"Oh don't get me wrong I appreciate that quality in you. It is what makes you a great pilot. Gordy and I can fly but you are a pilot and more than that you are a fighter pilot. Freddie told me that today you went head to head with the Red Baron and he didn't win. Do you know how rare that is? If that had been me or Gordy you would be picking bits of us up with tweezers. You can't change your nature but you should expect Beattie to get upset."

"The trouble is it is such a long time since I have seen her."

"Things quieten down just before Christmas. We will have leave then. Do something with her. Take her away somewhere."

"In December?"

"What? You want a bloody suntan now? It is the break that is important and not the weather."

I realised how right he was. "Thanks, Ted. You are right. You should get a woman of your own. You seem to know how to handle them."

"Aye, and that is why there are none in my life. It is complicated enough just staying alive in the air without worrying about a woman. I will wait until this damned war is over. If it takes ten years like Randolph said then at least an ugly bugger like me will have more chance of a good-looking woman."

"How so?"

He shook his head sadly, "Because almost every eligible young man will be dead and the land will be filled with wounded cripples who survive this madness."

Chapter 7

Archie flew his Bristol and led the stronger half of the squadron. Freddie and I led the eight Camels who had survived. Jack Fall looked to be more confident and assured. Part of that was the fact that he did not have to worry about Roger Jenkin who was still in sickbay.

We did not want to go but we were ordered into the sector where the Red Baron had hunted the previous day. I had advised Archie to take us as high as he could. The Bristols were a large inviting target. What worried me was that we were supposed to be clearing the air of Germans but, so far it was us who were outnumbered. Randolph had told us that other squadrons were outnumbering the Germans but the High Command felt that we were close enough to the French to operate as a single squadron. They were wrong.

For the first time since we had returned south, we saw troop movements in the distance. The lines of grey were moving towards the trenches. Although it did not necessarily mean an offensive it was worth investigating. Archie led the Bristols lower to ascertain numbers and to engage in some strafing. As fighter cover, we maintained our altitude and I was the one who first saw the twenty odd aeroplanes as they appeared like an angry swarm of hornets.

They were too far to identify but I felt my heart sink into my boots at the thought of locking horns with the Flying Circus once more. I had a handful of Camels under my command and the Bristols were totally outmatched by the Fokker Triplane. I led my flights east. I heard the machine guns of the Bristols as they swooped along the columns of grey. Archie and the others would have no idea that they were about to be jumped by overwhelming numbers and we had no means of communication. I had no choice. I could not remain high; I needed to intercept them before they cut Archie and the others to ribbons.

As I began to descend I saw that it was not the Flying Circus and they had no Fokker Triplanes. They were the Fokker Biplane and the Albatros. Both were sturdy aeroplanes but they could neither outturn nor outmanoeuvre a Camel. However, they outnumbered my Camels by over two to one. I cocked my Vickers. I had been profligate with my ammunition the previous day and I was determined to be more careful.

Freddie and I had decided that he and his flight would fly above me and to my left. It meant I would turn to starboard when I had finished my attack. I saw that the twenty-three aeroplanes were in lines of five stacked above each other. I watched as the first five dived to attack

Archie and the others. We swooped towards the rest of them. I hoped the rear gunners of the Bristols could handle the five Albatros who screamed towards them.

One of the Fokker pilots caught sight of us and he began to turn to face us. The others were a little slower and their tardiness meant that a gap appeared between the two end aeroplanes. The margins between success and failure are minute at eight thousand feet when you are travelling in excess of a hundred and ten miles an hour. I was slightly quicker on my guns and I opened fire at four hundred feet. My first short burst ripped into his engine and he peeled off to the north. When you were outnumbered then kills were not so important. You needed to rid the skies of the enemy aeroplanes. Roger gave him a second burst and I saw flames licking around his engine. The Germans had issued some parachutes to its pilots and I caught a glimpse of the pilot as he hurled himself over the side.

I adjusted my nose and fired a short burst at no more than a hundred yards from the second Fokker. I caught him side on and I fired a second burst. I was close enough to see him die and I had to jerk my nose up to prevent me crashing into his bus which flew straight in his dead hands. Another burst missed the third Fokker but my sudden appearance was like a fox in a hen house. The neat lines of the Germans were broken while our line astern ploughed through them. Each Camel gave the Germans a burst of .303. As I zoomed over the last Fokker I began to bank to starboard.

We could fly inside the larger Fokkers. The German pilots turned to port to match our turn but I was able to give a long burst to the second German line. I hit the wings and fuselage of one German who barely missed hitting me as he pulled his aeroplane up and over me. I felt the wind from Lieutenant Clayson's bullets as he gave a long burst into the surprised German. With smoke pouring from a wrecked engine he began to spiral to earth.

Freddie and his flight had had even more success. He had more aeroplanes and twice our firepower. I watched the last of the Fokkers heading east. I was tempted to follow them when I remembered Archie and the Bristols. I saw the four remaining Albatros as they nipped inside the less manoeuvrable Bristol. I saw two Bristols on the ground; their crews had their hands up as irate Germans captured and then prodded them towards the east with the butts of their rifles.

We screamed down like avenging eagles. I waved my arm to indicate to Jack and Roger that they should choose their own target. We needed maximum firepower. I gave one Albatros a long burst and Ted's gunner finished him off. The remaining three Albatros broke left and I heard the chatter of Jack's guns as he destroyed one. Roger was following a second and I turned my attention to the captured Bristol crews.

I dropped to the lowest altitude I could. There was a German vehicle and the guards were pushing the four airmen towards it. I took a risk and gave a long burst at the lorry. The Germans dived to the ground. As the lorry exploded I caught a glimpse of my four comrades as they grabbed guns and began to run to the British lines some half a mile away. I banked to starboard and swept over the four. As soon as I was over them I fired my two guns until they were empty. It was like firing a shotgun at close range. The grey-uniformed Germans were stopped in their tracks. As my gun clicked empty I pulled hard on the stick to climb away from the angry Germans' ground fire.

My detour meant that I was the last to land and the other flight leaders were waiting for me. Ted ran over, "Did you see Thomson and Lowe?" His voice betrayed his anxiety.

"They were captured but I fired at their captors and the last I saw they were heading for our lines." I shrugged, "Sorry Ted I didn't have time to hang around. I was out of ammunition."

He nodded, "Thanks anyway."

Jack Fall was so excited I thought he was in danger of bursting with joy. "I have a kill, sir, and I damaged two others! It is a marvellous feeling."

I smiled, "You did well. You both did well but, Lieutenant Clayson, it is Bates who gives me a haircut. You were just a tad close with the Vickers!"

"Sorry, sir. I just reacted. He came into my sights and I fired."

I laughed, "Don't worry Roger you just gave me a scare. Well done."

Senior Flight Sergeant Lowery was less impressed at the damage to my bus. "You are grounded tomorrow, sir."

"But she flew well enough and she landed well."

He nodded and pointed to the bullet holes next to the engine. "It just shows what a tough little bus these are. We will have to strip the engine and see what damage has been done inside." He pointed to the darkening skies. "Besides it looks like a weather front is moving in. I reckon we will have rain tomorrow, sir."

Bates confirmed the weather forecast when he gave me my whisky. "Yes sir, we have rain forecast for the next three days and it looks like a nasty storm. It will be good to give you a little rest."

As I lay in my bath I reflected that I did not want a rest. I wanted the war over so that I could go home and see my girl.

There was, however, a party atmosphere that night in the mess. Only Ted looked to be unhappy. We had shot down six Germans and only lost two. Our replacement Camels had arrived which showed us that we had a better rate of production than the Germans.

We were on the pudding course when Lieutenants Thomson and Lowe burst in. The old colonel would have reprimanded them for not changing out of their flying gear but Archie just shook his head. They came straight over to me and both saluted and then shook my hand. "Sir, we can't thank you enough. We both thought that we were in the cage for the duration and then you came screaming down. We both knew that you were too good a shot to hit us and when the lorry exploded we grabbed the bally guns, shot our guards and legged it and then when you came back you were so low I thought you were trying to pick us up! You saved us, sir. Thank you again."

"You are welcome Lieutenant Lowe but I was worried that I might hit you."

He shook his head, "Not even close sir! Marvellous flying and shooting!"

Archie nodded, "And now, gentlemen, go and get changed. The sergeants will have your meal ready when you return."

Ted was grinning, "Thanks Bill but I can see my little talk last night did no good. It has made you even crazier!"

The rain and inclement weather were a mercy on many levels. Our bodies and our buses were healed. The good feelings after our success continued for many days. Most importantly, Flight Sergeant Lowery discovered how to get a little more speed from the Camels. Since the saboteur, he and his mechanics had examined every piece of the engines. They had taken them apart and put them together so many times that they could do it blindfolded. They began to tune and adjust the engine to a sophisticated level. On the second day of our enforced holiday, I took shelter with him in the workshop.

"I think we can get a few more miles an hour out of the engine sir. You might get even more at higher altitude."

"That is good news. I hate not being able to catch the new Fokkers."

"Well when this awful weather lets up, sir, you can try it out." He nodded to the rain which was sheeting down. "Mind you I am happy. It means we don't have to patch up broken machines. I much prefer working on making a good machine even better expected rather than mending the damage."

As I left him I reflected that whilst they shared none of the glory or the medals, the ground crew were equally responsible for our success.

The second week of September was still as overcast. Archie and Randolph were summoned to Headquarters. I was left in charge. Doc Brennan released my injured pilots and I saw them in the mess. Lieutenant Jenkin sought me out for a quiet word.

"I have just spoken with Jack Fall, sir. He has his first kill. And he followed your orders to the letter." I nodded. I could not see where this was going. "The thing is, sir, I have been a bit of an idiot. I arrived here thinking I could win the war on my own and I resented being stuck where I thought I was out of the action. I was wrong and I have a lot to learn."

I smiled, "If every pilot arrived here as the finished article I would be surprised. We all have to learn. I am still learning. When we first encountered the Fokker Triplane I was flummoxed. I didn't know how to defeat it. I had to learn. The day that you stop learning is the day you should be worried."

"Why is that, sir?"

"Because that is the day you will die! This is a war fought by young men. Young men learn quickly. In this war, you are either the quick or the dead. Be quick, George, and learn all that you can."

When Randolph and Archie returned they were followed by a lorry which was carrying a great deal of new equipment. The packing cases were taken to a workshop and Archie sent for me and Ted. We sat down and Archie poured us a whisky each. He said nothing for a while then he smiled.

"That was a strange meeting. The general began by praising us for our skill in handling the Flying Circus."

"But they hammered us!"

"Apparently we got off lightly compared with the other squadrons. I had thought that the meeting was just a pat-on-the-back session. You know the sort of thing: *'You are all doing very well. Carry on with the good work'* that sort of thing. Then he told us that we were to be one of the first squadrons to try out the new radios. It is an experiment. There doesn't appear to be an ulterior motive behind it."

"Radios? In an aeroplane?"

"I know. It surprised me too. The lorry that followed us has the radios and the crews. There are three for the aeroplanes. Ted and I will have one each and you will have the third one, Bill. I am afraid that you will have the harder job. We can use our gunner to speak to the airfield but you will have to fly, fire your guns and talk on the radio."

"When do they fit my extra arms?" They laughed and I sipped the whisky. "What about the weight?"

"The weight?"

"Yes Flight has just managed to get more speed out of the old bus and the last thing I want is to carry a bunch of unnecessary radio equipment which will slow me down."

"There is no way out of this, Bill. The General wants it trialling. If it works then we could fit it to all the aeroplanes and, someday, you could talk to your pilots in the air."

I could see the advantage of that but I was still not convinced.

Randolph gave us the solution. "Look, Bill, we try it out without the stress of combat. If it adversely affects the performance of the Camel or the Bristol then we take it out and tell the general that we gave it a trial."

Ted nodded, "It seems to me it is worth a try. I mean it would allow us to reinforce our buses if we had a problem or warn the field that we had damaged aeroplanes coming in. I can see the potential."

I laughed, "The world is upside down. Ted is the optimist and Bill is the pessimist. Very well, sir. We give it a try when the weather clears."

"And that will be tomorrow. When we were at Headquarters the meteorologist told us the front was clearing from the west. We can try the radios in the morning and, if they work, have a sortie in the afternoon."

"Tomorrow sir? When are the radios being fitted?"

Archie chuckled, "Even as we speak!"

Flight Sergeant Kenny was the youngest flight sergeant I had ever seen. He looked even younger than some of my pilots. He was at my bus working under the critical gaze of Senior Flight Sergeant Lowery.

"Did you know about this contraption, sir?"

"I just heard about it, Flight. Do you think it will cause a problem?"

Before he could answer Sergeant, Kenny popped his head up from my cockpit. He looked at me, "It shouldn't be a problem, sir. You aren't exactly a big chap." He pointed to the space behind my seat. "We are putting the radio here in the centre of the aeroplane so that it won't affect the balance and the trim. I will run a cable from the engine to power it."

"Who said you could touch my engine?"

"Steady on, Flight. Let's hear the sergeant out. We are going to give them a go tomorrow and if they spoil the bus then they will come out."

Sergeant Kenny's head popped up again, "The General won't be happy about that sir!"

"The General doesn't have to fly these things. I do. Now how do I operate the bloody thing?"

"Well sir, it is one way only."

"One way?"

"Yes sir. You talk to us but we don't talk back to you."

"Then how do I know you have heard what I say?"

"Well you don't, sir, but the equipment will work. Trust me. It is pukka stuff!" He saw the look of doubt on my face. "You have this microphone around your neck and you just speak into it. The transmitter is set to transmit all the time so you don't have to switch anything on." I grunted. That was one thing at least. He chuckled, "Mind you, sir, it means the operator on the ground hears every word you say."

I found myself liking this cheerful and engaging young sergeant. "Well, they had better be prepared for some choice language, sergeant. I will not worry about offending your young operator."

He nodded, "Don't worry sir. That'll be me."

Sergeant Lowery and I stood to one side. I spoke to Lowery quietly. "How big is it?"

"It is bulky but it only weighs about the same as a Lewis gun and its ammo. What worries me, sir is that this is the thin end of the wedge. I hear they are thinking about fitting oxygen to them too. Sergeant Kenny is right to worry about the balance but how do you fit oxygen bottles too?"

"We'll worry about that when we have to. I can see the advantage of having these in the spotters though. We could direct artillery fire much more easily." I saw that Ted was wandering over and I headed towards him. "Carry on, sergeant."

"Well Bill, what does it look like?"

"Not as bad as I thought but it transmits only. The ground can't talk to us so we don't know if the message gets through."

"We will just have to try it. At least it is only in three aeroplanes. If we can't work it then it will go no further."

I sent Freddie up with the Camels to try out the improvements made by the mechanics while I went up to test the radio and to see if it affected the flight. Sergeant Kenny showed me how to fit the microphone around my neck. He had rigged up a hook above my head and it hung from the hook until I looped it around my neck.

"You just speak into it, sir. When you land I will tell you if I had any problems hearing you. I will be working with you and I have two lads working with the other officers."

"It seems an expensive waste of men."

He did not seem put off by my criticism. "Oh, don't you worry about that, sir. By the time they are fitted to every aeroplane, we will have improved the technology. This system is a hundred times better than the one we used last year. Don't worry, sir. It will be fine!" He gave me the words he wanted me to say. It struck me that it would not be a fair test if he knew the words I would be speaking but I bowed to his expertise.

Before I tested the radio I had a far more important task; I would test the modifications which had been made by the mechanics. I knew that it would not be an accurate evaluation. That would have to wait until I came up against the Fokkers but I would get a feel for the changes which had been made. I began to climb as steeply as I could. There was no loss of power which delighted me. I banked and flew straight. It seemed to be as fast, if not faster than it had been. The airspeed indicator said that I was going faster but they were notoriously inaccurate.

I descended to a better altitude and began transmitting. I said all that I had been told to say and then the naughty boy in me decided to test the equipment properly. I remembered a ribald song we had sung in the cavalry which I had taught to Charlie Sharp and I began to sing it.

I don't want the Sergeant's shilling,
I don't want to be shot down;
I'm really much more willing
To make myself a killing,
Living off the earnings of some high-class lady;
I don't want a bullet up my bumhole,
Don't want my cobblers minced with ball;
For if I have to lose 'em
Then let it be with Susan
Or Meg or Peg or any whore at all.

I had forgotten the second verse so I sang the first one again.

When I landed I went directly to Flight Sergeant Lowery and gave him my report. "Well, the good news is that the radio equipment doesn't seem to affect the aerodynamics and the modifications you made appear to work."

"Good. That is a relief then. Here are the two Bristols sir."

Archie and Ted came over with their gunners. "How did it work then, Ted?"

He shrugged, "Hard to say. Jack said all the words he was supposed to but we will have to see what the radio lads have to say."

When we entered their workshop Sergeant Kenny was laughing fit to bust. "Well sir, I hadn't heard that song before. I didn't know officers used such words."

I laughed too. "I was a sergeant before I was an officer. So it came over clearly?"

"Yes sir. Clear as a bell. It works."

The other operators had heard their messages too. "Good; then this afternoon we will have a shufti over the German lines. It is all very well using it when I can see the airfield but what about when we are over enemy lines?"

"It should work, sir. But we will see eh?"

Freddie had noticed an improvement in performance and we took off in the early afternoon to see if we could catch the Germans napping. With the Bristols to starboard and Freddie above us, we headed east. There were no troop movements this time but, in the distance, I saw the smoke from the railway line. They were resupplying and reinforcing the front line.

We flew down the German trenches. I took the opportunity to send a message back. It was not important, I just told Sergeant Kenny, what we were doing. It was more of a test than anything. The Bristols machine-gunned the trenches while we watched. It was something of an anti-climax when no Huns came to chase us off. We headed home when we had been aloft for two hours. We had the endurance of two and a half hours but there was no point in risking running out of fuel.

This time, when we landed, I went directly to Sergeant Kenny. "Well?"

"Loud and clear sir. I told you, it works."

Chapter 8

The lack of German aeroplanes was explained when Randolph reported to Headquarters. The German airfields had been overcast and they could not fly. It was an important lesson. The Bristols could have carried bombs and done even more damage to the trenches. My Camels could have engaged in a ground attack too.

We went up again the next day but without Archie. He and Randolph were summoned to headquarters. We presumed to report on the radios. Gordy took up Archie's crew so that his gunner could become familiar with the technology.

For the first time in over a week, I had a full complement of pilots. I was slightly less nervous than I had been. My pilots had all learned from the disasters of their first flights. Even so, I scanned the eastern horizon for signs of the enemy. Ted and Gordy led their flights at the same altitude. It proved to be a wise decision. Three German squadrons were waiting for us, expecting us to attack their trenches again. They were at the same altitude as we were. I did not see any triplanes and so I assumed it was not the Flying Circus. That was proved to be the case.

I sent the message back to Kenny that we had met over thirty-six Germans and that we were attacking. He could do little about it but I was anxious to use the radio in combat conditions.

We launched our attack in four columns. It contrasted with the wide waves of the enemy. They could bring more guns to bear but then they would risk collisions. Our method put the leader at the front in the gravest danger but as they were the best pilot it was a risk worth taking.

I saw that we were facing the Fokker D.III. It had two guns and was fast but it was not as fast as we were and did not have the manoeuvrability we did. I guessed that the Germans would choose the easier and bigger target of the eleven Bristols. If they did they would learn that Gordy and Ted had a nasty sting in their tails.

I cocked my Vickers and shouted, for no real reason, "Charge!" I suspect I was aware that someone was listening. I flew directly at the Fokker with the tallow propeller and spinner. We had learned that they were usually the leader. He must have been nervous for he fired too soon. His bullets struck my wings and my wires but a quick glance told me that they were still whole. This was an aerial game of chicken. Who would blink first? I raised my nose a little to invite another burst from him. This time I felt his bullets strike my wheels and then I dipped my nose and, as I did so, gave him a five-second burst. My sudden movement had thrown his aim and, at one hundred feet, the range was so close that my twin Vickers struck his propeller and then his engine. I must have struck something vital for he suddenly dived beneath me. I think my wheels must have clipped his tail as I flew over him. I felt a little judder.

The next flight was upon me and I turned slightly to starboard. It was a manoeuvre intended to allow the rest of my flight and Freddie's flight to fire obliquely across the enemy line. For that reason, I fired at two hundred yards. It was like a war of attrition. If each of us hit the same target with a short burst then we had a good chance of downing them.

I felt bullets strike my fuselage but we were a smaller target and they did little damage. I saw smoke appear from a Fokker in front of me and then he was past and I fired at the next one in line. I suddenly heard an explosion next to me and my Camel was thrown to the right as Lieutenant Clayson hit the fuel tank of the Fokker I had damaged. I no longer had a target and I began to climb. I wanted the freedom and flexibility to swoop down on the Germans and use our superior speed to maximum effect.

I saw in my mirror that some of the Germans were trying to match our climb. They were being left for dead. Flight Sergeant Lowery had certainly worked his magic. I banked to starboard and brought my flight down like avenging angels of death. I kept banking and brought us around to attack the climbing Fokkers. Their attempt to match our climb had been a disaster. I opened fire at the side of one and I raised my nose to fly over him and allow the others to fire at him. Once I had passed him I was able to descend and fire another burst at the next one in line. It was almost too easy. Had they been the Fokker Triplane they would have been a smaller nimbler target but these older Fokker Biplanes only had their two guns in their favour. We held all the other aces.

I checked my compass and saw that we were heading east. My fuel gauge showed we had used too much fuel already and I banked to port to take us home. I saw Freddie and his flight already heading west and, below me, the Bristols were chugging towards our lines too. My mirror showed that I still had my flight intact and I sent the message back to Sergeant Kenny that A Flight was coming home.

There was an exuberant mood on the ground. My flight had managed to shoot down three Germans and even George Jenkin had managed to make his first kill although he had to share it with Lieutenant Clayson. I noticed that Archie and Randolph had not returned and I went to take an early bath. I would enjoy a drink in the mess before dinner. The report could wait.

Gordy and I were on our second beer when we heard the car pull up outside. Sergeant Green came to the mess, "Gentlemen, Colonel Leach, asks if you could join him."

"Be there in a moment, Flight." As he left I said, "They have been at Headquarters longer than normal. Do you think something is up?"

"There is always something up but it never bodes well for us."

Ted and Freddie were there already. "Well chaps we now know why they asked to us check the trenches around Cambrai, there will be a major offensive there sometime in November. We have three weeks to photograph it and then three weeks to clear the skies of Germans."

"They do know that the Flying Circus is in this sector?"

"They do but Intelligence thinks that the Germans are having supply problems. At home, we are turning out the new SE 5 in huge numbers and that particular aeroplane is capable of over a hundred and thirty-five miles an hour. The General is confident."

I looked at Freddie and shook my head. That speed seemed impossible. Last year we had been flying the Gunbus and were happy if we could make eighty-five miles an hour.

Ted asked, hopefully, "Are we getting them?"

"Eventually we might but we are in a unique position. We have the Bristols which can photograph the ground and they can be protected by the Camels. We won't be getting any new aeroplanes until the New Year."

I didn't particularly want a new aeroplane. I liked the Camel but the extra speed meant we would have more chance of survival until this damned war was over.

Randolph said, "One bit of good news from the general though. After the offensive, the whole squadron is being given a three-week leave. By then the new SE 5 squadrons will be ready and they are being phased in."

The thought of leave made me smile. Both Gordy and Freddie looked equally happy. I saw that Ted looked almost indifferent. I suddenly remembered that Ted had nothing at home to look forward to. His conversation with me had told me that he was putting all thoughts of a woman in his life on hold until the war was over.

This would be the first time when the raid would actually be useful. It would be the opportunity for Ted and Archie to feedback directly about what they were photographing. For me, it would be the chance to call up reinforcements. I would certainly ask for help if the Flying Circus arrived.

That first morning was almost too easy. The Germans were not expecting us and our Bristols combed the battlefield as far as Cambrai.

The ground fire was annoying and I saw holes appearing in the wings of the Bristols but they could be repaired. We had nothing to do as no fighter appeared. The test would come on day two and three when the Germans would realise what we were doing. However, I was just grateful to get the extra hours flying with the new pilots. It was a luxury. We had not lost a pilot for almost a month and that was a rarity. We knew it could not last but the more hours in the air a pilot had the more chance he had of actually surviving the war. None of us believed that this offensive would be the one to end the war. We had heard that claim too many times but we would be able to measure our success by the ground gained.

I was right. The second day the Germans came to chase us away. I used the radio as soon as I saw the black crosses appear in the distance. We were further west on the second day. Someone had actually had the sense to begin the photography close to our target before the enemy forces were aware of what we were up to. I waved to Freddie and my flight. Cocking my Vickers, we began to descend towards the enemy formation. They would target the Bristols. They knew that we would not be using cameras. I felt sorry for the pilots and gunners of the Bristols. They were like the bait and they would have to take whatever punishment was dished out.

The Germans used a different tactic that day. They used two squadrons. One came for us while the other flew low and attacked the Bristols. We approached each other in our two totally different formations. Once again, I would be the focus of the German fire and I wondered when my luck would run out. When would I face a German pilot with the nerve to wait until the last minute and shred my propeller? It was not that day. The pilot of the Albatros who faced me was not a leader. I saw that he was struggling to maintain a straight line. That was the nerves. It told me he was a young pilot or a new pilot at least.

I used my usual trick of inviting the shot by lifting my nose slightly and then, as I jerked it straight back down, firing a hopeful burst. It worked. The young pilot fired as I lifted my nose and the bullets screamed over my head. My bullets smacked into the struts and the wires of his wings. Once again fortune smiled on me. I saw one of the wires severed. It would unnerve the pilot as he heard the twang and the port side of his aeroplane would be less stable. I moved my stick a little to starboard and Nat Hazell gave him a burst too. He made the mistake of pulling back on his stick and Lieutenant Hazell had another kill as his bullets stitched a line along the fuselage. The aeroplane continued in its loop. The pilot was dead.

I continued my bank to the right and it brought me alarmingly close to the next Albatros. I took a snapshot and my bullets rattled off the engine. I had to jerk my nose up and I felt bullets striking my fuselage. All that I could see were wings with black crosses. I had led my flight into the heart of the enemy. This would normally be fatal but the Camel was so manoeuvrable that I knew I could use its impressive handling to wrest the advantage back. I kept pulling on the stick. I felt the force of the wind as my Camel fought me but it kept coming around. We were a small target and we were moving very quickly. The mechanics had done a superb job. The hard part about pulling such a loop was keeping your orientation. I do not know why but I always found it easy. The pilots who followed me just had to keep on my tail.

I saw an Albatros below me as I came down. He was a perfect cross in my sights. At less than a hundred yards I pulled my triggers. Every bullet struck home. The pilot disappeared in a sea of blood. Such was the power of the twin Vickers that I saw daylight beneath his body as the bullets punched a hole in his fuselage. He was so close that my Camel almost collided with his tail. I came underneath him and found myself behind his leader. I fired again and his tail took many hits. I was in danger of ramming him and I pulled to starboard. I saw bullets strike his Albatros from the guns of Lieutenant Fall who was behind me. He began to spiral to earth.

I saw that Jack and I had lost the others. We were almost alone now. My loop had lost most of my flight and the Germans. I levelled out and checked the sky. The formations had disintegrated. I saw individual pilots chasing each other around the sky. To the west, I saw the Bristols as they headed home with the precious photographs. I started to circle. Jack and I would wait for the other Camels to rejoin us and I would keep the last of my ammunition in case they needed help.

One by one they returned. I was like a mother hen counting her chicks. We formed a circle. We would soon have to return home. One was missing. Nat had not come back. I radioed that one of my flight was missing and headed home. Perhaps, like Lieutenant Carpenter he had been forced down and he would rejoin us.

We were the last aeroplanes to land. Roger came over to me. "Nat bought it, sir. He went after an Albatros and flew into two Fokkers. He must have died instantly. Sorry, sir."

I shook my head, "It isn't your fault; it is war. And he had another kill today."

The death of such a likeable pilot had a demoralising effect. Although we had shot down more of the enemy we had lost one of the new pilots and I saw in the eyes of my flight the spectre of mortality. It was a sombre mood in the mess that night.

"Don't take it to heart, Bill. We did well and the photographs are top-notch."

"I know, Archie. You can't make an omelette without breaking eggs but I was beginning to believe that, if we avoided the Circus, then my lads might actually survive. What happens if the Circus comes to this sector? We will be massacred."

"No Bill. You have done a cracking job with your lads. Your Camels have a better kill ratio than any other flight on the western front. I heard that from the General. This is your first loss in a while. The Germans are losing more men than we are."

I shook my head, "I can't believe that we are hoping that the enemy will bleed to death before we do."

"It is a fact of life, or in this case death. Besides, we are producing more aeroplanes and when the Yanks finally get over here we might just have more men than the Germans."

I took a swig of wine. "I couldn't do what you do, sir. I couldn't send young men to their deaths. I wouldn't be able to sleep."

"And you think I do? I am just praying for this war to end so that I can get back to Scotland and my family. I have a nice little farm in the borders and I fall asleep at night making plans for what I will grow and what animals I will rear. That is how I get to sleep. You get to sleep thinking about your Beattie. All of us have different ways to cope. We just have to believe that this war will end before we are all dead."

And of course, he was right. That was the only way to get through the horror. Concentrate on the trivia and not the deaths. If you thought about the deaths then you would go insane.

Chapter 9

In the event, we were rained off the next day. It should have made life easier but we also received the news of an air raid over London in which twenty-one people died and seventy-nine were injured. The odds that one of them was either Beattie or Mary was slim but it did not stop Gordy and me pestering Randolph all day to find out if our loved ones were safe. We did not discover the truth until late at night by which time we were both nervous wrecks. It made us both more determined than ever to finish this war as soon as possible.

The late night and the worry made me grouchy the next day. Bates noticed it immediately. He was incredibly sensitive to my moods. He smiled at my snarls and nodded at my grunts. As he handed me my goggles, flying helmet and gloves he just said, "Try not to take it out too much on the young gentlemen, sir. It is a hard enough job for them without worrying if their commanding officer is going to bite their heads off."

I turned to snap at him and then I saw the look on his face. He was smiling but there was steel in his eyes. I knew that he was right. I forced a smile, "I will try, Bates, and thank you."

"It's my job sir and besides you are so even-tempered normally that one can accept the occasional aberration. Just so long as it is occasional."

We did not need a morning briefing. Until the photography was complete then we would be over Cambrai each day. Two of the Bristols were unfit to fly as was one of Freddie's flight, Lieutenant Duffy. It would make the task of the Bristols harder as they would need to cover a larger area with fewer aeroplanes.

As we headed east across the ground the troops would traverse I could not help noticing that it seemed to be solid barbed wire. I did not envy the infantry travelling over that. Our shells were supposed to clear a path but it only seemed to make it even more entangled. Until they had some way to walk over wire then the machine-gunners would be able to slaughter the advancing infantry with ease. The other noticeable feature was the number of abandoned farms and small villages. I wondered how on earth the owners would be able to move back once the war was over. I knew that many soldiers lay just a few feet from the surface buried in a sea of mud. This part of the front had not seen a major offensive yet but once it did then the war would seed the land with fresh corpses. Farmers in the future would have a grim harvest.

The Germans were waiting. We knew in our hearts that they would, inevitably, react to our daily sortie. This time it was they who held the advantage of height and they came down in waves of five aeroplanes. At least our Camels were a little higher and we did not have to climb steeply to counter the threat but the climb would eat into our fuel and shorten the time we could spend in the air.

It was not the Circus. Each time we went up I looked for the dreaded triplanes. When I did not see them then I knew we had some chance of success. They were the Fokker D. IV. I suspected they were the same ones we had met before for the livery on the aeroplanes looked the same. There were more of them which led me to believe that this was a Jasta.

The twin Spandau of two Fokkers converged on me. They had fired early but were trying to get me in a cone of fire. I lifted my nose and, as I dipped it again quickly, began to bank to starboard. I felt their bullets tear into my port lower wing but Lieutenant Clayson had a shot at them from the side. I saw a black cross appear as my nose swung around to the last aeroplane in the line and I fired at the cross. Miraculously I hit the cross. I did not think there would be much damage but the Fokker began to yaw. I realised that I must have hit his controls.

I banked to port. It was pure instinct which made me do so. The space I had occupied was filled with steel-jacketed parabellums as the Fokker from above dived down. I turned my bank into a climb and passed the German pilot. My move took me up above the dogfight but, when I looked in my mirror, I saw that I had lost my wingman. My Camels were engaged in deadly duels with the Fokkers. It was not a fair fight as we were outnumbered. I brought my Camel around and lined up on the two who were chasing Jack Fall. He was twisting, turning and attempting to loop. It made him a small target but each time they fired at him they were hitting his bus. It would only be a matter of time before they made a critical hit.

The height I had gained gave me more speed over the already slow Fokkers. I waited until I was less than fifty yards from the rearmost German and gave him a steady burst. My speed took the bullets along his fuselage and into the cockpit. I held the finger on the trigger as his aeroplane disappeared from my sights and was replaced by the next Fokker. As soon as my bullets hit his rudder I saw him jerk his head around and then he began to bank. I managed to hit him again before he flew from my sights.

Jack was in a bad way. His Camel was oozing smoke and his wings looked like a piece of Swiss cheese. I waved for him to get home.

"Jack Fall is heading back, Sergeant Kenny. His bus is badly shot up. Over."

It was the first time I had used the word '*Over*' in such a way and it felt weird. Sergeant Kenny had asked me to use it when I had finished a transmission to let him or another operator know that the message was complete.

I looked around the sky and saw that most of my pilots were following Jack home. I was still high enough to be able to look down on them. I began a slow descent; I did not want to waste fuel and I followed the three Fokkers who were trying to pick off the injured birds. I fired at a range of over three hundred yards as I closed with them. I wanted to discourage them. The tracer rounds showed me that I was slightly off target. I adjusted my direction and, at two hundred yards, fired again. This time some of my rounds hit the tail of one of the Germans. I made my descent steeper to increase my speed and I banked to port. I fired at a Fokker and then dived beneath him to come up under the last of the three hunters. My bullets hit his undercarriage. I saw one of the wheels come off and he jerked his Fokker around and joined his two comrades as they headed east.

I came up and flew alongside Lieutenant Clayson who waved a grateful hand at me. I looked along the line and saw Jenkin and Hickey. They had both survived but their buses looked only a little better than Lieutenant Fall's. Once again, we landed amidst a scene of confusion and action. Aeroplanes looked to be seemingly abandoned on the field. Huddles of mechanics and medical staff surrounded many of them. It is lucky for us that the Camel did not need much field to land in.

When I climbed out I saw that I had taken more damage than I had thought. The mechanics would have their hands full with my flight.

It looked like the Bristols had borne the brunt of the damage. I saw two gunners being stretchered away and Tony Alexander looked to have caught a bullet in the arm. Ted and Gordy trudged towards me.

"Well, we were definitely caught with our trousers down there. They were ready for us. There was ground fire as well as the damned Fokkers. We only got a couple of photographs before we had to take evasive action."

"It is our own fault, Gordy, we went over at exactly the same time and the same height. The Hun is not stupid, is he? Where is Archie?"

"He went to telephone headquarters. He wants us stood down to recover."

"That makes sense. A different squadron might vary it a little."

"How do you mean, Bill?"

We fly in a predictable way. We come in four lines at the same height each day. Even our little tricks like me raising my nose and then dropping it when I fire are known. I always turn to starboard and my lads follow me. I hate to admit it but if we had radios which could transmit and receive in the buses it would be much easier to vary things."

"Well, that isn't going to happen in our lifetime."

I shook my head, "The way things are going this war could last another ten years and we might just get them."

"Well, you are cheerful. Let's go and find Archie and see if we have got a reprieve."

We walked into the office and Archie waved us to the table where the whisky was already open.

"Yes General, I know but we took a beating today and we only have half of the Bristols able to fly." There was a silence and Archie rolled his eyes. "Thank you, sir. Even twenty-four hours will make a difference." After a moment or two, he slammed the phone down. "These desk wallahs haven't the first clue about what it takes to keep a squadron up to scratch. We have one day."

Ted nodded to me as he lit a cigarette, "Bill thinks we ought to mix things up a little."

"Go on."

"The Germans will be waiting for us when we go over in two days' time. We know that. Why not do things a little differently? Instead of going just after dawn, we should go after lunch. We will have the sun behind us and they will have wasted fuel waiting for us. If we climb to a higher altitude before we leave our lines then the Camels can have the advantage of height and if we use the two flights to come from two different directions we might just catch them napping."

"That's all well and good, Bill, but it doesn't help us in the Bristols."

"I know, Ted, but you have to go in low to photograph. We can't change that but by going in later we may throw them off. You only have a little more of the front to photograph anyway. If we can buy some time then you might be able to complete it this time. We could go before you so that we are ready to pounce on any Germans we see."

"The problem with that is that you will be outnumbered."

"So long as it isn't the Flying Circus then we can handle the biplanes. The Camel can mix it up close in." I swallowed the whisky. "If we do things the same way we have always done them then we will get the same results. Next time we might not be so lucky and the wounds will be deaths."

Archie nodded, "I don't have a problem with making that change, Bill. It doesn't make much difference when we fly. We only have two and a half hours over there anyway. We can't leave it too late or else night will be falling but just after noon works. We can be back by three at the latest. We will try it and hope it works. The brass is very keen on this offensive. Randolph…"

"Yes, it appears that we are going to be involved in the actual attack. It will be like Arras all over again. I think that is why we had the radios fitted so that we could liaise closely with the ground attack."

It all made sense now. Perhaps there was some planning going on at Headquarters. I hoped so.

The next day Archie gave us permission to go into Amiens for a well-deserved day off. Freddie drove and the four of us went, along with Johnny to see what we could buy to brighten up our lives.

After we had bought some cheese and French bread we found our usual bar. It was crowded and we were forced to stand outside. It seemed there were lots of men in the town. It was always the way before an offensive.

"Bill!" I looked around and saw our Bert and his mates. He was not wearing the uniform of an Engineer. I did not recognise it. He came and shook my hand. He tapped my medals, "This is my brother, the hero. See he has the VC and the MC!"

I heard the pride in his voice. I was just as proud of him. Anyone who burrowed away like a mole had my admiration! I tapped his uniform. "What's this then? Not in the engineers?"

He took me to one side. "All hush, hush, our kid." He took me to one side and spoke quietly. "I am in the Tank Corps. I got fed up with being underground and with my skills as a mechanic and the fact that I am small, well, they were desperate for me. I am in line for a promotion."

I remembered that a few metal contraptions had been used the previous year. I didn't know we had them in numbers.

"Are you involved in the next push then?"

He tapped his nose, "Can't say."

I nodded, "Well when you look up it will be our squadron keeping an eye on you."

"And that makes me feel a whole lot better." Gordy brought over our beers. "How is our Alice getting on?"

"She's struggling but I think she will get through it. I heard from Mum the other day. She says things are hard at the estate and she complained that you never write."

He laughed, "I was never much with the old pen and paper but I promise that I will write."

In the end, we spent the whole afternoon with them and a tipsy Freddie drove us back to the field. But it had been good for us. We had met some of the soldiers we saw from the air. We were all closer as a result. I was silent all the way back thinking about Bert and how much he had changed. He was now confident and seemed to be enjoying life. Perhaps the army had been the best thing for him. Our buses were all repaired and lined up neatly at the side of the airfield. That evening in the mess we had a happy buzz as we discussed our new plans for the next day. It was amazing how a little trip out could do so much for morale.

We heard that the two squadrons who had gone to photograph the front in our absence had lost six aeroplanes when they were jumped by the German fighters. I felt that my plan was worth a try. Had we gone up with fewer aeroplanes then we might have suffered even greater losses.

Our morale was even higher after a lie-in and a late breakfast. Freddie and I would lead our flights with a gap of half a mile between us. It had been some months since we had used the technique but we could fly long loops. We would intersect twice and never lose sight of each other. If there was danger we could respond quickly. We left slightly before the Bristols; we were faster anyway but we needed to be on station before they reached us. I prayed that I was right and the waiting German fighters had gone.

It was a dull day but the cloud was relatively high. I took my flight as high as I dared and began my loop. We saw the grey uniforms below and they took hopeful potshots at us. It was a waste of ammunition; we were too high. I saw the Bristols as they began to work across the fields. We were ahead of them. They had photographed the section over which we flew days ago. I was beginning to think that we had escaped notice when I saw the black shapes of the German fighters appear from the east. The ground troops must have sent a message and asked for support. I waved to Freddie and we began to descend.

"German fighters have appeared from the east. Engaging. Over."

We were above them and they were climbing to reach us. The Bristols would be invisible to them as they were flying so low and close to the ground. I knew that Gordy and Ted would know the danger when they saw our two flights heading east. They would have to make the decision about the best time to leave. I saw that there were at least twelve German aeroplanes. They were biplanes. Since my encounter with the Red Baron, I had found myself dreading meeting with him again. I felt I had been lucky the first time.

I cocked my Vickers and worked out who I would attack. The Germans only had a ragged line. Their field must have been close to the front. I was closer to the Germans than Freddie and his flight and so I aimed for the lead aeroplane. It would mean I could bank to port and rake their line. If they were expecting us to do the same as we had before we might catch them napping. Freddie was to starboard in any case. I flew, not directly at my intended target but the aeroplane next in line. The Germans would make their plans based on that.

At three hundred yards I banked to port to line up on the lead German. I fired at two hundred yards which was before his guns could come to bear and I did not have to flip my nose up. At a hundred yards I gave another burst. He turned to port to meet me and his Fokker ran into a hail of my bullets. I banked to port and I heard Lieutenant Hickey's guns as he fired at the German. As I fired at the next Fokker I saw that the lieutenant had managed to damage the Fokker which was heading for the ground and a crash-landing. I knew he would not make it as there were another three pilots who would take the opportunity to rake him.

My angle brought me towards the flank of the last Fokker in the first line. I fired a short burst and was rewarded by the sight of smoke and oil coming from the engine. He began to climb and I turned to starboard. I guessed that he would head due east. He must have thought he had avoided me as he descended and tried to nurse his wounded bird home. I fired a second burst and ripped through his tail and his rudder. He began to spiral towards the ground. As I completed my turn I saw that the Bristols had finished their work and were heading west. By continuing my starboard turn, I would be able to follow them.

I checked my mirror and saw that all my chicks were following me but out of the corner of my eye, I saw smoke. One of Freddie's flight was heading to the ground with smoke pouring from his engine. I recognised that Johnny Holt was on the tail of the German attacker. As Johnny downed the Fokker I thought that it would be little consolation to Jock Macdonald as his aeroplane exploded when it hit the ground. Another young man would not return to Blighty. What had been a successful mission now left a sour taste in the mouth.

I let Freddie and his flight land first. I knew what Freddie and the rest of his men would be going through. A flight was like a family. You watched over each other, quite literally and a loss would be keenly felt.

After we had landed I let Freddie and his pilots head to the mess together and I joined Ted and Gordy as we headed for Archie's office. Ted was actually smiling. I know he could not have been aware that we had lost a pilot. "Your plan worked, Bill, and we got the photographs we needed. Perhaps now we can stop being the Aunt Sally and go back to being fighters."

"You would think so wouldn't you?"

Randolph, too, was smiling. "Just one loss today. You did well."

"Don't say that to Freddie. He will be distraught."

"How many did we get?"

"Probably three or four."

"Then we are winning. Just losing one pilot for three or four damaged Hun is a good deal."

The others looked at me. I knew that they were right but it had been the Camel pilots who had paid the price for the photographs. I put on a brave face, "I suppose you are right. What are our orders for tomorrow?"

"Hit their rear lines. Headquarters is sending over some bombers escorted by the first of the SE 5 buses. We need to hit them all along their lines and spread out their defences."

I laughed, "I see. We are poking the hornet's nest with a stick so that Headquarters can count the number of bugs!"

"Crudely put Bill, but you are right. I think the General is hoping that the Germans will not be able to respond everywhere and will spread themselves too thinly."

At the back of my mind was the thought that poor Bert would be going up against these German defences. I would do my level best to make sure there were fewer of them when the push came.

Chapter 10

It felt strange to be flying so low. We had become used to using all the altitude we could get but we were hedge hopping. I had persuaded Archie to let us leave a little later than planned. I was being selfish. If the other squadrons hit first then the Germans might react to them before us. We also had to contend with a different formation. We flew in line abreast. It would maximise our firepower.

We hurtled over the German trenches. We flew so fast that they had no time to even lift a gun let alone fire it. We were heading for their rear areas. We would not have long over the target but with the Bristols dropping bombs and us strafing the ground it was hoped to cause as much disruption as possible. We were also to observe. The three of us with radios would report back what we saw and Randolph would be listening in and plotting our observations. It was a new way of gaining intelligence.

As soon as we flew over their trenches I armed my gun. "Crossing the German trenches. Over." It was beginning to feel marginally less silly to say '*over*'. As we wanted to hit together the camels were not flying at full power. I hoped the saved fuel would ensure we reached our field safely. I saw, ahead, a line of German vehicles and horse-drawn carts. There appeared to be a tented village and the vehicles were offloading. Machine guns began to fire at us.

I waited until we were just four hundred yards away and then began firing. I fired a longer burst than I would have in the air for my sights were filled with German targets. I saw a German lorry explode and the explosion threw me into the air. I remembered my radio. "We have found lorries and a storage area. Attacking. Over."

I knew that Gordy and Ted would drop their bombs on the tents and the roads. We needed maximum disruption. I banked to port and, as I saw German artillery pieces tracking me I gave them a long burst. I was so close that I saw their bodies as they disintegrated beneath the hail of .303 bullets. I hoped that the guns had been damaged too. I banked to port again and saw burning vehicles and tents which were on fire. I opened fire on an undamaged tent. When my guns clicked empty I pulled up my nose and waggled my wings to show the others I was leaving.

"A Flight returning to base. Over."

I glanced to my right and saw Jack Fall and Roger Jenkin. In my rear-view mirror, I saw the other two. They must have been slow to see my turn. I started to climb. The German gunners would be ready for us when we came back and I was not certain if German fighters were on their way. I saw the puffs in the air ahead which showed where the Germans were laying a barrage to try to hit us. They would be very lucky to do so. They had to adjust their guns for our height and our speed. Neither was easy. We had just crossed the German lines when I saw the black crosses in my mirror. The German fighters had arrived. They had no chance of actually catching us and I relaxed.

"A Flight approaching the field. German aeroplanes have just arrived. Over."

For once we were the first back and by the time the others had landed I was with Randolph and we were plotting the position of the camp we had raided. "From your speed and your reports, I put it to be about here." He pointed to a spot on the map.

"Yes, that is about right. The town we could see ahead must have been Fontaine." I shook my head. "That is worrying, Randolph. If I didn't know better I would say that they knew we are going to launch an offensive and were getting their supplies ready early."

"You could be right, Bill. We will have to hit it again tomorrow and perhaps bomb the crossroads."

"They will be ready for us tomorrow."

"I know. We were lucky today. I had a message from my chum at HQ. Some of the other squadrons had it far worse. The bombers were hit by the Flying Circus and they lost eight of them."

I could imagine the carnage the Circus could cause. "Then we will have to be vigilant tomorrow. How about if I take my flight in early and high? We can act as top cover. If the Hun fighters don't appear then we can ground attack when the others have left."

"I think it is a good idea. I will run it by Archie when he lands." As I rose to leave he said, "Oh your new pilots are here. Yours is Lieutenant Davies. He's Welsh. I left him in the mess."

Owen Davies was a very serious-looking young man. He did not come from a privileged background but was a farmer's son. He and I had much in common. We both came from the land and were more familiar with the sod rather than the city.

I held out my hand, "Major Harsker. I am your flight commander. How many hours in a Camel?"

"Six hours in training and the two-hour flight here."

It could have been worse but not by much. "I am afraid we will have to hit the ground running. We are doing ground attack tomorrow. You will fly astern of me and copy everything I do. Don't worry if you don't get the chance to fire your guns. You will need as many hours in the air as we can manage."

He nodded, seriously. "I won't let you down, sir. I am a good pilot."

"I am afraid that just being a good pilot does not guarantee your safety. I have known some damned fine pilots and they bought it and I have known some bloody awful pilots who have had kills and survived to get home. If you have any favours with the man upstairs owing then now is the time to call them in."

"Sir, I am Chapel and I do not like the lord's name being taken in vain!"

I laughed, "If you are so close to God then who knows, you might just survive!" He was a very serious young man. As I headed for my quarters I met Freddie. "Sorry about Jock. His replacement has arrived."

"I know sir. It was hard going up today. I kept looking in the mirror and he wasn't there."

"Well, I don't think it will be easy tomorrow. I have persuaded Randolph to let me give an aerial umbrella. They will be expecting us."

"It's the same target?"

"Exactly the same target. They will have more guns and the moment we cross their trenches then they will be sending messages to their fighters. I am just hoping that my flight can disrupt their attack."

He smiled, "If anyone can do it, sir, it's you. I don't know how you do it. You seem to have a charmed life."

"The problem with charms is that they rely on luck and that can run out." I gestured with my thumb. "My new pilot is a Chapel boy, a Bible thumper."

Freddie laughed, "Well he should fit in well!"

I called in to see the other pilots. Each flight bunked in together. "You all did well today, chaps. Tomorrow is the same target but we will be the umbrella keeping the other lads dry. We have our new pilot. Owen Davies. I have told him to stick close to my tail. You had all better stay out of his way. He has only had six hours in a Camel." I smiled, "And I remember what you lot were like!"

They had the good grace to look embarrassed. George said, "I can't believe how arrogant I was then. I thought I was going to win the war all on my own."

"There's still time, George, there's still time."

As I went to my quarters the laughter I heard in their room gave me a good feeling. They were a tight-knit bunch and I had managed to keep more of them together than any other flight I had commanded. Perhaps Freddie was right and I was lucky. I prayed that my luck would continue.

We took off first to allow us to gain altitude. As I climbed to just below the cloud cover I thought about the new radios we had fitted. If only they could receive as well then we might have an idea what was going on around us. It was frustrating just being able to talk and not hear. Because we had been climbing, the rest of the squadron, now led by Archie, reached the target just as we were on station. We were flying in line abreast with the new pilot tucked in behind me. It was not my favourite formation but I needed all of my pilots to be able to bring his guns to bear immediately.

We flew diagonal legs over the other aeroplanes and we were just turning when I saw, below me, the twelve German fighters as they swooped down on the rest of the squadron. "Enemy in sight. Over!"

I pointed down and began to dive. I made sure, by looking in my mirror, that Owen had followed me and I cocked my guns. The Germans had not seen us. Our altitude had given us the advantage but it also meant that the Germans would be able to hit the Bristols and Camels. I saw the tracer from the Bristol's rear gunners and watched as Freddie and his Camels looped and dived away from the twin Spandaus. They would all be low on ammunition.

I took the flight across the twelve aeroplanes. It minimised the chance of us hitting our own aeroplanes and gave us the opportunity of hitting the entire enemy force. We were touching almost one hundred and twenty miles an hour as we screamed across them. At that speed, you have the target in your sights for seconds. I held down the triggers as I zoomed over them. I was flying too fast to see what damage I caused but I knew that I was hitting them. I stopped firing when I passed over the last Albatros. I pulled my nose up to loop. I saw that my new lieutenant was desperately trying to copy me but the Camel needed a firm hand. At the top of the loop, I rolled to regain the horizon. It took the Welshman a little longer to realise he was flying upside down before he finally remedied it.

The Germans were chasing the Bristols west. I quickly counted and saw only eight Germans. Either some were shot down or they were elsewhere. Glancing to left and right I saw the rest of my flight were with me. I put the nose down and began to chase the Albatros with the green tail. He was a good pilot and he kept jinking from side to side. I was patient. He could not hit Gordy, whom he was chasing, whilst he was jinking. Gordy's gunner had no such problem and I saw his bullets hitting the Albatros. It must have irritated the German for he stopped squirming and flew straight to get his shot in. I was ready and I gave a five-second burst. His tail was shredded. He tried to pull up but, as he did so, Gordy's gunner let rip and the Albatros side slipped down to the ground where it exploded in a fiery inferno.

The rest had left and so we escorted the Bristols home. My flight had all survived. I was not certain that my new pilot had fired his guns but that was not important. He had another two and a half hours in the air and he had fought in aerial combat. Days like this were rare and to be savoured.

I sought out Lieutenant Davies as soon as we landed. He was wide-eyed and looked a little pale. "How was it, Lieutenant?"

"A little hard to know what you were going to do, sir. I nearly lost you a couple of times and after the loop…"

"You were disorientated. I know. Well, you survived your first flight over German lines and that is a bonus. The next time you fly you will be in the middle of the flight but you will do exactly what you did today. Stick to the bus in front like glue," He nodded. "Did you get to fire your guns when we were up there?"

"No, sir. I was afraid of hitting you."

"Next time we are up if you don't get the chance to fire them in combat then fire them on the way back. You need to know what it feels like."

"I have fired guns on the range, sir."

"Have you fired from a Camel, in the air?"

"No, sir."

I nodded, "It will feel different. We were lucky today, Owen, we caught the Hun with his trousers down. Sometimes they will be waiting for us. Remember to use your mirror and be aware of where the flight is at all times. Now if I were you I would go over your bus with your mechanic."

"Sir."

The early October weather was notoriously unpredictable and we were grounded for the next two days with overcast skies and sudden squalls. It was frustrating for all that we wanted was to get in the air and consolidate the good work. I used the enforced ground time to catch up on letters. I told Mum that I had seen Bert and that he was well. I did not tell her of his new regiment. She would not understand and it was, after all, still a secret. I wrote to Alice and Beattie too. My letter to Beattie was full of concern about the raids on London but I was able to promise her that I would have a leave at around Christmas time. I begged her to get leave at the same time. The last thing I wanted was for her to be working. When I reached London, I wanted every single minute with her.

The skies cleared and so were we. Headquarters thought that they might have repaired the storage area we had raided and destroyed and we were sent back. I took the decision to repeat the same tactics. Archie was certain that there was no need. "Listen laddie you mauled their fighters well last time. Besides, we were about to head home anyway. If you join in the attack too then we can leave quicker."

"If you don't mind sir I will take my flight aloft. I can still raid the supply depot but I will feel happier watching over you."

"Your instincts have never let us down, Bill. Aye, take your flight aloft."

I put Lieutenant Davies between Jack and Roger. They had proved dependable and I knew that Jack would watch over our new chick. We climbed over the trenches to take our position. I had just cocked my guns when I saw the enemy aeroplanes coming from the northeast to intercept us. It was the Flying Circus. I recognised the strange shape of the leading six triplanes.

"I have spotted the Red Baron and the Circus. Over."

It was a simple bald message but if anything happened to us at least they would know the reason. Below us, I saw the rest of the squadron as they began their runs. I waved to the others and aimed my bus directly at the eighteen fighters. Alarmingly they did not make for the buses attacking the supplies, they came for us. Out of the corner of my eye, I saw that a second squadron was approaching from the south to attack Archie and the rest. It was as fine a trap as I had seen.

The detached side of me thought that this would be a good opportunity to see if Sergeant Lowery's improvements had made us a better bus than the Fokker. With odds of three to one, it was unlikely that anyone would ever know.

"The squadron is being attacked by a second formation of German fighters. We are engaging the Circus. Over."

We were two very fast formations of flights and we were not flying the way that the Germans would expect. We were not in line astern. That was our only edge. The Red Baron's distinctive red livery was three aeroplanes along. I flew at the gaudily painted yellow and blue Fokker. I glanced to my left and right and saw that, for some reason, I was slightly ahead of Hickey and Jenkin. When I was three hundred yards from the Germans I moved my stick to starboard and then, as I corrected to return to my original course I fired my guns. I was gambling that the pilots we faced were the best and would have wonderfully quick reactions. It worked. The pilot of the yellow and blue Fokker tried to match my turn and his guns had no target. I hit his engine at two hundred yards and I could not miss. His Fokker fell from the sky as all power was lost. He was a good pilot and I knew he had a chance of crash landing. There was a gap into which I flew.

I banked to starboard. I was in dead air. The second wave of Fokkers could not fire for fear of hitting their own pilots and I could attack the unprotected rears of the Fokkers who were being attacked by my brave young pilots. I kept the turn going and raked the rear of a green, white and black Fokker. I saw that the next aeroplane was that of the Red Baron.

"I have just shot down a triplane. I am engaging the Red Baron. Over."

It might be my last message but it was important for Randolph to have a picture of the fight.

As I pulled my nose around I saw the red tail and I fired. Richthofen had good reactions and a sound tactical sense. He began to pull a loop to get away from the danger and to allow his second wave to hit us. I had to adjust my turn and climb with him. This would be a test. He did not pull away. He kept jinking as he climbed and I had no shot. I had the tiger by the tail and I hung on. When he got to the top of the loop I knew what he would do. He would not continue down but he would roll and then either turn to port or starboard. I had to gamble. When he rolled he was, briefly, flying level and I fired for the two seconds he was in my sights. I do not know why but I turned my bus to starboard. It could have been a disaster. If he had turned to port he would have been able to get on my tail but he turned to starboard too and I fired again.

I was suddenly aware that we were in clear air. The clouds were close to us but the rest of the combats were taking place far below us. The sound of the guns seemed muffled. This was a game of cat and mouse. I saw that I had damaged both his tail and hit his fuselage although it did not appear to affect the handling of the lively little Fokker. He had begun to move his bus from side to side trying to draw fire and waste my ammunition. I was less than a hundred and fifty yards from his tail and I could be patient. I looked at my compass and saw that he was drawing me east. Perhaps Randolph was right and they had a shorter range.

Suddenly he jerked his Fokker and disappeared into the clouds. I had no choice but to follow. I knew that he would turn once he was in the clouds. I gambled and turned to port. It was the opposite of the move I had anticipated earlier and it took him away from his base. I had met the man and knew his calculating mind. When the turn was complete I dropped my nose and saw him below me, heading south. I discovered I was heading east. He had not seen me and I banked and dived to starboard. As his aeroplane became a cross beneath me I fired. I hit his top wing and his Spandau. I must have damaged his guns for he turned to port and began to descend as he headed for home. I looked at my fuel gauge. I was running out too. I gave one last burst and then turned to head west.

As I flew over the scene of the fight I saw the Fokker I had hit, burning. There were also two burning Bristols and a Camel. I think I saw the wreckage of three other aeroplanes but I could not identify them. If we had lost just one Camel and two Bristols then we had edged a draw with the Circus.

"Returning to the field. Over."

I did not know what to feel. I had survived a second encounter with the Red Baron and shot down a Fokker but nothing was decided. We both still lived. I had this feeling that the Circus was a squadron bound up in the myth of the Red Baron. If we could only shoot him down then the myth would be destroyed.

My engine began to cough a little. My aerial exertions had almost used all of my fuel. I was lucky. I saw a gap on the airfield and managed to land my bus before it ran out of fuel. As I stood in the cockpit I surveyed the field. All of my Camels were there although all of them looked to be damaged in some way. Freddie had lost his new pilot. He had lasted just three hours over enemy lines. Our life was exciting but could be very short.

My flight raced over to me once my propeller had stopped. "Did you get him, sir? The Red Baron?"

"We saw you disappear into the clouds and then..."

I shook my head. "No he escaped but I hit his guns. It may be he won't be flying in the morning. Did you get any kills?"

They all looked disappointed. "No sir, although we winged a couple of them and George made one of them smoke a little."

Jack Fall was ever generous with his praise. "Well done, George. Claim that as a possible eh?"

"No, sir. I'll wait until I see that they are down. Don't worry. I'll get there. We took on the Flying Circus today! And they ran."

I nodded, "I think that they do have a problem with endurance and I also noticed that while they can climb they don't dive so well. Keep them flying around and they will run first."

Once again our damage grounded us but the Circus was noticeable by its absence. Randolph and Archie were summoned to Headquarters. I wondered if it was for a dressing down. They did not like our squadron to be stood down.

In the mess, we managed to catch up on old newspapers. We read how Werner Voss, one of the other leading German aces, had been shot down by Captain McCudden in an SE 5. I shook my head. The British ace had had seven other aeroplanes with him and the German had managed to damage three before being shot down. The Germans had some remarkable fliers.

Freddie took me to one side. "Sir, my new pilot lasted just two flights. How do you manage to keep your pilots in the air longer than I do?"

"You should know, Freddie, you flew with me. Protect them while they are new. Even if they think they are ready to take on the Germans don't let them until they have hours in the air. I was worried sick about Davies. But Fall and Jenkin looked out for him. My flight may not be claiming many kills but they are damaging the enemy and they aren't dying. That is a victory in my book."

"The lads say you took on the Red Baron again."

"He is a damned good pilot. I was lucky up there. I managed to second-guess him. Next time I might guess wrong."

The next morning we had a briefing from Archie and Randolph. They had been at Headquarters until late in the night.

"Well, it wasn't a telling-off as we expected. It seems we hurt the Germans the other day. They sent a couple of reconnaissance aeroplanes to photograph their field and it looks like they were damaged worse than we were. Well done; and now the good news. We are being rested. A and D flights will be given a week's leave and then B and C flights. That way we will have both Camels and Bristols. We need to be ready for an offensive in November. Until then we will just patrol our own lines and stop the Hun from watching what we are up to." Everyone cheered. Archie nodded, "And Bill here has been recommended for a bar to his MC." He chuckled, "He will need a bigger uniform soon."

Ted asked. "When do the first lads go on leave, sir?"

"Tomorrow Ted. If you and Freddie can take your flights up today for a patrol then Gordy and Bill can pack." He smiled at me, "Oh and Bill the general said there is an investiture at the Palace on Thursday. The Prince of Wales will be presenting you with your VC." Everyone cheered but part of me resented the fact that I would have a day less to spend with Beattie.

"Right, sir."

"Contact the General in London when you arrive and his chaps will give you the details."

It was good news but I was not certain if Beattie would be able to get time off. However, any time I could spend with her was better than nothing and a week's leave was not long enough to get home to

Burscough. I told Bates the good news. "Leave sir? How delightful." He hesitated, "Will you need me, sir?"

"I don't think so. What have you planned?" I knew that he had no family.

"Well sir, I thought I would take the opportunity of exploring the old buildings of London. When I heard that the Germans were bombing the old city I realised that I needed to see them while they were still standing. Who knows what mischief they might get up to?"

He was right but I would have no time for sightseeing. "Well enjoy yourself."

"Will you be in London, sir?"

"I think so." I hesitated, "I have to go to the palace on Thursday to get a gong."

His face lit up. "Well done sir! Will you be staying at a hotel or the Army and Navy club?"

It was a good question but I didn't want to be around soldiers. My medals drew too much attention and I wanted to be able to be with Beattie as much as possible. "A hotel I think."

"Well if you would not mind, sir, I would like to arrange that and then I would still be able to keep your uniform looking smart for the investiture."

"You don't need to you know."

"I know sir. I want to."

"Good, then I will leave that in your hands. One job less for me to do."

"And I will pack for you, sir."

Chapter 11

I had no time to contact Beattie and, when the boat train arrived in London, I left Bates to arrange the hotel while I went to the hospital. He told me that the hotel would be close to Buckingham Palace. There were many hotels in Victoria. I arranged to meet him outside the gates of Buckingham Palace in an hour. It was a relief not to have to worry about such mundane things as arranging a room in a hotel. It was late when we reached London. I ran across Hyde Park to reach the hospital. If she was on duty I could wait for her to finish her shift and if not then I could go to her quarters.

The orderly who was standing outside having a quiet cigarette recognised me. He stubbed out his cigarette and wafted away the smoke. "Major Harsker! What are you doing here?"

I smiled as I sought for his name. "Just a quick leave, George. Is Miss Porter on duty?"

He scratched his head. "I am not certain, sir. If you wait here I'll find out."

I cooled my heels and looked around at the peaceful streets. One change I noticed from my earlier visits was there were more sandbags around the doors and the windows were taped. The German bombers were more than a nuisance; they were deadly.

George wheezed back to the door. "Er yes, sir. She's on duty. She's in theatre at the moment. I left a message to say you were here."

"What time will she be off duty?"

"Ten o'clock."

I looked at the clock in the hallway. It was six-thirty. "Right, I'll be back at nine-thirty. Make sure she knows I will be here waiting for her."

"Don't you worry, sir. We'll make sure." He nodded towards my ribbons. "Well done for the medal, sir." I nodded. There was little to say that didn't come out as either false or arrogant. I had found a polite nod worked.

I found Bates peering at the Palace through the gates. "It would be a great shame, Major Harsker if this was to be damaged by the Hun. It is a wonderful building."

"It certainly is." As he led me back to the hotel he had found, the Mayflower, I said, "I am allowed two guests on Thursday, Bates when I come for my medal. I would be honoured if you would be one of them."

He turned and for one moment I thought that he would embrace me, "Really, sir?"

"I only have Miss Porter in town and I don't think that Captain Hewitt would appreciate being dragged away from his wife and child."

"Then I accept. That would be wonderful. It might be my only chance of visiting the home of the King and Queen."

I thought it was true and it was sad at the same time. Bates and soldiers like him would do their jobs far better than I did mine but they would never be rewarded. It didn't seem fair.

The hotel was comfortable and quiet. It was an old Georgian building which had been converted into a hotel. At one time it would have been the townhouse of some aristocrat. Times had changed and this one had become a pleasant little hotel which was close to Buckingham Palace. I suspected that in peacetime it would have been popular. The bombing raids had meant that fewer people visited the capital.

I had a bath while Bates pressed my uniform and he gave me one of his special close shaves so that I left the hotel feeling as smart as paint! He was more than happy to go around the corner for a quiet meal in the local pub, The Grenadier. Food was the last thing on my mind.

My supposed stroll across the park proved to be almost a run and I reached the hospital at nine-fifteen. I lit my pipe and smoked a whole bowlful. I tapped it out at ten to ten. I just had a few minutes to wait. As I had hoped she was the first one out of the doors and she threw herself into my arms. I heard the giggles from the other nurses as they passed us. I didn't care.

"This is a surprise!"

She linked my arm and we followed the other nurses towards the nearby nurse's home. "It was a reward for our work. It is only a week. Bates and I are staying at 'The Mayflower'."

She turned and kissed me, "That is just across the park!"

"I know. John picked it."

"He is a treasure."

I have to go to the Palace on Thursday for my gong."

She stopped and looked at me. "How wonderful! You are clever."

"Could you get the morning off and come with us?"

"If I tell matron that you are getting a medal at Buckingham Palace then I am sure she will give me permission. If not, I will swap with Sally. She owes me tons of favours." Her face darkened, "I am afraid I am working every day for the next week. Today is my last late shift though. The rest are all mornings. I start at six and finish at two."

"Perfect!"

We had reached the Nurse's Home where she had her room. "And I am afraid we have to be in by ten-fifteen each night."

I glanced at my watch. We had just ten minutes left. "We'll have to make good use of the time we have." I kissed her full on the lips.

"Bill! You will get me in trouble."

I laughed, "You know, I don't care! Why shouldn't a fellow kiss his girl?"

She giggled, "You know you are a bad influence on me. I don't care either." She kissed me back.

The light from the door shone on us as it opened and a hatchet-faced harridan glowered at us. "The door will be locked in two minutes, Nurse Porter!"

"Just coming."

I kissed her again, "I'll be outside the hospital at two. Decide where you want to go!"

She kissed me and went up the steps. "Anywhere so long as it is with you!"

As I walked back across the park I reflected that I had had but a few minutes with Beattie; I had not eaten and yet I was happy and content. I would make sure that every moment we had was worthwhile. That evening my sleep was disturbed by the distant explosions of German bombs. It was another reminder of the proximity of the war.

I visited General Soames in the building that would become, in the following year, the Air Ministry. I was treated far better than I had expected. Apparently, the award of a VC to a pilot who was still alive was considered a rarity. Lanoe Hawker had been the last one! Our three passes and precise instructions were given to me along with a rapid course in court etiquette. As I left, the young lieutenant told me that there would be someone at the palace who would ensure that I didn't make a mess of things.

John had gone off to see Somerset House and the fine buildings down by the Strand. I slowly sauntered around Trafalgar Square before grabbing a Ploughman's and a pint at a little pub just off the Square. After my meal, I wandered the streets and I found a good tobacconist just along Piccadilly where I spent half an hour with a most knowledgeable tobacconist who helped me to select a pound of good smoking tobacco. He made up a mixture of black shag, an aromatic leaf from the Dutch East Indies and a slow-smoking Virginia. He even supplied a humidor to keep it moist. He gave me a great deal of his time and a most reasonable price.

"Thank you very much."

"No sir, thank you. My son was killed at Arras and his mates told me what a good job you fliers did. I am sad that my son is dead but proud of heroes like you. God Bless you, sir."

Once again, I was at the hospital well before two. Beattie was the first out. In the daylight, I could not get over how beautiful she was. She linked me and began to lead me to the Nurse's Home.

"Why go to your quarters?"

"I need to get changed, silly Billy!"

"Get changed later. I want more than ten minutes with you before you disappear again!"

She giggled, kissed me and we headed off into Hyde Park. If you had asked me what we talked about I could not have told you. We both gushed out the words which told the other of what had been happening lately. Before I knew it, dusk had fallen.

"Now I will need to get changed but I promise I will just take fifteen minutes, no more!"

I smoked a fine bowlful of my new tobacco as I waited for her. She was a picture worth waiting for when she came out. I took her to the Ritz. Part of it was because we loved the atmosphere but it was mainly because it evoked memories of Charlie and Alice when they were happy. We toasted them in a celebratory bottle of Champagne. It cost a fortune but I rarely spent the pay of a major anyway. I was remembering all my dead comrades as well as the sadly doomed relationship of my little sister.

As the evening wore on I began to feel frustrated. I wanted Beattie to be with me. She had promised, already, to be my wife and I was waiting patiently for that day, whenever it arrived. I looked at the couples who were dancing, the women with rings on their left hands and they looked happy. I would have to take her back to the Nurse's Home and they would be sharing a bed together. I thought of Gordy and Mary and how happy they were and then I remembered Alice's letter. I wanted no regrets and I took the plunge.

"Let's get married on my next leave."

"What?"

"I know I said I wanted to wait but I don't or I won't! We have to have banns or something read, don't we?" She nodded. "Well, let's get them done and then when I get a leave we can just get married."

"But the war will still be on and it won't be a big wedding."

"I don't care. Who wants a big wedding? I want you to be Mrs Harsker and I want to be able to hold you all night and not say goodnight at the door of your digs. That is all that I want. That and the chance to be a dad and watch our children grow up."

"You are sweet and I would love to but I don't know how to go about these things."

I looked at her in surprise. "But you are a woman!"

She laughed. "That doesn't mean I know everything about getting married. If I had sisters or my mum was still alive then it might be different. All the girls I live with are single. The only married woman I know is Mary Hewitt."

I slumped in my seat. "Sorry, you are right. I didn't know how to do this sort of thing but…"

She sipped her Champagne. She suddenly sat upright. "I know, I'll see the Chaplain in the hospital tomorrow. He will know what to do. Uncle is a nice chap."

"Uncle?"

"That is what everyone calls him. I don't know why. He is a lovely man. You will like him."

It was a long lonely walk back across the park after I had taken Beattie home. John was sitting in the lounge catching up with the news by reading the Times. "Things are not looking good in Russia, sir. I fear they will be out of the war soon and then goodness only knows what that will mean."

I smiled at my manservant. He was so clever and could do so much more than he did. I often wondered what he would do when the war was over.

"Did you have a good night, sir?"

I nodded, "Yes I told Miss Porter I wanted us to be married on my next leave."

He stood and grabbed my hand in his. "Oh, good show sir! What wonderful news!"

I shook my head, "The trouble is neither of us know how to arrange such things."

"Pish posh, sir. It must be easy. Why, hundreds do it every month and they aren't as clever as you and Miss Porter."

"Well, she is seeing the Chaplain tomorrow. He will know how to go about things."

"There, you see, you are a pair of clever things." He became serious. "Now don't forget that your mother and father are getting on in years and they will need to be here for the wedding!"

"You are right, John, but I am not certain when my leave will be. This one was unexpected. We had thought we would have one in December but…"

He nodded. "What do you think of this hotel, sir?"

It seemed a bizarre question which was unrelated to our previous conversation. "Fine. I like it. Why?"

"I was talking to the manager, he is a nice chap and he was impressed when I said you were going to get your VC from the Prince of Wales. I bet he would hold a couple of rooms for us and we should have a week's notice at least eh sir? And I can get in touch with your lovely sister and she could make the travel arrangements."

"But it would be wrong to get their hopes up of a wedding Bates."

He shook his head and wagged his finger, "Sir! I am surprised at you. I can be discreet. Leave the arrangements to me!"

He was as good as his word. Once we were back in France he took on all the details.

The Chaplain was a lovely man. Major Osborne was a career Chaplain. He had been wounded at the First Battle of Ypres and had a limp. I saw the pain of that battle etched on his face. Had the war not still been on I daresay he would have retired but he was the perfect person for us to talk to. He was an old soldier and understood our motives from the off. He was more than happy to get the banns read in the local church. "And if you don't mind being married in our little chapel here then we can use that for the ceremony."

For some reason, that seemed like Fate. The hospital was where we had first met and there was something almost perfect about the arrangement. It seemed to have symmetry about it. The next few days passed in a blur and even the investiture seemed dreamlike. I think Bates and Beattie were more affected than I was. Certainly, they both cried. The Prince of Wales seemed a nice chap and asked some knowledgeable questions about our buses. After the ceremony, the three of us were photographed outside and I was happy about that. Bates would have a permanent reminder of his visit to the Palace. The chap who took it said that the photograph would appear in papers like The Times and The Daily Mail. Mum and Dad would be as proud as punch.

Bates took care of the bags and found us a carriage on the boat train while I said goodbye to Beattie. "I will get a message to you when my leave is to take place and John will make the arrangements for mum and dad. I am sorry that all the rest will be up to you."

"Oh, you are a silly Billy! That is no hardship. I shall see Mary and she is a whizz at such things. She did a marvellous job of her own wedding." She kissed me. "You concentrate on staying safe! And I will concentrate on becoming Mrs Bill Harsker."

Chapter 11

The reality we returned to was that the squadron had taken casualties. Lieutenant Thomson and his gunner had gone west while Lieutenants Carpenter and Duffy had both been wounded. They would have a leave with bandages to mark them as warriors. Randolph returned and Archie left leaving me in command for a week. I told Gordy about the wedding and he was delighted telling me that he would write to Mary immediately. My young pilots returned brimming with confidence but Owen Davies still refused to smile. The mess orderlies were in despair- he had no mess bill. When we paid our mess bills we normally included a tip. It ensured us prompt service and augmented the pay of the orderlies. A teetotaller from the Chapel did not please them.

Archie had left us a report of where the problems had occurred. The casualties had all come three days after the patrols had started. I knew why as soon as I read them.

"They were too predictable. They flew the same patterns at the same time for three consecutive days. Fritz is not stupid. I intend to mix it up." I began to fill my pipe. "Headquarters just want us to stop the Hun coming over our lines?"

"As far as I can see, yes."

I pushed my tobacco pouch over to Randolph as I lit mine. The aromatic smell of the new mix filled the room. "Then I think we use the box system Freddie and I used. That way Gordy and I can keep in touch with one another while covering a large part of the front."

He filled his pipe and lit it. "This is damned good stuff. You must tell me where you got it from. Yes, well, you are in command, old boy." He tapped a manila envelope. "Things will get hot around the middle of November though. It looks like we are going in with the artillery and the tanks. It seems some Johnny at Headquarters thinks it might work. Instead of a barrage which warns them we are coming, they want a creeping barrage ahead of the tanks. We keep the artillery informed about the tanks' progress and we use ground attack to keep the Hun's heads down. It might work."

"Our Bert is in the Tank Corps now."

"Oh, sorry about that. I didn't know. Still, they are supposed to be a great invention and they are being used in greater numbers than ever before in this little shindig. He should be safer in one of those rather than burrowing under the ground."

"They only travel at four miles an hour and you can bet that the Germans have been working out how to destroy them. They were used on the Somme, remember?"

"If we can make a breakthrough…"

"I suppose you are right. Now listen, Randolph, this has nothing to do with operations but I intend to marry Beattie on my next leave."

He shook my hand, "Well done old chap."

"The thing is I need as much notice as I can and I need to be able to tell Beattie. What do you suggest?"

"Well, Archie will know a fortnight before the leave starts when it will be. He normally tells you chaps a week before in case anything comes up but I daresay he could make an exception. I have a chum at Headquarters. He could send a message to the hospital she works at. How about that?"

"You are a brick. Come on let's go to the mess and celebrate."

It was a party atmosphere that night. I couldn't help noticing how much Jack, George and Roger had grown over the last month. They were all different men now. I just prayed that they would survive to the end of this war… whenever that day came.

Gordy was happy with my plan and we headed to Flesquières flying in two lines with the Camels above the Bristols. Once we reached our area then Gordy flew to the south-east while we flew to the north-west. After two miles we turned around. It meant we could keep an eye on each other and minimise the chance of being jumped. I would devise a different plan for the next day. We saw the German aeroplanes but they were close to Noyelles and they did not attempt to close with us. They flew in five flights of five stacked one above the other. The flight they used was a north-to-south one. We left each other alone but I knew that they would report on how we flew.

There were just three of us in the office as we mulled over the patrol. "What do you think Gordy? Should we shake a stick at these hornets?"

"Leave well alone I say. In a couple of weeks' time, we are going to need every bus we can get."

"I agree. Tomorrow, though, we will fly in one line. Your lads can be at the back. The rear gunners will come in handy. Let's see what they make of that. I did notice that they outnumbered us. They may decide to chance their arm. You know they have good intelligence. I am betting they know an attack is in the offing. Some Hun at staff will be demanding that they come and see our dispositions so we will keep a sharp eye out for them."

We left half an hour later than the previous day. If the Germans were as efficient as they usually were then they would be there ready to watch us and I wanted them wasting fuel if they did. If they decided to venture over in our absence we would still arrive in time to attack them.

I took us in higher than the previous day. It was irritating to have to wait for the Bristols to catch us up. We had a much faster rate of climb. The Germans were in position but this time they were venturing across No Man's Land.

"German formations approaching the British lines. Over."

My message would not help anyone unless they telephoned the trenches to warn them. In my experience, the presence of RFC aeroplanes normally alerted the ground troops to danger anyway. We were slightly higher than the Germans and I led my long line of aeroplanes towards the amalgamation of Fokkers and Albatros. I saw that the squadron had a number of different types. There was the D III as well as a couple of D. IV. There was even an old DII which was struggling to keep formation.

As soon as they spotted us the first wave banked to attack. I felt more confident facing such an eclectic collection of fighters. I was faster and more manoeuvrable than all of them and I had twice the guns of half of them. The hard part would be facing the initial firestorm before I was through. The Camels and Bristols behind me were stacked up a little and when I dived they would each have a clear shot. By the time the Bristols came through their rear gunners would be able to sweep both sides. That was the theory. It never worked out that way in practice.

The older aeroplanes might have recognised the horse painted on my cockpit; I don't know. But the pilots in the first wave all fired too soon and too inaccurately. Bullets zinged around my bus but none came close. I held my fire. I knew, myself, how nerve-wracking it is to have an enemy come at you with silent guns. It exacerbated the tension. I waited until they were less than a hundred yards away. By that time the first aeroplane's gun was hitting my bus but then the pilot pulled up his nose. I gave a short burst as his nose filled my sights. I actually saw pieces of metal flying off as my twin Vickers shredded his propeller and then ripped into the engine cowling. It fell sideways causing the next aeroplane to have to veer to port in order to avoid a collision.

There was confusion in the German formation. As the Fokker D III fell to its death I saw that the second rank was made up of the Albatros D III. They all had a twin Spandau but they were almost twenty miles an hour slower than I was. I opened fire at two hundred yards and then dived so that the Camels behind me could have a shot at the green Albatros with the wavy red line as it tried to adjust its flight to attack me. I was so quick that I was gone before he could fire his guns. I immediately brought my nose up. The third line was made up of the Albatros D II and Fokker D II. These only had one machine and were much slower. However, more importantly, the radiator was so high that it could obscure their view at the front. I had a similar problem when I changed from the Gunbus to the Camel. They didn't see me and I came up under the yellow-painted Fokker. He seemed so slow after the triplanes that it appeared to be stationary. I gave a short burst as I zoomed up at a hundred and ten miles an hour. My last bullets ripped into him from less than twenty yards and I had to adjust my Camel to avoid smashing into him. He too tumbled to earth.

I saw in my mirror that I only had my Camels with me. Our climb had been too fast for the Bristols but the Bristols were now finishing off the front two lines of German fighters. The slower ones we now faced turned and ran. There was no order to their flight. It was every man for himself. I took snapshots at them as they departed and was gratified with a few hits but no more were shot down.

As we banked to return home I saw that none of our aeroplanes had been hit but there were at least six aeroplanes either burning on the ground or tumbling from the sky. The losses of the last week had been avenged.

There was an exuberant atmosphere in the mess that night. Although we were not overly competitive my young pilots were delighted to have shot down more German aeroplanes than the rest of the squadron. It did them no harm and I knew that their confidence would be up. More importantly, was the time in the air they had spent fighting German fighters. They might not have been the best German fighters but they had done well to sweep them so imperiously from the skies.

We must have frightened them for they never ventured across our lines for the rest of the week. From captured Germans in other sectors, we discovered that our squadron was seen as a British version of the Flying Circus. It was a compliment but I knew the dangers. They would send their best to shoot us down.

The rest of the squadron arrived back on the 19th of October. They came back bubbling with excitement. Leave did that for you. They had only been away for a week but I know that it would have felt like a month. It was a party in the mess as everyone shared the news of a fortnight spent apart.

The next day we were brought back to reality when we were ordered into the air. We would be used to spot for the artillery. While we had been on leave Freddie's bus had been fitted with a radio so that the four flights could each go to a different sector and direct artillery fire. It was a trial of the new technology as well as an attempt to deceive the

Germans. We were directing the fire to the south of the intended offensive at Cambrai. For once someone at Headquarters was actually thinking. We would find any problems with the radio communication and the Hun might move his troops to face a phantom attack which would never materialise.

We took off on the twenty-first and headed for Le Catelet. The sector had been quiet and we each only had a battery of six guns to direct but it seemed a good idea to me. The batteries had been given our frequencies but to ensure that it worked Sergeant Kenny and his magicians had been sent to the batteries to assist the operators. It had been one reason for the delay in the barrage.

"A Flight on station. Over."

While the rest of my flight climbed above me to provide cover I flew over the German lines. I had a map in front of me with grids marked on it. I had been told where they would shell first and I would direct them once I had seen the fall of shot.

The first shells all screamed over. They were closer to each other than I would have expected but they were short of the trenches by a hundred yards. It was just some barbed wire which had been hit.

"A Flight. One hundred yards short. Repeat one hundred yards short. Over."

I had to admit this was faster than flashing with an Aldis lamp but it would be much easier for Ted and Gordy for they could watch the skies and just fly. I had to do both. As I waited for the next fall of shot I glanced up to see that my umbrella was still in place. Each of the flights was sufficiently far away from each other that there would be no confusion with the fall of shot.

The next salvo was much better. Two of the shells struck the trench and the other four straddled it. The chap from the artillery who had briefed us had told us to send back the word 'straddle' when that happened.

"A Flight. Straddle. Over!"

The next shots had five hits.

"A Flight. On target. Over."

This was where it would become more complicated. I flew up and down in a small loop as I watched the fall of shot. When a section of the trench was destroyed then it would be my call to change the target. It only took six salvoes and the trench looked like one huge shell hole.

"A Flight target destroyed. Over."

I saw that there were command and secondary trenches just fifty yards further east. I deduced that the artillery would find it easier to hit a target further away rather than adjusting to left and right.

"A Flight. New target. One hundred yards east. Over."

I had no idea how the artillery could hit something they could not see but when the next shells came over three of them hit and three straddled.

"A Flight. Straddle. Over!"

It took another four salvoes to begin to destroy it but I heard the sound of the Vickers and glanced up to see my flight being attacked by ten Fokker D III.

"A Flight. Under attack. Aborting. Over!"

We had been told to break off if we were in danger. This was a trial and there was little point in risking valuable aeroplanes and pilots. I began to climb. The Germans were after me, as the spotter. I would not be the pigeon for these hawks. I saw that Jack Fall was leading the line well and the five aeroplanes kept a tight formation. He must have seen me climbing for he began to turn and lead the flight west. They started to drop so that I could join them. I saw that Owen Davies' bus had been damaged but the rest looked intact.

Two Fokkers came screaming down at me. I fired a short burst and rolled the Camel away from them and then pulled it into a steep climb. They were past me in a flash and I had a clear sky. I banked to starboard and dived after them. I was so fast that I soon caught them. I fired at two hundred yards. I hit the tailplane of one of them and they diverged. My fuel gauge told me to get the hell out of there before I ran out and I climbed to join the rest of the flight who were busily seeing off the enemy. Anything but a Fokker triplane or the D V was no match for us. We headed home, unmolested.

The patrol the following day was two miles southeast of Le Catelet. It proved to be as easy a target. Nor did we have the problem of fighters curtailing our task. We had just finished when they appeared. We headed safely home; I daresay the German pilots were frustrated to have missed us.

Headquarters gave us two days off and then began again. I could see what they intended. The Germans would see a pattern and assume that we were trying to disguise our point of attack. As this was happening over a fifty-mile front it would be hard for them to pinpoint the precise location of the offensive. That we were going on the offensive was no secret. I had no doubt that they had agents in Amiens and other large towns. They would be sending back reports of the influx of new troops. Eventually, they would go on the offensive but the methodical Teutonic mind liked to work things out.

We were over Le Catelet again but this time we flew above the support trenches. I knew from my own visits to the trenches that these contained supplies and provided shelter for troops moving to the forward areas. If we destroyed them then it would leave the front line a little weaker for a while. Our problem would be that the German fighters would be closer. However, the fact that only four of our aeroplanes were spotting while the rest provided protection gave me hope that we might emerge unscathed again.

The problem was that the Germans had fitted out a squadron with the Albatros D.V. Although not the fastest of buses it had twin Spandau and they were fast. We had only seen them in ones and twos. That day we saw eighteen of them as they descended to discourage my spotting efforts. I told the artillery I was breaking off and I climbed to meet them. I had not fought them often enough to be confident about predicting their performance. It certainly looked like a neat aerodynamic aeroplane.

Jack and the others either didn't see them in time or they were flying a leg which took them away from the fighters. Either way eight of the aeroplanes screamed down towards me. I did not panic. I cocked my Vickers and aimed my bus at the third fighter from the right. It minimised the number of guns which could be brought to bear on me and it took me towards my flight. As I closed I feinted to port and then jerked my nose around to starboard. I fired a burst at relatively long range and then began to climb. The Camel is a small aeroplane and it is fast. The three Albatros I was facing tried to emulate me. That was the day we discovered why there were not many of these new aeroplanes in service; they were new and they were dangerous to fly.

As I looped I saw in my mirror that one of them tried the loop. I saw something which I had never seen before. His lower wing began to sheer away. It was too flimsy. The poor pilot could do nothing about it and he plummeted to his death.

I continued my loop and swept into the Albatros. The disaster of the broken wing must have unnerved them. I flew through them, firing my guns without a bullet in reply. I threw the Camel around in a shallow bank and opened fire on them again. This time they began to stream east. It was ridiculous. I was a single Camel and I had outflown eight Albatros. My flight screamed through the others and I saw four downed before the whole Hun squadron fled east. We could have pursued them had we not been so low on fuel.

My young pilots were positively bouncing when we landed. Four of them could claim a kill and one a probable. I was astounded. When I told Randolph, he did not seem surprised. "I didn't know it was an Albatros but we had reports of new fighters falling apart in the air. We thought it was sabotage."

"No, they are just a poorly made aeroplane. Thank God they don't have many Fokker Triplanes."

We moved down the line again the next day and did not run into any Germans. It was when we returned that we discovered the reason. The whole of the Red Baron's Jasta had been on patrol. He had four Jasta under his command, 4, 6, 10 and 11, the Flying Circus. Although only Jasta 11 had the triplane the rest were all equipped with the Fokker D.IV and the Albatros D. IV. They had knocked two squadrons out of the air. Although they were flying SE 5 and DH 4 aeroplanes they were no match for the German formation. Our comrades had paid the price for our success. It was a sombre message to pass along to our young pilots. The Red Baron was back and that meant pilots would die.

Poor weather grounded us until the twenty-seventh of October. I was pleased to see that our young pilots spent their spare time with their mechanics and riggers around the aeroplane. Their encounter with the poorly made Albatros showed them what a fine bus we had. We had learned it was hard to get to know its idiosyncrasies but once you did then it was the best aeroplane in a dogfight. None wanted the faster SE 5. They had learned that our small size and superb aerodynamics more than compensated for the speed.

Randolph waved us over just before dinner. Archie looked down. "Bad news chaps. The Tsar has just been overthrown. The Bolsheviks have taken over the country."

Gordy asked, "How does that affect us?"

"A number of ways. Remember the French mutiny? Some British units also had a low-key rebellion of sorts. This kind of thing can spread. We even heard that some of the Kaiser's sailors refused to fight, but the real problem is that it means Russia will be out of the war. The Kaiser can move those Divisions to the Western front. The American Army is still coming over and will be nowhere near as big as the army the Russians could field. I am afraid this has lengthened the war by years."

Everyone was as depressed as I had ever seen them. I struggled for something positive. "I know that it means there will be the Eastern aeroplanes coming over but what do we know about them?"

Randolph brightened, "From what my chum said they have inferior aeroplanes on the Eastern front and yet they still manage to defeat the Russians and in terms of numbers then it will not add many to their Jasta."

"There you are, the war might go on longer than it should but we have the same problem. How do we defeat the Red Baron and his menace?"

Ted laughed, "Well only you have the answer to that. No one else has given him a run for his money yet."

I began to fill my pipe. I looked at Archie when it was going. "Then sir, you need to call in all the favours you have and have the Bristols replaced with Camels. If everyone wants the new SE 5 then they might let us have the older Camel."

"You have that much confidence in it?"

"Yes, sir. With Senior Flight Sergeant Lowery's modifications, we are a better aeroplane than the triplane and with our greater endurance we can make sure that Fritz breaks off the fight before we do and if we chase him back to his fields we have more chance of shooting them down."

Ted shook his head, "You said yourself that they were a bugger to learn how to fly."

"If these young lads can manage then I don't think an old goat like you should have any problem."

Archie nodded, "I will get on to General Henderson. Don't get your hopes up. I think we will need to get this offensive over first. They will need the Bristols to bomb the German lines."

Randolph began to write out the request. Archie might well telephone or visit the General but the RFC liked its paperwork. "Let's hope then, that by January 1918 we are a Camel squadron!"

Chapter 12

A mixture of bad weather and luck meant that we escaped the carnage of some of the other squadrons in the lead-up to the Battle of Cambrai. We had a full squadron and, more than that, an experienced squadron. The two days before the battle we pored over the maps and the detailed orders we would have to follow. Sergeant Kenny and his team left on the eighteenth to join the artillery batteries. Ted and Gordy would be responsible for directing the artillery fire as General Henderson had found a spare Camel for Archie. He would be with the Camels and our job was close support. We were told to stay over the battlefield and snuff out any attempt to destroy the tanks. It sounded easy. It was not.

The battle began, well before dawn at six a.m. with a creeping barrage. Perhaps if we had been able to support them earlier on then things might have gone differently; I am not sure. As it was we took off before dawn to join the battle.

The two British Corps, III Corps and IV Corps were supported by four hundred tanks. I had seen them before, of course, but not in such numbers. There were the males with two six pounders and the females which were armed with Lewis guns. It was a strange feeling, knowing that Bert was in one of those metallic leviathans. We flew high. I kept silent as the radio operators only needed to hear the voices of the two observers in the Bristols.

The tanks were not moving quickly; about the pace of a man marching quickly but they were relentlessly eating up the ground. They just rolled over the barbed wire as though it was not there. I could hear the bullets of the German machine guns as they pinged off the thick armour. The danger to the tanks lay in a lucky shell hit. Soon the artillery was raining down on their gun positions. I saw groups of Germans emerge from the trenches and run purposefully towards one of the males. I swooped down and machine-gunned them before they could get within grenade or flamethrower range. One of these contained my brother.

As I zoomed up to rejoin my flight I saw the German fighters as they appeared from the east. I knew that our night bombers had done some damage to their fields which explained their tardy arrival. We did not have the advantage of height but we did have the advantage of speed. I signalled for line abreast and we swept towards them. Shells were exploding all around us but, for once, there was no ground fire. The tanks were the centre of attention. I fixed a Fokker in my sights; they were trying to get to the Bristols and I had a free shot. I remembered the effect of a pair of Vickers machine guns at less than thirty yards and when I fired I almost cut the Fokker in two. I felt something strike my lower wing and saw a line of bullet holes. I pulled up my nose and began to bank at the same time. As I edged to port I saw an inviting tail appear with a perfect cross on the fuselage. I fired. I must have hit some controls because it began to waver up and down. I fired again and it descended. The pilot was trying to land. I admired his optimism. There was not an inch of flat ground beneath us. I rolled to starboard and saw some smaller German artillery pieces. I knew that they could damage the tanks and I flew as low as I dared. I was so low I saw one German officer with a wonderful Franz Joseph moustache. Then I let rip. Had I had bombs, even a Mills bomb, I could have put all six of them out of action. As it was I did not leave one crewmember without a wound to remember me by. It would take some time to bring that battery back into action.

The tanks were crossing the support trenches. I saw a couple of the crew leap out and hurl fascines of wood into the trenches to make the passage easier. Someone had thought this through. And still, the tanks rolled on. I banked to starboard to clear a path for them. To my amazement, a head popped out from the hatch of a male. I was just fifty feet above him and I saw that it was Bert. I noticed that the tank had a Union flag tied to an improvised jackstaff. It made my task even more important and I waited until I was almost on the machine-gun position before I opened fire. The gun was thrown into the air and the crew was destroyed. The six-pounder, on our Bert's tank, flashed as it fired and I saw another machine gun disappear in a shower of H.E.

I knew that I was running low both on fuel and ammunition and I climbed so that I could turn. My speed and my course took me half a mile from Bert's tank. I decided I would fly back over him in case he would wave again. To my horror, the tank was stopped and I could see, as I approached, that the tracks had come off. Some stormtroopers were racing towards it with a flame thrower. I saw the officer climb out of the tank only to be shot by a stormtrooper with a hand-held machine gun. Then Bert appeared and he held the Lewis gun like a rifle and emptied the ninety-six bullet magazine at the stormtroopers. The flame thrower blew up and threw Bert and his crew to the ground. I later discovered that it must have been ammunition on the soldier rather than the flame thrower tanks which caused the explosion. I might have been running out of fuel and ammunition but I was not going to leave my kid brother in the lurch.

I flew over the damaged tank and banked to come back around. I saw that Bert and four of his crew were running towards me but behind them were another two groups of storm-troopers. I flew directly at one group and destroyed them with one long burst. Then I was over them and I had to bank to come back around. I saw them in my mirror. I will never forget the sight of Bert, some three hundred yards from me aiming his pistol at the advancing soldiers and trying to keep them at bay so that his men could escape. I was so proud of my little brother. It made all my exploits seem pathetic by comparison. Then the flame thrower sent out a column of flame and my little brother was engulfed in fire. As his body collapsed to the ground I knew that he was dead. I used the last of my bullets to kill the remaining stormtroopers. But it was too late for Bert. I was now the last of the Harskers.

I was perilously short of fuel and out of ammunition. I headed home, oblivious to the bullets whizzing around me. I was aware of nothing. My whole body was numb and I think I must have flown on some sort of auto-pilot. I still cannot remember landing. My flight all rushed up to me to praise me but I said not a word and headed for the office. I had to get a message so that someone was there when my mother received the telegram. I knew Bert was dead but the authorities would not send a telegram for a couple of days. It would kill her to receive a brown telegram alone.

It is strange, now, to think the way my mind worked. I just wanted to avoid the pain of the telegram. I remembered how badly she had reacted when the telegram came to say I was dead. I needed to get in touch with Alice, or Sarah or Lady Burscough! Someone had to be there.

Randolph was grinning when I went in. "We heard that we have made great advances and we have not lost a single aeroplane. This has been a wonderful day!"

"My brother, Bert, was in one of the tanks. I saw him killed."

"Oh, my God! I am sorry, Bill I ..."

I waved my hand to shut him up, "That's fine you weren't to know. I'm not upset. Listen, Randolph, I have to get a telegram sent to the Burscough estate. How do I do it?" He gave me a puzzled look. "I want family there when Mother gets the telegram telling her that Bert is dead!"

I saw understanding dawn. "Listen I have a chum at Headquarters. They have a telegraph office there. I am sure that he could send it." He pushed the whisky bottle over and began to work the handle on the telephone. I was oblivious to what he was saying. I just stared at the amber liquid in the bottle. I heard voices outside. They were laughing. The door opened and Archie and the others stood there. They could see that something was the matter. I saw Randolph shake his head and wave to the seats. He continued talking. The four of them sat down and poured themselves a drink. I knew they were desperate to know what was amiss but I couldn't tell them; not yet. I swallowed the peaty, fiery liquid in one and filled my glass again.

Randolph put his hand over the telephone. "We can do it. Which telegraph office should it be sent to?"

"Burscough, Lancashire."

He repeated everything I said, "Right Bill. You dictate, slowly and I will tell Harry."

"Bert killed today stop Telegram from the army not sent for two days stop Someone needs to prepare Mother stop Death was instant stop Bill stop."

Gordy came over and put his hand on my shoulder. The hardest thing I ever did was to stop myself from bursting into tears. "I am sorry Bill. We didn't know…"

Archie nodded, "We were just well… you know."

Randolph finished dictating and said. "They are sending it now." He paused. "You are certain he is dead. I mean…"

I looked up and I knew that my eyes were dead for that was how I felt inside. "A flame thrower killed him. He's dead but he saved his crew. He was a hero." That was the point when I broke. That was the moment when I ceased to be a man and became a broken-hearted child. I don't remember how I got to my quarters. I just found myself on my bed looking up at the ceiling.

I glanced at the candle burning on the bedside table and I saw Bates there. "How long, John?"

"Mr Hewitt and Mr Thomas brought you here three hours ago." He stood and felt my forehead. It was the sort of thing my mother might have done. "Are you hungry, sir?"

I shook my head, "I could do with a drink."

"No, you couldn't, Major Harsker. That is the downward slope and we can't let you go there. You have a good night's sleep and tomorrow, well, tomorrow the sun will come up and your life will go on."

"But not Bert's."

"No sir, not Bert. Another fine young man like Mr Sharp will not be going home and that is a tragedy but we will still go on because you and I know that Bert, like Charlie, would have wanted it." He took a letter out of his pocket and held it before me. "Your mother sent me this last week. She said that she got a letter from Bert. She knew that you had instigated it because Bert would do anything for you. He was your brother and he loved you. You have your whole life to live, sir. I think that your decision to get married on your next leave was almost prophetic. You and Miss Porter will have children and Bert and Charlie will live again in them. You will be good parents. You will always remember the sacrifices that soldiers like Bert and Charlie made. That is why you need to go on sir." He sighed, "Because if you don't, then their deaths will have been in vain."

He put the letter away and stood. He suddenly looked very old. "When I came here, sir, I felt as depressed and as down as you are now but you and the boys in this squadron have given me hope. Take some back, sir. Get up in the morning. Climb into your Camel and live for Bert."

I didn't see him leave for my eyes were closed and I was crying. I heard the door close. I lay in the candlelit room and I thought about his words. I thought about his words. The best memorial I could make for Bert was to help win this war and then win the peace. Bates was right, some spirit had guided my thoughts and made me decide to marry Beattie. I would live for my dead comrades and when the war was over then I would remember them. Until then I would hide them in a recess in my mind.

Chapter 13

It was strange as I walked into the mess. Everyone looked at me as though I had two heads. The mess sergeants spoke in hushed tones. Archie and Gordy came to sit on either side of me.

"Listen, Bill, if you aren't up to flying today we will understand. I will lead your flight for you."

"Thanks, Archie. I can fly and I am sorry for being such a baby yesterday. Soldiers die every day. Bert was a soldier and damned good one."

Gordy put his arm around my shoulders, "You saw your brother die, for God's sake. It would upset anyone."

"You are right Gordy and last night I was upset. Today I am ready to get aloft and help to win this war. Bert's mates are still out there in their tanks. I can't protect Bert any more but I can help his pals." I forced a smile. "I will not let you down. Any of you. That I swear."

Archie shook his head and murmured, "That was the last thought on our mind. If you are sure, mind?"

"I am." I forced a smile, "What is it today? More of the same?"

"Aye consolidate our gains. Apparently, we made more territorial gains yesterday than in any other battle. They rang church bells in England. It is seen as a great victory."

"But it isn't, at least, not yet."

"Then let's get in the air and see if we can win it now!"

I smiled as I went to my bus. I was getting fed up with the sympathetic looks. Sympathy didn't get you anywhere. It certainly wouldn't bring Bert back.

I saw my flight. "Right, lads. Let's get up in the air and watch out for fighters. I can't imagine Fritz letting us have the freedom of the skies today. Watch for the Hun in the sun."

None of them knew Bert and none of them knew me well enough to offer condolences but I could see, in their faces, that they were itching to say something.

I was glad when we were in the air and heading, in the darkness, towards the rising sun and Cambrai. I saw the flashes from the guns as the barrage crept ever further forward.

By the time we reached the front, dawn had broken and I saw the damaged tanks from the previous day. I also saw the remnants, there appeared to be less than two hundred of them, as they chugged east to take on the Germans again. They were slowly eating up the ground. It was ponderous but they were still making good progress. We began the day with luck and geography on our side. The western skies behind us were still dark but we could see the German fighters approaching from the east.

"German fighters. Engaging. Over."

I waved to Freddie and pointed. He had seen them too. We both climbed and led our men, this time in line astern, towards the Germans. For the first time in a long time, I didn't care who we met. If it was the Red Baron then he had better watch out because that day I would kill as many Germans as I possibly could. It might not bring Bert back but it might bring the end of the war closer.

As we climbed I felt the cold. November was almost over. Normally we would have ceased operations. It showed the planning of the high command. The ground was not muddy but was frozen in places. The tanks had made more progress because of it. I did not think the Germans had seen us and I took us as high as I dared. They would be looking for our spotters who would be at a lower altitude. Today we would surprise them. We had breached their vaunted Hindenburg line and now we would destroy their Jastas.

We were five hundred feet above them and some thousand yards from them when I led my flight down. I waited until I was less than a hundred feet from the leading aeroplane before I fired. I jerked the nose up as I fired and hit the pilot. The bullets stitched a line across the top wing and then made his head disappear. I kept lifting the nose and fired at the second aeroplane. He was just forty feet behind the leading aeroplane and my bullets hit his propeller, his nose and his top wing. He peeled away. I suspect I had not only damaged his bus but wounded him too.

I banked to port and saw a line of Fokkers. They were in disarray and I flew imperiously along the line hitting every German I saw. No more fell to my guns but, with five Camels behind me each firing his twin Vickers, it became a slaughter. Our manoeuvrability and small size had once more given us an advantage.

As the survivors fled I led my flight to machine-gun the troops on the ground. By flying obliquely across the front, we minimised the chances of hitting our own tanks or troops. I husbanded my ammunition. The bursts were one or two seconds in length. The Americans I would later meet called it a turkey shoot and it was an appropriate term. We could not and did not miss. When I clicked on empty I turned to port and led my flight back to the west. We had done all that we could and could do no more. It was time to go home.

We had not escaped unscathed. Lieutenant Hickey's bus had holes in the wings, the fuselage and his cockpit. Miraculously all had missed him. Our dour Welshman had not been so lucky. I do not know how he managed to get his bus down. He had been shot in the right arm and right leg. By another miracle, they had missed all the vital arteries but he would not fly again for some time. The Bristols had fared worse. Ground fire had brought down two. No one could remember seeing their buses go down and we were left in the dark.

In Randolph's office, everyone assiduously avoided mentioning tanks but we could not skirt around the offensive. "Well, it looks like we have stalled a little." Randolph had a map on the wall. "We are within two miles of Cambrai but the bridge we were counting on using proved weaker than we thought and the tank which tried to cross it destroyed it in the process. The General is digging in."

"But that is still a bigger gain than we have made before."

"You are right, Freddie, but we believe that the Germans are already transferring soldiers from the Eastern front. They will take some time to get here but it means they can move soldiers from quiet sectors and reinforce their line around Cambrai. The French are going to attack around Verdun." He sat down. "And we have been ordered to attack their roads beyond Cambrai."

I noticed Archie watching us. The two of them were a good team. Archie let Randolph explain things and it gave the colonel the chance to look at our faces and gauge our reactions. I had learned, long ago to keep my face neutral. Poor Gordy always spoke from the heart.

"But that means we will be on the edge of our endurance! And I assume you want the Bristols to bomb which means we have to go in low. We will be easy meat for any German fighters."

Freddie ventured, "We could keep the Camels as an umbrella. When we have used that tactic before then we haven't lost any buses."

Freddie was right it had been effective. Gordy stubbed out his cigarette angrily. "You are right, Freddie, but it doesn't help us with the ground fire. They are getting more accurate. We are the victims of our own success. It was inevitable. If we keep flying low they get constant practice at shooting at us. We'll do it but we won't be bringing a full complement of buses back."

Archie nodded, "You may be right. How about this as a compromise? I'll join Freddie and we will ground attack their gunners. Bill here can be the umbrella."

"Freddie and his flight have the more experienced pilots. My young lads have been lucky up to now but if we meet a decent squadron then it could be a slaughter."

They all looked at each other. I could almost see Archie weighing up my state of mind. "The difference is you, Bill. If you lead the Camels against anyone, Richthofen included, then it gives the rest of the pilots more confidence. We all know that confidence can make a difference. Of course, if you don't want to be the umbrella we will all understand."

I shook my head and tapped out my pipe. "No, sir, I didn't mean that. We will be your umbrella and we will watch your backs."

The relief on their faces surprised me. "Good." As we rose to leave he added, "Oh and you got your bar for your MC. Well done, Bill."

The awarding of the bar seemed to mean more to the rest of the squadron than it did to me but I saw a lively side to them that night. The sombre, deflated mood of the previous day was replaced by high jinks. I just watched and listened. Bert was still at the forefront of my mind but I knew that I dare not show that I was upset. I wouldn't have been able to stand the commiserations and sympathy. Instead, I looked at the young men I led. They were not much younger than I was but they came from disparate backgrounds. In a world, without war, I would have spent my life knuckling my forehead to them and calling them sir. In this topsy-turvy world in which we lived, they called me sir and looked up to me. It was bizarre.

Archie sidled up to me and slipped a glass of whisky in my hand. "Here laddie, it is from my special bottle; a quarter cask Laphroigh."

I could smell its peaty fumes as he handed it to me. "Thank you, sir."

He shook his head, "Its Archie, laddie. We both know that I am the commander of the squadron because I am colonel but the leader is you. You had us all worried yesterday." I opened my mouth to speak but he held his hand up. "No laddie, let me speak. I am not going to give you sympathy, we all know you hate that. You are important to this squadron because you are an ace. You have one of the highest totals on the western front and we both know how rare it is for you to be still alive. Randolph's chum told us that young pilots request a posting here just to fly with you."

"You must be joking!"

He laughed, "Have you never noticed that we get replacements really quickly? That is not just the General being kind. So your moods and your opinions are important."

"I hope you don't think that I will be moping around sir? I will do my duty."

"I know but you have to be true to yourself too. Don't hide behind this mask all the time. When this offensive is over you will be going home to get married. When you are with your young lady then be yourself. Put away the mask and the armour." He downed his whisky. "Because if you don't, you will crack and I dinna want that when you are twenty thousand feet in the air leading these young laddies." He gave me a sad stare. "You hear what I am saying, Bill?"

I nodded, "I think I do sir. And I won't let anyone down. Least of all myself."

Chapter 14

I had only four aeroplanes with me as I climbed high above the rest of the squadron. The two Bristol pilots had both been captured. At least Lieutenants Fox and Aston along with their gunners would survive the war. It meant we were a small squadron which headed east. We saw the new front line as we neared Cambrai. We had come tantalisingly close to ending the war. Had we made Cambrai then the Hindenburg line would have been irrevocably breached and the end of the war would be that much closer.

The ground fire was bad and I could see holes appearing in the huge wings of the Bristols. Had they been Gunbuses then I fear that those slow-moving leviathans would have all been shot down. I peered ahead as I led my four young pilots. We had to spot the Germans before they spotted us.

I saw eight crosses appear as Ted and Gordy began to drop their bombs on the road junction. My heart began to sink as I realised that they were four triplanes and four biplanes. Then a sudden flash of sunlight from behind a cloud showed me that they were not gaudily painted. This was not the Circus! My elation was short-lived. It might not be the Red Baron but they were the only bus which could worry us and we were outnumbered. I remembered Archie's words. We needed to stop them from hurting our ground attack. I waggled my wings to tell my flight we were going into action and then I said, "Engaging four triplanes and four biplanes. Over!" If anything bad happened then Randolph would know the reason.

We had the advantage of altitude. The Germans had taken off from their own field not long earlier. We found ourselves heading into a flurry of sleet. The shower had come from nowhere but it made the visibility poor. I knew it would be as hard for the Germans but, as it was coming from behind them, it was adding to their airspeed and slowing down ours.

They came up at us in two banks of four. The biplanes were at the fore. They were the Albatros D. IV. I began to sway my bus from side to side to make myself a more difficult target. We were small and the sky behind was still a little dark. The longer I could delay their fire the better. I was already planning my next move. When we were amongst them I would not turn to either port or starboard as I normally did; I would take us up and use our superior climb to loop and come down upon them again. If they knew who we were then they would expect either a left or right flight and I might just throw them off.

I saw the flames from their Spandau as they all fired at me. It was a waste of ammunition from the ones the flanks and the two in the middle merely hit my wings. I turned slightly to port and fired at forty yards. The Albatros was so big at that point that I could not miss and smoke began to pour from his engine. I returned to my course and braced myself for the gauntlet of fire from the Fokker Triplanes. These were a smaller target. Their bullets were more accurate. I felt a couple ping off my engine cowling and then I fired. I hit the undercarriage of the leading Fokker and saw it judder. No matter what happened next that was one Fokker which would not be flying the next day.

As soon as I had fired I pulled my nose up. As I did so I saw the four triplanes split into pairs and go to port and starboard. They had anticipated my next move. Had I turned in either direction I would have found myself attacked by three or four aeroplanes for the Albatros had done the same. As it was they had to try to avoid each other. As I climbed I looked in my mirror. There were just three Camels behind me. One was missing. I could not worry about the lost chick. At least the other three would find it easier to hang on to my shirttails.

I banked to port as I turned to dive on the German fighters. There was confusion below me as the seven remaining aeroplanes tried to regain some sort of formation. I saw an Albatros come into my sights and, as I screamed down upon him I fired a short burst. I had to pull up to avoid hitting him and, in my mirror, I saw George Jenkin finish him off. Then I was on the tail of a triplane. I fired a burst and missed for he began to dive towards the earth. I pushed my stick forward and followed him. I suddenly realised that he was not running away from me. I was gaining on him. I had found another weakness in the Fokkers; they had a slower rate of descent. Later I realised it must be because of the three wings which would act as a giant air brake. It gave me the opportunity to wait a little longer to fire.

He kept twisting and turning and still I closed with him. The ground seemed to be looming up and I knew that he would have to pull up soon. I waited until I saw the small profile become large and I fired at a range of forty feet. I scythed through his fuselage and his tail simply fell off. The front half plummeted to the ground and I fought to pull up the nose of my Camel to avoid the same fate.

As I rose I saw that I was alone in the sky with my three Camels. The sky was empty and when I looked at my fuel gauge I saw that my Camel was also nearly empty too. We headed home. I was able to identify the missing pilot by looking in my mirror. It was Stephen

Hickey. He had been a good pilot with five kills to his name. I had hoped not to lose any more young men but another had joined Charlie and Bert.

My engine was coughing and spluttering as we finally landed. I rolled the last ten yards without power. The fight had taken us to our very limits.

Although we had done well and exceeded our expectations the ground offensive came to a halt and we had begun to lose ground as the Germans counterattacked. The French had also attacked, successfully at Verdun and overall, we had more ground now than before. However, the loss of so many men and the new tanks did not seem a fair swap. Randolph had been to Headquarters and discovered that the Brass Hats were more than pleased with themselves. They saw it as a victory. It seemed largely hollow to us.

The last week of November 1917 saw us wearily climb into our buses each day and attempt to hold back the German counterattack. We were no longer raiding their rear trenches and their lines of communication we were attacking their aeroplanes and their advancing troops. I even heard that the Cavalry, which had been meant to exploit the gains of the tank assault had been drafted in as infantry. In a way I was pleased for the horses would not be needlessly slaughtered. The constant sorties took it out on the buses and, for once, we did not receive either replacement aeroplanes or pilots. The end of 1917 was dragging out.

Both Archie and Ted had had their buses damaged so that on the last day of November I led the squadron on its daily meeting with death. There were just five Camels left airworthy and four Bristols. We flew in line astern. Johnny Holt was back as my wingman and Freddie guarded the rear. Jack Fall and George Jenkin made up the rest. Gordy and his Bristols flew behind Freddie. That was the day when the Germans attacked with twenty divisions and almost all of the gains of the first day were wiped out.

As we arrived over the front I saw the brown uniforms flooding west. "A Flight. British forces retreating towards the canal. Over."

The Canal du Nord was a vital part of the gains we had made. By holding both banks we controlled large parts of the area before Cambrai. The Germans were racing over the ground. The lack of artillery damage and the frozen ground meant that they moved quickly. There was no time to waste and I led my squadron down to machine-gun the advancing Germans. My pilots were experienced enough to know that they had to fly in line abreast. Gordy led the Bristols obliquely across the battlefield so that his rear gunner could rake the ground. The Germans hit the ground and took whatever shelter they could.

I banked and took us across the German advance. It looked to be all the way from Bourlon Wood down to Honnecourt. As far as I could see, as we machine-gunned our way south, only the 6th Division at Ribecourt appeared to be making a stand. The bullets ran out before the fuel and I led us back to the field. As we landed I shouted, "Get them fuelled and armed we are going back up."

I ran to the office. "Archie, they are flooding over our lads. I'll have to take us back up. Get on to Headquarters and have the artillery ready to launch a barrage. I'll get Gordy to coordinate it."

"Have a rest, Bill. Just an hour or so."

"In an hour or so we may find Fritz knocking on our door. What you could do is have any spare pilots to take over when I come back."

"You want a third sortie?"

"Want? No. Need? You bet your life!"

I ran to Gordy who was examining his undercarriage. I saw that it had been hit by ground fire. "Direct the artillery, Gordy. I'll lead your lads."

"Righto, Bill. Bit of a cock-up eh?"

I shrugged. "Nothing changes."

I almost threw myself into my cockpit and screamed along the airfield. My squadron made a ragged take off. This was no straight line and regular formation. I did not wait for the stragglers to catch up. I flew the reverse of our earlier flight. I was appalled by how much ground had been lost in an hour. I flew low and my Vickers took a heavy toll on the advancing Germans. I saw the Camels behind me as they exploited my success. I saw that every German had taken cover. To my left, I saw a line of our tanks advancing. There were fewer of them than on the first day of the battle but they might be able to hold back the enemy.

As I neared Bourlon I saw that we had lost the village but it looked like a retreat now and not a rout. I turned to fly south. My ammunition lasted one more burst. I saw Jack Fall in my mirror. Ground fire hit him and he began to descend. He was lucky, he was able to turn and head west. The frozen ground might mean that he would survive. I hoped so. He was too good a pilot to lose.

I was the first to reach the field and replacement pilots were waiting. Archie said, "I'll fly your bus, Bill."

"No sir, with respect. I have been there all day and you haven't. I know where to go. Jack Fall has crashed. He should be near to Graincourt."

"I'll send a lorry for him."

Bates scurried up with a cup of something hot and a sandwich. "Here you are, sir. You are not leaving until you have drunk this soup and eaten your sandwich."

I could not argue with him and I was hungry. "Go and get a couple of Mills bombs from the armourer, Bates."

He rushed off. I watched the rest of the squadron as they landed. George's Camel spluttered its way down and Gordy's bus twisted and plopped to the ground as the undercarriage collapsed. I would be leading six pilots. Fresh pilots jumped into the buses despite the protests of Freddie and Johnny.

"Gentlemen you have done well. It only needs one of us to lead this handful of aeroplanes. That will be me."

Bates handed me the Mills bombs and examined the mug to ensure that I had drunk all of the soup. "Now you be careful Major Harsker. Your mother has had enough bad news she couldn't cope with more." He waggled a finger at me and I nodded.

"I'll do my best. That was good soup. Thank you."

This time I had to wait until the other five buses were ready. They would have to follow. Lieutenant Carpenter was the most experienced pilot I had left and he flew in the middle of the flight. I did not know the Bristol pilots but they were all reliable types.

The line was beginning to stabilise. Dusk would fall in less than two hours. I headed for Ribecourt. The 6th Division looked to have been holding and were digging in. I led the squadron east from their position. As soon as I saw the advancing grey uniforms I banked to port and flew along the line. They raised their guns to fire at me but I was too small, too low and too fast for them to hit. My bullets tore through them. I swayed the nose from port to starboard as I kept my fingers on the triggers. The Vickers' reliability saved many a Tommy that day. They just didn't jam.

When they clocked empty I banked to starboard and then flew towards their lines. I saw the flash of a mobile artillery piece. I prepared the Mills bomb and as I flew over I dropped it. I missed the gun but hit the ammunition tender. There was a whoosh behind me. The concussion knocked my Camel to the side. It saved my life as a machine gun stitched a line in my port lower wing. But for the exploding ammunition that would have been me. In retaliation for the death of Bert, I took out the second Mills bomb. I banked to port and, as I flew over the machine gun dropped the bomb and then climbed. I saw the gun and crew in my mirror as they were torn apart by the explosion.

I headed home.

Two of the Bristols did not return. One was shot down and one suffered engine failure. Senior Flight Sergeant Lowery shook his head, "I am sorry Major Harsker but they can't cope with three sorties in one day."

"I know Flight but it was either that or lose all that we had gained. It was a sacrifice but it worked."

And it had worked. The Germans had been halted. It had not just been our aeroplanes which had done it; the tanks had been sacrificed too and the Guards thrown in. That and the heroism of Tommies who refused to fall back even though they had lost meant that we held on to some of our gains. The Battle of Cambrai had not been a failure. Bert had not died in vain.

Chapter 15

We flew no more in 1917. Weather, aeroplanes flown beyond the limit and pilots on the edge of a breakdown meant that we spent the next week recovering. By the third of December, the battle stopped and on the fifth, we heard that Germany and Russia had signed an Armistice. All the Eastern Front troops would be heading west to reinforce the west. We were granted leave. General Henderson had no choice. As a squadron, we needed both aeroplanes and pilots. The leave would begin on the twelfth of December and I used Randolph and his contacts to send messages to the hospital to tell all that the wedding could go ahead. I had almost forgotten the hotel and my family in Burscough when John said, as he packed my bags, "I have let Miss Alice know of the wedding and the rooms are booked." He smiled sadly. "It will not bring your brother back but it might soften the blow for your mother." He nodded. "I am looking forward to seeing them both."

I was pleased that I had written to both Alice and Sarah to warn them of the impending wedding. I hoped that Mum would be as understanding.

He was now more of a friend than a servant and I do not know what I would have done without him.

I had persuaded Ted to attend the wedding. In all honesty, I do not know how he would have filled in the leave otherwise. Gordy and Mary would be there, of course. I knew that Mary and Beattie would be working as hard as possible to ensure that everything went off without a hitch. I had told Beattie by letter of Bert's death and she knew how devastated Mum and Dad would be. From her letter in reply, I knew that we had made the right decision. This was meant to be.

It took two days to reach London. The effects of the Battle of Cambrai lingered on and the casualties took priority on the trains. We still reached London before Mum and Dad and the rest of the family. At least I hoped they were on their way. I had not spoken to anyone and it was more an act of faith. Suppose I got to the chapel and there was no family there? Each time I thought that I glanced up and saw Bates. He would not let me down. They would be there. Randolph and Archie were torn. They both wished to attend the wedding but the chance to be with their families was just too tempting to turn down; they would have little enough time as it was. Poor Archie always wasted three days of his leave getting home.

We reached London on the fourteenth of December. I did not expect Beattie to meet me for she was at the hospital. Mary and baby Hewitt did meet us. Bates amused the baby in the perambulator while Mary and Gordy embraced. She turned to me after they had kissed and threw her arms around me. "Sorry to hear about your brother. You and Beattie deserve to be happy. This will be a lovely wedding."

"When will it be?"

That made everyone laugh. Even the baby chuckled although I think that was down to the funny faces Bates was pulling.

"Honestly Bill! You need a minder! A week today. The shortest day. It was the only one we could get. The Chapel will be busy with Christmas services after that but everything is organised. We are having the wedding breakfast at our house, Gordy."

"Suits me! I can just roll into bed when I have had too much to drink!" He turned to Ted and said, "Mary this is Ted. It's all right if he stays with us isn't it?"

I saw Ted about to object and Mary embraced him too and said, "Of course it is. Now Beattie is on lates tonight so you will have to wait until tomorrow to see her. You are both to see the chaplain at ten o'clock and he will run through the service with you. Beattie has three days of earlies and then she has been granted a week's leave." She hesitated. "Have you anywhere in mind for the honeymoon?"

I must have looked confused. Honeymoon?

John piped up, "It is all arranged Major Harsker. You and your bride are booked in at the Imperial Hotel, Blackpool for three days. We thought that it would mean you could travel north with your parents and then visit them on the way home. I know they would appreciate it."

I was amazed at my manservant's ingenuity. "Thank you, John. You should do this for a living."

"Who knows sir? When this madness is over anything will be possible."

Bates and I took a taxi to the Mayflower and he filled me in on the details. "Your sister and Lady Burscough will be here on the 17th sir with your parents. I have booked them in the Mayflower until the 22nd. I will book the trains north tomorrow while you and Miss Porter see the chaplain. I took the liberty of booking you a double room sir. I know you will only need a double for the one night but…"

I caught the twinkle in his eye. "Very thoughtful Bates. Thank you." He nodded as though he was just doing his duty.

Beattie had told the chaplain about Bert. "My condolences, Major Harsker. I seem to say that every five minutes these days. Old men like me survive and fine young men like your brother die. It seems obscene somehow. Now then let us move on to more joyful events. Miss Porter has made all the arrangements. The service will be at eleven o'clock. I am sorry we had no choice over the day but..."

"That is not a problem padre. I am just grateful that things have moved on so quickly."

"I am sure you bright young things have got better things to do than talk to an old man like me. Now normally we have a rehearsal for these sorts of things but I am sure that you and your best man will..."

I slapped my head. "Best man!"

Major Osborne laughed, "Don't tell me you haven't got a best man yet? The next thing you will tell me you haven't got a ring either."

I stared at Beattie who smiled and looked down, "We haven't had time yet, Major."

"Well 'pon my word." He put his arms around our backs and said, "Shoo! Go this minute and get her a ring, Major Harsker!"

I think the fact we had thought so little about what other people took to be essentials showed that we were marrying for the right reasons. Beattie wanted just a nine-carat ring saying it was harder wearing. I was having none of that. I barely touched my Major's pay and I bought her a twenty-two-carat one. I also bought her an engagement ring with a single diamond.

"Bill this is extravagant!"

"No, it isn't and you only get to show it off for a few days but I want everyone to know we are to be married."

We barely had time to get back to the hospital for the last of her late shifts. As I walked across the park I ran through the options for best man. In the end, there was but one choice. Had Bert been alive it would be him. It couldn't be and so I chose the next best choice. Bates was reading The Times and drinking cocoa when I arrived.

"Everything tickety boo then, sir?"

"Almost. There were a couple of things I forgot, Bates."

He looked crestfallen, "Oh dear sir. I am sorry. What did I forget?"

"You forgot nothing! I forgot the ring."

"Oh dear, sir. Still, you have had a lot on your plate. I take it that problem has been remedied?"

"Yes we went to Burlington Arcade this morning but there is one more task."

"Sir?"

"I need a best man. Would you do the honours?"

For the first time since I had known him, he looked positively dumbfounded. "But sir, what about Major Thomas and Captain Hewitt?"

"If you don't wish to then…"

He looked offended, "Sir! I would be honoured."

I nodded and shook his hand. Reaching into my tunic pocket I took out the small box. "Then you had better look after this for me eh?"

Beattie, John and I were at Euston station early for the four o'clock from Liverpool Lime Street. Beattie had fretted that she had not enough time to make herself look presentable. John was superb and he eased her worries. The train steamed in and the platform filled with smoke. I had expected them to emerge from First Class but they appeared through the smoke with the second-class passengers. Money had to be tight. They had engaged a porter.

I had time to watch them as they headed towards the ticket barrier. All of them had aged. Lady Burscough was going grey and even my little sister had a streak of white in her hair. Mum and dad looked shrunken and weary and all four of them wore black. I had to wait until the ticket collector had taken their tickets before I could take my mum in my arms. She was crying even as I approached her and she sobbed heavily into my chest, "Oh Billy, our Billy."

I had no words. Any attempt at speech would have meant I cried too. I had to be strong for them all. Bates had told me that. It was like aerial combat; everything seemed to be in slow motion. Alice was in Beattie's arms crying while Bates was helping Lady Mary to support Father. People stared at the outrageous show of affection but I did not care. Eventually, the sobs subsided and she stepped back. "Eeeh, but you do look smart and your young lady is a picture!" She held her arms out, "Come and give a silly old woman a hug. I don't want to spoil your big day."

"You couldn't. We are just glad you could make it."

I shook my father's hand and saw that he too was tearful. "Good to see you, son, and I am right proud of you. Everyone in the village is."

I turned to Alice and picked her up in my arms. She was as light as a feather and I could feel her bones through her coat. I kissed her on the cheek. "Thanks for doing this, our kid."

"We have to stick together, Bill. We are a dying breed." And then she burst into tears.

Bates took charge. "If you will all follow me I shall get a taxi for us."

I turned to Lady Mary. "I can't thank you enough."

She shook her head and hugged me so tightly that I found it hard to breathe. "Nonsense. His Lordship thought of you as a son and we were as fond of your parents as anyone could be. I am just pleased that you have been spared." She stepped back. "And I know that John would have been as proud of your medals as anyone. I hear you are a leading ace now?"

"It is all luck, your ladyship. All luck."

She took my arm. "And I don't believe that for a moment. I am still in touch with many of John's old comrades and they sing your praises constantly." She nodded to Beattie, who was with Alice and Mother. "She is the best thing to happen to your family. Alice thinks she is wonderful and I do too. Look after her, Bill. You never know when happiness will be snatched from you."

"Lord Burscough?"

She nodded, "He was with me for far too short a time and we kept putting off things we should have done. You have done the right thing. Goodness only knows how long this war will go on. Grab what you can while you can."

While the ladies freshened up I took Dad to a pub around the corner from the hotel. I saw the pride in his eyes when everyone deferred to us. My uniform and my medals did that. I bought two pints for us and we sat in a corner.

"Bert!"

"Bert!"

We touched glasses and drank half of the beer in one long swallow. We both took out our pipes and I gave him a fill of my new mixture. He nodded approvingly when he began to puff on it.

After a while, he looked at me and said, quietly, "Our Alice says you saw him die." I nodded. "Mother isn't here and she won't want to know anyway but I do. What happened?" I drank some more of the beer. "Come on son, I served. You can tell me. I won't be any more upset than I am already. John and Tom, well we had drifted apart but Bert. He was like you. He loved horses and … well, you know."

"I know." I sighed and took a deep breath. "He was in a tank. It broke down. The officer was killed but Bert got the crew out. I gave a hand with my Camel and shot some of the stormtroopers trying to get him but I was only over him for seconds and then I had to turn around. When I came back our Bert was holding the enemy off with a pistol but then…"

I paused and took a drink of my beer.

Dad said quietly, "Go on son. This is helping, believe me."

"German stormtroopers attacked and they had a flame thrower. He was dead in an instant."

Dad looked confused, "Flame thrower?"

I tried to simplify it. "Imagine a pipe and it spits out burning petrol."

I saw Dad's eyes close and I put my hand over his. His fingers tightened on mine. He said quietly, "Did he suffer?"

I couldn't know but I gave him the answer he needed. "He died instantly. It wasn't pretty but I don't think he suffered."

He opened his eyes, "And you saw it?" I nodded. "I am sorry about that, son but at least Bert knew you were there at the end and you were trying to help him."

I nodded, as I rose to get two more pints, "I killed them all." I said it flatly.

"Good! The bastards deserved it!"

It was not just the venom in my father's voice which shocked me but the swearing. He never swore.

When I returned with the beer we spoke of other things: Beattie, the wedding and John. "Your mother is very fond of your Mr Bates. She sees him as a gentle soul. She thinks he is good for you."

"He is that. He is to be my best man. It would have been Bert…"

"A good choice!"

That evening at dinner there was an artificial air of gaiety. The spectre of Bert hung over the table but everyone tried hard to be happy and cheerful. Over the next few days between Bates, Alice and Lady Mary we had a guided tour of the sights of London. When we reached Buckingham Palace, John regaled them with every detail of my investiture. Rather than making my parents jealous as I had feared, it made it seem as though they had been there. That was a good day.

And then the rest of the leave flew by. The wedding dominated all. The ceremony in the chapel was perfect. Beattie's colleagues had decorated it and the small chapel was filled with off-duty hospital staff. Even the fierce Matron appeared. As I had expected Mum and Alice were in floods of tears. For Mum, I was the only son she would see married and for Alice, I was a reminder of what she and Charlie might have experienced. As Beattie said, later on, "Everyone cries at a wedding, the difference is that those two were not crying for us but for a personal loss. I can share that. The important thing is that we are married and not the reason people cry."

The wedding breakfast was cosy and intimate. Ted was touched by the interest everyone showed in him. That day saw a change wrought in him. He became less solitary and more outgoing. I think he saw in the two married couples something that he wanted. Gordy enjoyed playing the host and he and Dad got on like a house on fire.

The next day we headed north on the train. We changed trains at Liverpool Lime Street. John went to Burscough and Beattie and I were alone. Even when we arrived in Blackpool we were alone. It was

December and there was a war on. Apart from a handful of permanent residents, we were the only guests but a combination of my uniform and the fact that we were a honeymoon couple meant that we were treated like royalty.

We spent the few days walking along the prom either in a gale or a storm of sleet but it didn't matter. In the evening, after dinner, we would listen to the pianist in the residents' lounge and then have an early night. It was idyllic.

The idyll continued at Burscough where mum showed off to Beattie cooking all of my favourite foods and Beattie responded as I knew she would be asking for the recipes.

One day, while they were in the kitchen and Dad was in his shed I sat and spoke with Alice. "How are you really, our kid?"

"I am getting there." She lowered her voice and held my hand in hers. "I thought about, you know, ending it all after … but then I thought what it would do to mum and dad. I tell you this, our Bill, there isn't a day that goes by when I don't think of him and what we had. It was, well, it was just right." She leaned in. "You and Beattie getting married has been the best thing that has happened to me. Have tons of kids because I am going to be the best auntie in the world."

I kissed her on the cheek as John came back with some scones he had made. "I never doubted it for a minute."

"Fresh out of the oven! Come along leave the kitchen!"

When the three of them came in to join us I knew that my world was complete. I closed my eyes and prayed that the war would end that minute and I could stay here and all would be well. There would be no more deaths. I opened my eyes and the world was the same and there would still be months of slaughter. My prayers went unanswered.

Chapter 16

Beattie was back on duty by New Year's Eve and John and I stayed at the Mayflower. We did not have long. We received our telegrams asking us to report to the field on January the third. After hurried goodbyes outside the Nurse's Home, John and I took the boat train back to the war: back to reality.

I was largely silent on the way back to France. I resented having to leave my new bride. I suspect Bates understood such things, for he chattered the whole way back. My grunted and curt responses did not upset him at all. He spoke of my family and Lady Burscough. He even spoke at great length about the pub and the men he had met there. By the time we were on the last leg, From Calais to Amiens, I realised that he was chattering away not to take my mind away from Beattie but because he was a lonely man and he now belonged to my family. He had had nothing before and, in his mind, he now had everything. War was a strange beast and changed every man- just in different ways.

Ted, Gordy, Johnny and Freddie had been on the train from Calais to Amiens and it was good to catch up with them. I could be silent with Bates: he was like my confidante but I had to be sociable with the men with whom I flew. The train to Amiens had been a transition from the world of peace to the world of war. One topic of conversation was the attitude of the press and the public to Cambrai. At home, everyone viewed the battle as a great victory. We knew that it was not. It showed how the newspapers were being manipulated, perhaps even controlled. I never trusted them after that.

Randolph had arrived back early along with the senior warrant officers. Consequently, everything was in order by the time Bates and I arrived. There were stoves strategically placed pumping out heat and there was hot food available. January was cold. I had no idea why we had been summoned back for there would be little flying for the next month or so. Archie arrived back a day late. His train had been delayed in Scotland and he had missed his connections. I took charge on that first day.

The new Camels had been delivered and Randolph and I assigned them. Ted and Gordy were a little upset that they had not said goodbye to their gunners. They had been sent to their new squadrons already. It was sad because a pilot and a gunner formed a relationship which was as close as that of a married couple. The two of you became one. The

Brass hats which had decided that would not understand such considerations.

The pilots walked warily around their new buses. They knew them, of course, but they had never flown them. I had told all of them that they should treat it with a great deal of respect, at first. This was not an easy bus like the Bristol. This was a thoroughbred and required delicate handling. Ted had laughed at my terminology. "This isn't the cavalry you know!"

I smiled, "Perhaps if you treat the Camel like a horse you won't get thrown. In the cavalry, if a horse threw you then you fell six feet." I patted the Camel. "This beastie might throw you ten thousand feet."

Ted had changed and he nodded sagely, "Point taken."

While the pilots discussed the Camels and examined them I went to the office. I had bought more of my special mix at the tobacconists and gave Randolph a pouch of it. We lit our pipes. When they were going I asked, "Why the rush to get back Randolph?"

He went to the door and closed it. He spoke in a hushed voice. "This can go no further, Bill." I nodded. "I thought the same things as you and I telephoned my chum at Headquarters. It appears that the Germans have had a competition to build new aeroplanes. Your old pal, the Red Baron, had the idea. They will be ready by the spring. The Germans are also making more of the large Jastas like the Flying Circus. They are being fitted out with the Fokker Triplane. My chum reckons that they are going to try to sweep us from the skies."

I tapped the loose ash from my pipe. "A Spring Offensive."

"Exactly. There are hundreds of thousands of troops on their way back from the Russian front. They will outnumber us and do you remember those chaps with the flame throwers?" He shook his head, "Sorry, insensitive of me, of course, you remember."

"You can't keep pussyfooting around my feelings, Randolph. I am dealing with it."

"I know. And you are doing a damned fine job of it. Anyway, they are called Storm-troopers and the Germans are going through all their Divisions and selecting the best soldiers they have to form small Storm-trooper units. We saw what they could do at Cambrai. Well, there will be thousands like that. The men not only have flame throwers they have small portable machine guns too. So, you can see that the new Jastas, the new aeroplanes, and the new German Units all point to a Spring Offensive. We have to be ready and we have to be able to stop the attack whenever it comes."

That was a tall order but at least we now had twenty-five Camels and we could hold our own against the triplane. When Archie returned,

I would ask him for permission to begin training the pilots in tactics to use against the Flying Circus. The Germans looked to have created another two of them. We could hide no longer.

Once Archie returned we threw ourselves into our new work. Randolph briefed Archie but the rest of the squadron were in the dark They could not understand the frenzied training regime we put into place. Every day when the weather permitted we took them up and had them all practising dogfights. It took a week for Ted and Gordy to be confident that they could fly the new bus. Ironically it was the younger pilots who took the change in their stride. The older pilots could not understand it. By February Archie and I felt that we were ready to take on the Germans. We had patrolled all through January but we had not seen the German Jastas. It was as if they were hibernating. Archie and I had discussed the real reason with Randolph whose chum kept us well informed. "When they launch their attack, they will come with everything at once. With all of these extra men from the east, they can afford to be profligate with their losses."

"You are right Randolph. You can bet that the infantry who make the initial attack will not be the best. They will be the ones to weaken us and then these new stormtroopers will exploit the gaps."

"And we have heard that they are building their own tanks. They captured some of ours. It is highly likely they will use our own weapons against us."

"And you can bet they will have made them work a little better too!"

We were sent over enemy lines on February 4th. It was a squadron patrol but we flew in four flights a mile apart. We were looking for evidence of this spring attack. The rumour at Headquarters was that it was called Operation Michael. I didn't care about the name but I did worry that if it worked we could have a front line forty miles west of where we were.

It was so cold I was tempted to have a nip from the hip flask of whisky I always carried in my flying coat. I knew that was the slippery road to ruin. I would ask Bates to make a flask of soup for me next time. The repaired and serviced Camel purred beautifully as we flew at ten thousand feet. It was too cold to venture any higher and the visibility was good. Knowing what I did, I viewed the German lines with heavy suspicion. Hidden from view there were hordes of grey uniformed soldiers ready to fill the forward trenches. There were superior squadrons of German fighters ready to pounce.

As we turned on the southern leg of our patrol I was glad that they had not upgraded us to the SE 5. It might be faster but it was bigger and did not have the turning ability of the Camel. When the push came I knew that the Fokker Triplanes would turn them inside out and have them for breakfast. I caught a glint of sunlight. It reflected on something in the east. The odds were that it was a German aeroplane. We had spent many hours practising aerial signals. I waggled my wings and pointed to the east. I knew that the signal would be repeated to Jack Falls in the rear.

I began a gentle climb. If it was a flight of Germans I wanted to be able to swoop in and out quickly. We were too high for ground fire but the Germans had some smaller artillery pieces and they began to hurl hopeful shells into the air. It was a waste of ammunition.

I saw that it was a flight of six triplanes. Did I attack or run? I decided to try something new. Freddie and his flight were a mile to our south. I flew a little further east until the German formation was just three miles away. I knew that we had been seen and I feigned flight. I banked to starboard and headed south-west. The Germans had the advantage of height and I saw them, in my mirror, as they swooped after us. I knew that my young pilots would be thinking that I had lost the plot but I was putting myself in the leading German's head. This was not the Flying Circus, they all had the same livery, therefore they had just acquired the triplanes. They would think themselves invincible and that our flight showed fear.

I kept descending slowly. I wanted them below Freddie and his flight. As soon as I saw the six Camels ahead I levelled out but maintained my course. The leading pilot fired early. I saw Jack begin to move his bus from side to side. It would take a lucky shot at distance to hit him. More importantly, it distracted him from the line of six Camels which were diving towards him. I pulled my nose up sharply and banked to port. My flight followed immediately and the move took the Germans by surprise.

I kept banking so that I could bring my flight into the centre of the German formation. With Freddie's flight cutting off their escape east we had our best chance to make a killing. The third Fokker in the line was desperately pulling his nose around to align his sights on me. I managed my turn first and I gave a short burst. I hit one of his wings. His turn took him from my sights but directly into the sights of Lieutenant Jenkin who riddled the Fokker with a burst. It began to smoke and turned east. George followed him.

We had practised this and I knew that Lieutenant Fox, my new pilot, would tuck in behind me. There would be a gap but I knew I would have support. I kept my turn going and saw the tail of the second Fokker hove into view. I fired and hit his tail. He twisted to port. I had expected that for a turn to port would take him east. I continued my turn. He was better at turning and I only hit him with a handful of bullets but he was hit. As we came around I saw Freddie's flight swarming all over the last two Fokkers. They had hit one for I saw it plummeting to earth. The leader had had enough and was heading home. My target twisted and turned. I kept hitting him but I failed to do enough damage to bring him down. I checked my fuel gauge and saw that I was down to a quarter of a tank. I turned for home. Two Fokkers escaped but the rest found a grave in No Man's Land.

"Well done, sir. That was brilliant the way you took the Germans towards the captain."

"It made sense, Mr Fox. Six to six might have meant we shot down fewer and we may have lost a couple ourselves. Two to one is better if you can manage it."

The young lieutenant looked disappointed. "I thought the war in the air was supposed to be noble."

I stared at him, remembering the fiery death that Charlie Sharp had suffered, "There is nothing noble about this war! Get that idea out of your head now! Our job is to shoot down as many Germans as we can manage and to survive the war! Understood?"

He recoiled in the face of my anger, "Yes sir."

As I strode towards the office I noticed Jack walk towards him. He would explain my venom. There had been a time when I might have been gentler. I had lost too many friends for gentleness now. I wanted all of my young men to survive.

"So the intelligence was correct for once. They have fitted out their Jastas with triplanes."

"Yes. We were just lucky that it was a small patrol. I don't think we will be as lucky the next time."

Archie nodded, "Still four Fokkers destroyed in one action is pretty good going. Well done, Bill."

"It wasn't me who got them it was Freddie and my flight."

"You are the leader. If you weren't up there then they might have had less success."

I shook my head. "I don't believe that for a moment."

The next day Bates handed me the flask of soup. "Here you are, sir. Piping hot soup."

"What kind is it?"

"Best not to ask, sir. Probably the leftovers from a few days ago. Still, it is hot."

We had the same patrol area. As we climbed into the skies over No Man's Land the burnt-out Fokkers were a stark reminder of how close death and destruction lay.

I kept a wary eye east but saw nothing and I was beginning to think that it would be a dull day when I saw Freddie's flight coming towards us. Behind him, some half a mile distant, were six Fokkers. I began to climb. As I did so my eyes were drawn to the cloud cover which was a little lower than it had been the previous day. I caught a brief glimpse of an undercarriage and a wing. It had to be Germans. I increased my angle of ascent and my speed. There was no signal I could give to warn Freddie of the danger he was in. I only had one option. I opened fire. Waggling my wings I signalled for my flight to return home. I waited until they began to peel off. I knew that they would think that Major Harsker had finally cracked but I knew the Germans. When they laid a trap, it was usually lethal.

Suddenly eighteen Fokkers descended like a flock of vengeful Valkyrie. I saw that five of the Fokkers had joined those chasing Johnny and were swooping down on him. He would have no chance. I banked to starboard and did the only thing possible: I flew into the heart of the formation. My hope was that I would disrupt them. I did not think they would be able to fire at me for fear of hitting their comrades and the biggest danger would be a collision. I had to pray that my reactions were quick enough.

I opened fire at a hundred yards and, as I swept in from their flank, kept firing. Hopefully, I would hit something. I felt the wind from the Fokker, which had to pull its nose up to avoid a collision with me. I was so close I could see where the painter had missed a bit. The pilot then had to swerve to avoid a head-on collision with a colleague.

I heard the sound of multiple Spandaus. Looking to my right I saw Johnny swerving from side to side as he tried to throw off the aim of the two triplanes which were on his tail. I banked to starboard and fired as I did so. I hit one in the tail and it banked to port. As my nose came around the tail of the Fokker appeared just feet before me. I pulled the trigger and braced myself for the impact of the crash. I was so close that I severed the tail and the nose-heavy Fokker fell. Johnny waved and banked to port.

The sense of relief I had was short-lived as I felt the judder of parabellums in my tail. I tried to bank to starboard but the controls were sluggish. From my left came a double judder and bullets poured into my engine. I dipped the nose. I had to get down as quickly as possible. As I looked in my mirror I saw five Fokkers lining up to hit me. I tried to jink from side to side and up and down but I was so sluggish that I was hit more than missed. As the propeller stopped smoke began to pour from my engine. I fought to keep her level but it was hard. The ground was racing towards me and still, my Camel took the punishment from the Fokkers. I was paying the price for spoiling their party.

As I raced towards the British lines I found that the Camel wanted to turn right. Ahead of me, I saw a burnt-out farmhouse and a half-shredded barn with the remnants of a hedgerow between. I was so close to the ground that the Germans were forced to pull up and the deadly punishment ceased. I had almost no control but I knew that if I let go of the stick then I was dead and I had to hang on as long as possible. I saw the barn looming up and knew that I was going to hit it. I braced myself. Perhaps the Camel tried to save me for, at the last minute it veered to port a little and I hit what had been the door. The wings were torn off and then the undercarriage hit something and I was flung into the air. My seat belt had given way. I thudded into the far wall of the barn and then all went black.

Chapter 17

When I came to I could smell burning. I saw that the Camel was smouldering. I tried to struggle to my feet but my left leg would not bear the weight. Suddenly a sheet of flame leapt up as something inflammable caught fire. I dived and rolled out of the opening my bus had made. The ground fell away sharply and that saved my life as my Camel and the barn erupted in a huge sheet of fire. The concussion of the explosion made it hard to breathe. I rolled further down the bank and found myself nestling in a ditch close to some shredded bushes. The pall of smoke from the fire rose high in the sky. I daresay pilots on both sides would be reporting my death- again!

I forced myself into an upright position and took stock. I always kept certain items in the flying coat: whisky flask, compass, three bandages, spare ammunition for the Luger and the Webley, a spare pipe and some tobacco. Thanks to Bates I also had a flask of soup. Miraculously it had survived. My first task was to ascertain my wound. I rolled my left trouser leg up. It was easy as it was split along its length. I saw blood oozing from the wound which was there. The fact that it was oozing and not spurting told me it was not an artery. There was some rainwater in the bottom of the ditch. I fished some out in my goggles and then soaked my scarf. I sponged away the blood. I was intrigued as to what I would find beneath the blood. A long, thick splinter of wood from the barn wall had been forced into my shin, calf muscle and, from the pain, into my knee. As I sponged away the blood I felt shivers of pain in my left knee each time I touched it. It did not fill me with confidence.

I started to pull the splinter out. I nearly passed out with the pain. That was no good. I took out my jackknife and poured a little whisky on the blade to sterilise it. I also took a mouthful of the whisky; I felt I had earned it. The warming malt made me feel better. I took the knife, which Bates kept sharp for me, and I slowly cut up the skin which covered the splinter. Luckily it was not too deep and I did not have to cut very far. When I reached the top of the calf I stopped. There was little point in hamstringing myself. I tried to pull the splinter out again. It was less painful but the offending piece of wood was reluctant to come out. I was about to give up when one last tug brought it free. The blood began to flow freely and I jammed the soaked scarf next to it to stem the flow.

I put the splinter to one side and had another sip of whisky. I wiped the wound with the scarf and then dripped the whisky over the wound.

The pain was excruciating but I gritted my teeth. I had to clean the wound. Holding the flask in my teeth I bandaged myself. I had three such dressings and I knew that I would have to replace it sometime.

That done I put the top back in the flask and slipped it into my pocket. I drank half of the soup and felt better. I also felt sleepy and knew that was the last thing I should do. I was in No Man's Land. My best chance of reaching the British lines was to do so in daylight. At night twitchy sentries would be more likely to shoot first and ask questions later. The barn was still burning. I picked up the splinter. It was a sizeable piece of wood but when I looked at it I saw that the end had broken off. I still had a piece of wood in my leg. I touched my knee and it was tender to the touch. I now knew where the broken splinter resided.

I fished out the compass and worked out where our lines were. That done, I checked that both my pistols were loaded and in working order. I jammed my goggles and my helmet in one of the pockets in my coat. Using the stumps of the trees I pulled myself up. I tried to put weight on my left leg and I nearly passed out with the pain. I rested against the broken hedge and looked around. The Camel had burnt and I could not see anything which I could use as a crutch or a stick. I saw that not ten yards away was a brown uniform. It was a body. I hopped along the ditch until I reached it. I held on to the hedge with my right hand while I pulled up the body by the webbing. It came away really easily and I saw, to my horror that it was just the top half of a body. I laid it gently on the bank. It was a young soldier. He only looked about eighteen although his body was decomposing and it was hard to tell. I saw that in the water at the bottom of the ditch, there was his rifle. I prayed that it was whole. I reached down to pull it out. I caught my left knee and I was convulsed with paroxysms of pain. I persevered and pulled out the rifle. It was whole. I ejected the bullet that was in the spout. I was in enough trouble without shooting my own foot off.

I put the rifle, barrel down and tried to take my weight on it. The muddy bank made it sink a little but it held. I was about to start to move west when I stopped. I turned to the young dead soldier and removed his identity tags as carefully as I could. If I made it home then there would be one soldier who would not be missing in action. I saw that he was Private John Lane of the 1st Battalion 6th Gordon Highlanders. I remembered that they had taken part in the Battle of Cambrai. He and Bert might have died on the same day. Pocketing the tags, I began to limp west.

The ditch was too wet and I forced myself to climb the bank. It was not easy and I was bathed in sweat when I reached the top. The fierce fire had almost burned out but the smoke hid me from the Germans. They had not come to investigate. The conflagration must have convinced them that I was dead.

I prayed that the soldiers ahead would not be trigger-happy. I saw that there were lines of barbed wire before me but I also knew that they would not be continuous. The men who laid them left gaps so that they could make forays at night. It was another reason why I had to move in daylight. I needed to see where the gaps were. I began to move down one line of wire. After sixty yards I found a small gap and slipped through. It was now a lottery. I chose left. Thirty yards later I found another gap and so it went. I could see the British lines or at least sandbags which indicated a defended position. It was more than three hundred yards away. I glanced at the sun. I had less than two hours of daylight left. It had taken me an hour to move fifty yards to the west. I had travelled more than two hundred yards but that was up and down the wire. I had travelled further north and south than west.

An hour later and I stopped. I was exhausted and my leg was in agony. I took out my flask and drank some. I could feel blood dripping down my leg but I dared not stop to repair the dressing. Darkness was falling and I dreaded being shot by my own men. I realised that I had walked over a hundred yards and found no gap. Perhaps there were no more gaps. How would I get across?

Suddenly I heard, "Halt or I fire. Put up your hands! Hands Hoch, Fritz!"

I held up my right arm.

"Both of them or I will shoot."

"I am Major William Harsker of the Royal Flying Corps and I need my left hand to hold the rifle I am using as a crutch."

There was silence. Then another voice said, "Stay there and don't move."

Four heads peered over the top of the trench and the four soldiers ran towards me. They halted just ten yards away and I saw then that there was a removable piece of barbed wire.

One of the soldiers said, "It is him, Sarge, I recognise him." The young soldier grinned at me. "You are Bert's brother. I met you in Amiens."

"Right Radcliffe let's leave the pleasantries until we get the officer back. Give him a hand."

One took the rifle and the soldier called Radcliffe put his arm around my back and took the weight off my injured leg. Another soldier did the same on the right. It was such a relief when I did not have to move.

"How is Bert? I haven't seen him since I transferred."

"He was killed at Cambrai."

"I am sorry. He was a good bloke."

They lowered me into the trench and the sergeant shouted, "Stretcher bearer!" He offered me a cigarette but I shook my head. "Were you in that aeroplane that crashed?" I nodded, "We thought you were a goner. You were bloody lucky, sir."

"I know. Believe me, sergeant, I know."

I filled my pipe as we waited for the stretcher-bearers. Two cheerful young men arrived. They looked at me in surprise. "Blooming heck! A flier!" He looked to the heavens. "Did you just drop from the skies, sir?"

The sergeant shook his head, "This is what we are down to sir. Dozy buggers like this. Get this wounded officer to the first aid station and be bloody quick about it. He is wounded." He nodded to me, "And in case you hadn't noticed he has a VC so this a hero." The sergeant saluted, "Proud to have been able to help sir."

I nodded, "Thank your lads for me eh, Sarn't." As they began to lift me I remembered the identity tags. "I found these on a soldier out there. His family should know."

"Thank you, sir. You can leave them safely with me."

The two young men were strong and they jogged down the trenches. I saw why it had taken them so long. They twisted and turned every few yards. Finally, we reached a dugout where a white-coated doctor waited for me.

"Now then Major, what have we done?"

I pointed to my knee which now hurt far worse than when I had been hobbling. I could see that it was swelling, almost while I watched. "I had a splinter in my leg. I got it out and bandaged it but..."

He frowned and rolled up my trouser leg. He cut away the bandage and sniffed. He chuckled, "Good use of antiseptic Major. I take it you took some internally too?"

I nodded, "It seemed to help."

He quickly swabbed my leg and then applied a bandage far tighter than I had done I winced with the pain. "You need a major hospital for this. I do not intend to go poking around in the trenches. I could do more harm than good. Orderlies." The two soldiers reappeared. "Get this officer to the base hospital at Amiens and be quick about it." He looked at me as they loaded me on the stretcher. "I have a feeling, major, that your war is over now."

My heart sank. I had to be there at the end. Who would lead my boys if I were not there?

The doctor had given me a draught to drink. As the ambulance headed west I slowly drifted off into sleep. When I awoke I was in a bed with clean sheets and a smiling nurse peering over me. "Ah, you are awake, Major Harsker."

"Where am I?"

"Well at the moment you are in Amiens but within the hour we shall whisk you off to Blighty." She smiled. "I think your war is over."

"My leg?"

"Oh it is still there," I noticed she had a Scottish burr, "but the doctors here are a wee bit concerned about a possible infection. They got out the wee piece of nasty wood that was causing you trouble but the kneecap is giving them some concern. Don't you worry Major, for an officer with a VC and an MC you have no need to worry. You have done your duty already

I was not certain I liked that. My medals should not grant me any special treatment. "Thank you, Nurse...?"

"Nurse Stewart. And you are welcome. It is lovely to treat a hero."

I closed my eyes. I was no hero. Charlie, Bert, they were the heroes. I was a sham. I slowly drifted off to sleep. I was awoken by the motion of a train. I looked up and saw a medical orderly smoking a cigarette. "Good morning, Sleeping Beauty. By but you can sleep. We will be in London in the hour and then we will have you in a hospital bed before you know."

"Could I have some water?"

"Of course, you can sunshine, sorry, Major." He poured me some water and then lifted my head so that I could drink. It felt so cooling as it went down. I emptied the mug. "Thirsty eh? I'll get you another." After the second I felt better. The orderly knew his business and he took my pulse before nodding. "I'd get your head down for a bit longer sir. The hospital is a couple of hours away."

I closed my eyes again and began to imagine life away from the squadron. I couldn't. All of the faces from the past flashed before my eyes. It was like a slide show and there were so many faces. Some faces I couldn't put a name to, and that frightened me. Bert and Charlie kept looming up before me.

"Major Harsker." I opened my eyes. A smiling bespectacled face greeted me. "Ah good, you are awake. I am Doctor Bentine and I am going to try to solve your problem. Now I know that you are hungry but if we operate now we might save your leg. You have an infection. No one's fault but I have to get in quickly and clean out the wound."

I tried to speak and the words came out in slow motion. "Save the leg. Need to get back." I did not like the way people kept saying that my war was over. I would decide when my war was over.

He smiled and it was a sad smile, "We'll do our best Major but I think this country has had all that it can expect from you. Your war is over. Now close your eyes and count back from ten." I felt the slightest of pricks and I tried to count. I got to nine.

Chapter 18

I dreamed. I dreamed that I was high in the air and suddenly I was surrounded by German triplanes and they were all red. I twisted and turned but no matter which way I went there was the Red Baron. The engine on my Camel cut out and I was falling; I was going down and no matter how hard I pulled on the stick my bus would not pull up. The ground was so close that I could see it and then there was silence.

"Bill! Bill, are you awake?"

Dreams are strange. I could have sworn that I heard Beattie's voice but that was impossible for I was dead. I tried to turn over to sleep some more but I felt a hand on my shoulder and, strangely, I could smell Beattie's perfume. This was the weirdest dream I had ever had. I forced my eyes open and looked up into the face of my wife.

I saw a single tear drip from her left eye. She wiped it away and quickly kissed me. "You had us worried, Bill. You have been out for a whole day. Sir Michael was really worried."

"Sir Michael?"

"The surgeon. He was summoned because he was the only man for the operation."

I tried to sit up. "My leg!"

"Is still attached but you were lucky. There was a great deal of damage to the nerves and the kneecap." She leaned over and kissed me again. "You will walk with a limp for the rest of your life."

"But can I fly?"

She stepped back and I could see the horror on her face. "But my love, you could be out of the war!"

I took her hand in mine. "I have to see it out. You know that!"

She shook her head. "Bill Harsker, why did I have to fall in love with such a noble and dedicated man?"

"I don't know but I know that I am the lucky one."

Sir Michael was equally incredulous the next day when he visited me. "But good God, man! You have the chance to survive this war. No one will think any the less of you for what you have done. They are thinking of giving you a medal for what you did and you already have the VC, MC and bar! What are you trying to do? Win the war all by yourself?"

"No doctor but I owe it to all the men I have flown with to see this through."

He shook his head. "I hope that the British public will realise what the likes of you chaps have done and will remember them." He grabbed my hand, "I am in awe of you." He turned to Beattie. "You have a remarkable husband, Mrs Harsker."

She laughed, "Why do you think I grabbed him with both hands? We can't change him we just have to fix him up so that he can go back and do the same thing again. It is in his blood and, no matter what happens, I wouldn't change him."

Doctor Bentine nodded and then added seriously, "There was, is, some serious damage to your knee. We have repaired what we can but I am afraid that you will have pain in your left knee for the rest of your life. It will be prone to arthritis when you are old. And you are not out of the woods yet. We still have to get rid of the infection!"

"But at least I have two legs. My old gunner lost a hand! So when can I start walking on it!"

"Walking?" He shook his head. "We can let you out of bed in two weeks or so."

"No doctor, in two weeks I shall be walking out of here and spending a night in the Mayflower Hotel with my wife!"

"Impossible!"

"Doctor I may not know much about the human body but I know horses. When we had a horse with an injured leg, if we didn't shoot it then we kept it on its feet and began riding it within a week. It should be the same with a man. Get me a couple of sticks or crutches and I will exercise each day."

"But the damage to your knee…"

"Is repaired, you told me that. Thanks for all that you have done, doctor. I promise you that if I think I am doing more harm than good then I will rest."

He just shook his head and as he left, said, "Nurse Harsker, I think your life with the major will be interesting, to say the least."

She sat on the bed when he had gone and held my hands. "He knows what he is doing, Bill. I don't want to have you crippled for life."

"And I won't be. Look, from what he said the splinter went into my knee and damaged stuff inside there. Right?"

"The stuff is tendons and ligaments. And the knee cap was cracked."

"Bones heal, I know that. So the ligaments and the tendons might not work. I heard what he said, I will have a limp. He may even want me to have a stick. That is fine but when I am flying the knee will not be a problem. I will just build up my muscles to support my weak knee." I pulled her towards me and kissed her.

"Bill! If Matron sees me she will change my ward!"

"Go to the Mayflower when you are off duty and book a room for us. A fortnight today!"

She looked at me doubtfully. "I think the room will be empty."

"Well I shall be there and, hopefully, so will you!"

I started my training regimen the next day. One of the male orderlies brought me crutches and I took to marching around the bed. The rush of blood to my foot took me by surprise and I nearly passed out with the pain but then I found that I could drag my left foot on the ground and, after a while, it did not hurt as much. By lunchtime, my armpits and my hands were red raw but I felt I had accomplished much.

By the time Beattie came on duty, I had had enough exercise and I was in bed. I felt like a cheat when she smiled and said, "There, I told you it was too early to be using them. I'll put them in your cupboard."

"No! I find it less embarrassing if I use them to take me down to the toilet. A bedpan is …"

She nodded. "I can see that. Well, I have other patients to attend to." At the door, she paused and said, over her shoulder, "I booked the room at the Mayflower!"

I worked alone in my room. Every day I put more weight on the left leg. When the nurses shooed me back to bed I lay on the top and raised and lowered my leg until the muscles screamed their objections. I had nothing else to do. The alternative was to read the newspapers and that made for depressing reading. There was an air of doom and gloom amongst the British press. The dreams of a quick victory had evaporated by 1915 but the hope of a victory after Cambrai had been snuffed out and replaced with pessimism.

I had been in the hospital for a week when I had visitors. It was General Henderson and an aide. He waved me to my bed when I tried to rise. "It seems I am fated to ever see you here." He chuckled, "Well done Major Harsker. You are a bright light on a foggy night. This is Captain Bellerby, you don't mind if he takes notes, do you?"

"Notes? Of course, not but notes on what, sir?"

"You, Major Harsker. Even within your remarkable squadron, you stand out as unique. You alone appear to have the measure of these Fokker Triplanes." He shook his head, "We got rid of them but the Germans seem to be able to make them do things we never could. You not only manage to shoot them down, take on the Red Baron and survive, good God man you actually flew into a whole squadron of them shot down two and damaged four others. The captain here will make notes on how the devil you manage to do it!"

I didn't really know and so I just told them both how I flew and the reasons I had done what I did.

When I had finished the General nodded. "You know that in a month or so we are amalgamating the RFC with the RNAS. We will be the Royal Air Force. It has taken some time but we have finally convinced everyone. When this war is over I want you to help make the pilots of the future. You need to come up with a plan and methods of training to give all of them the reactions that you have."

"I am not certain if I want to stay on after the war sir."

He stood and waved an imperious hand. "Of course, you do." He jabbed a finger at my tunic with the medals. "It's in your blood man. You are a hero and you want to serve your country. You can still serve your country in peacetime." He laughed again, "You might actually spend less time in the hospital then!" His face became serious. "You should have got a meal for what you did but you have your bar already. In case you didn't know your brother was given the Military Medal for what he did at Cambrai. You are all a fine family."

After he had gone I wondered why he had bothered to take the time to find out about Bert. As for me, I didn't need any more medals. When Beattie came on duty I told her what he had said. She seemed to approve.

"From what Gordy and Ted told me, that sounds like a perfect job for you. They both said how the pilots you trained and led were the best in the squadron."

"But I thought I would be out of the service after the war."

"Doing what?" She looked at me and I knew then that I had married the perfect woman. She knew me better than I knew myself.

"Well, I thought I could go back to working with horses."

She shook her head, "Where? Lady Mary has had to sell off most of the estate to pay the death duties and as for horses well I am sorry Bill but the automobile is here to stay. The few horses that come back from the war will be put out to pasture."

I slumped back in my bed. "But I thought…"

She came and fluffed my pillow, "You have changed since the war began Bill. I didn't know the old Bill but Alice and your mother told me what you were like and you have changed. You are neither better nor worse but you are different. The old Bill would never have been an officer. He would have been like Bert and stayed a sergeant and followed orders. You don't follow orders you give them."

I shook my head, "That is Archie."

Laughing she said, "I have spoken with Gordy and Ted, remember? When Major Harsker says something then that happens." She paused at the door. "It would be a crying shame if you threw the baby out with the bathwater. Grab your opportunities in both hands, who knows where they might lead."

By the middle of the next week, I had managed to use sticks. I still found it hard to put weight on my left leg but I was getting there. Even Doctor Bentine was impressed. "Remarkable! It shows that the human mind and spirit can overcome what we doctors think is impossible."

However, I found that I had bitten off more than I could chew. At the end of the two weeks, I could walk a little but not enough for me to leave and go to the Mayflower with Beattie. That took two more days.

Doctor Bentine arrived and I threw one stick on to the bed. I walked to the door and down the corridor while he watched. I returned and said, "Tada!"

He laughed, "I can see the sweat on your face Major and I know the effort and the pain that cost you but you can be discharged." He waggled an admonishing finger at me, "If you weren't married to such a fine nurse I would not allow it but I know that Nurse Harsker will manage your walking."

"When can I return to active service?"

He cocked his head to one side. "I think I should have examined your head as well as your knee. You would rather go back to the western front than have a week's leave with your wife?"

I blushed, "Well, I mean…"

"Have a week's leave and then report to your doctor. I will leave that decision to him." He shook my hand, "I am pleased to have met you, Major. I have had to change my opinion on many things."

Chapter 19

It was the end of the first week in March before Beattie would countenance my return to the war. I was impatient to get back. This was not because I wished to leave my wife; far from it. The time we spent in the Mayflower was idyllic but the newspapers were full of the losses in the air. I had no contact with the squadron and I feared for my lads. Beattie eventually agreed when I was able to walk around Hyde Park without wincing every hundred yards or so. Inside I was in agony but I had learned to be the consummate actor.

As I waited in Amiens for the car which would take me back to my squadron I found my eyes drawn to the sky. I convinced myself that I could see aeroplanes there. Of course, there were none. It was just my imagination and the desire to get up there again. I was now convinced that I knew how to defeat the Fokkers. My reckless charge in amongst them had disturbed their Teutonic order. If we used their own strength against them then we might just win.

It was Quarter Master Doyle who came for me. He grabbed my bag and threw it in the back. "You are a sight for sore eyes, sir. The lads, all of them, have been asking after you since you crashed. You are looking well." He noticed the stick and a frown passed over his face. "Are you not fit yet sir?"

"I am as fit as I will ever be Quarter Master. Don't worry I can still fly it's just I may be a little slower getting in and out of the bus."

"Well, that is a relief."

On the drive to the field, I learned the news and none of it was good. We had lost five pilots since I had been away. I knew none of them for they were all replacements; that made me feel guilty. If I had had them under my wing who knows what might have happened.

"We are having a hard time sir and that's no lie. I am not an airman but from the *Griffin,* it seems the Hun is coming over in greater numbers than ever. I think the bastards are up to something."

"I agree Quarter Master. It seems I came back just in time for the kick-off then."

It was late afternoon when I arrived back and the Camels were all down on the ground. Alarmingly I saw riggers and mechanics swarming around them. The Quarter Master saw my look, "Aye sir, that is the result of the sortie this morning. I'll take your bag to your quarters. Good to have you back, sir."

I limped to the office. The drive had made my leg stiffen a little. Beattie had warned me to expect that. I walked in the office and Randolph stood up and grinned at me. "Like a bad penny, you keep on turning up." He grabbed my hand and pumped it. "Good to see you back." He glanced at my stick. "Are you fit to fly?"

"That depends upon the doc but as I argued Beattie and Sir Michael Bentine out of grounding me I shall not take no from the Doc!" I threw a pouch of tobacco on to the desk. "Here, a little present and I have a couple of bottles of malt in my bag. I'll have Bates bring them over later."

"He will be more than glad to see you. When you were reported missing he was the one who was convinced that you were not dead. He badgered the life out of poor Archie. He wanted search parties sent out!"

I laughed, Bates was a force of nature.

Archie came in, "When I heard the laughing I hoped it was you. You are riding your luck you know. Johnny Holt told us how you plunged into the middle of a horde of Fokkers. Madness!"

"I don't know sir. General Henderson came to see me and asked about my tactics. It has made me think about it. I know it was daft for one bus to do what I did but if I had done that with my flight then even six Camels could upset eighteen or even twenty Fokkers. We can turn inside them and they hate their order being upset. I reckon it is worth trying."

"Well, I dare say the Quarter Master filled you in. We are losing too many young pilots. They are surviving for hours not days."

"I heard. Can we rearrange the flights? I'll keep Jack Fall and put all my experienced lads with the other flights."

"You want the novices?"

"I have had a lot of time to think as I was strolling around Hyde Park. I think I can help the young lads and keep them alive." I looked Archie in the eyes. "It has worked up to now: Freddie, Johnny, George, even the dour Welshman have all survived. I must be doing something right. I am not certain what but…"

"You are right but first you had better go and see the Doc. He has to clear you to fly."

I stood. "I know. But I am confident."

They both laughed, "Confidence is never lacking in you, Bill. Sense? Yes. Confidence? No."

As I headed towards the sickbay Johnny and Freddie ran up to me. "We heard you were back." Freddie looked at the stick. "How is the leg?"

I nodded to Johnny, "I thought that we could be a pair of pirates! One-Eyed Holt and Peg Leg Harsker!" They laughed. "I am fine."

Johnny stared at me, "Thank you for what you did, sir. You saved my life and I have never seen anything so magnificent and so heroic."

I shook my head, "And so bloody mad that if anyone in my flight had done that I would have had them on a charge! I have to see the Doc. I will catch up with you all at dinner."

Doc Brennan frowned when he saw the stick. I held up my hand. "Before you start I don't need a stick to fly. This is just until my knee gets a little stronger."

In answer, he waved a manila envelope at me. "Sir Michael sent me the report. You are lucky to be walking! You do know he is one of the top surgeons in the country?"

"Well, there you go! My knee must be fine then!"

"You are incorrigible. Get your trousers off and let me have a look at this knee."

He put me through my paces but I was prepared. I had been through this with Beattie and Sir Michael. I never showed any discomfort even though it was agony. He nodded, "You can put your trousers on. Well, Bill, I guess you can fly but take a tip from me; when this war is over get yourself on the stage. You are a marvellous actor!"

Bates had a worried look on his face when I went to my quarters. He had unpacked my bags already. He said nothing but I saw the concern in his eyes. "Thank you for looking after my gear so well and for being so concerned. Mrs Harsker sends her regards."

That made him smile. "Did you find time to be together, sir?"

"We stayed at the Mayflower!"

He grinned, "Excellent, sir, excellent!"

"Could you take two bottles of that whisky to the office please, Bates?"

The next day I met my young pilots. I had seen them the previous night at dinner but Gordy and Ted had monopolised my time as they quizzed me about my escape. I did manage to see my old flight and told them of the new arrangements. I was touched by the disappointment on the faces of the three who were to leave me. I took Jack to one side before either of us had consumed too much whisky. "I need you to be baby minder for these lads. Keep them tight to me. You are the one they will be able to talk to. I will be the bastard who shouts at them."

He had smiled, "They won't mind that. The fact that they are in the flight of a leading ace with a VC is like their birthday and Christmas have come together. They will be fine."

"Right boys. My orders are simple. We fly line astern and you follow me and do as I do. You can fire your guns, just so long as you don't blow my arse off in the process!" They laughed, as I knew they would. "If we meet these invincible triplanes I intend to get right among them. That may frighten you but you are young lads and if I have the reactions then you should have them in abundance. If you have to fire then a short burst will do the trick. Jack and I have found that snapshots work the best isn't that right lieutenant?"

"Yes sir. A couple of bullets in the right place can do serious damage to the Hun. You stick with the major and you might survive and remember that I am watching your back. You just concentrate on staying close to the Major."

Their takeoffs were a little wobbly but I had more to worry about than a couple of bumps. This was the first time I had flown with my dodgy knee. I did not need to use my left leg a great deal but I did need to use it. As I climbed to reach a good altitude I decided to ask Flight Sergeant Lowery to see if he could move the seat on the new Camel back a little. I had hoped that the new bus was as carefully tuned as the one I had crashed. As we climbed it purred like a kitten. The ground crew had not let me down.

Randolph had briefed me and told me that the Germans were trying to bully us out of the air. They were coming mob-handed. They never sent over less than twenty-four aeroplanes and normally over seventy per cent were the triplanes. At least that was the picture in our sector. It was why we were flying as a squadron. We needed protection in numbers. Freddie and I flew higher than the other flights and we flew line astern. Archie led the other Camels at a slightly lower altitude in line abreast. I hoped that this combination might just work.

When I saw them, I realised that they were higher than we were. I waggled my wings and began to climb. Freddie and I had the flanks of our formation. I intended to repeat my charge into the heart of them again. I had yet to have Freddie paint my horse on my cockpit and, as far as the Germans were concerned, there was nothing to identify me. My tactics might only work once but if it bought my pilots another two and a half hours in the air then that would satisfy me.

The Jasta we faced was not the Circus; the aeroplanes all had a squadron livery. They were green with what looked like a black and white checkerboard design on the side. I stored that for future reference. It was cold as we climbed. I hoped that the young pilots behind me would not be overawed in this, one of their first combats. Archie had wisely kept them on the ground the previous day.

The Fokkers were stacked in four lines of six. It meant that, if they chose, then all of them could open fire on Archie and the two flights he led. I thought it unlikely that they would do so for it would be a waste of ammunition but I did work out how they would attack. Each six would fire and then climb to loop and come around again. In that way, all four lines could fire at Archie and his eleven aeroplanes. Inevitably they would knock some out of the air. It was how they had gained air superiority. I hoped to throw a large spanner in their works!

I began a slow bank and headed for the second line of six Fokkers. I heard the Spandau of the first six as they opened fire and the deeper chatter of the Vickers as they responded. I held my fire. The pilot on the extreme right of the third line tried a hopeful burst at me. It was a waste of bullets. At fifty yards I gave a short burst and then pulled my nose up. I heard Lieutenant Grey behind me as he fired his guns for the first time in anger.

If the Germans thought I intended to fly across their second line they were wrong. I banked to port and kept climbing. I was rewarded by the aeroplanes from the first six as they tried to turn out of their loop. I had a flank shot at them. Head-on they were small but side on they were a bigger target and I fired a long burst. I saw the stays and the wires as they parted. The bullets continue on and hit the fuselage. The Fokker began to dive. The pilot was struggling for control. I left him and turned to starboard. I had a sudden flash of déjà vu. Fokkers were appearing all around me. I snap fired as each triplane appeared. As had happened before I had no idea of what damage I was doing but this time I had the reassurance of my young pilots as they fired at every triplane that came before them. Suddenly a Fokker appeared less than fifty feet from me. I pulled my triggers and then braced myself for the crash. The pilot was a gifted one for he managed to pull up his nose. It did not save his life for the twin Vickers pumped a hundred bullets into the base of his cockpit. As he soared, trapped in a death loop, his Fokker slammed into an Albatros which was trying to bring his bus around to hit me. In my mirror, I saw that a gap had appeared. Poor Lieutenant Grey could not keep up with me. I began to bank to port to make it easier for him. The combat had lasted almost thirty minutes and the Nemesis of the Fokker came to our aid. They had to turn to return to their field.

It was not worth risking my young pilots in a pursuit and I led them back west. I counted my five chicks in a line and I was happy. They had survived. Sadly, I saw two Camels burning on the ground. We had not had all the rub of the green. I had seen two enemy aeroplanes go down and I hoped that we had managed to get more in our wild charge.

I circled the field with my flight to allow the others to land and to get a few more minutes for my novices. When lives were measured in minutes then even extra seconds in the sky would help. When we landed I left Jack to listen to them. They were chattering like school children. I lit my pipe and wandered towards Gordy and Ted.

"Who did we lose?"

"Bell and Robinson."

"Any chance they walked away?"

Ted shook his head. "Both were dead before they hit the ground. Not everyone has your luck, Bill."

We strolled towards the office and Freddie ran to catch us up. He was grinning, "That was better! We gave them a shock this morning and no mistake."

I gave a word of caution, "And we know that they will learn from this. I would expect two Jasta tomorrow."

Freddie's face fell. "Really?"

I nodded. "I had the chance to read the papers back in Blighty and I spoke with General Henderson. The Germans have brought whole divisions from the east. They must be massing behind their lines already. Fritz is stopping us from having a look-see. They will do anything to knock us out of the air."

"Well, they might wait until they have all of their men here."

"The Yanks are coming. It will take a few more months until they are at full strength. They will want to beat us before the Americans arrive. I think they are only waiting to get as many new aeroplanes as they can."

We had reached the office and Ted said, "You seem remarkably well informed."

"Like I said I had time to read and I visited the Army and Navy club a couple of times." I tapped my medal ribbons. "These loosen an amazing number of tongues."

Archie was there already and he had opened one of my bottles of malt. "Well done for today and thanks to Bill we have a new malt so cheers."

I toasted them and asked, "How many did we knock down then?"

Randolph looked up from the tally sheet he had before him. "Three Fokkers and three Albatros; better than any other day this or last month."

I noticed that they all looked at me. "It was luck and using new tactics. Now we need to work out what to do when they send thirty odd birds after us tomorrow."

In the end, the weather closed in the next day and we had a short storm of Biblical proportions. Some of the enlisted men's tents were blown away and one Camel was damaged when its mooring peg came loose.

The storm gave me the chance to get to know my new pilots. "Well, Walter what was it like hanging on to my shirttails?"

"Er, it's Wally sir and it was scary. I didn't want to lose you."

"And you didn't."

"I nearly did. I pulled back to avoid a collision."

"Understandable."

"But you just fired when you were going to collide."

"Did you get to fire your guns?"

"Yes sir."

"Did you hit anything?"

"I am not certain but I think so. Not enough for a kill. I will never get the number that you have sir."

"I can remember when I was desperate for my first kill. It will come."

I waved to Jack and sat with him. "How did they do?"

"Better than when we first arrived, sir. I can understand that they were frightened. I was. It seems unnatural to fly into the heart of the enemy."

"I know but it seems to work. We are turning the tide. Their better pilots are being killed. The ones they are bringing from the east haven't faced a bus like the Camel yet. They are in for a shock."

When we did fly again we saw no Germans in our sector which was strange. Archie led us, tentatively, towards the German lines. Their guns blasted away at us. We noticed they had far more than they used to. It was always dangerous; all it took was one lucky shot. Once we reached their rear areas we saw trucks, vehicles and horses filling the roads. We went in for a low-level attack and soon the roads were emptied as the soldiers and vehicles fled to the safety of side roads and ditches. When we were empty we climbed high and returned west.

All the way back I was wondering why we had seen no German aeroplanes. It was not like them. My unease was lessened somewhat by the knowledge that we had given the new pilots more hours in the air and they had fired their guns at the enemy. Confidence was all.

Randolph gave us the bad news when we landed. The German aeroplanes had been over our lines. They had bombed the area to the west of Bapaume and several airfields had been attacked. It was a disaster and it told us, quite clearly, where they would attack; it would be the Somme and we were in the line of their advance. Someone at

Headquarters was thinking and we were sent a company of machine-gunners. It was not as good as artillery but it was effective at keeping aeroplanes at a distance. We advised the soldiers on their sandbagging. We were the poacher turned gamekeeper.

Things began to escalate from then on. Between the tenth and twentieth of March, we were in the air every morning fighting to keep the Germans at bay. Although we lost no aeroplanes in the dogfights we did have damage to both pilots and Camels which had a debilitating effect on the morale of the squadron. On the seventeenth, St Patrick's day, we had twenty Camels in the air. We found ourselves facing twenty-four Fokkers. Twenty were the triplane while four were a new bus we had not seen before. This was the Fokker D.VII. It proved to be a dangerous opponent.

We flew in four lines astern. Our aim was to keep the Germans guessing. They seemed more than happy with four lines of six abreast. Freddie and I were in the middle. He and his flight were to my right. We had varied our line astern by stacking each Camel just ten feet above. I had more confidence in my pilots and Wally knew to fire a heartbeat after I opened fire. In the first few moments of combat, our plan seemed to be working. The triplane fired at me and I felt the bullets as they hit my top wing and then I fired. As soon as Wally joined in we had a cone of fire from four machine-guns. The propeller disappeared and smoke started to pour from the engine.

The next Fokker was just fifty yards behind the first and we were soon upon him. He fired first and I felt the camel judder as his bullets struck my undercarriage. Once again, our combined fire hit him although less spectacularly. We tore into his underbelly as he pulled up his nose to correct his aim. He kept on rising and I was not certain if this was deliberate or if he was already dead.

The third and fourth Germans suddenly lifted their noses as they looped up and over us. We had no target. The last three Camels in my flight fired at them as they climbed and banked to the east. They had outnumbered us and we had only destroyed four of them. I could not understand why they had fled. As we headed back to our field we saw the reason why. They had been keeping us in the air. Other bombers and fighters had raided our field. The Hun had not had it all his own way and we saw three downed bombers and two downed fighters. The airfield was too badly damaged to land. Randolph fired the Very pistol which told us to land at the next airfield. That was close to Amiens and, by the time we landed there we were flying on fumes.

The adjutant, Captain Moncrieff came to us. "Get refuelled sir and take your Camels to your new field at Abbeville." He handed me a map.

"Here is where it is. Your field is being abandoned. Intelligence seems to think that it is in the direct path of the German advance."

"But they haven't started advancing yet!"

"Sir, they have bombed all the forward airfields. Your squadron was lucky, your buses were in the air. Two squadrons have been destroyed on the ground. General Trenchard is taking no chances." He swept an arm around the field. "We are getting ready to move out too."

"But we are forty miles behind the front here."

"I know, sir and we are now the furthest forward field in the Somme area."

As we flew west I reflected that the Battle of Cambrai had done more harm than good. We had lost good men and the gains we had made had been given back and weakened us. Until the Americans joined the war there was a better than average chance that we would lose the war before summer.

Chapter 20

The field was a windsock and some tents. It was, however, flat and free from potholes. We landed. The lorries did not arrive until it was dark. We saw their headlights as they meandered along the road. I breathed a sigh of relief when I saw Bates in the car with Randolph and another three batmen. John smiled at me. "I saved all of your stuff Major!"

"Thank you, John, I am just glad that you are unscathed."

"It is only thanks to your bath that I am though, sir."

Archie and the others turned when they heard Bates' comment. "My bath?"

"Yes sir. The first bombs blew the windows out so I hid under the tin bath. It is a good job too, sir. It looks like a giant colander now. I fear that you will never use it again. Your quarters are a mess."

I saw Archie and the others smile. I, too, found it funny but Bates had a close encounter with death and it would not do to minimise its importance. "Well done Bates. I am afraid we will be in tents for a while."

He sniffed imperiously. "I will go and claim one for you, sir."

As the warrant officers arrived they did what they did best, they took charge. As we smoked our pipes and waited for the tents to be erected and for the cooks to make some sandwiches Randolph told us of the raid. "They came from nowhere and used the big Gothas as well as two-seaters with smaller bombs. They strafed the gunners. Those sandbags stopped the bullets but they couldn't stop the bombs. The Quartermaster was killed and Percy Richardson." He looked at me, "Geoff and Joe, your mechanics, were also killed. We lost thirty men all told. The doc is still at the field with the wounded. He refused to leave. He will join us in the morning."

Archie shook his head. "Well, this a fine how do you do! No ammunition. No fuel and the Hun is about to begin an offensive. Randolph, get in touch with Headquarters and find out what they expect of us. We need some sort of telephone."

"Yes sir. I'll drive to Abbeville. There must be someone there who can help us."

As he sped off Ted said wryly, "The Channel isn't far over there. It will only take an hour and we will be back in Blighty!"

Gordy shook his head, "I wouldn't joke about that. It might well happen."

Archie tapped his pipe out. "Let's not lose our heads. They have hit our fields but there is no offensive yet. We haven't lost any ground at all!"

I agreed with Archie but this was ominous. Like everything the Germans did this was well thought out and well-executed. Their offensive would be just as well thought out. They had sat back and soaked up all of our attacks. Our best soldiers, like Bert, lay buried in the fields of Northern France. We had planned for an aerial war and we had been outwitted. They had bided their time and waited for the soldiers to return from Russia. They outnumbered the allies now and they would use that advantage ruthlessly.

Inevitably it took us some time to get organised and we were not able to fly a patrol again until the nineteenth. We had further to fly to reach the front and a shorter time over the combat zone. It was not a satisfactory arrangement. Each sortie showed the devastating effect their aeroplanes were having.

We were sent towards Bapaume and then Cambrai. That battlefield still held bitter memories for me. As we flew over the battlefield I saw the detritus of battle. There were wrecked aeroplanes littering No Man's Land. It had been fought over as though it was a pot of gold.

That morning it was lucky that we were at altitude else we would have fallen foul of Von Richthofen and his Flying Circus who were on the prowl. I prayed that my young lads would not be upset at the thought of fighting such a renowned Jasta. The Red Baron was clever. He knew that the sight of his garishly painted buses inspired fear in the enemy. He had the advantage as soon as he appeared. My lads knew how to fight Fokkers. They had done so before but it was the psychological aspect which I could not predict. What was in their heads?

We had retained our four line astern formation and I was happy with that. The Flying Circus had not seen how we worked. The stacked Camels above me worked and gave us a marginally better rate of fire. I hoped it would be enough. Once again Freddie and I were in the middle and slightly ahead of the other two flights. This time we had no height to make up but we would have the same endurance issue as the Germans. We would have no more than thirty minutes to defeat them and then we would need to break off.

I saw that the Red Baron was in the centre of the line. It would either be me or Freddie who had to come against him. I hoped it was me. I had fought him three times. Perhaps this would be the day when it was decided. I waited until I was but fifty yards away. I fired just a heartbeat ahead of the Red Baron. Such are the margins of victory. Smoke began to drift from his engine and, more importantly, his nose dipped as he lost power. That dip saved his life for it took him away from Wally's guns which would surely have ended his life. Grey's bullets hit his upper wing and his fuselage. I had no time to fire at him again as I saw another triplane ahead. I fired and, this time, Wally did too. I felt the German's bullets strike me but the Hun drifted to port as some wires gave way and he lost some control. I fired again before he moved away as did Wally and this time we hit his cockpit. I could see that he was in trouble. I slowly banked to port to continue to pour bullets into him. This time Roger Stuart, in the third Camel, had a shot and he managed to hit the pilot. The triplane plunged to the ground.

I turned to starboard to tackle the other Germans but they were descending as they headed east. I saw another damaged Fokker to port and headed after him. I saw Archie lead the rest of the squadron to pursue the Flying Circus. The Fokker I chased twisted and turned. I kept firing. I hit him again and again. Eventually, a hand came up and he descended. He was surrendering. I kept my eye on him but I was suddenly aware of a barrage to the east. The Flying Circus had led Archie and his two flights into a trap. There were machine-guns and artillery waiting for them. I saw one Camel explode in the air and another two spiral to earth before Archie extricated the squadron and headed west. We had come within a whisker of a great victory and we left with a draw; it was honours even.

It seemed an inordinately long flight home. Perhaps that was the maudlin thoughts which filled my head. I had had a brief moment when I thought we had had a victory. The sight of the Flying Circus fleeing had filled me with the hope that we might win. Instead, we had been led into a trap and two pilots lay dead. The tents which lined our new field did not look welcoming. I thought of the bottles of malt which waited at our old field and yearned for them.

There were few comforts on that cold field. However, we had bowsers for our fuel and parts were arriving to repair our buses. Jack Fall showed himself to be a good leader. He jollied along the younger pilots. It was hard to believe that he had but a few months more experience than they did. It showed what aerial combat did to a young pilot. If you survived the first few weeks then you became a changed man. We made the best of our new home. I think Bates was upset by the new arrangements more than anyone else. He disliked dirt and he positively hated anything which upset his ordered life. Our short time on that field was the low point in his life.

We were awoken on the morning of March twenty-first by the sound of a barrage. The noise was so intense that we knew it could mean only one thing; the offensive had started. The cooks had breakfast already going but we ate on the hoof. We had to be in the air by dawn. We were on the receiving end but we understood how these things worked. The German fliers would be in the sky to direct the fire of their guns and to support their infantry.

We sat in our buses watching the first hint of dawn peer over the eastern horizon. We could see the sky punctuated by the flash of artillery and Archie fired the Very pistol when it was still dark and we trundled down the grass. The German guns guided our flight.

As we flew towards the front we realised that there was thick fog. We had assumed, at the field, that it was a sea mist. As we flew beyond Amiens we saw that it looked like a low cloud which covered the earth. It would make observation difficult. The nearer we went to the front the more terrifying became the noise from the barrage. Archie began to fly higher to avoid the shells. There were so many that the air seemed to be filled with flying metal.

When dawn did break all that we saw was the fog below and explosions as the shells struck. We were helpless to aid the soldiers who must have been suffering hellish conditions. We saw no one and had to return to the field to refuel. Our new home was safe but we had a longer journey.

The barrage stopped shortly before ten o'clock. It had lasted five hours. We took off again and the mist and fog began to dissipate. To our horror, we saw that there were brown uniforms fleeing west. The Germans had broken through. The barrage had ceased and it was safe to descend. Not all the British soldiers had fallen back and we saw islands of soldiers fighting desperately in redoubts. I saw pockets of the dreaded storm-troopers, *Stoßtruppen*, attacking with flamethrowers, bombs and hand-held machine-gun.

I led my flight down to machine-gun the Germans who had surrounded one beleaguered island. By the time our guns were empty the redoubt was surrounded by a sea of grey uniforms and the corpses of the elite *Stoßtruppen*. We saw the rest of the squadron supporting other such redoubts and we headed back to the field.

Randolph was waiting with mess orderlies. Piles of sandwiches and buckets of hot tea awaited us. While we ate Randolph filled me in, "It is bad, Bill. HQ knew it was coming and most of our soldiers had been pulled back from the front-line trenches but the barrage caused huge damage to our advanced positions and they have exploited it. What did you see?"

"There looked to be redoubts holding out but the Hun is using those storm-troopers you told us about. I don't think our lads can hold out."

"It looks like they are heading for Amiens. If they capture that we are scuppered. That is the main rail link for the whole of the front. If that falls then so do we. Those redoubts have been specifically built to hold out and slow the enemy advance down. I hope they work!" I nodded and washed down the bully beef sandwich with hot sweet tea. "Did you see the Hun in the air?"

I shook my head, "Not yet and that surprises me."

The other flights began to land. "Headquarters wants a third sortie this afternoon. I know that causes problems but we have to hold them, Bill."

"I know. I'll go and brief my lads." I waved Jack over. "Lieutenant, get the lads gathered around. We are going up again."

They had all taken off their goggles and their helmets. I wondered if I looked as amusing. There was a blackened area where oil and dirt had spattered and then two white patches where their eyes were. We looked like owls!

"We are going back up, chaps. Now the Hun is breaking through. We have to stop them from reaching Amiens. This time keep your eyes open for Fritz in the air. We may not be able to keep formation. If we are attacked then I think we will be outnumbered." I smiled, "You are not raw recruits any more, you are pilots. You can handle anything the Germans throw at you. Yesterday we sent the Flying Circus packing!" I saw them stand a little taller at the memory. "When you are low on fuel or out of ammunition then get back here as soon as you can." I looked at them all one by one, "Our backs are to the wall but then British soldiers have had their backs to the wall before and we have always come through. Your ancestors were outnumbered at Poitiers, Crecy, Agincourt, Blenheim and Waterloo." I paused, "We always won and you lads are going to win today." I nodded when I saw the sparkle in their eyes. They would not let me down.

Bates had been standing to one side. He handed me a flask which I knew would contain something hot. "Make sure you come back today, Major Harsker. The men who led in those battles you spoke of all came home and made our country a better one. Make sure you do too."

It felt a little lonely leading the six Camels over the enemy lines. We reached the front far quicker than we had done which showed the speed of their advance and we arrived as a mixed force of Albatros and Fokkers were dive-bombing and machine-gunning the redoubts. I waggled my wings and led my flight down. We were outnumbered but the enemy aeroplanes were busy machine-gunning our soldiers. The first they knew of our presence was when I opened fire at twenty yards range. The pilot of the Albatros knew nothing for my first burst, delivered from above, hit and killed him instantly. I pulled the nose up and fired at the tail of the next German. We were faster than the Huns anyway and our altitude had given us even more speed. It meant we had seconds only to fire but there were six of us pouring round after round into the Jasta and receiving nothing in reply. After I had passed the last Fokker I pulled up the nose and began to bank to port.

As I looked to my left I saw the devastation we had caused. At least five German aeroplanes were burning. Ground fire must have accounted for some of them. I came around and saw that the rest of the German squadron were heading east. I did not think that six Camels had made them do that; it was probably a need to refuel and rearm which had prompted it. I was faster than they were and I had more height. I followed. Inexorably I gained on them. I did not want to waste ammunition and I waited until I was thirty yards away from the rearmost Albatros before I fired. I could not miss him but he kept swinging his bus from side to side in an attempt to shake me off. Suddenly he plummeted to the ground. Either I had hit him or something vital. I sought my next target. As I did so I glanced below me. We were over what had been the front lines just eight hours earlier. It was now German territory.

I saw an Albatros a hundred yards away. I would need to return home soon anyway and I tried a hopeful burst. I hit his tail and his wing and then my guns clicked empty. That was one lucky German pilot. I turned and headed west. I saw the rest of the squadron; they were to the north. My flight was spread all over the sky and was heading west. I counted five of them. I saw that David Dundas' engine was smoking. I headed in his direction to keep an eye on him. As we flew over Amiens it was as though someone had kicked open an ant's nest. Brown uniforms were scurrying around but I could see purpose there. They were shoring up the defences and preparing to make it expensive for the Hun to take it. Although Lieutenant Dundas dropped lower and lower he made the field at Abbeville and landed safely. I was relieved.

The mechanics were around his bus as I taxied. By the time I reached him, Flight Sergeant Lowery was wiping the oil off his hands. "This one won't fly tomorrow sir, sorry."

"Do your best, Flight." Dundas looked crestfallen, "Don't worry David, you'll be up the day after. Did you get any today?"

"I finished off two sir, does that count as two halves for one kill?"

I patted him on the back. "No, young man! If you finish them they are your kills. Congratulations, they are yours."

"But sir you hit both of them first!"

"And I didn't finish them off. They are yours. Well done!"

He raced off to join his fellows and tell them his news. I had never subscribed to this numbers game the press liked to play. It didn't matter to me who shot down Fritz; just so long as someone did.

It had been a long day. The tent Randolph used was not like the office at our old field but he had the whisky ready for me as I strode over. I gave him the figures and he nodded. "We did well today; I say we and I mean this squadron. As an army, it has been a disaster. Still, the plans they put in place have saved many men but I just wonder if this is the beginning of the end."

I puffed on the pipe I had just lit, "That is a little pessimistic Randolph. You sound like Ted."

"I guess it is because I get information from my chum at Headquarters and I see the bigger picture."

I shook my head. "My dad told me about a story he had heard when he served in the cavalry. It was in the Zulu Wars and the Zulus had just slaughtered a whole British army. There was a little outpost with a hundred soldiers and twenty wounded and they held out and defeated four thousand Zulus. It was at a place called Rorke's Drift. Those Welshmen knew that their army had been beaten and yet they still hung on. That is why no one has conquered Britain in almost a thousand years. We never know when we are beaten and the British Tommy has more steel in him than the Forth Bridge. The redoubts we passed were still hanging on despite the Hun using their best soldiers. Wait until we are crossing the Channel before you give up."

He laughed, "I think I should take up flying, Bill. It seems to inspire you pilots. I'll take you at your word. Here's to Rorke's Drift!"

"Rorke's Drift!"

We were laughing when Archie and the others came in. "Well, I am pleased that someone is happy!"

Randolph poured a whisky for the others and said, "It was just Bill here giving me a history lesson and telling me that we will hold on here."

Ted shook his head, "I think you need a new bloody crystal ball, my old son. All I saw today was a beaten British army."

Archie shook his head, "Bill is right. We are not beaten but we are retreating." He waved his hand around the room. "We didn't lose a single bus today." He threw his report down, "And how many Hun did we claim?"

Randolph quickly scanned the lists. "It looks like twenty."

"There you are, Ted. Can you think of another day where we shot down twenty Germans and didn't lose any?"

"Well no but what about the lads on the ground?"

"They will dig in and gradually we will regain the ground we have lost."

However, things got worse before they got better. By the end of the next day, the front line was a mile or two from Amiens. As we climbed to our patrolling altitude I knew that we would not have it as easy again. They were making Amiens a fortress. We saw the Germans as they headed for our front lines. The two-seaters which would bomb and strafe were protected by twenty triplanes. We would have to work to clear the skies.

We did not have the luxury of time and I led my flight directly towards the Fokkers. Archie would make the decision about the two-seaters. If I was leading the squadron then I would detach one flight to destroy them. The Germans had good two-seaters but they were no match for the incomparable Camel.

It was not the Circus we were attacking but it would not do to be overconfident. I looked in my mirror and saw the four Camels were stacked one above the other so that Jack, at the rear, was fifty feet higher than I was. I knew that Freddie was to my right and we would perforce divide the enemy fire. We needed to exploit that advantage quickly. I held my fire even when the triplane fired at me. I just dipped my nose so that his bullets ripped into my top wing and when I brought my guns up he was just fifty yards away and I was able to give him a short burst before he was forced to pull up and avoid a collision. Wally was able to give him a long burst and he continued a smoking loop away to the east.

I banked slightly to the left and came up along the side of the third Fokker in the second line. I fired a hopeful burst at a hundred yards but only hit his fuselage. He turned to bring his guns to bear and I fired before he had aligned his guns. Wally's guns chattered out too and the combined cone of fire hit his engine. As he tried to climb Lieutenant Stuart finished him off with a longer burst.

We had two Fokkers isolated on the right side of their line and they turned to face my five aeroplanes. In my mirror, I saw Jack Fall hit by the fire of two Fokkers and he dived his damaged bus towards the ground with the two triplanes in hot pursuit. The Camel had a better dive than the triplane and I hoped he could outrun them.

Wally and I fired almost together and I saw the German pilot slump in his seat. Stuart and Fielding concentrated their fire on the last Fokker. I banked around to go to the aid of Jack Fall. I saw the tracer from the Fokkers as they tried to hit the elusive Camel. I fired at over three hundred yards. I had virtually no chance of hitting them but I wanted them to look in their mirrors and see two Camels coming after them spitting bullets. As we closed with them our bullets started to strike them and they banked away and headed east. Wally and I shepherded Jack safely back to the field.

Once again, we had a damaged bird that would not fly the next day but there was worse news to come. When Freddie landed he had two Camels missing. It was Tom Carpenter and Harry Duffy. Both were experienced pilots it would be hard to replace. Joe Dodds and Brian Hargreaves had also been shot down. We had lost four of the most experienced pilots we had. Although we had downed more than ten aeroplanes it was a heavy cost to bear.

When Randolph told us that the Fifth Army was in full retreat and we should be prepared to leave our new airfield there was a mood of doom and gloom about the place. We knew that we could do no more and yet we were losing and we were losing badly. The Germans were within a hand span of taking Amiens. We also discovered that we were an isolated pocket of success. The Circus and the other Jasta had destroyed vast numbers of the DH 4 and SE 5 squadrons. The triplane ruled the whole of the front apart from our sector. It was worrying.

Chapter 22

We heard, during the night, the lorries taking reinforcements to Amiens. We knew that more were arriving by train as the Generals tried to shore up the line. When we had flown back across the battlefield we had seen the wrecked tanks and artillery pieces. We had lost a large quantity of supplies as well as men. Amazingly our old field was still intact. The machine-gun company still defended it although their guns were now traversed to the east and not the skies. It seemed unlikely to us that we would ever return there.

Freddie and his flight flew with me when we took off the next morning. Archie led the other two flights. We had decided that Freddie and I would take on the triplanes while the rest destroyed the two-seaters. We had had no plan the previous day and our pilots had paid the price. Freddie and his depleted flight were tucked in behind Lieutenant Dundas who had to replace Jack Fall. As we headed towards Amiens I took heart from the fact that there appeared to be more order. The streams of soldiers heading west had now halted and I saw columns of Australians and Americans heading east to plug the gaps.

I climbed to just below the cloud cover. This time I knew that Archie and his ten Camels would be strafing the enemy infantry or attacking their two-seaters. We would not have to climb to find the enemy. The artillery was silent. Perhaps the Germans were afraid of hitting their own rapidly advancing storm-troopers or perhaps they had expended too many shells already. Randolph said that someone at HQ had calculated that more than a million shells had been dropped in the five-hour bombardment. I could understand it.

We had reached the front quicker than the Germans and the thirty odd two-seaters were snaking their way west at a low altitude. I peered above them and saw the fourteen triplanes. They were higher than the two-seaters but lower than us. They were flying in three lines. The first two each had five Fokkers and the last had four. I waggled my wings and we dived.

It was an incredible feeling to be diving at over one hundred and twenty miles an hour. The airspeed indicator was useless at high speeds but I could feel the power of my Camel as the wind rushed past my face. This was when a pilot needed lighting reactions.

We had been seen and the Germans began to climb. The Fokker Dr I could out-climb anything in the air but we had the edge in terms of position. Stacked as we were and approaching at a combined speed of over two hundred miles an hour Wally and I would only have seconds in which to fire. I waited until we were eighty yards apart and pulled my triggers. Wally followed a second later. The German bullets struck the underside of my engine and the four Vickers tore through the propeller and the engine of the triplane which peeled away to twist and turn towards the earth. I saw oil dripping from my engine. He had damaged me.

The second Fokker approached and, this time, I fired first. It must have been the worry over my engine. Between us, Wally and I managed to hit his engine and his guns. There was no fire in return. I banked to starboard after I had fired, my engine felt rough already. It meant we approached the last four obliquely from the side and we had a free shot at the Fokkers. With a stack of eight Camels descending through them, the last four Fokkers stood no chance. I could not stay in the air much longer and I signalled to Wally that I was heading home. The oil was now pouring from the engine and I needed to get down before it seized.

I saw our old field before me and I headed for it. Our new field was too far away. I could not last much longer in the air. The machine-gun company had actually repaired a couple of the bomb craters and I managed to bring the smoking Camel down. They raced over. I struggled to clamber out of the bus. My leg was giving me shooting pains.

"Are you all right, sir?" Despite the engine propeller not turning there was still smoke as the oil dripped over the hot engine.

"Yes sergeant; just my gammy knee. Any chance of a brew while I fix this?"

"Yes sir." He gave me a worried look, "Sir, you can fix this?"

I laughed, "I began life as a sergeant gunner. I can give it my best shot."

The workshops were a mess but not everything had been taken. I found some hose and some oil. I had some spanners in my Camel. By the time I was back at the Camel, the sergeant had my tea ready. "There you are, sir."

"Thanks, Sarn't." The hot sweet tea was so strong you could have stood a spoon in it but it was welcome. "How are things going?"

"It's been quiet since you left sir. They came over the day after you left but when they saw it was deserted and we discouraged them a bit they left us alone."

I nodded. There was less damage than I might have expected. Half of the buildings were intact and it was just the potholed airfield and craters which were the problem.

I took off the engine cover and saw that the German's bullets had severed an oil hose in two places. I removed the clip and replaced the hose. I took off the filler cap and, using a funnel, refilled the sump. The engine was too hot to take off and I went to the workshop and found a half-full can of fuel. I returned and topped up the Camel's tank. I heard the roar of engines and looked up. Gordy and his flight were flying above. I waved to show that I was safe. Had I still had the radio I could have told Randolph but the receiver was still in the burnt-out wreck of my old Camel close to Cambrai.

I handed the cup back to the Sergeant. "Are we winning sir?"

"Not yet but we have stopped losing." He laughed. I waved my arm across the field. "Keep your eye on it for us. We'll be back!"

I started the engine, with a little help from a private and then gingerly took the Camel to the end of the field. The test of my repair would be when I lifted the nose at the end of the field. Thankfully I had done a good job and I waggled my wings to show the machine-gun company that all was well. I was happy to see the temporary airfield. I would let Flight Sergeant Lowery make a proper repair.

There was a happier air that night. We had not lost any Camels and Archie and his flights had decimated the bombers. Randolph spoke with Headquarters and announced that we had not lost any more territory that day. As we toasted our success I said, "We could go back to our old field you know."

Archie shook his head, "Too risky."

"I don't think so. When I spoke with the sergeant he said that Fritz had not bothered with it since the day before the offensive started. Conditions are better there and the field would not take much to repair it. We would have longer in the air and it is still behind our lines. The Germans are a good five miles away."

"Yes but if they push…"

"Then we get back here." I saw that Gordy and the others agreed with me but Archie was not convinced.

Randolph, like us, wanted to be home, "I'll tell you what, sir. How about I ring Headquarters and see what they say?"

We left Randolph and went to eat. The cooks were doing their best but the field kitchen we had meant that it was largely bully beef and mash that we were eating. We were used to better.

Randolph arrived and frowned at the sludgy mess that was his dinner, "Headquarters says that if we can repair the field we can go back." He nodded at me. "You must have a crystal ball, Bill, Headquarters says that the German advance has been halted. The Yanks and the Aussies have made a difference."

"Good," said Ted, "because I am fed up of being a happy camper!"

Gordy laughed, "You have never been a happy camper."

The next day as we went to discourage the German fighters we saw a line of lorries as our mechanics and riggers returned to our old field to repair it. They were as keen to return as anyone. They hated the idea of running.

That morning we met the same squadron we had been fighting for the last few days. This time they had no reconnaissance aeroplanes and when they were faced by eighteen Camels they turned tail and headed home. We outnumbered them and we had the upper hand. War in the air was often won or lost in the mind. As we flew back we saw that the old airfield was already in better shape. Our men had filled in most of the shell holes and bomb craters.

They arrived back, weary but happy in time for the evening meal. Senior Flight Sergeant Lowery looked dirty and dishevelled but he had a smile on his face. "Major Harsker was right sir. It didn't take much to repair it. We could go back tomorrow if you wanted."

Archie looked at us and nodded, "Well done, Flight. You and the others can leave tomorrow morning after we have taken off. We will return to our old field."

We had been lulled by the flight of the Fokkers the previous day. When we reached the front line we saw, high in the sky, freshly painted Fokkers. There looked to be two squadrons of them and we were well outnumbered. Archie signalled for us to climb and assume a defensive position. It was a sensible move for it drew the triplane to us and the Germans would have to leave quicker than we would.

We spiralled to a higher altitude as the Fokkers made their purposeful way towards us. They came in lines of five abreast. It meant we had two lines of five and then three more lines of five. We would have a gauntlet of steel to face. We just had three columns of Camels. I led eight while Archie and the others were in two columns of five. As we reached the right height I positioned my flight in the centre of the line. We headed to meet the Fokkers.

I checked in my mirror and Wally was in place. As we approached the triplanes I felt anxious. I still do not know why but something did not feel right. I held my fire. Suddenly at a distance of less than a hundred yards, the two Fokkers before me peeled to port and starboard and I had no target. The next five Fokkers came directly for me. I felt the bullets from the first two Fokkers as they raked both sides of my fuselage. How they failed to hit me I will never know. Perhaps I was moving too quickly and they had not turned enough however they managed to hit Wally and I saw him falling from the sky. And then I was hit by the bullets from the second wave of triplanes. I fired my own Vickers but I had no supporting fire from behind me. Lieutenant Dundas and Lieutenant Field were fending off the attack of the first two Fokkers. More bullets struck my engine and my propeller. The pitch of the propeller changed. It had been damaged.

I had had enough of this. I banked sharply to starboard. I needed to get down but first I had to clear a path. My sudden move took the German ahead by surprise and his bullets sailed above me. I saw a triplane less than fifty feet ahead of me and he was broadside on. I gave him a long burst. I hit his fuselage and then his cockpit. I saw his body shaking as though he had St Vitus' dance and then his bus fell to earth. There was clear air before me. My Camel was struggling. I did not want to lose my propeller and I descended as quickly as I could. I found myself amongst the triplanes. I fired whenever I saw one and I felt the bullets as they hit my wings and my fuselage. I was taking too much punishment.

I saw our old field ahead. The machine-gun company were lining their guns up. I wondered why until I looked in the mirror. Two Fokkers were diving towards me. This would not be a graceful landing. I just needed to get down. I hit the ground hard but I heard the Vickers as they sent a wall of death towards the Fokkers. One was hit immediately and plunged to earth, making another crater. The second rose and I thought the pilot had escaped but, when it continued its loop I knew that the pilot was dead. It exploded in the next field. As I clambered from my Camel I saw the lorries with the ground crews beginning to arrive. When the propeller juddered to a stop I saw that it had lost the tip on one side and there were holes in the blade. I had been lucky.

I turned to watch the fight in the air. The Camels and the Fokkers were twisting and turning. It looked like we might lose when the Fokkers headed east and home. Their Achilles heel was their endurance and it had saved us once again. As the Camels landed I saw much damage to our precious aeroplanes. I also saw that Phil Lowe had not made it either. With Wally gone we had lost two pilots and there were at least five badly damaged buses.

Just then I saw Wally as he sauntered into the field. He waved cheerily. "I thought you were a goner there old son."

"So did I but the wrecked Camel is just two fields away. It is a write off I am afraid."

"But you are alive! The bus we can replace!"

Archie walked over to me. "You have had a hard two days Bill. Your last little manoeuvre saved your lads. You upset Fritz."

"I told you, they learn all the time. We made the mistake of repeating ourselves and you can't do that."

As we headed towards the office he nodded, "Well at least we are home."

As we neared the office I stopped Archie and pointed. There was a freshly painted sign. It said. '***Doyle Airfield***.' Senior Flight Sergeant Lowery was nearby and he shrugged. "He was responsible for most of the camp anyway. He scrounged what the engineers couldn't build. The lads thought it was a nice way to remember him."

He was right. We had yet to mourn our dead comrades. Things had been too hectic but this would be a good memorial and a sobering reminder of how close were the margins between life and death.

Chapter 23

Everyone had to set to, making the field habitable again and we had to make do with sandwiches and whisky. The late night and the fact that we only had five serviceable aeroplanes meant that we could not muster a patrol the next day. The mechanics had just recovered Wally's wreck when the German bombers appeared. Freddie led the five Camels into the sky while everyone else grabbed any weapon we could to throw a hail of bullets in the sky. It was an amazing sight. It was as though the whole squadron had decided that enough was enough. Even the cooks stood outside their tents shooting their Lee Enfields into the sky. The combination of ground fire and five Camels proved to be too much for the Halberstadts which were driven off with the loss of five shot down and only two new craters.

It energised the squadron and by the end of the day, all the damage of the two raids was repaired. However, poor Bates was distraught that he could not draw me a bath. The giant colander was a reminder for me that I had nearly lost not only a servant but a damned good friend.

Wally's propeller was serviceable and meant that I was available to fly the day after we were bombed. That was the day our new Camels and pilots arrived. Thanks to the mechanics we had nine Camels on patrol. We were not needed as the Hun did not return. We heard later that the French had launched an attack in the south and that had drawn the German's venom. We just needed time to regroup and reform.

The new pilots who bumped their way along our runway were welcome reinforcements but we knew that we would have a great deal of work to do with them. Archie took the decision that they would be spread amongst all the flights. "It is about time we started doing what Bill has done. We need to make the young lads into pilots."

On the day that we became the Royal Air Force, April the first, we were ready to become operational again. Ted was the one most amused by the change of name on April Fool's Day. Of all of us, he was the one who had changed the most since the war had begun. He was now rarely the pessimist and even tried to look on the positive side more often than not. We were all different people from the ones who had come to France in 1914. Ironically all of our new pilots had still been at school when the war had started.

We did not have the luxury of time to train the new pilots. Although the Offensive was slowing down it was not over. It would peter out by the fifth of April. I was lucky. I needed no replacements. It was decided that, when we went out on our first patrol on April second, I would provide top cover. We headed east. The line below us was now stable. Worryingly the Germans had not made an appearance for a day or two. This was partly because of the action close to the French sector and partly because we had hurt them. What I did know was that they would return and with a vengeance.

It was a cool day with cloud cover. I hated cloud cover. The Germans had a habit of hiding there. I led my flight; now the most experienced in the squadron, just below the clouds. I saw the rest of the squadron this time in lines of three as they headed north to south. I had enough confidence in my flight to head into the cloud. I waggled my wings so that Wally knew I was about to do something. The lower edges were thin enough for Wally to see me and the rest to see him. I used my watch to time myself. We were travelling at about two miles a minute. We were flying a leg of ten miles and then turning east. After five minutes I turned. I could see Wally behind me and I breathed a sigh of relief when he, too, turned. After another minute I waggled my wings and I descended.

As I came out I saw, below me, the Flying Circus. They were diving to attack Archie and the rest of the squadron. They had been seen for the Camels were climbing to engage them. I waggled my wings and then pushed the stick forward. We would have no time to stack our Camels. We would have to attack as soon as we could. Travelling from such a height gave us added speed and we began to catch up to the Fokkers which had a slower dive than we did. I doubted that they would be looking in their mirrors. After all, the only thing above them was the clouds!

It was the full Circus and I saw the Red Baron. He was too far away from me to attack but I saw one with a yellow rear which I targeted. This was the hardest part. I had to wait until I could not miss. If I fired too early then I would warn them and I might miss. These were the best pilots the Germans had. Voss had taken on eight pilots and nearly beaten them. Every one we shot down was irreplaceable. For the first time that I could remember we were trying to kill them. They were like a dangerous animal. They could not be caged; they had to be destroyed.

I waited until I was fifty yards from his tail and I gave him a good burst. His tail disappeared and he went into a spin. I left him. He was out of the battle and would be lucky to walk away even if he could get it down. I banked to port and aimed at the centre of the next triplane. He had seen me and he was desperately trying to lift his nose and bank towards me. He was flying superbly but I had a bead on him and I gave him a long burst. The bullets hit his fuselage and, as he turned, they stitched forward until they tore into his wing and his engine. I must have hit the pilot too for it began to spiral a death dive to earth.

I kept the turn going and, as each Fokker came into my sights, I fired. Wally could not fire at the same time but our oblique attack meant he, too, could fire at each Fokker as we passed.

I jerked the stick to starboard. To this day I still do not know why but bullets cracked along my port upper wing and the Red Baron screamed by. I took a snapshot. I have no idea if I hit him but I turned my Camel to follow him. If he was in my sights then I was not in his! He twisted and turned as he tried to evade me. He could not out-dive me and so he began to climb. The climb on the triplane was tremendous and even Sergeant Lowery's modifications could not catch him. His Achilles heel kicked in, his fuel ran low, and he began to head east. I started to catch him. I knew that I would have to give up the chase soon but I wanted him finished. Psychologically it would be worth more than a Fokker downed. He was an icon. I fired and hit his tail. He twisted and began to climb. Then he thought better of the waste of fuel and dived a little. As he did I fired again and hit his undercarriage. I was certain that with a few more minutes in the air, I would have had him but my fuel gauge screamed that I was running short of fuel. I turned and headed west. A hand came from the side of the cockpit and waved. He was ever the gentleman.

That was the last time I saw and fought the Red Baron. He died on the twenty-first of April shot down by an Australian machine-gunner. He was the best pilot I ever fought but our war became much easier the day he died. It seemed fitting that the finest fighter pilot on the Western Front was not shot down by a fellow flier but by a gunner with a lucky bullet.

Two of the new pilots did not make it. That was not a surprise but both Ted and Gordy were upset that their new pilots had lasted but one flight. Archie was just delighted that I had had the presence of mind to hide in the clouds. "Well done Bill. We knocked out four of the Circus. I know we lost two pilots but…"

I looked at Archie. It was too cynical. "I would rather we shot down fewer but that those two lads were still alive."

"So would I, laddie, but that isn't the way of the world. We can replace Harrison and White but the Germans will struggle to replace those four pilots."

It is sad that I did not even know that those were their names. The battle drifted to a quiet end. We had no more aerial battles and by the eighth, it was all over. We even had our two replacement pilots and

Headquarters were cock a hoop about our victory. It did not taste like victory to me.

We had little respite for, on the ninth, the Germans attacked further north. Seven thousand Portuguese troops were casualties as the Germans punched a hole towards the coast. At one point they were just fifteen miles from the sea. However, we were too far away to be involved in the defence of the ports and we were given the task of going on the offensive. Our job was to get over our old stamping ground of Cambrai and cause as much damage as we could to their supply lines. It was back to ground attack.

I saw the new armourer, Sergeant Raymond White. He was not Percy but he seemed a competent chap. "I need a couple of Mills bombs, sergeant."

He raised both eyebrows but his voice was calm, "Mills bombs sir?"

I sighed, I hated having to explain. Percy would have known why I wanted them and not questioned me. "Yes Sarn't, we are going to ground attack and I want something to lob over in case I find a defended gun position."

"I could fit some bomb racks, sir."

"No. It would add weight and affect the flying. I can carry the bombs in my coat."

"It isn't very safe."

I stared at him. "I have used Mills Bombs since 1915 and I am still here."

"Then you have been lucky, sir."

"Look, just get me a couple and that is an order!" I was aware that I had barked at him but he didn't react. "And I suspect some of the other more senior pilots may want them too." I smiled, "It is why we are so successful."

He sniffed, "Yes sir!"

I did not react well to change.

We knew that there was a railway line to the east of Cambrai. We were going to escort ten Airco DH 5 fighter bombers. Although designed as a fighter the strange position of the top wing made it vulnerable to attack from the rear. However, it was much faster than the Bristol and had a synchronised Vickers. I think HQ thought we might draw aeroplanes from the area around Messines. We would be bait.

Cambrai was now well behind the enemy front lines. All those gains of November had been lost and more. A few artillery pieces popped ineffectually at us. When we reached the railway line we let the Airco go in first while we watched for Huns. There were none.

As we were watching I saw smoke to the east and as soon as the Airco began to machine-gun the marshalling yards I led my flight east. It was a train. There were two machine-guns at each end and it had ten wagons. The driver had sensibly halted when he had seen the attack and as we approached he put it into reverse. It was a futile gesture as we raced along at over a hundred miles an hour. I took out one Mills bomb. There was little point in wasting bullets on an armoured train. I flew low and then lifted the nose to rise above the train. The machine-guns tried to fire at me but I was gone before they could bring their guns to bear. I dropped low when I had passed the train and I dropped my grenade before banking and sweeping around. I saw that the grenade had damaged the track. I flew just feet from the ground and sent my bullets into the two machine-gun crews. My flight was raking the train. Suddenly the rear carriage hit the twisted rails and the end wagons slewed off to the side. The engineer tried to brake. I had my second grenade ready and I dropped it into the engine. It must have bounced into the firebox for, as I zoomed away, the whole boiler erupted sending my bus into the air.

By the time I had recovered and turned the train was a burning shambles of twisted metal. We flew west looking for another target for our guns. We saw nothing worth wasting our bullets on and we headed back to our field. As we came over the German trenches I saw guns behind sandbags. I dropped to fifty feet above the ground and machine-gunned it. In my mirror, I saw the rest of the flight fire too and when we had resumed our flight the gun and crew had been destroyed. In many ways our action was petty but it would serve to make the Germans look to the area around Cambrai and bolster their defences.

When we landed there was an air of euphoria. We had managed to do our duty and no one had been hurt. Randolph had been surprised when we had returned to the field that the two bottles of whisky were still there. We opened one to celebrate. Randolph pointed to the map. "That is where the Huns are attacking. The squadrons up there are experiencing what we did."

It was not said with any joy. They would be suffering the kind of losses we had suffered. They would be losing young inexperienced pilots and they would be the fodder for the Fokkers.

Archie smiled as he lit his pipe. I knew that he was happiest when we had no losses. As the oldest man in the squadron, he was almost old enough to be the father to some of the young pilots. "Well, Randolph what do our lords and masters have planned for us tomorrow?" He frowned as a worry entered his head. "The buggers aren't sending us back to Cambrai, are they? The bloody Germans will be waiting for us."

"No, sir. It's the Albert canal. The Airco will drop the bombs on the bridges and any barges and we will deal with anything that comes our way." He toasted me, "Like Bill's train."

I smiled as I tapped out my pipe. "And I shall be asking the armourer for more Mills Bombs too!"

"He is right Bill, you would be better off with bomb racks. You could do more damage."

I shook my head, "We are a fighter and it would spoil the manoeuvrability of the Camel."

"Well far be it for me to argue with an ace but I am having a couple of racks fitted. I'll do whatever I can to end this war quickly."

Eventually half of the squadron chose to have bomb racks. It is like many things it worked at first but none of the pilots who had the bomb racks bothered to have them removed. It proved to be a mistake for they were not as manoeuvrable but that was in the future. We became a squadron with two roles ground attack pilots and then the others, A and C were the fighters. That evening, after dinner Freddie and Randolph sought me out.

"You know Bill that A and C have shot down more Germans than the rest of the squadron. If you look at the pilots who flew with you then you are responsible for seventy-five per cent of all the downed aeroplanes. That is quite a record."

"I didn't know that."

Freddie said, hesitantly, "I am thinking of staying in when all this is over sir. What do you think?"

I remembered my talk with the General. "I wasn't going to but you never know there may be a role for me."

Freddie became quite animated. "That is good news, sir. I think it would be a shame if the RAF lost your talents!"

"Yes, but will my talents be of any use in peacetime?"

Randolph began to fill his pipe again. My new mix was proving popular. "I think it is a little premature to think of peacetime. I thought that the war wouldn't last beyond 1916 but since the Russians made peace I can't see this war ending until the twenties."

"That is a depressing thought."

"The Germans are less than twenty miles from the sea. If they get to the coast then…"

I nodded, "Then we shall have to make sure that doesn't happen."

The Albert canal was a useful way to move heavy goods towards the front. Since their gains in the first weeks of the offensive, it was even more useful and provided their new gains with a direct supply route.

We took off before dawn. This was the closest target to Doyle Airfield and we were there as the sun came up. The Airco squadron arrived shortly after we did. While we waited we took the opportunity of shooting up the barges we found. They all sank to the bottom of the canal, effectively blocking it. They could be recovered but when the Airco arrived they bombed the bridges and the locks. The bomb racks had still to be fitted to Archie's Camels but they were not needed that day,

We were so close to our home base that we were able to sweep up to Vimy Ridge where the Canadians had lost so many men. It was just south of the new German offensive. I saw that the Germans had a spotter aeroplane up and so, while Archie and the rest of the squadron strafed the artillery I took my flight after the spotter. It was a Halberstadt. The pilot stood no chance in his slow bus and he headed for the ground as soon as we appeared. I let them land and then, as they ran from the aeroplane I dropped a grenade to blow it up. I would not claim it but I was pleased that I did not have to kill a pilot and observer. It didn't seem sporting.

We machine-gunned the ammunition for the artillery and headed home. Once again, we had hurt Fritz and escaped injury. April was beginning well. As we flew back we heard the enormous guns that the Germans were using to shell Paris. The war had suddenly come a lot closer to Britain and to the heart of France.

Chapter 24

For once what we were doing was working. A senior staff officer came from Headquarters to brief Archie and Randolph. We just had a patrol over Cambrai that day and we saw little of the enemy. The sector had quietened down. As we landed we saw the staff car heading back to Amiens. Curiosity got the better of us and Ted and I hurried to the office.

Randolph and Archie were studying a map. "Good, we need you chaps." Archie pointed the stem of his pipe at the map. "General Haig is rushing every soldier he can muster here, towards Loos and Festubert. It will be a Division cobbled together from British, ANZAC and American forces. Fritz has left his flank exposed. There will be no barrage. Instead, they will use us and other squadrons to ground attack. The Airco did a fine job the other day. We also have a couple of squadrons of the D.9. Our job is to keep the Hun off their backs. We leave before dawn so that we can be on station before the bombers and the ground troops go in. Freddie and his flight will be in reserve and will take off an hour after we do so that we always have a flight over the battlefield. We will be in the air all day tomorrow. Randolph will warn the ground crews. I am afraid it will be tea and sandwiches tomorrow."

I didn't mind. If it meant we got the offensive over sooner rather than later then I was happy.

Bates was ready with a flask as I headed for the bus. "It might be the middle of April sir, but it is still nippy. The soup will come in handy."

He was right. As I taxied and I rubbed my knee which always ached in the morning I reflected that his soup might well have been the difference between death and survival when I had crashed. The knee had not got much better nor had it worsened. Sir Michael had been right about the aches but at least I could manage without a stick now. I knew that if I did a lot of walking then I would need it but when I was flying it was unnecessary.

It was a chilly morning as we headed north. The first part of the German offensive had brought their front line to within five miles of where we were flying. Fortunately, they had not moved their squadrons forward yet. Their Fokkers, we had learned, could only stay in the air for an hour and a half. It had saved us thus far. We flew by dead reckoning and spiralled into the air when we reached the rendezvous area. I watched the sky lighten and then redden as dawn broke. I heard the throb of the Airco's engines as they flew from the west. With an endurance of over four hours, they could afford a safer airfield than ours. It would be the bombers who would initiate the attack. Once they had dropped their bombs then the ground troops would go in.

There were three squadrons of bombers. Two were the D9 and one was the D5. They went in waves. It was light enough to see that the Germans had captured territory and trenches but they had yet to improve the defences. The bombers were far more accurate than artillery. Each successive wave could see what the previous ones had achieved and they sought new targets. Even from our altitude, we could see the machine-gun companies being shredded by the bombers. When they had completed their work, it was the turn of Archie, Gordy and Ted to dive and use their Vickers to keep down the heads of the Germans. Although we were kept aloft watching for Germans I glanced at the ground from time to time and saw the waves of brown uniforms walking purposefully north. Thanks to the bombers and to the Camels there were no machine-guns to turn them into mincemeat.

Archie and the rest of the squadron headed south to refuel and rearm while we kept watch for German aeroplanes. It was hand to hand fighting below us but the allied forces had the advantage that the Germans had suffered an aerial bombardment and were weakened because of it. The whole intent of the attack was to weaken the flanks of the Germans and make them halt their advance. It looked like it was working.

The Fokkers arrived just fifteen minutes after the departure of Archie. They were the triplane along with a few of the older Fokkers. I waggled my wings and led my six aeroplanes down to attack them. The triplanes climbed to engage us. They would have to leave the party sooner than their comrades. We were stacked and I intended to make one pass over the triplanes and then engage the older buses. I pulled my triggers and banked to port at the same time. My bullets hit the wings and struts of the leading Fokker. Wally behind me was luckier. As I turned I saw that he had hit the pilot and the triplane tumbled to the ground.

As I fired at the next Fokker I felt bullets hit my fuselage. You learned to ignore them. I hit the tail of the Fokker which banked away, to starboard. I continued my bank and saw, below me, the three older Fokkers as they began to fire at the advancing allied soldiers. We were able to fly more than twenty miles an hour faster than they were and our altitude meant we were even quicker. We reached them before they had expended more than a dozen bullets. As we swooped we each fired in turn. My banking manoeuvre meant that I crossed all three of them. I kept firing knowing that they would have to endure the fire of six Camels.

When I passed the last, I began to climb. In my mirror, I saw that all three had been badly hit. None would reach home. Jack Fall had also been hit. I saw smoke coming from his engine and he was surrounded by triplanes. I led the other four to attack the Fokkers from underneath. As we fired I saw, to the south, Freddie and his flight as they came on station. The Fokkers stood no chance. Freddie was the hammer and we were the anvil. When three had fallen from the sky the remaining seven fled east pursued by a vengeful Freddie.

We headed south. I signalled for Wally to lead and I flew next to Jack. His bus coughed and spluttered but it kept going and when we saw the field ahead I knew that he would make it.

That first day we took off four times. Our numbers became depleted as the day wore on. It was not due to losses from enemy fire but the wear and tear of air time. The umbrella of Camels stayed aloft until dusk and the Germans were pushed back. Their offensive had stalled.

By the end of April, we felt that we had halted the German advance. We were, for the first time in a long time, stood down. Leave was granted, at least for some of the younger men. Gordy was a little resentful but I explained that many of the younger pilots had yet to have a leave. We were left with a skeleton squadron. We would only be needed if the Germans began another attack. Many of the ground crews were also given leave and the rest spent their time finishing the repairs to Doyle Airfield.

We also received mail. The German Offensive had upset the postal service and I had a whole day's worth of reading. It was a pleasant May morning and I sat outside my quarters. There was news in all of them but one had the most important piece of news.

Hyde Park
April 5th 1918,
Dearest Husband,
I hope that you are well. The newspapers are full of the news that the Germans have broken through! As I have not had a telegram and you haven't turned up injured at the hospital I assume that you are, at least, alive. I hope your knee is not giving you too much pain.

I have some wonderful news, at least I believe it is wonderful, we are going to have a baby in the autumn. You are to be a father. I know that you will be as happy as I am.

I have told no one yet, save Mary. They have rules about that sort of thing and I will have to leave the hospital. I am not showing yet and so I can carry on working. I would like to carry on for as long as I can.

Mary has said that I can stay with her in the short term but that is not an answer. What do you think?

I pray that God watches over you. You have even more reason now to survive this war.

I love you and go to bed at night thinking of you and yearning for your arms around me.

Your loving wife,
Beattie
xxx

I read the letter a dozen times to make sure I had understood it. I was to be a father. I would not be the last of the Harskers! I read the other letters from Alice, Sarah and mum but the only one I went back to was Beattie's. Then I thought of the ramifications. Where would she live? She was quite right she could not stay indefinitely at Mary's. It was not a large house and, besides, it was my responsibility. I saw a solution almost immediately. Burscough; she could stay with mum and dad. When the baby was born then I could look for a house although I had no idea how to either rent or buy.

I put pen to paper and wrote to mum, Sarah and Alice. I told them the news and then asked mum if Beattie could stay with them. I knew what the answer would be but I knew that they would expect to be asked. I then wrote a very long letter to Beattie. I think I managed to convey my joy and I told her of my plan. I almost ran to the office to have them sent. I knew that Randolph would have to censor them and so I told him my news. He was delighted for me and said, "I will do these in a jiffy! We celebrate in the mess tonight!"

Bates was even more pleased than even Randolph. He approved of my ideas and my plans. You would have thought he had a vested interest in the birth. It was as though the new baby would, in some way, be related to him! Needless to say, I had a distinctly bad head the next morning, as did the rest of the squadron. The fact that it was all the older pilots was reassuring. We had so much in common.

Archie had been particularly garrulous. He had three children of his own. He regaled us with stories of their childhood and his dreams and hopes for their future. It made all of us think, for the first time, of life after the war. Gordy was adamant that he, like Archie, would leave the service. "I shall open a garage. Trust me there will be a fortune to be made and I am still a handy mechanic."

"I will go back to the family farm. There's little on it now but I have saved a wee bit of money and I shall buy some sheep and highland cattle. I will be a laird."

The rest of us were all keen to stay in the new RAF although my impending responsibilities put some doubts in my mind. I would wait until the baby was born and then decide. There was little chance of the war being over by autumn. I would have plenty of time to make up my mind.

The young pilots returned from leave at about the same time that we heard the news that the Red Baron had been shot down. Surprisingly enough there was neither elation nor celebration. We all knew that he was a good pilot and when we heard he had been killed by ground fire it made us more aware than ever of our own mortality. Ground fire was like luck; it struck indiscriminately. Even the best pilot could die at the hands of a lucky machine-gunner.

May brought renewed attention from the German Jastas. They began to probe and attack the area just to the east of our field. Headquarters sent some heavier artillery pieces to deter the Hun. No one wanted us to decamp to a tented village again. At first, the Germans were cautious. Their numbers were too small for them to risk a combat with our twenty aeroplanes but their daily presence was a sure sign that they were up to something.

After one such patrol, I found Freddie talking to one of his young pilots, Jamie Fox. He was a likeable young pilot and he came not far from my home in Ormskirk. I waited until he had finished and then approached Freddie. "Problem?"

"Possibly. Before he went on leave he was reliable and very popular. Since he has returned he has become withdrawn and he has had a couple of fights and arguments with the other pilots. I caught him and Owen squaring up to each other this morning after the patrol."

"Can't have that."

"Quite. You know the Welshman, he is just serious. He isn't belligerent."

"Do you want me to have a word?"

He smiled, "No sir. It is my flight and my problem."

"Yes, Freddie but we can't have one bad apple at fifteen thousand feet. Pilots could die."

"I know. I will deal with it."

It was strange for the young pilots normally got on well with each other. We didn't have to deal with petty squabbles which I knew happened in other squadrons. I would let Freddie work things out but if it continued then I would do something about it.

It was in the second week of May that the Germans began to increase their aerial activity. Perhaps they had been stunned by the Red Baron's death and forced to reorganise but when they came they came in numbers. We were over La Fere. It was now well behind the German lines but it had been the front line a month earlier. We were looking for targets to strafe but Fritz had become warier and we saw no targets as we patrolled the skies. Freddie waggled his wings to signal that the enemy had been seen. I peered east and saw twenty odd German fighters. Half of them were the triplane but the other half looked different. They were not the older fighters we were used to. They were a new bus.

Archie led us higher to match their altitude. The Germans climbed higher. That was a worrying development. The new fighter looked to have a greater ceiling. I wondered if they had oxygen or heat in their cockpits for once you were above twenty thousand it was hard to breathe and almost impossible to keep warm. Archie wisely kept us circling rather than risking the higher altitude and its attendant dangers.

The Germans swooped down. I saw that the new bus had twin Spandau like the triplane. It appeared to be out diving the Fokker; that set alarm bells ringing in my head. Then we were amongst them and all such thoughts were driven from my mind as we just tried to survive.

The new bus was a bigger target. My first shots hit his wings but then he was passed me and firing at Wally. I banked to come around and get on his tail. My smaller size and turning circle meant I was able to do so quite quickly; he was not a triplane. I fired a second burst and hit him. I felt bullets cracking into my own tail and saw, in my mirror, that I had two triplanes close behind. I pulled up my nose to loop. The first Fokker was slow to take his fingers off his guns and I saw him hit the new German fighter. As I reached the top of the loop I flicked my Camel around and then side slipped to port. The move threw off the aim of the Fokker which was behind me. I banked to starboard and saw the second of my pursuers ahead of me, side-on. I gave a long burst. I hit his stays, his wires, his wing and finally the cockpit. The triplane seemed to disintegrate in the air. I kept the turn going and the first Fokker started to dive. I had more speed and I brought my Camel around to line up on his rear. He headed east. His fuel was running out. I fired again and hit his fuselage. Although twisting and turning I was hitting him.

Suddenly I felt my Camel judder. I looked in my mirror and saw the new fighter on my tail. He had a superior dive to me and I pulled back on the stick. I let the triplane go and I looped to get behind the new fighter. He could not out-turn me and he descended and headed east. It was over. We had met the new Fokker D.VII. The earlier ones we had fought in April had been improved. They were a formidable fighter. The Germans had regained their advantage.

I followed smoking Camels back to Doyle Airfield. I stayed well back as I was not certain that all of them would make it. I saw that Pearson and Herris, two of the new pilots had not made it but as I passed over the German lines I saw one pilot being marched east with his hands in the air. At least one of the new boys might survive the war.

I left the casualties being dealt with by Doc Brennan and his staff and a rueful Sergeant Lowery looking at the damage he would have to repair. Archie had the whisky open as I entered the office. "They are a nasty fighter!"

"And they have a better rate of descent than we do."

"Was it tough?"

"And then some, Randolph. They have a higher ceiling than we do."

"They must have oxygen and something to keep them warm."

"I don't know, Bill. Perhaps they are tougher than we are!"

Gordy and Ted came in. "Freddie is out of action for a couple of days and the miserable Welshman too. Both copped a bullet."

Gordy nodded his agreement. "I have three buses that will need serious repair before we can go up again."

"Right. Bill how about your lads?"

"I haven't checked yet but I think they were all down safely."

"Then tomorrow you take up Freddie's flight and I will go with Gordy and Ted." He held up a piece of paper. "We have to patrol two sectors tomorrow. They are sending down another squadron, SE 5s this time." He pointed to the west of us. "They are building them a field there. I think that was why they put the bigger guns here. I have a feeling we are going to be at the sharp end soon."

Chapter 25

It was worse than we had feared. Freddie would be grounded for a week and Owen for ten days, at least. Two of my Camels were out of action as they both needed new engines. It would be a depleted flight I led the next day. Poor Freddie was mortified. "I am sorry about this, sir." He held his bandaged arm up. "I am sure I could fly with one hand. You did."

"That was a Gunbus and I was stupid. You get better Freddie I will look after your boys. It is just Johnny and Jamie anyway."

He frowned, "I hope Jamie sorts himself out. We need him more than ever now."

"I'll have Jack chat to him. He has this ability to get on with anybody. It was him who turned George Jenkin around." George was now one of the most reliable pilots in the squadron.

My flight was given the task of flying over Noyon. It had been under our control some months earlier but now the Germans were doing something there and we were given the job of finding out what. The BE 2s who had been given the task of photographing it had been shot down. We would not have to take photographs but we would need to see what was going on. As we headed east I thought I could work out what was going on. Noyon was close to the section where the French and British lines met. Although there was close cooperation between both forces the language issue always caused a problem.

As we flew over I kept my eye to the east; I was wary of German fighters. I had the luxury of Johnny at the rear and he was the most dependable pilot in the flight. Jack flew behind Lieutenant Fox. I had not told him why but I asked him to keep an eye on him. As we neared Noyon I saw German tanks. They looked very similar to the ones that Bert had driven. The main difference was that they had sloping armour at the front. I saw many German vehicles and they appeared to be disgorging storm-troopers. We now recognised these for what they were; the prelude to an attack.

There were no fighters in the sky and I led my flight down to strafe the troops on the ground. As we swooped towards them they took cover behind the tanks. It was too late to pull out, we were committed to the attack and we all fired. Surprisingly the fact that our bullets struck the sloping sides of the German tanks worked in our favour. The bullets pinged and ricocheted and flew in all sorts of directions. One lucky ricochet managed to hit an ammunition truck and it exploded in a fiery ball. We had annoyed them enough and we headed home.

I left the pilots to examine the Camels for damage while I reported to Randolph. Archie still had the rest of the squadron out on patrol. "Something is up, Randolph. I saw tanks and storm-troopers. They have an attack planned and if I was a gambling man I would say it would be between us and the Frogs."

"I think you might be right. I'll get on to John."

I headed back to my quarters. As I was passing Jack's room I heard a commotion and Lieutenant Fox came hurtling out, nearly hitting me. He looked at me in horror and then ran outside.

I looked in Jack's room and my pilot was rubbing a red jaw. "What happened, Jack?"

"I am not certain, sir. I asked him into my room, like you said, for a chat and he chinned me when I started to ask him about home! I was just trying to get to know him."

"I'll have charges brought."

Jack shook his head, "No sir. Please. I was talking to his mates and they reckon this is girl trouble. Something went on at home. He seems a nice lad. I wouldn't want to get him in bother."

"He is in bother, Jack. No one hits one of my officers! But I will get to the bottom of this before I decide what to do."

I left the quarters and saw one of the mechanics. "Smith, did you see Lieutenant Fox leave here?"

He grinned, "Aye sir, he ran out as though he was a rabbit with dogs after him. He ran into yonder field." He pointed to the east.

"Thanks." I took out my pipe and began to fill it as I followed him. I was angry and annoyed. The pipe and the tobacco would take the edge off my tongue. Both Freddie and Jack had asked me to go easy on the young man. I would try.

I saw a tendril of smoke coming from behind the hedgerow. I left the field by the gate, walked along the lane and entered the next field. I saw the lieutenant with his head down, smoking next to the alder tree.

I walked towards him. He saw me and threw away the cigarette. In my mind, I had decided to have him arrested if he ran. He looked as though he was contemplating running but thought better of it and stood dejectedly waiting for me to reach him. The pipe had calmed me a little. I stood and looked at him. His head was down. I thought back to my childhood and I used the disappointed voice my father had used when he was talking to one of his sons who had done something wrong.

"It's Jamie isn't it?" He nodded. "Then look at me and give me a sir unless you are some sort of donkey!"

His head snapped up and he came to attention, "Yes sir, Jamie."

"That's better. Now before I really lose my temper, as you just did, and before I think of all the charges I could lay on you would you like to tell me what is going on? What happened on your leave to change you?"

He looked terrified. I remembered driving with Lord Burscough and almost hitting a deer which stared in terror at the headlights of his Singer. Fox had just such a look. The look was replaced by resignation, "It doesn't matter anyway sir. My life is already a mess. It can't get any worse."

I nodded and puffed on my pipe. "I can't see the wound, Fox."

"Wound sir?"

"Yes, I am thinking this must be a terrible wound you are concealing to make you sound so depressed. I mean is it worse than Mr Holt's eye? You didn't know him but is it worse than the loss of the hand that Lumpy Hutton suffered?"

"No, sir. No wound."

"And unless I am talking to a ghost then you are still alive so for the life of me I cannot see what is wrong."

He raised his voice, "Sir, you don't understand!"

I used my sergeant's voice as I barked, "Then damned well tell me and do it in a polite tone or so help me God I will forget myself and give you a good hiding myself!" He suddenly began to weep. It took me aback and I changed my tone to a more conciliatory one. "There's a girl I believe."

"I am sorry, sir. I shouldn't have shouted at you. There is no one I respect more than you. You are the reason I joined the Corps. My dad knows you. He drinks in your village pub and I wanted to be like you." I nodded. He was talking now and I didn't want to stop him. "There is a girl. She is lovely but her mum and dad are posh and think that a lad whose dad works on the land isn't good enough for her. Caroline, that's her name, loves me but she is only nineteen, like me. I wanted to marry her but her parents wouldn't let her."

"You just have to wait two years and then you can marry her."

"I can't wait. I mean too many lads die so young and I wanted… well, we couldn't wait." I waited. There was more to come. "We ran off to Gretna and we were married. That was the first day of my leave. We stayed in Carlisle as Mr and Mrs Fox." He looked embarrassed. "I didn't want the marriage annulled so…"

"I understand. Then what is the problem. You are married. It is what you wanted."

"I know, sir but when we got back to Ormskirk and told them they went off it. Her dad is the local magistrate you see. They wouldn't let her leave the house and the magistrate sent for the police."

"You didn't hit them, did you?"

"No sir, I'm not that daft. I went home and told me, dad."

"What did he say?"

"Just what you did, sir. That I should have waited."

"Well, you are going to have to wait now." He nodded. My pipe had gone out and I tapped the ash against the bole of the alder. "Right this is what you are going to do. First, you are going to go and apologise to Jack Fall. Then you are going to start doing your job. You are a pilot and a damned good one according to Mr Carrick." He started to open his mouth. "Now shut up and listen for once! You and I have a lot in common. I know how you were brought up and I think that this magistrate is wrong but your wife will be safe at home. They will not mistreat her, will they?" He shook his head. "Good. Now Lady Burscough is a friend of mine. I will write her a letter and ask her to see this magistrate. What is his name by the way?"

"Jeremiah Ramsden, sir."

"Well, she will have a word. I am not saying it will do any good but she is a well-known lady and has influence. If that does not work then I shall go with you on your next leave and we will try to sort it out. How's that?"

His face brightened, "That is good of you, sir."

"I am not certain it will do any good and I suspect that you will have to wait two years but it is a plan and is better than you going around trying to take on every pilot in the squadron."

He grinned, "Sir."

"Now go and apologise to Lieutenant Fall."

As I walked back to my quarters I began to write the letter to Lady Mary in my head. I felt sorry for Fox. I understood him. After all, I had got married on the spur of the moment. The difference was I had not gone against the wishes of anyone's parents. I hated snobbery but I was not sure if I had the power to change anything. The world was changing but not that fast.

Chapter 26

That evening in the mess, Jack sat next to Fox and he nodded and smiled when I entered. All was well. I would wait until I had my reply from Lady Mary until I spoke with Freddie. The real test would be when we were in the air again. If Fox was more reassured then his flying should show his old qualities. I knew that Freddie had confided in Johnny Holt and I asked him to give Fox the once over in the air. Johnny nodded and said, "I'll keep an eye on him, sir… my good one!" Nothing ever got Holt down.

We were ordered to go deeper into German territory and spy upon the build-up. The French had captured some German prisoners who reported an offensive in the offing. Headquarters had not known where that would be likely to be but our information made the southern Somme the favourite choice. If we could find more evidence from the German rear then we could prepare for yet another offensive. As we headed east I cursed the Russians for making peace. The war might have been over but for the cursed Revolution.

We headed for the area east of la Fere. It was within ten miles of the new front line and would provide evidence of enemy preparations. We flew in a stacked formation and I told Johnny Holt to watch the skies for enemy fighters. As soon as we crossed their front line I knew that they would be sending a message to the German Jastas. To aid confusion we flew south-east as we crossed the front line and then I headed northeast. We would still be spotted by any Germans but they would waste fuel searching in the wrong area.

There was a steady trickle of grey uniforms moving along the country lanes. They were heading west. As we flew over, they dived for cover, expecting the chatter of machine-guns. It was their lucky day; we sought bigger fish. We were ten miles from the front when we saw the tents which filled the empty fields. Here was the army which would launch the offensive. We banked to move south where I saw tanks and vehicles too. The only thing missing was cavalry. That was strange because if they made a breakthrough then cavalry were the best force to exploit a gap.

As we headed west I realised that a crucial breakthrough could take the Germans to Paris. Already being shelled an attack by Ludendorff might force the French to make peace and then Britain and Belgium would be isolated.

I glanced in my mirror and saw Jack and Johnny waggling their wings. It meant only one thing, German fighters. I could not see them but I knew that, in all likelihood, they would be coming from the southeast and that they would be higher than us. Our field was to the northwest and I gambled. Instead of rising to meet them, I began to bank and to dive towards the ground. We would outrun them. We were on the limit of our fuel anyway and it was not worth risking a fight with the information we had discovered in our heads. As we reached fifty feet I waggled my wings and waved for the pilots behind me to fly on. They waggled their wings to show they understood and, as I slowed down they overtook me until there was just Jack, Johnny and myself as the three rear Camels.

I could see the Fokkers in my rear mirror. There were ten triplanes and four of the new Fokkers. I signalled the other two to take station on either side of me. We were close enough for me to shout but our signals worked well and they obeyed. If I could get back without fighting I would but the moment I heard their Spandau I intended to loop and attack them head-on. The younger pilots were already half a mile ahead of me. I was certain I could hold the enemy up long enough for them to reach the field.

Suddenly ground fire erupted. The flight of the other Camels had alerted the soldiers and they were firing indiscriminately. I remembered what had happened to the Red Baron. The only way to stop them firing was to get amongst the Fokkers. I signalled for a loop and I pulled back on the stick. It was not a moment too soon for the Fokker D VII began to fire as I did so. The other two joined me and the bullets sailed harmlessly by. Our sudden move and the fact that they, too, were hedgehopping meant we took them by surprise. As I turned the top of the loop I saw them below me and I opened fire at the Fokker triplane below me. He was trying to loop too and my bullets struck his top wing and his cockpit. I finished my loop and found that I was behind a D.VII. He twisted and turned to avoid my bullets but the Camel could out twist anything but a triplane.

The D.VII was a tougher aeroplane than the triplane and it took a great deal of punishment. I felt bullets striking my bus from the Germans behind. Ahead I could see the airfield and I increased my speed to close with the D.VII and make it harder for my pursuer to shoot me and not hit his comrade. I did not have the luxury of being able to slow down for my landing. The German had to pull up suddenly when the machine-guns and artillery which ringed the field began to fire at him. The field was thankfully empty and I landed diagonally to give myself the maximum grass upon which to land.

Johnny and Jack had not attempted my foolhardy landing but they had split left and right to allow the gunners to pepper the air and the Germans with their fire. They peeled away with at least three smoking aeroplanes and headed east. Johnny and Jack were able to land more sedately than I did. My landing had taken me so far away that they were out of their Camels before I had taxied over to the rest of the aeroplanes.

"Interesting landing, sir!"

"I know Johnny. I hoped that the gunners could get a couple of them."

He nodded, "It looks like there is a push sir and it is coming in this direction."

"I know. I shall tell the Captain. Well done you two. I hope you suffered no damage."

"No, sir. Just a couple of holes in the wings. Nothing that can't be repaired."

Our news was confirmed by other spotters and we were ready on the twenty-seventh of May when the Germans attacked between Soissons and Rheims. The French bore the brunt to this attack along with six resting divisions. The whole front collapsed almost overnight and the Germans made the Marne River. Paris was now a possibility.

We spent every day from the twenty-seventh until the advance stopped on the eleventh of June in the air. We were fighting for our lives. In all that time we found ourselves fighting not German aeroplanes but German ground troops as we were used as aerial artillery. After the initial loss of territory, the French counterattacked with their own tanks. We went in with them. We had learned how to deal with the German counterattacks. We flew low over the tanks and machine-gunned the storm-troopers who tried to surround each tank and kill its crew. The storm-troopers were brave and they were tough but .303 bullets from a pair of Vickers can reduce a man to a bloody wreck in seconds. Gradually we wore them down and the attacks stopped. By the time we had beaten back the hordes, we were down to four Camels which were able to fly. The rest needed the care and attention of more mechanics than we had at our disposal. Our sister squadron, flying the SE 5 had suffered even more. Their larger size had meant that four had been shot down and they only had two serviceable aeroplanes left.

We all thanked God when, on June twelfth, we were stood down.

Once more the Offensive had disrupted the flow of letters from home and I received a large number. They were all out of order. Beattie's told me that she was now staying with Mary and that her days as a nurse were, temporarily over. I had arranged to have some of my pay sent to Mary's for I did not want my wife living on charity. Mum, of course, had said that she would be delighted to have Beattie staying with her and I found, in my letters, the letter from Beattie telling me that she would be travelling to Burscough in June. I felt a deep sense of relief. I was not unhappy with Beattie staying with Mary but family was family. My two sisters and my unborn child's cousin lived close by. It was right that a Harsker should be born at Burscough. The letters from my sisters showed their unbounded joy. I left Lady Mary's letter until last for I was dreading reading it.

Lieutenant Fox had been a changed man since my talk with him. When Freddie returned to duty he was as delighted as anyone that his fine young pilot was back in the cockpit both physically and mentally. Like me, he worried about the future. I was a coward. I did not want to read the letter alone and I sought out Freddie. We went to an empty mess and had a beer while I read it. The letter did not make pleasant reading.

"It seems that Jeremiah Ramsden is as dour as his name sounds. He was polite to Lady Mary but refused to countenance reconciliation with Lieutenant Fox. As far as he was concerned they would not be together even when she was twenty-one." I read the next paragraph and threw it down. "Damn!"

"What is it?"

I picked it up again. "Apparently Lady Mary managed a few words with this Caroline. She told Lady Mary, in confidence that she was convinced that she was with child. She has not told her parents."

"Surely that will make a difference."

"Lady Mary thinks not!" I finished off my beer. "That leaves us a problem. Do we tell young Fox that his wife is pregnant?"

"He might run."

"He might. The thing is the baby won't be born until almost Christmas. Much can happen in the meantime." I looked at Freddie. "He is in your flight. I leave the decision to you." It was the most cowardly thing I ever did and one of the few decisions which I came to regret. Freddie nodded.

The next day began what was to become an attempt to retake the land recently captured by the Germans. The Americans had entered the war in greater numbers and were supporting the French. General Foch counterattacked the Germans at Soissons. I suppose we should have felt honoured that we were requested as support for the French but it did not feel that way. To be fair to the generals at Amiens we were close to the French sector and we had supported them before. I had been honoured for my work with a medal but it would also bring us into contact with

Jasta I. Although the Red Baron was dead his legacy remained and we would be going up against the best pilots the Germans had. They were replacing the Fokker Triplane with new buses and although they did not have them in large numbers they were highly effective as fighters. General Trenchard kept trying to get Archie to change to the SE 5. He said he would keep the Camels. We liked them.

Our role was simple. We had to keep the German aeroplanes away from the French and Americans. It meant two sorties a day and tiredness soon became a factor.

We were back to full strength and our wounded pilots returned. The replacements had arrived and, once again, I had the most experienced flight. We took off at the beginning of July and headed south and east. We now knew that we could not get above the German fighters and we had to resort to other tactics. Each flight had a different sector but we were close enough to see the others. I was in the centre with Freddie to my starboard and Ted to port. I kept the line astern stacked above me. My pilots liked it and it had been lucky for us.

I saw some Rumpler bombers escorted by a mixture of the new Fokkers and the older triplanes. They were heading west for the Marne. Waggling my wings, I led my flight towards them. The newer fighters came directly for us while the Fokkers gave close protection to the vulnerable two-seaters. There were eight of the Fokker D. VII. I hoped that Freddie would see the bombers and deal with them. We would have our hands full.

The only slight advantage we had was that the Germans were a bigger target but they could fly slightly faster than we could and were damned hard to knock out of the sky. All the fighters we met these days had fantastic paint schemes and it was hard to tell who you were fighting. Some of the ones we fought that day had a strange design we later discovered was called a Swastika. The design actually helped us for you had another target apart from the German cross.

The extra height and speed of the German fighters brought them down to us remarkably quickly. They seemed to fill the air. The ones on the extreme side of the flight fired their guns at me at the same time that the leader did. I felt the bullets as they hit my wings and my fuselage. I was lucky for I did not detect any damage or deterioration in performance. I kept my nerve and did not fire until we were just forty yards apart. My bullets hit his engine and then Wally's hit the pilot. His garishly painted Fokker went into a dive beneath me. In my mirror, I saw Wally's Camel struck by many bullets. He was not as lucky as I was and his engine started to smoke. He was now an old hand and he banked to starboard. He would head home.

Without my wingman, I had little choice. I flew my Camel directly at the Fokker to my right. Once again, I risked a collision and, once again, the German pilot took evasive action. As he presented his side to me I fired from close range and saw his struts and wires severed. His top wing began to flex alarmingly and I saw the pilot trying to control his damaged bird. He pulled the aeroplane to port and I fired at his Swastika. I was so close that my twin Vickers tore a hole in the side. I had to jerk my nose up as I nearly collided with a third Fokker. I saw the one that I had damaged spiral slowly to earth. He might land but it would not be at his own airfield. I turned to starboard to attempt to fire at the Fokker I had just missed. He must have flown into Jack Fall's gun sights for his propeller disappeared as the .303 tore into it. Another Fokker fell from the sky and then it was empty.

I was feeling pleased with myself when I saw Lieutenant Fielding's Camel burning on the ground. I had lost one of my young lads. I had hoped to have them all last until the end of the war but it was not meant to be. Poor Gordy's flight had fared even worse; Lieutenant Wilson and Lieutenant Smart had both died. They were new pilots who had lasted a mere week in France. The Western Front was a cruel teacher.

The messages from the French were appreciative. We had stopped the bombers getting through. All of them had been destroyed. This would be the last throw of the dice for the Germans and they were throwing all that they had at the Americans and the French.

We went up again the next day and this time we were joined by SE 5s and Spad VIII flown by Americans. This was the largest force we had flown with. We encompassed a large part of the battlefield. Our task was to knock out any German aeroplanes and then ground attack. That July morning was an air battle! A whole Jasta came to sweep us from the air. There were well over fifty German aeroplanes of varying types. The three allied squadrons each adopted different formations while the Germans relied on their line abreast. That difference was to prove crucial.

Once a battle in the air begins it becomes small. A pilot sees the enemy before him and his comrades in his mirror. I had no idea how the Americans and the SE 5s fought that day. I did not know what had happened to my squadron until we landed. We just flew, fought and, in some cases died. When we ran out of fuel we returned home. It was a very personal battle.

We were on the extreme right of the line while the Americans were on the right. We had begun to climb as soon as we saw the Germans but the Americans were new to this deadly battle in the air and were slower to rise. Our climb and the Germans coincided so that we reached ten thousand feet at the same time. Once again Freddie and I were the centre of our line and we both fired at the same time. We were a hundred yards from the enemy. It was a longer range than we normally used but there were so many German aeroplanes that I thought we might get lucky and hit some in the rear. Wally fired a moment after I did. We both hit the struts and the wings of the Fokker. I threw my Camel on to its side and the manoeuvre threw off the aim of the German pilot. His bullets hit the space where my wings had been a moment earlier. I banked slightly and fired from a range of just forty feet as he sped by. My bullets punched a hole in his fuselage. I straightened up. The next German's bullets zoomed over my head and, in my mirror, I saw them strike the undercarriage of Wally's bus. I fired a long burst as we closed with each other. The tracer showed me that I was hitting him and he flew into my bullets. Smoke came from his engine as Wally added to my fire.

Suddenly there was an empty sky before me. I banked to my right and watched as my four pilots attempted to follow me. Jack's Camel was riddled by the fire of three Germans but I saw no smoke and we were through. We were behind the Germans who were trying to get to the larger formation of SE 5s. I could not see Freddie but I guessed that he was engaged with his own personal battle.

There were five Fokker triplanes. They were holding their line well. Our speed had taken them by surprise and they must have thought that the air to their starboard side was occupied by the D.VII we had just attacked. Whatever the reason we had a clear shot. I flew obliquely across them so that all five of us could fire at each one in turn. That one attack in July 1918 resulted in more kills for my flight than any other day of the war.

I opened fired and just held down the triggers. The Fokkers tried to dive away from the barrage of bullets but we could out dive them. As I came behind the last Fokker on the extreme left of the five I followed him down. He twisted and turned but to no avail. I stopped firing only when my ammunition ran out. I had begun to think that the pilot had a charmed life when I saw the ground approaching rapidly. I pulled the nose up. The concussion from the crashing Fokker lifted me into the air and I headed west.

Below me, I saw the storm-troopers running into the brick wall that was the American defenders of the wood close to Soissons. The Americans had not tasted defeat and had not retreated almost to the sea as we had. They had stood firm. I waggled my wings as I passed over them.

Having fired my bullets so quickly I was the first one back and I filled my pipe as I anxiously awaited the return of my boys. All four appeared but Jack's had smoke coming from his engine and I remembered that Wally had had his undercarriage hit.

"Senior Flight Sergeant Lowery, Mr Grey has had damage to his undercarriage. He may need some help!"

"Sir! Right you lot, get ready. We might have to get the young officer out in a hurry!"

I saw them watching for Wally's bus as the four of them touched down. As we had feared the damage meant that the wheels collapsed as it hit the ground. The nose dipped alarmingly and I feared that the Camel would cartwheel but, instead, the tail dug into the ground and it slewed and spun across the field. It made a giant fairy circle in the grass. The mechanics were close enough to race and pull the pilot from the wreckage before it exploded. Fortunately, it did not and I could afford a smile. That day had been a good one. We had lost no pilots!

Ted had lost one pilot. Paul Ferry had been with us for some time and I had begun to hope that he might survive the war. We had lost almost a quarter of our pilots in the last month. That was the last time we went aloft in what became known as the Spring Offensive. The German High Command had gambled and lost. Not only had they lost many of their elite ground troops they had also lost the initiative in the air. We had knocked out many of their new fighters and a lack of fuel would restrict their flights until the end of the war. It was the middle of July and we had held the German war machine. August would bring a huge change both in our tactics and our lives.

Chapter 27

It was lucky that we were not required the next day for we could only field four serviceable aeroplanes. The ground crews worked around the clock to repair them. We were told that the replacement Camels and pilots would arrive by the first week in August. It should have been a pleasant time. The weather was fine and we had no enemies to fight. The SE 5 squadron took over the patrols and they saw no one in the air. The Germans were licking their wounds and, like us, awaiting replacements.

Freddie took the lull to tell Fox of his situation. He did not take it well. The last month had seen a change in him but after Freddie told him the young man stormed off. He was like a petulant child. Freddie was quite upset. "I hope I did the right thing, sir. I mean, perhaps I shouldn't have told him."

"He was bound to find out sooner or later. I'll have a word with him." Freddie looked at me questioningly. "I am going to be a dad too." I shrugged, "Perhaps it can be a bridge. It is worth a try. The alternative is to relieve him of duty and he is too good a pilot to lose."

I knew where he would be. The tendril of smoke gave him away. As I walked up to him I shook my head. "You can't just keep running away can you, Jamie?"

"But my wife is going to have a child and I cannot be with her!"

"And Captain Hewitt was over here when his child was born. In case you didn't know, Jamie, my wife is expecting and I haven't seen her since February. There is a war on and we all have to make sacrifices." He took the stub of his cigarette and ground it into the soil. "You may not like her mother and father but she is safe there is she not?" He nodded. "And you could do nothing even if you were there. I am in the same boat. I daresay that by the time I get my next leave my child may be months old."

His shoulders slumped, "You are right, sir."

"Come on let us get back to the field. I cannot believe that they will leave us inactive for too long. We shall have new pilots coming soon, Jamie, and they will look to you for help and advice. Do for them what others did for you eh?"

"Yes sir."

We were given less than three days to recover and then we were sent with a flight of Bristols to photograph the German lines. It did not take a genius to work out that the brass were looking at the weaknesses.

There would be an offensive. It turned out to be an easy patrol. The Germans came nowhere near us. Although we were a depleted squadron the Germans had come to respect our Camels. As we flew high over the Somme I could see the weaknesses for myself. The Germans had salients. The straight lines they had left to advance were now bulges in our lines. With the extra troops from America and the reinforcements who had joined us from the Middle East, we were now in the position of the Germans when the Russians had made peace. Because we were not disturbed the Bristols managed to photograph the whole sector.

Archie had not flown with us. His Camel had required an engine replacement. We sat in his office and showed him what we had seen. "Then it looks like this will be a short holiday for us." He looked at the four of us. "I wish I had let you four go on leave when it was quiet. I can't see us having time for leave any time in the near future."

I shrugged, "If it brings this war to a close then I am willing to make the sacrifice."

Gordy shook his head, "My child is growing up and I am not there."

Archie stood and poured him a whisky. "Laddie I went away with a bairn who was still gurgling and came back to a son in short trousers. If you are serving then that is the way of the world. The days of wives tramping all over the world after their husbands is a thing of the past."

"And that is why I am not staying in. As soon as I can I am getting out."

"And I don't blame you. For me, it was a career and my brother was running the estate. It'll be mine now and I like you Gordy; the minute hostilities cease I will put in my papers. I will become a gentleman of leisure."

Two days later Archie and Randolph were summoned to Headquarters and, ominously, our replacements arrived. The Offensive was on. We did not know it at the time but we would be attacking until the war ended.

They arrived back too late to brief us. We had spent the day organising the new fliers and finding out how little experience they had. When we were briefed we saw the enormity of our task.

"We have to keep the Germans behind the Hindenburg line occupied so that they cannot reinforce their front!"

Ted almost choked on his whisky, "But that is twenty miles behind the German lines!"

"I know Ted but the offensive is going to begin here in this sector. It has to be a complete surprise. The Hun will think we are licking our wounds after their offensive failed. The troops and the tanks go over the top on August the eighth!"

"Bloody hell that doesn't give us long."

"I know. For that reason, we are flying as flights. We fly staggered so that there is always a flight in the air. We fly from dawn until dusk."

I tapped out my pipe. "Of course we have a bunch of new pilots too, sir."

Archie nodded, sadly, "I know and we can do nothing to protect them. Number 15 squadron will help us out and hopefully, the new Yank squadrons will fill in further south. We are not alone and thanks to buses coming back from Palestine we have almost thirty-eight squadrons. It is not as bleak as you might think."

There was a distinct lack of enthusiasm. I was luckier than the rest. I just had one new pilot, Lieutenant Ralph Carter. I had Jack Fall keep an eye on him.

When I got to my quarters Bates was in a particularly good mood, "You are happy, Bates."

"Yes sir. I had a letter from your mother. She is so happy now that your good lady is living with them. With your nephew in the house too she sounds like a young woman again. I think it has been a very wise decision."

I couldn't help thinking about poor Lieutenant Fox. I had a supportive family and my wife was happy. Jamie's wife was unhappy and kept a prisoner so that she could not even send a letter to her husband. I thanked my lucky stars.

We were the first flight up the next day and we headed towards Bapaume. I kept us as high as I dared. The days were almost fourteen hours long and this would be an incredibly arduous day; especially for the new pilots.

We had half an hour left before we were relieved when we saw the five Albatros appear on the horizon. Our early start meant we were on station before they were. We had been told to be aggressive and I led my stacked flight east. I frowned when I saw that my new pilot was not as high as he should have been. He would not be able to add his fire to that of Lieutenant Dundas. Still, it was his first flight and we would have to have a word when we landed.

The five Albatros came on. We knew we had the beating of them and they must have had the same feeling we had once had when facing the triplane for the first time. I saw that they were struggling to climb. It was a fault on some of the older German fighters. It meant we had the height and when I dived our acceleration was so great that we must have appeared to be a blur. I aimed for the bird on the extreme left of the German line. I fired and began to bank at the same time. The German line tried to react but their slow rate of climb and our speed

1918 We Will Remember Them

whipped us from their sights in an instant. Wally's bullets killed the pilot as I lined up on the second one. The remaining four Albatros had no targets for we were coming in at an angle. It was as though someone had startled some gulls. The Germans flew in every direction. I saw two falling to earth and another smoking. Only one had evaded being damaged.

I turned to starboard and headed for the rendezvous point. We were too low on fuel to chase them.

When we landed we had time for food but I took young Carter to one side. He was exuberant, "I say, sir, that was easy! Is it always like that?"

"No Lieutenant Carter." I sighed. I hated to deflate him but I had to for his own sake. "This is not training, Lieutenant. You have to keep station."

"But I did sir. I was on Lieutenant Dundas' tail as I was ordered."

"But you weren't stacked above him." He looked puzzled. "If you are stacked then you can add your fire to the Camel in front. If the Hun tries to climb then you get an easy kill."

I saw enlightenment dawn, "That is how the flight managed to down three of them so quickly. Sorry, sir. I didn't realise."

"This is a hard school, Lieutenant. You learn quickly or you are dead. Watch it when we go up again later on."

He looked surprised, "We are going up again, sir?"

I laughed, "Welcome to the sharp end of the war."

It was a war of attrition in those five days before the offensive began. It took its toll on the Camels and, after the first day, we flew with fewer buses but we still kept knocking down the Germans and they saw nothing of our preparations. We never saw more than eight of them. Perhaps it was true that they were running out of fuel or perhaps we had knocked too many of them from the sky and they couldn't replace them. Certainly, the first week of August was an easy time for us. It would not remain that way.

One thing we noticed about the new pilots was their new uniforms. They were RAF. They were not vastly different to ours but they showed a change. Our world was changing.

We only had twenty Camels ready for the day of the offensive. It would begin at four o'clock in the morning. There would be a creeping barrage and then an attack by tanks, infantry and ground attack aeroplanes. We knew, from flying over the battlefield, that the Germans had not consolidated their new gains. They had only had them for a few weeks. They liked to make formidable defences and so far, our attacks had not allowed them to do so. It was hoped that the surprise would work in our favour for once.

We waited behind the British lines as the barrage began and the tanks rolled forward. We were high enough to see the shells strike the German trenches and destroy the machine-guns. The ground over which the tanks trundled was flat and it was dry. Cambrai had been boggy and lessons had been learned. As the barrage crept forward we flew diagonally across the battlefield machine-gunning any storm-troopers who attempted to attack the tanks. There were fewer of these elite troops this time. They rolled on with a mixture of Australian, Canadian and British troops marching steadfastly east. By the time we had to return to refuel the offensive had managed to punch a hole fifteen miles wide. It was unprecedented. As we returned to the battle in the afternoon we saw that the SE 5s had had a dogfight with the Germans and there were damaged and destroyed aeroplanes littering the battlefield but still the tanks rolled forward. They only stopped when they ran out of fuel and we turned for home with the soldiers digging in for the night.

It went on like that for three days. Finally, the offensive stopped, having gained twelve miles. We had outrun our supplies but, for the first time, we had defeated the Germans. We had made substantial gains. Over thirty thousand Germans had been killed wounded or captured for the loss of just six and a half thousand. We began to dream that we might win the war.

Of course, Fate has a way of waiting until you dream before giving you a nightmare. Poor Lieutenant Fox received a letter from home; a letter from his wife. Fortunately, he was in the mess when he read the letter. He suddenly stood and shouted, "Bastard!" He tried to run out. Enough of the pilots now knew of his dilemma and Jack and Jonny restrained him. Johnny had a laconic manner about him and he said, "I say, old boy, what's the matter?"

I was seated in an armchair and I saw that Jamie was weeping. He thrust the letter at Johnny. Johnny read it and then put his arm around Jamie. "You ought to read this, sir."

Freddie had walked over to his young pilot and he took the letter. He shook his head in disbelief and came to me, "It is from his wife sir. It seems her father found out she was pregnant and threw her out on the street. She is in the workhouse in Wigan."

If I had had the magistrate before me I would have done more than horsewhip him. However, I needed to do something more positive. "Freddie, I shall try to remedy this situation but you and the others need to stop him doing anything stupid. Tell him that I have a plan and he has to trust me."

"Sir, and thank you." This was something way out of Freddie's experience.

I ran to the office. "Randolph, I need to get to Amiens. I'll be back as soon as I can."

Randolph knew me well enough not to question me. "Of course. Anything I can do?"

"See Freddie and then you will understand."

By the time I got back, I had missed dinner and it was late but I had done what I could. The mess was like a funeral parlour. Everyone was there and Archie was glowering at Jamie who sat between Freddie and Gordy. There had obviously been words exchanged. I just hoped that Jamie had not been insolent. Archie was a fair officer but he had been in the service his whole life. Insubordination did not sit well with a career officer. Jamie looked up as I entered. It was bizarre because everyone was waiting for me to speak. I should have spoken with Jamie privately but there was no way I could do that.

"I have sent a telegram to my wife and Lady Burscough I have asked them to go to Wigan and bring your wife to my home. They won't be able to get there until tomorrow." I spread my arms. "It was the best that I could do, Lieutenant Fox but I believe your wife will be both safe and cared for."

In a small voice, Jamie said, "Thank you, sir. I owe you more than I can say."

I looked at Archie as I said, "Well you had better get to bed lieutenant we are flying tomorrow."

"Yes sir." He faced Archie, "Sorry sir I…"

Archie waved an irritated hand, "Oh get to bed you wee silly man!"

After he had gone Archie said, "He came within a whisker of being put on a fizzer! What an idiot!"

Freddie shook his head, "Sir, he is young and life has not been kind to him."

"You make the best of what you have. Look at Johnny there. He lost an eye and he doesn't let it upset him."

I knew what Archie meant but it was like comparing apples with oranges. I was sure that if Jamie had suffered an injury like Johnny then he too would have dealt with it. This was different for someone he loved was being hurt and he could do nothing about it.

On the eighteenth, we prepared to take on the Germans east of Amiens. We knew from our recent visits to Amiens that the Tommie's tails were up and confidence was high. Had it not been for Jamie Fox then ours, too, would have been high. As it was we went about work efficiently rather than enthusiastically.

With a full squadron, we flew toward Albert. The tanks were eating up No Man's Land and the lines of soldiers were marching purposefully behind them. We flew in four lines abreast machine-gunning the area just in front of the tanks. I kept glancing to the east and I saw the twelve Fokker D.VII's as they dived towards us. I began to climb, knowing that my flight would follow me. I knew that I would have to be careful with my guns as I had probably expended half of it already.

The Fokker fired early and I felt his bullets as they hit my struts. I had to hold my fire a little longer and so I used my old trick of dipping my nose and then bringing it up sharply. It seemed to work as the Fokkers Spandaus sent their bullets below me. I saw him begin to turn to his left. I mirrored him with a turn to starboard. As soon as I saw the German cross in the fuselage I fired. The nippy little Camel turned quicker than the Fokker and my bullets stitched a line towards his cockpit. I saw him clutch his arm and swing to port. I fired again and hit his tail. My guns were empty and I too turned to head home.

As I levelled out I felt bullets strike my tail. I looked in my mirror and saw that I had a German behind me. I had no wingman and no ammunition. The Fokker was faster than I was. I pulled back hard on the stick and looped. I gave the Camel all the power that I had. The Fokker tried to copy my turn but he was bigger and heavier. I turned inside him. I reached into my greatcoat and took out my Luger. As he looped above me I held up the gun and emptied the magazine. I must have hit something for, in my mirror, as I zoomed beneath the slower Hun, I saw him wobble and it took him some time to right himself. I had bought myself some time and I headed to ground level as quickly as I could. When he levelled out, the German headed east. I daresay his mess would be surprised when he told them of my actions. Perhaps they would wonder why a British pilot was firing 9mm bullets at him.

Chapter 28

Once we had captured Albert our job became easier. We just had to fly patrols above the Allied soldiers who were consolidating their gains. We made sure that the German reconnaissance aeroplanes kept their distance and that they did not attempt to retake the trenches. We had learned the lessons of Cambrai.

I walked into the mess on the twenty-third of August holding a telegram. Lieutenant Fox was chain-smoking. "Your wife is safe, Lieutenant Fox. Lady Burscough and my wife have taken her to my parents' home. She will be looked after."

Even before he spoke I saw the gratitude in his eyes. His fellow pilots looked relieved. It must have been like sitting with a ticking time bomb. Before he could speak I said harshly "I have done what I promised now stop feeling sorry for yourself and start to do your job."

He stiffened to attention and said, with a smile on his face, "Yes sir!"

The French began their own advance in the south and soon, they too, along with the Americans were driving the Germans back to the Hindenburg line. Their Spring Offensive had backfired. They had lost all the ground they had gained and far more troops than we had. Their army was bleeding to death and there was no one to staunch the wound.

We, too, were suffering. Two flights a day took it out of the pilots and the Camels. Even the new pilots were exhausted whilst those who had not had a leave since February looked like walking skeletons. There were many petty arguments and we were in great danger of losing our esprit de corps.

Archie called his flight commanders into his office on the evening of the twenty-fourth of August. "Look, laddies, we have to go up again tomorrow. Arras this time. We need to lift the men's spirits. Any ideas?"

"Sir, when we stand down again how about a party? If we tell the chaps now it will give them something to look forward to."

"Good idea, Freddie."

"I will get Bates to go into Amiens and get some decent wine and some cheese. Make it special."

"That's the spirit, Bill. I have seen this before. The lads are like a piece of steel it is tough but one more bit of pressure and it could snap. I thought that when the Fox thing was sorted out everything would be hunky-dory but I was wrong."

Randolph tapped out his pipe on the ashtray. "They are exhausted sir and exhausted men bite too easily. Perhaps if we were less snappy in the mess…"

Archie glared at Randolph, "Do you mean me, Captain?"

No one said a word but we all remembered the way he had dealt with Lieutenant Fox. Archie was a good man at heart and I saw him gradually subside as he realised that what we were saying was true. "Aye, it might be true. I wonder if the fact that this war seems to be drawing to a close is making me demob happy. You might be right. Aye well, I shall be a happy chappie in the mess from now on. I might even wear my kilt!"

Ted shook his head, "No need to go so far, sir. A smile will do! I am not certain I could cope with your bare legs!"

As we moved east to clear the skies of the Germans again we noticed the heavy ordnance being moved forward. There was purpose on the ground below us. We had been briefed to press as far to the east as our fuel would safely take us. It was a provocative move intended to make the Germans come from their fields to attack us. What we had seen was the lack of ground fire. Perhaps Intelligence was right and the Germans were not just running out of fuel but also ammunition. We all began to believe that there was a chance that this war might be over by 1919. I might see my child before he started walking.

German fighters were summoned when we neared Cambrai. We saw stiffened defences around this town which guarded the approaches to the railway which was so vital to the Germans. We had no doubt that it had been repaired since our raid. The proximity of the aeroplanes and the guns which ringed the town were a testament to that.

Having flown so far, we only had a short time over the town and so we were profligate with our bullets. We could afford to fire at range. We had the luxury of plentiful fuel; the Germans did not. We still had yet to see vast numbers of the new German aeroplanes and we faced the usual eclectic mix of fighters. I fired at a hundred yards range and I flew directly at the Albatros I chose to attack. He was conserving his bullets and he held his fire until he was much closer. Wally's bullets poured into him before he had fired a couple of rounds. He peeled off with a smoking engine. I banked to starboard and gave a long burst at the old Fokker D. II. The .303 tore through his struts and into the fuselage. Something must have been damaged for it began to fall to earth as the pilot struggled to control it.

We were not getting all our own way however and I saw Lieutenant Garrington tumble to the ground. It looked like he would land but he would be a prisoner. I emptied my guns at the last Albatros in the line and he took flight east. He must have realised that there were ten other Vickers machine guns coming his way.

After two more days of such fighting, the ground forces were almost at the Hindenburg line and we had time for a party as we were stood down. The Germans were reeling from attacks which had begun at the start of August. Now as August drew to a close we had regained all the land we had lost in the Spring Offensive and more. More importantly, we had barely lost either men on the ground or aeroplanes in the air. Every day, as we returned to our field we saw lines of prisoners being led west.

The mess sergeants enjoyed organising the food for the party. It was something different and they knew that there would always be a surplus for them. As Bates laid out my dress uniform he commented, "This was a good idea, Major. I had noticed many of the young gentlemen having a hangdog look of late. This will reinvigorate them."

Bates was the most wonderful observer of human behaviour. He was like the squadron barometer and I had learned to listen to him whenever possible.

He coughed discreetly and asked, "Has Lieutenant Fox's dilemma been solved, sir?"

"Dilemma?" I cocked an eyebrow.

Bates looked a little embarrassed, "Sir, it is no secret that he married and his young lady was taken away from him. Everyone saw the change in him. Why I even heard that he and Lieutenant Fall had an exchange of views."

I smiled at the euphemism, "Yes Bates, the dilemma has been temporarily solved." I knew that he would receive a letter from my mother soon and then the cat would truly be out of the bag. "If you must know Lieutenant Fox's wife is staying at the cottage in Burscough with my wife and mother so you can put your mind to rest. She will be well looked after."

He beamed, "Oh sir, you are like Solomon. You can solve the most difficult of problems!"

I shook my head and left for the party. I was not in the mood for a party and I stayed on the side-lines so to speak and observed them all. Part of it was sadness. The last party we had held had been some time ago and Charlie had still been alive. He had been the life and soul of the party entertaining all with his ribald music hall songs. I had even sung one myself when testing the radio with Sergeant Kenny. Would I have the spectre of Charlie's memory hanging over me each time we had a party? Would it spoil the chance of silly fun in the future? As the young officers, some of whom I did not know yet, horsed around I saw the other pilots whom I had flown with; the ones who would fly no more. They had been full of life and they had partied like there was no tomorrow; for many there had been no tomorrow. I sipped my whisky, smoked my pipe and I remembered them.

I did not notice Archie sidle up to me. "What's the matter, Bill? You were all for this and it is a great success."

"Just thinking of Charlie and the ones who are dead sir."

He nodded and began to fill his pipe. "I have been in uniform since before the South African wars. Not always in the Corps, you understand but I was like you once. I had young friends who died. Then when I became a more senior officer I led those men and ordered many to their deaths. I know what is going through your mind. You have to resolve to get through it and honour them in peacetime by being better than you were when you came into the war. You will have to live your life for your dead comrades who cannot. It is a great burden and a great responsibility."

He lit his pipe and I sipped my whisky, "But worth it."

"Oh yes, Bill, worth it." He tapped his head, "Every friend and officer I left live in here with me. I use them to judge my actions."

"Thank you, sir. I have a clear mind now."

"And you shall need it, Bill. Tomorrow we begin to push Fritz back to Germany and I do not think he will go quietly. Keep your young pilots on their toes for they will need to be sharper tomorrow than in the weeks leading up to this."

The orders were clear. We were to clear the skies around Cambrai. As we headed east and north we saw the columns of brown heading to the support trenches and the supplies being laid in for the next assault. It seemed to me we were playing leapfrog. One Corps attacked and held while another prepared for the next assault. It was wearing the Germans down.

Flying high I realised that this was the fifth September of the war. I had been barely more than a boy when I had ridden across Flanders on the back of my mount, Caesar. What a change had been wrought. I wondered how many remained of the ones who had gone to war in September 1914 so full of hope. It terrified me that I could barely remember their names. I wondered about their undone years. Would they have gone to war with their caps set at such a jaunty angle if they had known the result? I suspect so. That was the calibre of the men who went to war all those years ago.

My reverie was cut short when I saw the twenty Fokkers flying in fingers of five and heading for us. The party was over and the war had come knocking once again.

They were the D.VII and a new bus we later learned was the SSW D. IV. A smaller aeroplane than the Fokker, this would be our first encounter with it. I was in the middle and I headed for the pilot of the purple Fokker. I checked in my mirror that Wally was in position. He had flown with me long enough to be able to react to my moves and to anticipate what I might do. I knew that I still surprised him from time to time but that day I made what was for Wally, a predictable move. I dipped my nose and, as the German snap fired brought up my nose to fire at the Fokker. Knowing my move Wally fired at the same time as I did and we hit both the propeller and the engine. I continued my climb and rose to meet the smaller aeroplane we later discovered was the SSW. It, too, had the twin Spandau and I felt the bullets rip into my top wing. I held my fire and suffered even more hits. I fired at thirty feet, just before we would have crashed had not my bullets torn into the side of the cockpit and he plunged to earth.

His wingman began to climb away. I found, to my great relief, that the SSW had a poor rate of climb and I began to catch him. I fired at twenty yards and hit his tail. He twisted and turned as he descended. They were a very agile bus and it kept twisting from my sights. I followed him as long as I could and kept hitting him with bursts from my Vickers but the SSW was a difficult bus to bring down and my fuel gauge told me to head on home.

I saw a Camel being pursued towards me by two Fokkers. He was under fire and his engine was smoking. As we closed I saw that it was one of my flight, Roger Stuart. He had grown into a competent pilot but two Fokkers would be too much for him. I did not know how much ammunition I had left. I would need to be careful. I flew directly for Roger and hoped that he would know my moves. As we closed with each other I dipped my nose slightly. He knew what I was about and he dipped his so that, when I rose I had the closest Fokker just forty feet from me. I gave a short burst from my Vickers. I had taken the Hun by surprise and I saw smoke from his engine. The second Fokker opened fire and I felt the bullets as they hit my struts. Knowing I had few bullets left I flew directly at him. He blinked first and as he climbed I riddled his undercarriage with the last of my .303. He rolled away east.

I glanced over the side of my Camel and saw Roger heading along the ground. He was smoking heavily and I was not certain he would be able to make Doyle Field. I did not have enough fuel to watch over him and I waved as I left him.

Flying on fumes I landed my damaged bus. I was the last to return. "Mr Stuart will need some assistance when he lands Flight. He was badly shot up."

"Sir." Sergeant Lowery put his fist through one of the holes in my wing. "A bit like you eh sir?"

The office was like a funeral parlour. After I had made my report I soon learned that two officers had been killed, Wood and Newton. "How about you Bill?"

"Just waiting for Stuart. He was badly shot up. He might have to crash land."

Randolph nodded as Archie pushed over the whisky. "It has been a black day all over. The SE 5s lost five today. The Germans have brought new buses to the front and they are faster than what we have."

"How many did we get?"

"It looks like three kills and five damaged." He looked at me. "You say you damaged two of the D.VII when you helped Stuart?" I nodded, "Then that makes seven damaged."

We spent some time talking about the new SSW and the telephone rang. Randolph looked up. "That was the Australians. Roger Stuart was killed by ground fire. They recovered his body but he was already dead. Sorry, Bill."

Every loss was a bad one but my flight had been together for some time and I had had the foolish dream that we would all survive the war. I stood, "I'll go and tell the lads."

My flight were in the mess happily miming their actions and talking of their successes. My face must have warned them for they all watched me intently and in silence. "Roger Stuart was shot down today by ground fire. He is dead."

Their euphoria evaporated like a morning mist; they looked like a deflated barrage balloon.

"Listen, lads, we have to watch out for each other. I found Roger all alone and being chased by two Fokkers. There are four of you left. Jack, you watch Ralph's back and David you watch Wally's. Stick like glue to each other."

Jack said, quietly, "And what about you sir? Who will watch your back?"

I shook my head and said, "Every pilot who has ever flown with me and is now in the great mess in the sky. I have dozens to watch over me."

Chapter 29

That first day was a foretaste of what would come. It became known as Black September. More pilots and crews died that month than any other month in the war. Even Bloody April in 1915 was not as bad. The squadron came within a whisker of a breakdown. That was a couple of weeks down the road. We put the bad day down to bad luck and when we heard that the French had begun to advance in the south, and an air of optimism returned. We even had a day without seeing a German aeroplane. We saw a steady trickle of German prisoners heading west. We watched our front line creeping slowly forward as the pressure mounted.

September the third saw us to the south of Cambrai. The French were advancing and we were asked to support the American fighters operating in that region. We were without the SE 5s. We had become used to seeing them on our wing. That may have been an omen.

Freddie was the only one of us with a full flight and he took the lead. I was slightly astern of him. As we approached our patrol area we saw a formation of Fokkers attacking some SPADs of the 27th American Squadron. This was a large formation of Germans. It looked like the old Jasta I. The Red Baron might have gone but his influence still remained. Freddie led us down towards the dogfight. I lined my Camel up on the bright yellow and red triplane. I was surprised they hadn't changed to the D.VII but I knew that if he was in Jasta 1, he would be a good pilot.

He was firing at a SPAD which was twisting and turning to evade the deadly bullets. I noticed the American squadron had an eagle insignia. It seemed it was just the Royal Air Force which liked a plain livery. I could not afford to wait too long to fire as the German was scoring too many hits. The SPAD was a robust aeroplane but there was a limit to the damage it could take.

I fired at a hundred yards and I banked right as soon as I had scored my first hits. I knew that Wally would cover a move to port. I was lucky. He banked and climbed to starboard and flew directly into my gun sights. I hit his wing and then the cockpit. He spiralled to earth. I saw a hand waved from the American as he too headed home. Wally and Lieutenant Dundas had headed to port. I sighed with relief. They were heeding my orders and flying as a pair. It left me alone.

I looked for another German and saw a D.VII. This one was firing at Gordy. Gordy knew how to fly and he was banking, climbing and diving in an attempt to shake off his pursuer. I dived to catch them.

Gordy's manoeuvres made it hard for me to get the German into my sights. I had to be patient. I checked my mirror and saw that I was still alone. No one was trying a sneak attack on me. Suddenly Gordy made a mistake. He banked to port and tried to climb at the same time. Normally that would have worked but the Fokker was also banking to port. Gordy had flown port then starboard and then port too many times. The German anticipated the move. I saw the bullets thump into the cockpit and Gordy juddered. I had waited too long.

The German's move had given me a sight of his tail and I fired. I was lucky and I hit it. I saw him looking around for the danger. He banked to port and I watched Gordy as he recovered enough to head west. He was alive. I banked to port too. The German bus was slightly faster in the dive than I was. As I came around I fired again and, again, hit his tail. Even before he did I began to climb and bank to starboard. It is what I would have done in his situation. His tail was suffering too much. He would still be able to turn but it would be sluggish. As I corrected my turn his fuselage came into view and I gave a long burst. I was less than one hundred feet from him and the bullets hit both his struts and his fuselage. I saw that we were under a thousand feet above the earth. It sounds a lot but when you are flying at over a hundred and twenty miles an hour it is not.

He pulled his nose up. He rose but it was slower than he would have liked. I maintained my dive to gain speed and then I pulled up my nose when I was less than two hundred feet from the ground. I arrowed my Camel towards the underside of his Fokker. He was like a giant cross above me. I knew that he could not see me. He would be looking desperately for me in his mirror. I had the luxury of being able to wait until I could not miss. I fired at a point where the wings met the fuselage. It would be close to his cockpit and his tank. I hit both and the Fokker exploded throwing my Camel to starboard and the ground. I had to fight my aeroplane. My knee was aching from the use of the ailerons and I wondered if the tip of my wing would catch the ground. Someone was watching over me for the Camel righted herself and I was flying level. I scanned the skies and saw that I was alone. I turned west and headed home. That had been as close to a fatal crash as I come since I had crashed near to Cambrai.

The field showed that we had been hurt. If I was the last to return then we had lost another Camel. The skies behind me had been empty as I had headed home. I saw that Gordy's bus had landed but it looked a mess. When I came to a halt Ted ran over to me.

"It's Gordy. He has been hurt."

"He was alive. I saw him."

Ted nodded, "He was and he was conscious when he landed. When the propeller stopped he went out like a light. Doc is with him!"

I took out my pipe and began to fill it. "Who is missing?"

"One of the new lads from Freddie's flight, Johnson or something like that."

"It was his first time out."

"I know. He looked as though he hadn't started shaving."

We trudged to the office. Archie had the whisky already poured. "The Americans sent their thanks. They were getting a mauling."

I downed it in one. "That isn't a surprise. That was Jasta I, Richthofen's old squadron. They are bloody good pilots." We sat in silence with an unspoken question in the air. Eventually, I asked it. "How do you think Gordy is?"

Freddie said, "There was a lot of blood and he was as pale as..." he downed his whisky. "Damned white; like a ghost!"

An hour went by and I stood, "Well I am going to get changed."

Archie restrained me, "Bill, stay out of the sickbay. Let Doc do what he does best. He will tell us when he knows anything."

"I know Archie but I can't sit here. I have to be doing something."

After I had bathed and changed I did not feel any better but I was cleaner. I headed to the mess. I was not hungry but I needed a drink. As I passed the sick bay I resisted the urge to enter. I was a few yards beyond the entrance when I heard Doc's voice, "Bill!"

I whipped my head around, "How is he?"

"He will live but his kneecap was mashed by those bullets. I can't see how it can be repaired. He will have a stiff leg for the rest of his life."

"But he will live?"

"Oh yes. He is like you Bill, tough as old boots. His war is over."

I burst out laughing. I could have kissed the doctor. "Thank God for that. His hands are fine?"

He gave me a quizzical look, "Aye, why?"

"He wants to be a mechanic. He can do that with a gammy leg. Doc, I'll buy you a drink in the mess tonight. You have earned it!"

Considering that our friend was crippled the air of celebration that night might have been a surprise to anyone from outside the squadron. We knew, however, that Gordy had beaten the odds.

I didn't get to see him until we returned from our flight the next day. The Germans had fled when we arrived but two American fliers had fallen. We had been too late.

Ted and I were the first ones to visit him. He looked very pale and his eyes were closed when we entered. Perhaps he smelled the whisky on our breath for he opened them as soon as we stood next to his bed. He tried to smile, "Thanks for yesterday, Bill. I owe you my life. That bugger nearly had me. Did you get him?"

I mimed an explosion and said, "Boom!"

"Good I hope the bastard is burning in hell. I am a cripple now."

I laughed, "Join the club! Stop being as miserable as Ted here. You have your hands and you can still be a mechanic."

Ted snorted, "Aye and you have survived the war. Think of the poor buggers like Charlie and Lord Burscough. They would take a gammy leg any day."

He brightened, "Hey you are right. Sorry. Who is taking over my flight?"

"Forget your flight!"

"Ted, you wouldn't forget your flight, would you?" Ted shook his head.

"I am not certain. The next senior is Johnny Holt."

"He's a good lad. The one I would recommend is Roger Clayson. You trained him well, Bill."

"Leave it with us and you get better." I had seen Doc Brennan pointing to the door. We had overstayed our welcome.

Archie agreed with me and we offered the flight to Johnny. Surprisingly he refused, "Sorry sir but I would like to see this war out with Freddie. We started together and I would like to finish together. I got used to watching Major Harsker's back and now I watch Freddie's, I am happy enough."

And so Roger Clayson became a flight commander. He proved a good choice.

When we landed the next day, Gordy had gone. Had Beattie still been working then she would have seen him. I wrote her a letter telling her the news. I knew that she would be happy for Gordy while she would be terrified that my luck would run out too.

I suggested to Archie that we ought to take off earlier and be there when the Germans went up against the Americans. The Americans were brave but they were flying combat against the best German pilots. They needed time to get the experience.

On the ninth of September, we were there in the air when the American squadron met the Germans. They had made the classic error of not gaining enough altitude. The Fokkers were swooping on them and had the advantage immediately. We were even higher and we dived into the attack. We came in from their port side. It was a devastating attack. The Jasta was so busy trying to shoot down the SPADs that they failed to see us until our machine-guns chattered death and destruction.

Soon we were in a dogfight. Aeroplanes appeared from every direction. We just had to react. Although we had shot down three in our initial attack this was a big Jasta with the best German buses they had. I had just ripped a hole in a Fokker's wing when I saw two of them fall upon the rear of Freddie's bus. Johnny was busy engaging another Fokker. I aimed my Camel towards them but they were a good half a mile away. I saw Freddie's Camel judder as he was hit. I cursed for I could not reach him in time.

Suddenly Jamie Fox appeared from nowhere and he flew between the two Fokkers. Although he hit the one behind Freddie I saw smoke coming from his Camel and he peeled away west. The move had, however, allowed me to close with them and I fired a hopeful burst from distance. It attracted the attention of the rear Fokker who tried to turn to take me on. It was a mistake. As he rose I fired a long burst and hit his engine. He began to spiral towards earth. I banked to port and fired my last bullets at the Fokker damaged by Lieutenant Fox. I headed west and escorted Freddie back to the field. I flew next to him and he waved to show that he was uninjured.

I saw that Jamie had landed and I breathed a sigh of relief. I had seen the Fokker's bullets hit his cockpit. Alarmingly his bus was surrounded by the Doc and his orderlies. As soon as I landed I ran over to the Camel. They had not removed Jamie yet and that was a worry. The orderlies parted and Doc, who was applying pressure from the far side of the cockpit, shook his head.

Jamie opened his eyes. He smiled, "It's you, sir. It looks like I won't be going home to Caroline and my child after all."

I forced a smile, "You don't know the Doc here, he is a miracle worker."

"Sir, you have never lied to me before, don't start now. I am dying I know that but please, Major Harsker, as one Lancashire lad to another, promise me that you will look after Caroline for me. I know it is a lot to ask but, well you have been good to me and…"

His eyes closed and I feared that he would die before I could tell him. "I promise you that I will look after your wife and child as though they were my own family. I swear!"

I was pleading with him to live but the look on the Doc's face told me that he was going fast.

His eyes opened and he smiled, "Thank you, sir. I knew you would and tell her that…" His eyes glazed over and he died. Another brave young man with everything to live for had had his life snuffed out in a heartbeat.

Chapter 30

I had another letter to write that night. It was to my wife. I told her how Lieutenant Fox had died and my promise. I felt guilty as I did so for she was now many months pregnant but I knew I had to tell her. Poor Freddie Carrick was even more upset than I was. He felt he had let Jamie down and to have had his life saved by him seemed to make it worse. Bates helped us both. He almost nursed Freddie back to some kind of sanity. The end of that week was the one where all of us feared for the squadron. Gordy had been very popular and the manner of Fox's death and the events leading up to it made everyone become jumpy.

When we were in the air we all did our job but it was noticeable that in the two days after Jamie died we did not claim any kills. We damaged a couple but it was almost as though we were afraid of combat. I found myself firing too soon and that had an effect on the others.

By September the sixteenth things had got so bad that Archie called a meeting of the flight commanders. Poor Roger Clayson was visibly nervous. In normal circumstances, we would have tried to make him feel better but we had no time for such niceties.

"I know we have had a hard time of it lately but if we go on this way we will lose more buses and pilots than we save." He looked directly at me. "Bill, you are holding back and not taking it to the Germans as you once did." He paused, "Is it deliberate or do you not know that you are doing it?"

Everyone looked at me now. "I suppose it is deliberate. I made a promise to young Fox that I would look after his wife and child. If I die then I am condemning two wives and two children to a life without a father." I swallowed my whisky. "I need to survive this war."

I saw sympathy on all of their faces. They understood what I was saying. Archie's voice, however, was commanding. "That is nonsense Bill! The worse way to approach air combat is nervously. You of all people know that. My God man, you are one of the leading aces in the Royal Air Force. You have survived because you do fly on the edge. If you fly nervously then you will be shot down and then you will die. Do you understand me?"

"Sir, I agree with you but there are now just three of us still alive from the dozens of officers who have passed through this squadron."

His voice softened, "And you will survive. Of that, I have no doubt. When you fly as God intended then no one can defeat you. Even the

Red Baron was outshone by you." He leaned over and touched the back of my hand. "But even if that were not true then you owe it to the young pilots. They look up to you. If you doubt yourself then what do you think that does to them?" I felt the pressure building up inside me. He was right. "Roger, you are one of the younger pilots. Am I right?"

Captain Clayson looked at me and said, "He is right sir. I have heard it in the mess. The young lads are becoming more nervous because they see you acting nervously in the air."

"So you are all saying that this is my fault?"

Ted lit a cigarette and said, "No, you daft bugger, but we are saying that you are important to this squadron whether you like it or not. What you do and how you act impacts on everyone. I know what you are saying about being responsible for two women and two bairns but you could be condemning many more to that fate. If it makes a difference then I promise to look after the mothers and the babies if you die." He paused, "I would be bloody useless at it but you have my word!"

His words made us all smile and I nodded. "Then I will try to behave normally in the air; if only to stop the nightmare of you looking after Beattie!"

Bates must have had spies in the walls for when I returned to my quarters he said, "Just trust in yourself Major Harsker and trust in God. He will not allow such a fine gentleman as yourself die in the air."

I was not certain I could trust God but I could trust my own ability to fly and to fight. I determined that if they wanted a martyr and someone to follow then I would be that man. I knew that Ted would not let me down if I should fall. But I also remembered Bates' words and the last salutation on each of my wife's letters. I would trust to God.

The next day we were ordered towards Cambrai and the canal Du Nord. Once we captured this canal then we would have the Hindenburg line under our control and Germany would be within our grasp. I chose to lead the line as we headed for the canal. We knew we would draw the enemy and I was grateful to see the full squadron of SE5s on our starboard side.

The Germans were there the moment we began to machine-gun the German soldiers. For once their height did not aid them as much as it might. We were at ground level and they had to dive a long way to reach us. We climbed in our four lines with the SE 5s in echelon to starboard. As we climbed I chose my target. It was a Fokker with a red nose and propeller. I knew that every eye was upon me and I waited before I fired. However, I did not want to die and I used every trick at my command. I trusted Wally enough to know that he would watch my actions and then react. I feinted left and then right. I dipped my nose and I raised it. Each time I knew that the German was noting my actions. Even though we closed together really quick fighter pilots had quick reactions.

He opened fire and I feinted to port. He anticipated me then turned to my right and I did not. His bullets whizzed through my wings, striking a strut on the way. I fired at fifty feet as he tried to regain the initiative. Wally opened fire, too, and his bullets struck the German's tail while I hit the side of his cockpit and his engine. He began to go down as he lost power. I turned to port. The squadron on our starboard flank could mop up those on that side.

Freddie was being attacked by a purple Fokker. Wally and I came in from his flank and our four Vickers ripped into his fuselage. He tried to turn away and Freddie downed him. The loss of two leaders opened the door to us and we caused mayhem as we attacked them from the front and the side. They fought bravely and they damaged our Camels but we landed with every pilot intact and eight German pilots lay dead. We had won.

By the end of the first week of October, we had broken through the Hindenburg line and created a gap nineteen miles wide. It had been costly and we had but ten Camels in the air, the rest having suffered great wear and tear. For me, the most important part was that we had suffered no losses. Owen had been wounded again. Johnny had bad splinters in his arm but no one had been crippled or killed. In contrast, many other squadrons had suffered great losses. I suppose ours had come earlier.

Our last serious obstacle was the main railway line which ran from north of Ypres into the heart of Germany. During the last week in October, after a two day stand down to allow pilots and buses to recover, the sixteen remaining pilots took off. We had much further to fly these days and could only spend twenty minutes over our targets. It helped in one way for we did not need to save ammunition. We felt like a true band of brothers now. We had been to hell and back and survived. We could all see the writing on the wall now. This war could not last much longer and it looked as though we had won.

That day we saw no German aeroplanes. Below us, we saw lines of German prisoners heading west. Archie led us down to ground level. The Handley Page bombers above us were returning, having bombed the railway line already. Our job, along with fighter bombers was to disrupt any attempt to repair the line and enable the advancing Australians and Americans to capture the munitions in the warehouses. If the Germans had no supplies then they could not fight.

We flew into a scene from hell. Fires were raging and German soldiers were attempting to put out the fires. The railway line would take weeks to repair. Our task was simplicity itself. We attacked the column of lorries which were trying to rescue as much as possible from the burning buildings. Soon there was a traffic jam of destroyed vehicles. We had, literally minutes over the target before we had to return home.

That evening, in the mess, we heard the news we had been waiting for. We were to get new pilots and Camels the following week and we were to stand down until then. There was an air of relief in the mess that night. We had seen with our own eyes that the Germans were beaten. The Hindenburg line was breached and it was a matter of time before they surrendered. We discussed and pontificated when that day might come. The younger pilots all thought it would be over by December but we older ones were convinced that we would see the war still being fought in 1919.

Randolph speculated that we might have to move our airfield so that it was closer to the front line. None of us was happy about that; Doyle Field felt comfortable. He did point out that it would be unlikely that we would have to fly many sorties as the war had moved too far to the east and there were many squadrons.

Our last sortie was on the twentieth of October. A Jasta had attacked the allied soldiers who were moving towards the new front line and we were sent to Vervins to patrol there. It was halfway to the front and would allow us at least thirty minutes in the air. Other squadrons would replace us. As we prepared to leave I spoke with Archie.

"Well laddie, it was to be expected. The Hun is a good pilot and they wouldn't just sit back and let us have free rein. This way they hit back but I am not worried. We have the measure of these boys now. It isn't like 1915 when we nearly went under."

"We were a different squadron then."

He laughed, "Aye you were nearly court-martialled!"

"Don't remind of that. I wonder how Colonel Pemberton-Smythe is these days."

"Last I heard he was enjoying the country life. This was not the war for an old gentleman like him." he shook his head, "I am not sure it suited an old dinosaur like me either. Anyway, I shall soon be like the old boy walking through the heather and enjoying my family around me."

"You have been a great leader sir. I appreciate the latitude you gave me."

"Aye well it's like I said the night I gave you your telling off; you are a gifted pilot. You are without a doubt the best fighter pilot I have ever had the honour of serving with. It would be a tragedy if you left the service. I have had enough but you; you could make a real difference."

"Thank you, sir, coming from you I take that as a great compliment."

We took off on a chilly morning and headed east. Soon this would be a thing of the past. I would no longer have to take my pistols, hip flask, bandages and all the other paraphernalia. The war would be over. I would go home first, see my wife and my child and then make a decision about my future. I respected Archie and he had given me much to contemplate.

Once again Archie led. I frowned when I saw the low clouds. They were perfect for an ambush. I thought about moving up into them even though we were still ten miles from our patrol. Then I thought better of it. It was not fair on my young pilots. It was incredibly hard to stay on station in low cloud.

The Fokkers came without warning. Even as I was considering my course of action they plunged from the skies and attacked us from behind. In my mirror, I saw Jack Fall as his Camel began to spiral out of control. Ralph Carter in front of him was my least experienced pilot and it showed. He tried to climb and I saw his body judder as he was hit by two Fokkers.

I banked to port, looking for a target. As I did so I saw Archie's aeroplane as it exploded in the air. I had thought our war was over. I had thought we had suffered our last death and I was wrong. The bastards would pay. As I banked around I saw just twenty feet from me, a Fokker. I had no time to think and I just fired. His engine was hit and I saw the propeller stop. I fired again and hit him. He plunged to the ground as the next Fokker tried to turn and fire at me. Wally's bullets hit the pilot a moment or two before my bullets shredded his undercarriage.

As I came around I saw, to my amazement, that there were no German aeroplanes in the sky. We had been attacked by just eight aeroplanes and they had all been shot down. We had lost just the three aeroplanes but that did not make me feel any better. Archie had gone west along with Jack and poor Ralph. I turned the Camel around and headed back to the field. As I flew I ran through my conversation with Archie. I thought about poor Jack. He had planned on remaining a pilot in the new Royal Air Force; that would not happen now. Poor Ralph was due to be married at the end of the war and, like Jamie, his dream would remain unfulfilled.

1918 We Will Remember Them

Not a word was spoken as we trudged to the office. Randolph had a smile on his face and the whisky open as we walked in. One look at our faces and the lack of Archie made him slump into his seat.

"No, not Archie?"

I nodded, "And Jack Fall and Ralph Carter. We were ambushed." I raised my glass, "Archie!"

"Archie!"

I did not have the words to tell what had happened. Ted had been at the rear and he told Randolph what had occurred. I wanted to be alone and I emptied my glass and headed for my quarters. Bates had had his cat's whiskers working again and he was ready with the right words and a hot bath.

"Colonel Leach was a gentleman and he was proud of this squadron. Simpkins, his batman told me many times that he thought he was incredibly lucky to lead such fine young men. He regarded you, Major Harsker as his protégé. He was as proud of you as his own sons. He had been a soldier all of his life and he died a soldier. I hear he didn't suffer."

He said that as though it made a difference. Dead was dead. But I knew he meant well. "No, Bates, he didn't suffer."

"And sir, this makes you the Squadron Leader; they will all be looking to you. You will need some words tonight. It will be expected."

Terror filled me, "I can't say anything! I will make a fool of myself! I don't have the words!"

"Have your bath sir and another whisky. Trust in the lord and the words will come to you."

I did not believe him but I obeyed his orders. He was right; I had to say something. Either the whisky or the bath worked for I had the words. When I came out I said, "Send for Captain Marshall, I need to speak with him."

Randolph looked awful when he arrived. "I know it is hard but you and I, along with Ted, are the senior officers now. We have to set an example. I want formal dress tonight. We owe it to Archie."

He stiffened, "You are right… Squadron Leader." I looked at him. "General Trenchard was told about Archie. The promotion is premature; the ranks won't come into effect until January but that is your new rank sir and you are the Commanding Officer of this squadron. At least until hostilities cease."

After he had gone Bates said, "Congratulations. No more than you deserve."

The squadron looked magnificent in their dress uniforms. The mess sergeants and orderlies had broken out the best cutlery and they too were dressed impeccably. Before we began, Senior Flight Sergeant Lowery marched into the mess also in his full-dress uniform. He stood before me and saluted, "Sit, forgive this unwarranted intrusion but I just wanted to congratulate you on the promotion and to tell you, as a former sergeant," he allowed the briefest of smiles, "that the Sergeant's Mess will also be honouring a great man this evening." He stood to attention and then did a smart about face and left.

The meal was beautifully cooked. The cooks had gone to great lengths to make it perfect. There was just a murmur of conversation as we ate. I was flanked by Randolph and Ted while Doc Brennan sat on the other side of Ted. The doctor appeared to have aged ten years since the morning. After the meal, everyone looked at me expectantly. I stood.

"Gentlemen, charge your glasses." They all stood. "To Colonel Archibald Wilberforce Leach."

When they had toasted Archie, I waved them to their seats. "Bates said that I ought to say a few words about Archie." Everyone knew Bates and they smiled. "I was not certain I knew what to say about such a tragedy. I thought when my regiment was wiped out in 1914, that no greater tragedy could occur. I was wrong. This is the last in a series of deaths which has taken almost all of my friends." I looked down at Ted who raised his glass to me. "I will not list their names for it would not be seemly for me to break down before you. Rest assured that I will mourn them all in my own way. Archie was a great leader. He was quietly spoken but you knew where you stood with him. He was kind and he was thoughtful. I am most upset because I knew he had a future planned for his wife and his sons. He was to be a farmer. That was not meant to be. But today we also lost two more comrades. Captain Marshall has told me that since 1915 we have lost over eighty pilots and thirty gunners. We have rarely mentioned them. That was remiss of us."

I found my voice was breaking and so I took another drink of the whisky, "We also lost today a young pilot Ralph Carter. He had been with us for weeks only and yet he was as much a part of this squadron as Archie Leach. We will miss him. And poor Jack Fall who watched the rear of my flight for the past six months. What a tragedy that he will not fly again."

Just then the door burst open and Jack stood there with his arm in a sling. I did not know what to say. I knew I had to finish what I had started, "Give Lieutenant Fall a drink and I can finish my speech and we can celebrate his return from the dead!"

George Jenkin gave him a drink and sat him down. I saw smiles replacing frowns and felt the hope surge in the mess. "I had nearly finished. Let me see if I can get through this. Soon this war will be over. Some of us will stay in the service while others will move on to other things. I may never get a chance to command you again so let me give you one order now and I hope that you will all swear to obey it. For the rest of your lives live your lives for those who have no life to live. Each decision you make should be determined by a reflection on what our dead comrades would have done. The land we go back to will be broken. We owe to those who died to make it even greater in their memory. And when there is a quiet time each day, perhaps in the pub or watching the fire or looking at a sunset; we will remember them for if we fail to do so then their deaths will have been in vain."

Epilogue

The war ended a week later. We had no more losses. Within a week we were sent home. Many of the men took the opportunity to return to civilian life while those of us who would remain in the service were told to await orders. I will always remember the day the war ended for that was the day that Thomas Charles Albert Harsker was born. When I reached Burscough on the twentieth of November I walked into my home and saw my wife with a perfect baby. My mother burst into tears and hugged me. Even Beattie cried. Then she stood and put the child in my arms.

"Here is your son. We named him in honour of…" She began to cry, well you know… I hope you approve of the names."

I nodded, I too was close to tears. I looked at my son who stared seriously at me. I wondered if he would cry. Instead, his mouth creased into a smile which, as Ted had told me, meant he had wind. But his eyes glowed and that was not wind. "Well son, I am your dad. And you have been named after three of the finest men I knew. If I named you after every brave man with whom I have fought then we would take all day to speak your name. I can see in your eyes that you will be just as brave as they were and you will do your duty. That, in the end, is all that a man can do."

I cradled him in my arms as my father came to shake my hand. "Well done son. I am proud of you."

The door leading to the upstairs opened and there I saw Caroline Fox. She opened it fearfully. I could see that she was almost due to give birth. I handed my son back to Beattie and went to her. I took her hands in mine. "Your husband was a brave man who died well. He has been awarded the MC. It is no exchange for your husband but it will be something to show his child. It will be a memory to cherish. I promised him that I would care for you and his child as though you were my own. It was a promise made to a dying man and I swear that I will honour that pledge." I saw Beattie nod and knew that it would be fine.

I found that I could plan and organise far better after the experience of the war. I was helped when Bates came to Burscough a few days later. He had rejoined and would be my servant as long as I served. He helped to organise to rent a larger cottage on the estate from Lady Mary. Her ladyship, my sisters and my parents were all delighted. Emma Mary Fox was born on Christmas Day 1918 and she was perfect. As I strolled outside having a last pipe of the night I began to make plans. I was to take up my new post in March that gave me enough time to take Beattie and see Lumpy. What I had to tell him could not be put in a letter and besides, I wanted to see him in his new home. We would then visit Gordy and Mary. They would be anxious to see my new child too and then I would see Ted so that we could plan the squadron reunion. I had told the squadron that we would remember them and I planned to do so every year. They deserved the honour.

I looked up at the sky, "Well, Jamie, I have kept my promise." I put my arms by my side, "And to the rest of you I say, it was an honour to serve with you all. Rest in peace." I stood looking at the stars and saluted my comrades in the sky.

The End

Glossary

BEF- British Expeditionary Force
Beer Boys-inexperienced fliers (slang)
Blighty- Britain (slang)
Boche- German (slang)
Bowser- refuelling vehicle
Bus- aeroplane (slang)
Corned dog- corned beef (slang)
Craiglockhart- A Victorian building taken over by the military and used to treat shell shocked soldiers. Siegfried Sassoon and Wilfred Owen both spent time there.
Crossley- an early British motor car
Dewar Flask- an early Thermos invented in 1890
Donkey Walloper- Horseman (slang)
Fizzer- a charge (slang)
Foot Slogger- Infantry (slang)
Gaspers- Cigarettes (slang)
Google eyed booger with the tit- gas mask (slang)
Griffin (Griff) - confidential information (slang)
Hun- German (slang)
Jagdgeschwader – four German Jasta flying under one leader
Jasta- a German Squadron
Jippo- the shout that food was ready from the cooks (slang)
Kanone 14- 10cm German artillery piece
Killick- Leading seaman (slang-Royal Navy)
Lanchester- a prestigious British car with the same status as a Rolls Royce
Loot- a second lieutenant (slang)
Lufbery Circle- An aerial defensive formation
M.C. - Military Cross (for officers only)
M.M. - Military Medal (for other ranks introduced in 1915)
Nelson's Blood- rum (slang- Royal Navy)
Nicked- stolen (slang)
Number ones- Best uniform (slang)
Oblt. - Oberlieutenant (abbr.)
Oppo- workmate/friend (slang)
Outdoor- the place they sold beer in a pub to take away (slang)
Parkin or Perkin- a soft cake traditionally made of oatmeal and black treacle, which originated in northern England.

Pop your clogs- die (slang)
Posser- a three-legged stool attached to a long handle and used to agitate washing in the days before washing machines
Pickelhaube- German helmet with a spike on the top. Worn by German soldiers until 1916
Pukka- Very good/efficient (slang)
Rugger- Rugby (slang)
Scousers- Liverpudlians (slang)
Shufti- a quick look (slang)
Scheiße- Shit (German)
Singer 10 - a British car developed by Lionel Martin who went on to make Aston Martins
Staffelführer- Jasta commander
The smoke- London (slang)
Toff- aristocrat (slang)
V.C. - Victoria Cross, the highest honour in the British Army

Historical note

This is my fifth foray into what might be called modern history. The advantage of the Dark Ages is that there are few written records and the writer's imagination can run riot- and usually does! If I have introduced a technology slightly early or moved an action it is in the interest of the story and the character. The FE 2 is introduced a month or so before the actual aeroplane. The Red Baron is shot down, for the first time, six weeks before he really was. The Sopwith Camel arrived at the end of May rather than the middle. I have tried to make this story more character-based. I have used the template of some real people and characters that lived at the time.

The Short Magazine Lee Enfield had a ten-shot magazine and enabled a rifleman to get off 20-30 shots in a minute. It was accurate at 300 yards. Both cavalry and infantry were issued with the weapon.

For those readers who do not come from England, I have tried to write the way that people in that part of Lancashire speak. As with many northerners they say *'owt'* for anything and *'Eeeh'* is just a way of expressing surprise. As far as I know, there is no Lord Burscough but I know that Lord Derby had a huge house not far away in Standish and I have based the fictitious Lord Burscough on him. The area around Burscough and Ormskirk is just north of the heavily industrialised belt which runs from Leeds, through Manchester, to Liverpool. It is a very rural area with many market gardens. It afforded me the chance to have rural and industrial England, cheek by jowl. The food they eat is also typical of that part of Lancashire. Harsker is a name from the area apparently resulting from a party of Vikings who settled in the area some centuries earlier. Bearing in mind my earlier Saxon and Viking books I could not resist the link, albeit tenuous, with my earlier novels.

Radios were fitted to aeroplanes from as early as 1914. They could only transmit. The ground radios could only receive. By 1916 320 aeroplanes had radios fitted. Oxygen was introduced, mainly in bombers, from 1917 onwards. It was needed when the aeroplanes were operated at high altitude and by the end of the war, aeroplanes were capable of operating at 20000 feet!

Sopwith Camel courtesy of Wikipedia

Bristol F2b Courtesy of Wikipedia

This variant was faster than the F2A of which only 52 were built. Ted and Gordy's are the F2A variant and the later ones, the faster F2B, which could reach speeds of 80 mph.

Fokker Dr.1 Triplane

Baron Von Richthofen was actually shot down by an FE 2 during the later stages of the Battle of the Somme in one of his first forays over the Western front. In this novel, it is Bill who has that honour. The Red Baron is portrayed as the pilot of the Halberstadt with the yellow propeller. Of course, the Red Baron got his revenge by shooting down the leading British ace of the time, Major Lanoe Hawker VC. Major Hawker, was flying the DH2 while the Red Baron flew the superior Albatros DIII. The Red Baron took over Jasta 11 in January 1917 and he made a huge difference. Until he had arrived not a single aeroplane had been shot down by the Jasta. He had a kill on his first day. His squadron was known as the Flying Circus because they were all painted differently and in very bright colours. His was all red but every one of his aeroplanes had the colour red somewhere in the colour scheme. In the summer of 1917, the Germans reorganised their Jastas so that Richthofen was in command of four fighter squadrons. He was shot down while flying a Fokker Dr1 Triplane. It was painted in his favourite red colour.

The circle devised by Bill and Billy really existed. It was known as a Lufbery circle. The gunner of each F.E.2 could cover the blind spot under the tail of his neighbour and several gunners could fire on any enemy attacking the group. There were occasions when squadrons used this tactic to escape the Fokker monoplane and the later fighters which the Germans introduced to wrest air superiority from the Gunbus. It made for slow progress home but they, generally, got there safely. It was a formation that two-seaters could employ in the latter years of the war when they were faced with the newer, faster fighters.

General Henderson commanded the RFC for all but a couple of months of the war. The Fokker Scourge lasted from autumn 1915 until February 1916. It took the Gunbus and other new aircraft to defeat

1918 We Will Remember Them

them. The BE 2 aeroplanes were known as Fokker fodder and vast numbers were shot down. There were few true bombers at this stage of the war and the Gunbus was one of the first multi-role aeroplanes. The addition of the third Lewis gun did take place at this stage of the war. The Germans had to react to their lack of superiority and in the next book the pendulum swings in Germany's favour when the Albatros D.III and other new aircraft wrested control of the air away from the RFC.

I have no evidence for Sergeant Sharp's improvised bulletproofing. However, they were very inventive and modified their aeroplanes all the time. The materials he used were readily available and, in the days before recycling, would have just been thrown away. It would be interesting to test it with bullets.

The Mills bomb was introduced in 1915. It had a seven-second fuse. The shrapnel could spread up to twenty yards from the explosion.

The tunnels at Arras were astounding. Work had been going on underground to construct tunnels for the troops since October 1916. The Arras region is chalky and therefore easily excavated; under Arras itself is a vast network of caverns, underground quarries, galleries and sewage tunnels. The engineers devised a plan to add new tunnels to this network so that troops could arrive at the battlefield in secrecy and in safety. The scale of this undertaking was enormous: in one sector alone four Tunnel Companies worked around the clock in 18-hour shifts for two months. Eventually, they constructed 20 kilometres of tunnels, graded as subways for men on foot tramways which had rails and was used for taking ammunition to the front and bringing casualties back; and railways. Just before the assault, the tunnel system had grown big enough to conceal 24,000 men, with electric lighting. Bert and his company are part of this undertaking. However, the Germans knew of the tunnels and they were digging countermines. Both sides fought a deadly war beneath the surface.

The Battle of Arras was delayed because the French were not ready and consequently began during a snowstorm. Despite that, the British and Commonwealth troops made astonishing gains in the first few days. The German front line troops were, quite literally, shell shocked from the two-week barrage they had endured. The defences ceased to exist.

General Trenchard was in command in France although he was a controversial figure. He was not universally popular. He was the first Chief of the RAF. He was known for his penchant for offensive rather than defensive flying.

More aeroplanes were shot down by ground fire than other aeroplanes and I have tried to be as realistic as I can but Bill Harsker is a hero and I portray him as such. He does achieve a high number of kills. Lanoe Hawker was the first ace to reach 40 kills and he died just at the end of the Somme Offensive.

The Spring Offensive almost won the war for the Germans. With Russia out of the war and the Americans still feeding men across the Atlantic Operation Michael almost succeeded. The Offensive was four attacks. The first was in the Somme. It was followed by one close to Ypres. A third was to the south of the Somme and the final one was an attempt to enlarge the Somme salient. The Offensive cost the Germans almost 700,000 casualties whilst the allies lost nearly 900,000. It was stopped, in no small part by the RFC or, as it became on April 1st 1918, the RAF. The new German aeroplanes could not defeat the RFC. There were a few Fokker D.VIIs in the air but by the time they reached the front, the Spring Offensive had been halted. The battle cost many aeroplanes but once it was over then the RAF dominated the skies of Northern France.

I have tried to base the relationship between Bill and Bates on that of Frodo and Sam in Lord of the Rings. This is not as bizarre as it sounds for Tolkien served in World War 1 as an officer in the trenches and had a close relationship with his servant. It is widely believed that the Frodo/Sam relationship is that of Tolkien and his batman. For those readers who have commented to me about the lack of servants for the other officers, I say that all of them would have had a servant and the relationship would have been a similar one to Bates and Bill but I was trying to encapsulate in Bates a subplot to do with the stress of war and the remarkable changes it brings in the most mild-mannered of people.

I have taken the idea of Bill's injured legs from the true story of Douglas Bader who defied the odds in World War II not only to be able to walk again with artificial legs but also to fly a Spitfire and lead a whole wing of aeroplanes.

The swastika was used by pilots in Jasta 17 and appears to have been the personal emblem of Oblt Hermann Pritisch who was the acting Jastafuhrer. He scored one victory.

The war in 1918 surged one way and then the other. The Spring Offensive came within a whisker of succeeding but the German plan wasted their finest troops in their assaults. Ludendorff, in particular, did not use the elite troops well. Their job was to punch a hole through and then the rest would flood through the gaps they made. Ludendorff had these storm-troopers making costly attacks on the British redoubts. They could have been bypassed. Another crucial factor was the control of the air. The Germans were between their good fighters. The triplane was on the decline and the new Fokker D.VII was not ready in enough numbers. Even though the German air force was never defeated it could never control the skies because of their lack of production.

The Hundred Days Offensive began in August and lasted until November 1918. It ended with the allies in Germany. Ironically the worst month of the war was September when 560 allied aeroplanes were lost on the Western front. The previous worse month had been bloody April in 1917 when 305 Allied aeroplanes were lost. In both bloody battles, the bulk of the losses were amongst the pilots of the RFC/RAF. These figures pale into insignificance when compared with the losses on the ground and amongst the infantry.

WW1 Aviation Casualties				
Casualties	British	French	American	German
Killed	6166	2872	681	5853
Wounded	7245	2922	127	7302
Missing	3212	1461	72	2715
Total	16623	7255	880	15906

I used the following books to verify the information:
World War 1- Peter Simkins
The Times Atlas of World History
The British Army in World War 1 (1)- Mike Chappell
The British Army in World War 1 (2)- Mike Chappell
The British Army 1914-18- Fosten and Marrion
British Air Forces 1914-1918- Cormack
British and Empire Aces of World War 1- Shores
A History of Aerial Warfare- John Taylor
First World War- Martin Gilbert
Aircraft of World War 1- Herris and Pearson
Thanks to the following website for the slang definitions

- *www.ict.griffith.edu.au/~davidt/z_ww1_**slang**/index_bak.htm*

Griff Hosker February 2015

1918 We Will Remember Them

Other books by Griff Hosker

enjoyed reading this book, then why not read another one by the author?

Ancient History

The Sword of Cartimandua Series
(Germania and Britannia 50 A.D. – 128 A.D.)
Ulpius Felix- Roman Warrior (prequel)
The Sword of Cartimandua
The Horse Warriors
Invasion Caledonia
Roman Retreat
Revolt of the Red Witch
Druid's Gold
Trajan's Hunters
The Last Frontier
Hero of Rome
Roman Hawk
Roman Treachery
Roman Wall
Roman Courage

The Wolf Warrior series
(Britain in the late 6th Century)
Saxon Dawn
Saxon Revenge
Saxon England
Saxon Blood
Saxon Slayer
Saxon Slaughter
Saxon Bane
Saxon Fall: Rise of the Warlord
Saxon Throne
Saxon Sword

Medieval History

The Dragon Heart Series
Viking Slave *
Viking Warrior *
Viking Jarl *
Viking Kingdom *
Viking Wolf *
Viking War*
Viking Sword
Viking Wrath
Viking Raid
Viking Legend
Viking Vengeance
Viking Dragon
Viking Treasure
Viking Enemy
Viking Witch
Viking Blood
Viking Weregeld
Viking Storm
Viking Warband
Viking Shadow
Viking Legacy
Viking Clan
Viking Bravery
The Vengeance Trail

The Norman Genesis Series
Hrolf the Viking *
Horseman *
The Battle for a Home *
Revenge of the Franks *
The Land of the Northmen
Ragnvald Hrolfsson
Brothers in Blood
Lord of Rouen

Drekar in the Seine
Duke of Normandy
The Duke and the King

Danelaw
(England and Denmark in the 11th Century)
Dragon Sword *
Oathsword *
Bloodsword *
Danish Sword*
The Sword of Cnut

New World Series
Blood on the Blade *
Across the Seas *
The Savage Wilderness *
The Bear and the Wolf *
Erik The Navigator *
Erik's Clan *
The Last Viking*

The Vengeance Trail *

The Conquest Series
(Normandy and England 1050-1100)
Hastings
Conquest

The Aelfraed Series
(Britain and Byzantium 1050 A.D. - 1085 A.D.)
Housecarl *
Outlaw *
Varangian *

The Reconquista Chronicles
Castilian Knight *
El Campeador *
The Lord of Valencia *

**The Anarchy Series England
1120-1180**
English Knight *
Knight of the Empress *
Northern Knight *
Baron of the North *
Earl *
King Henry's Champion *
The King is Dead *
Warlord of the North*
Enemy at the Gate
The Fallen Crown
Warlord's War
Kingmaker
Henry II
Crusader
The Welsh Marches
Irish War
Poisonous Plots
The Princes' Revolt
Earl Marshal
The Perfect Knight

**Border Knight
1182-1300**
Sword for Hire *
Return of the Knight *
Baron's War *
Magna Carta *
Welsh Wars *
Henry III *
The Bloody Border *
Baron's Crusade*
Sentinel of the North*
War in the West
Debt of Honour
The Blood of the Warlord

The Fettered King
de Montfort's Crown
Ripples of Rebellion

Sir John Hawkwood Series
France and Italy 1339- 1387
Crécy: The Age of the Archer *
Man At Arms *
The White Company *
Leader of Men *
Tuscan Warlord *
Condottiere*
Legacy

Lord Edward's Archer
Lord Edward's Archer *
King in Waiting *
An Archer's Crusade *
Targets of Treachery *
The Great Cause *
Wallace's War *
The Hunt

Struggle for a Crown
1360- 1485
Blood on the Crown *
To Murder a King *
The Throne *
King Henry IV *
The Road to Agincourt *
St Crispin's Day *
The Battle for France *
The Last Knight *
Queen's Knight *
The Knight's Tale

Tales from the Sword I
(Short stories from the Medieval period)

Tudor Warrior series
England and Scotland in the late 15th and early 16th century
Tudor Warrior *
Tudor Spy *
Flodden*

Conquistador
England and America in the 16th Century
Conquistador *
The English Adventurer *

English Mercenary
The 30 Years War and the English Civil War
Horse and Pistol

Modern History

The Napoleonic Horseman Series
Chasseur à Cheval
Napoleon's Guard
British Light Dragoon
Soldier Spy
1808: The Road to Coruña
Talavera
The Lines of Torres Vedras
Bloody Badajoz
The Road to France
Waterloo

The Lucky Jack American Civil War series
Rebel Raiders
Confederate Rangers
The Road to Gettysburg

Soldier of the Queen series
Soldier of the Queen*
Redcoat's Rifle*

1918 We Will Remember Them

Omdurman
Desert War

The British Ace Series
1914
1915 Fokker Scourge
1916 Angels over the Somme
1917 Eagles Fall
1918 We will remember them
From Arctic Snow to Desert Sand
Wings over Persia

Combined Operations series
1940-1945
Commando *
Raider *
Behind Enemy Lines
Dieppe
Toehold in Europe
Sword Beach
Breakout
The Battle for Antwerp
King Tiger
Beyond the Rhine
Korea
Korean Winter

Tales from the Sword II
(Short stories from the Modern period)

Books marked thus *, are also available in the audio format. For more information on all of the books then please visit the author's website at www.griffhosker.com where there is a link to contact him or visit his Facebook page: GriffHosker at Sword Books or follow him on Twitter: @HoskerGriff or Sword (@swordbooksltd)
If you wish to be on the mailing list then contact the author through his website.

228

1918 We Will Remember Them

Printed in Great Britain
by Amazon